PRAISE FOR THE NOVELS OF SANDRA KRING

"Touching . . . surprisingly poignant . . . builds to an emotional crescendo . . . The book becomes so engrossing that it's tough to see it end."

—*The Washington Post*

"A beautiful, witty story that rings with heartbreak, hope and laughter . . . Kring's brilliance lies in her powerful reversals and revelations, taking readers and characters on a dramatic, emotional roller coaster."

—*Publishers Weekly* (starred review)

"Sandra Kring weaves an intricate and heartwarming tale of family, love, and forgiveness. . . . Kring's passionate voice is reminiscent of Faulkner, Hemingway and Steinbeck. . . . She will make you laugh, have you in tears and take you back to the days of good friends, good times, millponds and bonfires."

—*Midwest Book Review*

"A touching novel . . . Kring explores the far-ranging effects of family trauma with a deft hand as her child narrator uncovers the past, bringing light and hope."

—*Booklist*

"Sandra Kr … on Midwestern America . … s because it is so unpretentic …

—Salon

"Sandra Kring writes with such passion and immediacy, spinning us back in time, making us feel the characters' hope, desire, laughter, sorrow, and redemption."

—Luanne Rice, *New York Times* bestselling author of *The Deep Blue Sea for Beginners*

"Sandra Kring never fails to impress me."

—Lesley Kagen, bestselling author of *Whistling in the Dark*

"Sandra Kring has written a funny, deeply satisfying book; her characters finagle their way into your heart and when their story ends, you can't help but feel, 'ahhhh.' "

—Lorna Landvik, author of *Angry Housewives Eating Bon Bons*

Also by Sandra Kring

Carry Me Home

The Book of Bright Ideas

Thank You for All Things

How High the Moon

A Life of Bright Ideas

A NOVEL

Sandra Kring

BANTAM BOOKS TRADE PAPERBACKS

NEW YORK

A Bantam Books Trade Paperback Original

Published in the United States by Bantam Books,
an imprint of The Random House Publishing Group,
a division of Random House, Inc., New York.

Bantam Books and the rooster colophon are registered trademarks
of Random House, Inc.

LIBRARY OF CONGRESS CATALOGING-IN-PUBLICATION DATA
Kring, Sandra.
A life of bright ideas: a novel / Sandra Kring.
p. cm.
ISBN 978-0-553-38682-0
eBook ISBN 978-0-553-90802-2
1. Families—Fiction. 2. Wisconsin—Fiction. 3. Domestic fiction. I. Title.
PS3611.R545L54 2012 813'.6—dc22 2011017440

Printed in the United States of America

www.bantamdell.com

2 4 6 8 9 7 5 3 1

Book design by Ellen Cipriano

For the readers who would not let me rest until I went back to Dauber to find out what happened next

A Life of Bright Ideas

Prologue

I've always had an attachment to trees. Most likely because of my uncle Rudy, a farmer who knew the secrets of trees and seeds and wind and water every bit as well as my aunt Verdella knew the secret of how to love. He was always there to pluck an analogy from trees with which to assure me that hearts can sustain themselves in even the longest droughts of hope, and that something beautiful can take root and bloom in lives that have become wastelands. I clung to every one of his stories—dropped into my days like simple trivia—because, well, I guess it's like my first (and really, my only) true best friend, Winnalee Malone, said: "You have to believe in something, or what's the point?"

. . .

I don't remember much about the day my ma died, but I remember that night. Aunt Verdella stretching a sheet across the couch near midnight, and bringing Uncle Rudy a pillow. My two-year-old brother squirming himself to sleep between Aunt Verdella and me on a bed that smelled like vanilla and work clothes and sunshine, her hand bridged to my arm, stroking it when I cried softly, and squeezing it when my sobs jiggled the bed.

Aunt Verdella's hand didn't drift off until she did, and she moaned in her sleep. I lay still at the edge of the bed for hours, my eyelids slammed shut to keep in the tears. And when sobs formed in my chest, I bit the inside of my cheek until I tasted blood, which felt easier to swallow than grief. I knew that if Aunt Verdella woke, she'd only start crying along with me, and she'd already cried a river's worth of tears. Finally, when I couldn't keep quiet any longer, I slipped out of bed, circled the couch so I wouldn't wake Uncle Rudy, and went outside.

It was almost dawn and the sky was still wearing the stains of yesterday's storms. It was misting and foggy, and wet grass clung to my bare feet like hair clippings as I hurried to the tree that had been every bit a part of my childhood as Winnalee.

We called it our "magic tree" because it spun us off to faraway places, and brought us home by lunchtime. It kept our "adventure bag" (an army knapsack that held the items we believed we'd need when we snuck off to Dauber Falls in search of the fairies Winnalee was convinced lived there) hidden in the hole at its feet, safe from Tommy Smithy, Uncle Rudy's fourteen-year-old farmhand. And after the Malones left without warning, our magic tree kept Winnalee's Book of Bright Ideas for me until I found it. I'd read that book so many times since that summer, that I knew every "bright idea" by heart.

Just looking at the tree that had been the keeper of our innocence that summer of 1961 made my tears run like sap, and I ran stumbling to meet it, like people do when they're being reunited with family from across a sea.

I hadn't climbed that tree since Winnalee left, and my fourteen-year-old body, skinny and gangly as it was, felt heavy and awkward as I reached around a thick, low-hanging branch and swung my legs up to wrap around it. The bony bark scratched the inside of my thighs as I scooted down the limb, Aunt Verdella's nightie bunching around my hips.

The barkless platform in the fork of the tree that once held two pairs of dusty feet couldn't contain my ladies'-size-eights, but cupped my heels. I leaned back against one of the three thick limbs and looked up at branches that stretched toward Heaven, as if they, too, were reaching for Ma. Questions about why she had to go into the basement when she did played in my head like taps, and I had to bend my head forward or drown. I cried for my ma. I cried for my brother. I cried for my dad, my aunt, my uncle. And then I begged the magic tree to take me away. Far away, to lands where fairies played, and Winnalee waited. Where nothing could find me but innocence.

Instead, it was Uncle Rudy who found me. Sitting in the fork, straddling the limb I'd leaned against, my arms and legs wrapped around it like a child being carried. "Button?" he called.

I blinked awake and saw him below me, one hand extended and the other dangling at his side. The grass was bright from its washing and Aunt Verdella's nightgown was damp on my skin. "Come on, honey," Uncle Rudy said.

As he helped me down, I could see Aunt Verdella standing at the kitchen window, her hand pressed to her mouth.

Uncle Rudy put one arm around me and took a photograph out of his pocket. "I ever show you this, Button?" he said, handing it to me. "I took it up on Lake Superior, when your dad and I went up there on a fishing trip, right after he graduated." I stared down at the photo with the same skeptical wonder with which I once gaped at what appeared to be photos of real fairies. I squinted at Uncle Rudy, who had shrunken to five feet seven while I was growing, his eyes now level with mine.

"I know. I know," he said, nodding. "Looks impossible, don't it? A tree that size growin' on the top of a big rock jutting out of the water, no soil beneath it. But lookie here," he said, tracing his stiff finger along a thick rope that ran from the base of the tree across thin air, then disappeared off the edge of the page. "I didn't get it in the shot, but over here was a bluff some twenty feet from the rock, and these roots were stretched to it like an umbilical cord." He took his cap off, rubbed the top of his half-bald head, and pumped it back in place. "Anyway, I want you to have it," he said, giving me a pat.

I didn't get the chance to ask him how that tree knew which direction to send its roots in, or how it survived until it reached solid ground, because Aunt Verdella was already on the porch, her arms reaching, and all I wanted was to get to them. But later, four years later, to be exact, I came to understand for myself how that tree survived. And then, how it thrived.

CHAPTER 1

BRIGHT IDEA #62: If you want to go to Detroit because you think it might be a fun place to live, but you end up in Gary, Indiana, instead and your sister says, "Well that's life," then you might as well just accept that you are where you are for now.

I was upstairs in Grandma Mae's old house, in the room wallpapered with army-green ivy and a window seat, a stack of shirts on hangers bending my wrist, when Aunt Verdella shouted my name. She didn't call out "Evy"—short for Evelyn, which is what most people called me—but "Button," the nickname Uncle Rudy gave me when I was little. My stomach tightened from the fear in Aunt Verdella's voice, and I tossed the shirts on the bed and jumped over a row of cardboard boxes. I raced across the hall to the window in the pink flower-papered room facing my aunt and uncle's house, and butted my nose against the rusty screen. Aunt Verdella, shaped like a snowman made wrong for as long as I could remember, with only one big ball for her body, instead of two, and normal-sized limbs that looked stick-skinny in comparison, was almost to the dirt road separating her house from Grandma Mae's. "Aunt Verdella?" I called.

Her arms were going like two twigs caught in a windstorm as she gestured back toward her house, pointing high. "Boohoo!"

I looked straight ahead and saw my six-year-old brother, Boohoo (Robert Reece until Uncle Rudy dubbed him Boohoo, because of his ability to use a pout to get his way), walking along the peak of her roof, a red towel faded to pink draped over his shoulders—he thought Spider-Man wore a cape like Superman. Boohoo held a skein of pumpkin-orange yarn above his head. "My God!" I cried, then flew down the stairs like I was on fire.

I tore across the yard and into theirs and veered around Aunt Verdella, shouting at Boohoo to stand still *and* to get down—as if he could do both at the same time. He was twirling the yarn, sending long strands floating down over the gray shingles. My skin dampened with scared.

"He must have crawled out the attic window while I was on the phone," Aunt Verdella wailed, holding her pillowy, freckled chest. She pressed her hands to her flushed cheeks. "Boohoo, you're gonna fall and break your neck!"

"I'm not Boohoo," he said, "I'm Spideyman. And I'm making a web."

Boohoo walked with one sneaker "suctioned" on one side of the peak and one on the other, twirling the wad of yarn as he went. "Oh Lord, he's gonna fall!" Aunt Verdella cried, ducking, like each step he made was a boxer's jab.

"I'll go up after him," I said, because it was the only solution I could think of, even though I got woozy if I was more than a few feet off the ground. "Oh dear, oh dear," Aunt Verdella said. "Don't chase him or he'll run. Oh Lord. You're both gonna be landing on your heads!"

I'd just reached the front door when Aunt Verdella stopped me with a loud squawk. She pointed down the gravel road at Uncle Rudy's beat-up pickup lazily moving toward us in a haze of dust. I looked back up at Boohoo, who glanced down the road, too, then went back to his web-making. It was one of those moments when I just wanted to go back. Back to when our family worked as smoothly as the gears on the clock that Ma kept oiled.

Aunt Verdella ran to the truck, jogging alongside it before it could stop, huffing as she chattered, her finger jabbing at the roof. Relief pushed me to the truck, too. "Yeah, I see him . . . I see him," Uncle Rudy said as he opened the truck door, speaking in his usual still-as-a-lake-on-a-sunny-day voice.

"Hurry," Aunt Verdella said. "Do something before he breaks his neck."

I wasn't exactly sure what Aunt Verdella expected Uncle Rudy to do, since he was even older than she—him sixty-nine, her sixty-eight—and with a back that had him stiff and curled like the letter *S*. Uncle Rudy grabbed a hardware store bag off the front seat and waited for his half-blind, all-deaf lab, Knucklehead, to climb down from the seat. My uncle didn't look up. Not once. He just shuffled toward the house.

"Hi, Uncle Rudy!" Boohoo shouted. Uncle Rudy gave him a slow wave, still without looking up, while Aunt Verdella buzzed around Uncle Rudy like a housefly, verbalizing what I was thinking. "Where you goin', Rudy? You gotta do something! How's he gonna get down by himself?"

"Same way he got up, I suppose," Uncle Rudy said as he pulled the screen door wide open to let Knucklehead in. We followed them into the kitchen, where Uncle Rudy set his bag down on the cluttered counter, patted Knucklehead once he flopped down on his hair-matted rag rug, then went back outside.

Uncle Rudy was the only one who could make Boohoo do

anything. And Boohoo (when he was on the ground anyway) tagged after Uncle Rudy like Knucklehead used to. So when Uncle Rudy headed for the shed, Boohoo called down to ask him what he was doing. Uncle Rudy didn't answer. He just scraped open the wood-slatted door and slipped inside. And when he came out, he had his fishing pole and creel. "Rudy!" Aunt Verdella cried, flabbergasted. "You're not goin' off fishing and leave us in this predicament, are you?" Uncle Rudy just kept walking, his work boots crunching gravel as he made his way down the driveway, whistling as he went.

Aunt Verdella stopped, propped her freckly fists about where her waist should be, and watched him, her eyes stretched wide, her jaw dangling.

"Hey, Uncle Rudy?" Boohoo called, his voice thin and anxious. "You going down to the creek?" I glanced back at the roof. Boohoo was staring down the drive, the wad of yarn hanging limp alongside his knee. Uncle Rudy didn't even turn around. "Evy? He going down to the creek?"

Boohoo didn't wait for me to answer. He crouched down, and while Aunt Verdella and I held our breaths and pinched each other's arms, Boohoo shuffled his way down the sloped roof, his makeshift cape fanning the shingles at his back. He curled his leg into the opened attic window, tossed the skein in, grabbed on to the sill, and slipped inside.

Boohoo was out the front door in a flash. I gripped his forearm and jerked him to a stop before he could jump off the porch. I didn't know whether to spank him or hug him. Not that I had the chance to do either, because Aunt Verdella grabbed him and squished him against her belly. "Oh, Boohoo. You scared the dickens out of us! Don't you go on that roof again, you hear me? You could have broken your neck and been killed, or paralyzed, or—"

Boohoo squirmed as Aunt Verdella smothered his sweaty dark hair with kisses dropped like commas, in between a long list of near-fatal injuries he could have sustained had he fallen. He wormed his face free. "Hey, Aunt Verdella, Aunt Verdella," Boohoo said, patting her arm to get her attention. "Did you know that when you run, you don't go any faster, just higher? You do. Like this," he said. Boohoo demonstrated, his dirty sneakers scissoring baby-sized bunny hops, his head bobbing on a neck not much bigger than a wrist. Aunt Verdella looked at Boohoo, then at me, "I don't run like that, do I?" Boohoo assured her that she did, then headed for the shed, calling to Uncle Rudy to wait up.

Aunt Verdella mopped the fear off her brow as Boohoo raced to catch up to Uncle Rudy, then skipped down the drive alongside of him, his fish pole in one hand, his other hooked on the back of Uncle Rudy's suspenders. Aunt Verdella shook her head. "That boy's gonna give me gray hair yet," she said, as though she'd forgotten the duct-tape-width strip of silver that ran down the part of her *Shocking Strawberry* colored hair. "I swear, watching every child I ever babysat in one room, at one time, would still be less work than *that* one. He's a handful!" It didn't matter how upset Aunt Verdella was, her words always sounded like one long string of ha-has.

Aunt Verdella's eyes lifted then, and she said, "Sorry, Jewel, honey. Button and I are doing our best, but that boy *is* a handful!" Aunt Verdella did that often, talking to Ma as though she was standing right next to her.

"Did I tell you what he did when I dozed off watching TV last night?" Aunt Verdella asked. "He wrapped me up like a mummy in a good three, four skeins of yarn—my two new avocados, to boot! I woke up because I had to tinkle, and almost peed my pants trying to get my ankles free so I could get to the bathroom. My bladder isn't what it used to be, you know. That boy had the yarn so tangled that Rudy had to get the scissors and cut me loose. Course, all that little stinker did was laugh."

"That's what you get for telling him that bite on his leg this spring was a spider bite," I teased. Aunt Verdella chuckled and lifted her palms as if to say, *Well, what you gonna do about it now?*

"While they're fishing, how about I give you a hand unpacking?" Aunt Verdella didn't wait for me to answer. She just linked her arm with mine and headed me across the road.

"My little Button," she said, pulling me so close that our sides bumped. "All grown up and moving out of her childhood home . . . living right across the road from me." She got quiet suddenly, and stared down at her feet as we headed up my drive. No doubt, because she was thinking of how my move meant Dad would be living alone, with no one to make sure he ate, and to keep him from feeling lonely—as if *I* had the power to do either.

Aunt Verdella reminded me of a baby, the way her moods could go from sad or scared and circle back to happy again as quickly as a head turn. And that's exactly what happened when we stepped inside Grandma Mae's house.

"You know," she said, her whole body smiling, "after your grandma Mae passed, I couldn't come in here without getting all tensed up, remembering her with that frown pickled on her face. But when I brought over Rudy's tomato starter plants—I hope you don't mind. I don't have the window space at home—I just smiled, thinking of Freeda and Winnalee and the life they brought to this house. I was sorry, when after they left, your ma said she didn't want any more renters in here. I always thought having a young family across the street again would be nice. But now *you'll* be here." She wrapped her arms around her fat middle and shimmied gently.

Aunt Verdella followed me upstairs and took the shirts I'd flung on the bed, heading for the closet. "I'll bet every piece of clothing you own is something you sewed!" she called, her voice so loud that I swear I could see the windows vibrating. "Your ma would be so proud of you, Button."

Would Ma be proud of me? I wore that question at the back of my head like a ponytail. It was there when I'd packed Dad's lunches with store-bought bread instead of homemade because my crust always chewed like taffy (not that Ma was a good cook. She wasn't. But I knew she wanted me to be), and the question was there on nights Aunt Verdella and I tucked Boohoo into bed with sand in his hair and streaks on his legs, because time had gotten away from us and we were too tired to wrestle him to the tub. Sometimes, like when my English teacher complimented me on my latest essay, or when someone said what a sweet girl I was, I knew Ma was smiling down on me with pride. But other times, I knew better.

Like the night my friend Penny convinced me to lie to Dad that I was going to her house to help her paint her bedroom, and she told her mom the reverse. Instead we slipped off with a twenty-year-old guy Penny had the hots for, and his friend, even though both of us had a few weeks to go before we turned sixteen and neither of us was allowed to date until then. And certainly not guys that old.

That night, Penny talked me into rolling the waistband of my skirt like hers, making them minis that barely covered our butts. I didn't want to because of my skinny legs, with knees lumpy and big as cauliflowers, but she lifted a copy of her *Teen Beat* magazine to show me a picture of Twiggy, the model whose doe-eyed face and string-bean body was plastered everywhere. "She only weighs ninety-eight pounds," Penny said. "Girls are starving themselves to get as skinny as her—be glad you don't have to!" I could almost feel Ma's eyes burning two holes into the top of my head as I cuddled in the backseat with Trevor, who was cuter than I had ever imagined one of my dates could be, and drank the bottle of Pabst he shoved into my hand. He thought I was just chilly when I asked to wear his sweatshirt, pulling the hood up over my head so that it drooped down over my eyes, before letting him run his hand up my shirt and stroke my breasts a couple of times before I pushed him away.

No. I didn't think Ma was all that proud of me.

"How about this drawer for your socks?" Aunt Verdella asked.

I looked up and nodded.

"You tie your socks together. Now ain't that interesting," she said. "I always make balls. But then I guess your ma tied socks, too, didn't she? Course, she would. Balls make the tops stretch out, and your ma had those skinny ankles. Isn't it something how many things we learn from our mothers, though? I do all sorts of things like mine. Like cutting the ends off of bread when I bake it, and eating them while they're still hot. Even if I make four loaves!" She giggled. "And the way I can't throw nothing away. My ma was just like me. A real clutterbug."

Aunt Verdella had always slipped little things about her parents into our conversations, but until Ma died, I never paid all that much attention to them. Now I looked at things differently. It did me good to see her remember times without tears, because although I didn't cry every time Ma's name came up anymore, I'd still feel that horrible ache pooling in my center.

I smiled at Aunt Verdella as I picked up a box of my personal things, wanting to put them away myself. "I'm so glad your ma was good to you," I said.

Aunt Verdella pushed down the mound of socks and closed the drawer with her hip. "Oh, she treated me like a little princess. And Lord knows, it wasn't because I was so cute she couldn't take her eyes off of me, either! Though to her, I probably was."

Aunt Verdella noticed the leaning stack of sweaters I'd left on the window seat, and she hurried to grab them. "I'll put these on the shelf in the closet. How about that? The dresser's already full." I told her that would be fine, then opened the box of mementos I had wedged between my feet. Winnalee's Book of Bright Ideas was on top, alongside the empty urn Winnalee had left behind. I took the urn out of the box and set it on the floor, then picked up the book and sat down, smoothing my fingers over the embossed letters: *Great Expectations* by Charles Dickens.

Aunt Verdella was still chattering about my sewing when she stepped out of the closet and spotted the urn. "Oh my," she said as she crossed the room and picked it up. "I didn't know you had this, Button." She turned the urn in her hands, her eyes puckering with empathy. "I'll never forget the sight of that sweet little thing pulling this out of their truck and telling us her dead ma was in it."

Aunt Verdella looked like she might cry, so I lifted the Book of Bright Ideas to show her.

"Oh, I remember you two toting that book around! You girls were what, eight, nine years old?"

"Nine."

Aunt Verdella sighed wistfully. "I remember the day you found it in the bottom of the tree the two of you used to play in. You were so touched that she'd left it behind for you." Winnalee's "bright ideas" were written in chubby, irregular letters, the *i*'s dotted with circles and sometimes hearts. Aunt Verdella gave one long *awwwwww* at the sight of them.

Aunt Verdella sat down on the bed beside me, the urn cradled in her arms. "Now refresh me Button, 'cause my memory only holds things about as long as my bladder. Where'd she get that book from? And the things she'd write . . . what exactly was that about, again?"

So I reminded her of how Winnalee had swiped the book

from a rich lawyer's house where Freeda cleaned. How he had a whole collection of the classics in his library, all of them leather-bound prop books with blank pages.

"Now why would he have books like that?"

"For looks, I guess."

Aunt Verdella shook her head. "He must have been a little goofy in the head," she said.

I started to explain the notion Winnalee had that launched the bright ideas, then decided to just read the first entry, because it said it all: "Bright Idea number one: *If you don't want to keep making the same mistakes over and over again like Freeda says big people do, then you should find a book with nothing inside it and write down the things you see and hear that you think might be the secrets to life, because nobody's going to tell you shit. By the time you get to 100 you're probably going to know everything there is to know about how to live good.*"

"Ohhhh, isn't that precious," Aunt Verdella said, her hand warm on my arm.

My stomach suddenly got that hot sensation in it. The same one you feel when your eyes warm before you cry. "Aunt Verdella? Do you ever wonder why we think of the Malones so often, and still miss them? They were our friends over one summer. That's all. Penny was my friend for six years before she moved, and though I missed her for a time, I hardly ever think of her anymore."

"Oh, Button. It's not the length of time we knew someone that makes them so special. It's what they brought to our lives."

Aunt Verdella rested her head against mine. "You know, when the picture on your TV screen starts rolling. Or when your bread's coming out of the toaster with only one side brown, you admit the dang things are broken, and you either fix them, or you get a new one. But when your life is broken, you'll let that misery roll by for years, and ignore the side of you that isn't finished. Your uncle Rudy, who is, as you know, smart as a whip about most everything, says that's just human nature. And I suppose it is. But still . . ."

Aunt Verdella straightened up and stared across the room at nothing. "When Freeda and Winnalee pulled into town—Freeda with that fiery red hair and temper to match, and Winnalee, cute as a bug's ear in that big mesh slip and ladies' blouse, carrying this urn and that book—I brought them back to rent your grandma's place because I saw something in them that was broken that I wanted to fix. I don't know that I fixed even one thing in their lives, but what I do know, is that they fixed plenty in ours. Without even tryin'."

She made a soft *hmmmm* in the back of her throat. "I don't like thinking about those times, back before Freeda and Winnalee came and changed our family for the better—we were so broken then—but I can't help it sometimes. Your ma and dad's marriage had gone sour so long ago, that I doubt they even tasted the bitterness anymore. And your ma, so judgmental and jealous, and cold to you and your dad. I told myself that's just how she was made, because nothing ever seemed to change it. It broke my heart, though, the way she had you so scared of doin' something wrong, that you couldn't stop scratching yourself. Remember how you used to chew the insides of your cheeks until they bled?" I slid my tongue over to cover the jagged, tender skin in my mouth, as if she'd see the damage right through my cheek if I didn't.

"Auntie tried to help you loosen up—you were such a serious little thing. Like a little old lady in a child's body. But I couldn't do nothing to change that, any more than I could change Jewel's behavior. All I could do was love you both. But Freeda? She knew what to do."

"Yes," I said, remembering how, after Ma accused Freeda of having an affair with Dad, Freeda had flown into a rage and yelled at Ma for her jealousy, and for how she treated her family. Ma had cried so hard Freeda had to help her to a chair. That's when it came out that she felt ugly and undeserving of Dad, and Freeda helped her understand that she was putting those feelings about herself onto me. "But after Freeda took Ma under her wing, helping her fix up, loosen up, and feel better about herself, Ma turned butterfly bright and wasn't so hard on herself—or us—anymore." Of course, she never became as vibrant or as much of a free spirit as Freeda—nobody probably could—but she started giving Dad back rubs and me hugs. And when Boohoo came along, she cuddled him just like Aunt Verdella did, melding his little curled body against her every time she held him.

"Yep. Your ma was like a new person, after Freeda got done with her . . . and you got happier and more outgoing after Winnalee got done with you, too."

Aunt Verdella sighed. "That's why I got my heart so set on buying Hannah Malone a final resting place, like Winnalee wanted her to have. So that sweet little girl could set down this urn, and we could show the Malones how much we appreciated them. Remember when you and me went to Hopested, Minnesota, to buy the plot and stone, and how shocked we were when the funeral director told us that Hannah Malone was still alive? Lord, I couldn't hardly believe my ears! And then a few days later, after the funeral director told Hannah Malone that we'd come and why, there she was on our doorstep, wanting Winnalee back."

I flinched at the memory of Aunt Verdella and me learning—along with Winnalee—that Freeda was *not* Winnalee's sister after all, but her mother, and that she'd returned to Hopested to take Winnalee, only after she'd learned that her uncle Dewey was back living with Hannah. Freeda didn't want Dewey molesting Winnalee as he had her, and she was going to get her out of there even if she had to lie to Winnalee and tell her that *their* mom was dead, and put woodstove—

fireplace, cigarette, whatever kind of ashes they were—in an urn for Winnalee to carry so she'd go willingly, or not. And that night, after the secrets came out, Freeda and Winnalee pulled out of town. Without saying goodbye.

"I just wanted to do something nice for those two, you know?" Aunt Verdella repeated.

I nodded.

"We were so broken then," she said with a sigh.

I stared down at the Book of Bright Ideas. Then I asked in a whisper, "Do you know that we're broken now?"

Aunt Verdella put her arm around me and rested her head back against mine. Then she said, "Yes."

CHAPTER

2

BRIGHT IDEA #86: If you're scared of dead people, then you're probably scared of live people too. But you don't need to be scared of either.

On my first morning waking up in Grandma Mae's house—my second day of freedom from Dauber High—I stepped outside, my skin still damp from my bath, and checked the sky as I headed across the road. Boohoo was digging in his tractor tire sandbox. Uncle Rudy's truck was gone, and Aunt Verdella was coming around the side of the house with an empty laundry basket. "I need to go to Dad's to find my good sewing scissors. Do you think you could give me a lift?" I asked. "I went to get them late last night, but a warning light came on the dash and the car started smelling burny. I didn't know if I'd make it the six miles to Dad's house, so I turned around. Smoke was rolling out of the hood by the time I got home."

"Oh, I wish you had a more reliable car," Aunt Verdella

said. "That thing you're driving is nothing but a pill." Who knew what that expression meant, or if she was using it correctly. But if "a pill" meant an old, rusted heap of ugly maroon junk, then she was using it accurately. Dad had picked up the Rambler Classic right before I got my license. He paid two hundred for it, which is about how many times he'd had to fix it since then. "Course, I'll run you, dear. I could use some milk from The Corner Store, anyway," Aunt Verdella said. "Hopefully your dad will be home so you can ask him to look at your car."

"Yeah," I said. What I didn't say, though, was that I was relieved she'd be with me when I brought it up. Not that I anticipated Dad yelling if I was alone—either way, he'd only stare off and say with a sigh, "Well, bring it over, then"—but with her there, I knew I was less likely to turn into the big-eared kid I'd been, too mousy to talk to her dad.

"We going to Dad's?" Boohoo asked. I nodded.

Aunt Verdella told him to empty the dirt from his shoes and brush the sand off his bottom, then went inside to put the basket away. I watched Boohoo as he upside-downed his sneaker, letting the sand filter through his fingers as he made cartoonish sounds of a plane plummeting toward earth.

Once, Verdella had told me that Dad was a "change of life baby," meaning my grandma Mae—Dad and Uncle Rudy's mother—had him when she was old (forty-four, I think) and that she "never had the time of day for him." Some years after Uncle Rudy's first wife died, Uncle Rudy and Aunt Verdella got married and built a house across the road from Grandma Mae's. Dad was still just a kid, and he began hanging around more and more, and little by little, his toys and clothes moved across the road, until, without anyone verbally agreeing to anything, Aunt Verdella and Uncle Rudy were raising him. Just as now they were raising Boohoo.

Boohoo was too little to understand death, but the grief he

absorbed from the rest of us when Ma died, along with his missing her, caused him to wake and cry in the night. Nobody could comfort him except Aunt Verdella. Probably because after Ma opened her bridal shop, while Boohoo was still in diapers, Aunt Verdella took care of him during the day. Dad didn't seem to notice that Boohoo never came home after Ma's death. Same as he didn't notice that each night after our supper was finished and the dishes done, I got in my Rambler, crossed Highway 8, and drove down Peters Road to Aunt Verdella and Uncle Rudy's house, where I stayed until bedtime. So to Boohoo, it was "Dad's house," not his, and "Dad" was just a name. Obviously. Because when Aunt Verdella helped him make a Father's Day card last summer, he gave it to Uncle Rudy, and Uncle Rudy had to explain to him that it belonged to Dad.

After Ma died, her sister Stella came, wanting to take Boohoo. She claimed I was old enough to get along without a mother, but that Boohoo wasn't. Dad threw her out of the house, shouting, "Are you fucking nuts? You think I'm going to give my son away?" I wondered if Dad realized by now that he *had* given Boohoo away.

As far as Boohoo went, it was déjà vu all over again, proving that not only do people repeat the same mistakes *they* already made, but sometimes, the same mistakes their *family* already made.

"Okay, I'm ready," Aunt Verdella called as she came down the steps, swinging her crocheted purse, and carrying a paper plate covered with Reynolds Wrap. "How you coming there, Boohoo?" she called, and he answered, "One down, one to go!" Aunt Verdella sent a string of ha-has floating through the air like pollen.

"I brought your dad some supper," she said, handing me the plate once we got in her Buick. "Chicken from yesterday, which is what we're having tonight. And some German potato salad."

"Ew, I don't like that stuff," Boohoo said, wrinkling his nose as he hung over the seat. "It's snotty."

Aunt Verdella told him that she had mashed potatoes for him, and I told him to sit down. When he wouldn't, she said, "You don't sit down, and Button and me are gonna give you a love sandwich!" Since Boohoo turned six, he claimed he didn't like kisses anymore. Still, he hovered over the seat until Aunt Verdella and I smothered his cheeks with smooches, one pair of lips for each side. Boohoo shrieked and threw himself back against the seat.

Dad was sitting on the couch when we got there, looking groggy from working the graveyard shift at the paper mill—his preference since Ma's death. He tried to show enthusiasm when Aunt Verdella peeled back the aluminum foil. "You want me to heat it up for you, Reece?"

"Nah, I just had a sandwich. I'll have it after a bit."

I took the food from Aunt Verdella, offering to put it in the fridge so she wouldn't see the other plates she'd left him in the past week or two, or realize that Dad didn't have anything with which to make a sandwich.

Boohoo ran toward his bedroom to search for the Tonka truck that he'd forgotten when Aunt Verdella and I were packing my things. "No running in the house, Boohoo," I called. Dad didn't glance up as Boohoo raced by.

As upset with Dad's neglect of Boohoo as I was, I couldn't

help but feel sorry for him as he sat there staring at the television set, smudges of blame the color of bruises under his eyes, his body sunken with regrets. But I felt sadder still for Boohoo. Dad had gotten more approachable after the summer the Malones were here—when Ma was happier, warmer—and for a time, Dad and I had conversations like a real dad and daughter, even if they were short and not about much of anything. But not anymore. Now Dad hardly ever talked to anyone in the family, but for Aunt Verdella when she barged in, and Uncle Rudy when he ran into him. That made me sad for all of us, but especially for Boohoo. I remembered what it felt like to be little and have him look through you as if you were made of fog. Dad should have remembered how it felt, too.

Aunt Verdella plopped down on the couch and chattered to him—about Tommy Smithy asking to pasture some of his cows at the farm for the summer, about the tomato plants she'd started—while I went to my room to dig for my good pair of sewing shears.

I hated being in that house. The ambush of memories, and the thought of Ma cringing as she looked down from Heaven over her ruined house overwhelmed me. Ma's floors were gritty, her end tables littered with old newspapers and coffee cups. The kitchen linoleum was scraped in the shape of a fan because the back door no longer hung level, and there was a stained, bubbled patch in front of the sink, two feet in diameter, where water had leaked from loose pipes. Dirty shirts were bunched over the backs of chairs, and socks pried loose with the opposing big toe lay in crusty balls where they'd fallen. That is, until Aunt Verdella came along once a week to scoop them up and take them home for washing.

I would have continued to show up every day to clean the house for Ma's sake, had Dad not stopped me. Aunt Verdella explained it and I think she might be right. Maybe when Dad came home to kitchen sounds or the whir of the vacuum, he forgot for a moment that Ma was gone, and the truth, when it came, was just too jolting. In spite of how Dad felt, though, I vowed to sneak into the house once a week after he left for work to take down Ma's bells and dust them. Ma loved her bell collection.

I found my scissors and stalled in the hall until Aunt Verdella called for me, then gave me a reminder nod toward Dad. The insides of my left arm itched, and I scraped it with the cold edge of the scissors as I told him that my car was broken again.

"It overheated," Aunt Verdella said.

Dad glanced up, but only for a second. He sighed as I knew he would, and I wondered if he showed the same annoyance when other people asked for his help. I had my doubts. "Have your uncle Rudy fill the radiator, then bring it over Saturday. It's probably just the thermostat," he said.

"Okay, I'm ready!" Boohoo announced as he roared through the living room carrying his Tonka dump truck and a ratty Nerf ball wearing a bite-sized gouge—both finds from last summer's Community Sale, even though Aunt Verdella's house was already stuffed with so many toys that it would make the stash in Santa's workshop look skimpy.

"Well, I suppose," Aunt Verdella said, giving her thighs a quick clap. She stood up, leaned down, and gave Dad's forehead a kiss, then ruffled his hair like he was a boy. "Boohoo?" she said, "Aren't you gonna give your daddy a hug? . . ." But the screen door was already slamming. I hurried along Boohoo's trail, holding my breath for fear that Aunt Verdella would ask me the same.

Maybe it was seeing Fanny Tilman, dressed too warmly as she was that day back in '61, heading through the doorway of The Corner Store where I'd first met Freeda and Winnalee, that suddenly had me thinking of the Malones again. It was a day like this one. Early June. Warm. Breezy. Winnalee was refusing to get out of the truck, and Freeda had "to pee" and thought Winnalee should do the same. It was the first time I'd ever heard a woman cuss, or seen a girl in dress-up clothes. The memories made me smile, and Fanny gave me an odd look, like she thought I was smiling at her—fat chance of that!

"I scream, you scream, we all scream for ice cream!" Boohoo shouted, bumping Fanny's side as he zipped past her to get to the freezer.

Fanny shook her head. "That boy could use some manners."

Aunt Verdella ignored Fanny's remark, asking her how she was, while I went to grab the gallon of milk. Ada Smithy was behind the counter, as she'd been for years. She asked me if I'd be working full-time at Jewel's Bridal Boutique now that I'd graduated. I told her yes, but that I'd be working from home. I was shy around most people, but not Ada, who was sunshine warm like Aunt Verdella, though softer-spoken.

"Button's living in Mae's place now," Aunt Verdella added, even though she was still over near the bread rack with Fanny.

"How nice. You and Verdella will be good company for each other."

I told her I'd be doing some beading and other trim work on the bridal gowns, and sewing some of the bridesmaids' dresses, then bringing them in to Linda. "We're making mother-of-the-bride dresses and soon we'll be adding prom dresses, too, so Hazel and Marge are working in the shop now instead of from home. It's crowded in the work room, so Linda might look for a bigger place. Until then, me working from home works best for all of us." Ada glanced at Boohoo, who was ripping the wrapper off an Eskimo Pie, and she nodded. "Of course."

Aunt Verdella was heading to the counter, the ice-cream

wrapper Boohoo dropped as he ran outside bunched in her hand. Fanny followed behind her, looking like the Grim Reaper in her long wool coat and dark scarf. "You stay right out front where Auntie can see you, Boohoo!" Aunt Verdella shouted.

Aunt Verdella asked me if I wanted an ice-cream bar as she veered to the freezer, adding that she was having one. Fanny Tilman scrunched her face. *"She,"* Fanny said—never calling me by name, not once in my whole life— "could use one. But I'd think twice before having one myself if I were you, Verdella. No offense, but you're getting as big as a house."

Ada gasped, and my jaw tightened. I'd never liked Fanny Tilman, who smelled like horehound candy and had a personality equally as repulsive. Fanny didn't like many, and she certainly never liked me. Not even when I was a shrimpy kid with short, brown permed knots, and ears the size of dessert plates, who was always quiet and polite.

"That wasn't very nice, Fanny," Ada whispered.

Fanny shrugged as if to say, *But it's true*. Then she said to Ada, "She keeps this up, and Rudy will be looking elsewhere."

I wanted to shout at her that Uncle Rudy loved Aunt Verdella just the way she was, but of course I didn't. Because even though I'd just celebrated my eighteenth birthday, I still felt like that shy, big-eared kid most of the time. Especially around people like Fanny.

Aunt Verdella looked down and patted her poochie middle. She'd been the same size since I could remember, though her belly hung lower now. "Oh dear," she said. "I was wondering if I'd gained." She pulled the elastic waistband from her pink polyester pants and gave it a snap. "These did feel a little snugger when I put them on this morning. I guess I'd better stop having a treat every time I give Boohoo one," she said with a laugh. She glanced outside, then gave the window a rap when Boohoo wasn't in sight.

"I'll go look for him," I said, eager to get away.

The door was propped open with a chipped brick, and Fanny's scratchy voice tagged me outside. "You have to think of those things, Verdella. Bad enough that Rudy's been tripping over somebody else's kids all these years—the least you could do is not let yourself go." I hurried so I wouldn't have to hear any more.

I found Boohoo behind the station chasing a grass snake that had slipped between two large barrels. I hauled him back to the car, kicking and complaining. "Let me go! That snake's gonna be my pet. Knucklehead don't play with me no more."

"Well, a snake won't play with you, either. Now come on, Boohoo. Get in the car." I got Boohoo inside and slammed the door, but he just slid across the seat and slipped out the other side. He wouldn't give up on the snake until me and Aunt Verdella lured him back with a Bonomo Turkish Taffy *and* a Mallo Cup.

When we got home, Aunt Verdella went into the hallway near the bathroom and rooted around in the linen closet. I heard something clunk to the floor, and then "Oh my Lord!"

When she came into kitchen, her mouth was hanging open like she'd just seen a car wreck. "I'm two hundred pounds!" she announced. "I never thought I'd see two hundred pounds! I'm only five three and a half. That's just too heavy!" And Boohoo, who was standing at the table, twisting off a long string of banana-flavored taffy to give to Knucklehead as Uncle Rudy came through the door, turned to him and said, "Uncle Rudy, Aunt Verdella is as fat as Fred Flintstone!"

"Boohoo!" I hissed.

He turned to me. "It's true. That's what Fred said he weighs. Two hundred pounds! And that's just how much Aunt Verdella is."

CHAPTER 3

BRIGHT IDEA #23: If an apple is sour and has rot spots, don't think you can make it sweet by putting sugar on it. It will still taste sour and probably give you the shits.

I told myself to let go of the mean things Fanny Tilman said, but that night as I brushed my brown hair into a ponytail at the top of my head before bed, I remembered every single thing she'd said, and how she treated me. It always bothered me, the way I'd let belittling or insensitive comments simmer under my skin.

I stared in the mirror and wondered what about me always made people talk around me, not to me, like Fanny did. Like Dad did. Winnalee told me once that Ma and I were "gray people." I still didn't know exactly what that meant, but I knew that I'd been one before the Malones came, that I ceased to be one by the time they left, and that after Ma died, I tarnished again like neglected brass.

I studied my face in the mirror as I brushed my teeth. I wasn't homely anymore. Not once I grew into my ears like Aunt Verdella said I would, and let my hair grow long and stopped getting it thinned (though I did think it would look better if I lightened it with Sun In). And my friend Penny always said that I had pretty eyes. But my guess was that being a gray person was probably more about personality than looks. Try as I might, though, I just wasn't one of those bubbly, whirlwind people who exuded personality. Nor was I gray *and* outspoken, like Fanny Tilman. No, I was plain and quiet. Ordinary inside and out. Too self-conscious about myself to be vibrant. Mostly because I had boobs the size of coconuts, on a trunk the width of a knitting needle. Penny told me more than once how glad I should be that I wasn't flat like her, but who could be glad about having old, creepy men gawk at your chest, and high school boys making vulgar comments, as if there wasn't a human being attached to those breasts. If she had my boobs, I knew Penny would have understood why I kept my shoulders hunched, in spite of Aunt Verdella's warning that I'd end up with a bad back like Uncle Rudy, and that my internal organs would start drooping (which, I told her, probably accounted for my big, knobby knees).

I crawled into bed, my arms itching as I recalled Fanny Tilman's rude remark about Aunt Verdella's size. *As big as a house?* And telling her that Uncle Rudy would stray? Granted, Aunt Verdella thought Uncle Rudy was handsome in a Johnny Cash sort of way, but he was almost seventy years old!

Even as I stewed, I had to admit to myself that what bothered me most was Fanny's insinuation that Boohoo and I were a burden on Uncle Rudy and Aunt Verdella. Yes, I knew that they loved us and that we filled a void in their lives, but they were old now. And since Uncle Rudy retired, it seemed that he spent as much time searching for solitude and silence as he once spent looking for his cows. So I told myself that I'd hurry and finish cleaning a room for Boohoo, and I'd sew during the day and keep him with me at night. After all, it didn't matter if I felt like a scared kid inside, I *was* grown-up now. And Boohoo was *my* responsibility.

On Sunday Aunt Verdella ran me over to Dad's to pick up my car, and I headed to town to buy groceries so I could have Aunt Verdella and Uncle Rudy over for supper.

The sun was bright when I headed east, so I yanked down the visor. An envelope fell onto my lap. It was addressed to me, in care of Dad, which meant he must have wedged it on the visor for me to find. I squinted at the envelope, made blazing white from the sun. The edges were trimmed in red, white, and blue, and "airmail" was stamped on the front. It was from Jesse Dayne, the boy who became my best friend after Penny moved away. Well, if you could consider a best friend to be one who continually seeks you out for advice about his love life, and you share nothing about yours because you don't have one, aside from the secret fantasy one you're having with *him*. I pulled the car over and put it in park. The letter came all the way from the U.S. Army base in Mannheim, Germany. There was a photo of Jesse tucked inside, dressed in his uniform, the American flag behind him. Even with his hair cropped to almost-bald, he was still cute enough to make my stomach flip.

The letter was short, the print small, but for the *l*'s and *t*'s that tickled the bottoms of the letters above them.

> *Hey Evy. How's my best girl? Bummer that I missed you while I was on leave last May. I spent ten days of it in Santiago with my family for my sister Tracy's wedding, then headed back to Dauber for three. I spent most of those days arguing with Amy—what a waste! I stopped at your place the morning I shipped out, but you were gone. Your dad said*

he didn't know to where. Anyway, I was missing my friend so decided to write. Want to (pen) pal around with me?

Your friend, Jesse

P.S. I thought you'd get a charge out of this picture. Dig the hair.

As upset as I was to know that Jesse *had* made an effort to see me, and that Dad hadn't bothered to tell me, I was also filled with tingles that made my face feel flushed. I felt stupid for being happy—not like it was a love letter. No doubt he was only writing so he could fish for information on Amy Collins, his pretty girlfriend who had unwrapped the fluffy angora string she'd wound around his class ring in the parking lot of the A&W the day after they graduated, and handed it back to him. Or so Jesse's mom, Rita, told Aunt Verdella when they ran into each other at the post office, on that, their first (but not last) breakup. Aunt Verdella—oblivious to how I *really* felt about Jesse—told me that he was crushed. And the next thing any of us knew, Jesse was heading out west to stay with his sister and look for work. Six months and another girlfriend later (according to his mother), he enlisted in the Army. Jesse came home to spend a few days with his family before he headed for basic training, and I went to see him off as he'd asked me to. I stood back a few feet waiting for his family and buddies to say their goodbyes, and after they did, Jesse noticed me and came over. I don't remember what we said to each other, but I'll never forget that he kissed me. A quick peck maybe, but right on the lips.

Jesse went to Oklahoma first, to Washington state next, then to Texas for some special training in missiles, before heading to the base in Mannheim, Germany. I kept tabs on him through Aunt Verdella, who got her information from

Rita. Once, I almost got up the nerve to call Rita to ask for his address, but before I could actually get the phone off its cradle, I reminded myself of what was true—Jesse knew where to reach me, so if he'd wanted to stay in touch, he would have.

I tucked the letter into my purse—thrilled that he finally wanted to be in touch!—then drove to Ben Franklin to buy some pretty stationery before getting groceries.

When I got back, I hurried into Aunt Verdella's to invite them for dinner. The only supper food I knew how to cook was meat loaf and baked potatoes with sour cream, but I had picked up stuff for salad, too.

Boohoo was on the phone when I walked in, the TV blaring as usual. Aunt Verdella was shouting from the stairs, "Who is it? Ask them who it is, Boohoo. Button . . . that you? Take the phone from him, will you?" But before I could, Boohoo said bye and hung up.

Aunt Verdella came into the kitchen, winded from hurrying. "Boohoo, what did Auntie tell you? You're supposed to answer the phone, 'Peters residence, Robert Reece speaking.' "

"I said that!" Boohoo shouted, as he whipped dirty yarn from the ball that Aunt Verdella probably wound ten times already in a futile attempt to keep her house from turning into an even worse web of chaos.

"No you didn't, honey. You said, 'Peters house, Spideyman speaking.' "

Boohoo clunked down on his knees to wind the yarn around the legs of a kitchen chair.

"Oh well. Who was it, honey?" Aunt Verdella asked.

"I don't know. Some lady."

"Well, what did she say?"

"Just if Rudy Peters was there."

"She used our last name?"

"Yeah," Boohoo said, then he went on to make *whooshes* and *whams*, as he ducked under the chair.

"Did it sound like the same lady who called yesterday?" Aunt Verdella asked, her hands propped on her knees as she bent over her belly and peered under the chair. Boohoo didn't answer.

Aunt Verdella straightened up. "Ada gave my number to a lady who's looking to have an afghan made to match her new living room set. I hope that wasn't her . . . though why she'd ask for Rudy instead is beyond me. Oh well, hopefully she'll call back."

I gave her a kiss, then headed toward the door. "I'm making meat loaf for us tonight," I said. "So don't start any supper."

"Oh, how nice," she said. I was on the porch when she called, "You invited your dad, didn't you?"

I hesitated. "He wouldn't come," I called back.

"Oh, I think he would. He doesn't work tomorrow. I'll give him a call."

It was fun cooking in my very own kitchen, even if the pots and pans were scuffed and dented. I cranked the radio up high, since I didn't need to worry about waking anybody, and while I chopped onions I waited for slow love songs to play.

Jesse was cute. Real cute. Six feet tall, so I didn't feel like an Amazon when I stood next to him. He had straight dark hair that he used to let grow past his ears every spring after basketball season, since the coaches were the only ones who enforced the dress code.

When I was a freshman, Jesse's family moved to Dauber and built a house on a forty they bought from Mike Thompson—Freeda's old boyfriend—after he married a woman from South Dakota who missed her family too much to stay in Dauber. Jesse was a junior. He rode my bus for a few months as he worked to buy another car, after the engine blew up in the one he had. I still remember looking up from my book when the bus slowed down to pick him up that first day, and how my head filled with whooshy noises when he boarded. He was cuter than any boy in Dauber High—and he actually smiled at me.

I thought Jesse liked me, the way he sought me out on the bus, and even in the halls. But it turned out his attention was only meant in friendship, because two weeks after he came, he was suddenly going with Christine Conner, his first in a long string of girlfriends before he graduated.

One day, just weeks after Jesse moved to Dauber, he rode his bike over to get the book report I'd written for him, since he didn't even have a book picked out, and the reports were due on Monday. Dad called Jesse a "long-haired hippie" after he left, but Jesse wasn't a hippie. He didn't run around high, shouting antiwar slogans and making peace signs. He listened to Bob Dylan, but that was about it. "Not exactly the kind of boy I want to see you date," Dad grumbled, a year later, when Jesse dropped me off after school one night. I smiled inside because Dad thought Jesse *could* be my boyfriend.

The day I learned that Jesse had enlisted in the Army, I told Dad—even though it felt awkward since about the only exchange we ever had was about my car, or which one of us would pick up something at the store. Dad's dark brows dipped when I told him. "Jesse who?"

"Dayne. The ones who built a house on Mike Thompson's property. The one you called a hippie when you met him?"

"Well I'm glad to hear that he felt enough responsibility to his country to enlist, even if that might mean fighting in 'Nam. That's more than I can say about the rest of that goddamn hippie bunch who are running off to Canada." I stood quiet in my awkwardness, then left the room as soon as Dad looked down again.

That night, Aunt Verdella and Uncle Rudy and Boohoo came over a few minutes before six, and I could tell that it took everything short of another yarn-wrapping for Uncle Rudy to keep Aunt Verdella from coming earlier to help. Dad wasn't coming, of course. "He sounded tired," Aunt Verdella said. As if that was an anomaly.

If they noticed that the meat loaf was on the dry side, or that the skins on the potatoes were tough, they didn't say so. Uncle Rudy ate seconds, while Aunt Verdella, who normally did, too, stuck to a bowl of salad (swimming in a sea of French dressing). "She's gonna get skinny now," Boohoo said. "Because she's fat as Fred."

"Don't say things like that," I scolded. "You sound like Fanny Tilman."

"Well Aunt Verdella said it!"

I gave Boohoo's plate a turn so he'd stop dropping corn kernels on the floor, and told him to hush and eat.

Aunt Verdella swallowed another gob of salad. "He did hear me say it, Button. Well, not the part about Fred Flintstone, but the part about being fat and needing to diet."

By the time we finished our ice cream, Aunt Verdella was peacock proud of herself for skipping desert. The corner of Boohoo's mouth cranked to the side when she bragged, though. "You finished mine, Aunt Verdella. My plate stuff, *and* my bowl stuff."

"Just a couple of bites," she said.

Uncle Rudy shook his head. "All this fuss over a few pounds, Verdie."

"That's not just a few, Uncle Rudy," Boohoo said. "Two

hundred is a lot!" Then Boohoo started counting. "One . . . two . . . three . . ."

Aunt Verdella helped me do dishes, even though I told her she didn't have to, and Uncle Rudy dozed in the living room. He probably would have snored until Aunt Verdella woke him to leave had Boohoo not taken a leap from the back of the couch and landed on his belly. We heard Uncle Rudy's loud grunt. When he recovered, he shuffled into the kitchen. "Boy, I don't know," he said, patting his big belly. "Two good cooks on my corner now, I'll be *twice* the size as Fred by winter. Now if you ladies don't mind, I think I'll head home and turn in."

He thanked me for the meal and gave my shoulder a pat. Aunt Verdella grabbed him to smooch his cheek. "I'll be home after I help Button clean up," she said.

Boohoo started tagging Uncle Rudy to the front door. "You stay here now so your uncle Rudy can sleep," Aunt Verdella told him.

"But I wanna go with Uncle Rudy," Boohoo whined.

"Why don't you go upstairs and look at the room I'm putting together for you? I brought toys over from Dad's that you haven't played with in a long time. Monkey is up there." Monkey was the crocheted monkey Aunt Verdella made him when he was about three. The one with crocheted-on plastic eyes that were humorously cocked. Monkey had been Boohoo's playmate and sleeping companion for a couple of years.

Boohoo wasn't up there but ten minutes when he came down, Monkey in hand, and said he had to run "home" to get some yarn. He asked for some leftovers to bring to Knucklehead, since the dog was "too tired" to hike over with them, then headed out the door.

"Watch for cars," Aunt Verdella and I called in harmony,

even though we lived on a road that only saw about four vehicles in a whole day, and three of them were usually ours. "And you let Uncle Rudy have his nap," Aunt Verdella added.

I poured two cups of coffee and handed Aunt Verdella one. She looked down at my cup and frowned. "Oh, Button. Coffee? It'll stunt your growth."

"Aunt Verdella, I'm five feet nine already. How tall do you want me to grow?"

We had just settled into the living room when Boohoo returned, Monkey dangling from a yarn leash, a ball of ratty yarn in each hand, and his elbow wedging another two skeins against his belly. Yarn Aunt Verdella had unraveled from old afghans so he'd leave her new skeins alone, since those were for making the blankets and clothing and appliance "cozies" she'd sell at the Community Sale again this summer.

"You didn't wake your Uncle Rudy, did you?" Aunt Verdella asked.

"No. He wouldn't get up. Even when I tried to wake him 'cause somebody was on the phone."

"Oh? Who was it, Boohoo?"

"Probably Crackpot," Boohoo said as he headed out of the room.

Aunt Verdella and I exchanged glances and I stifled a laugh.

"Crackpot?" she said, then hurried after him. Boohoo was right, she didn't go any faster when she ran, only higher. I followed them both. "Boohoo," she was saying. "You shouldn't call people crackpots."

Boohoo was thumping up the stairs, Monkey banging behind him, stopping only when he dropped the ball of yellow yarn and it bounced down the steps. "Oh dear, not my new Harvest Gold," Verdella said. I grabbed it, holding it like a baseball. "Stay out of Aunt Verdella's new yarn," I scolded. "And don't talk rude about people."

Boohoo stuck out his chin, which wore a glossy finish of dried, dribbled milk. "That's what Uncle Rudy calls people on the phone!"

"Boohoo, honey. All Auntie wants to know is who called."

"I told you. A lady. Now give me my string, Evy, or I'm gonna kick you."

"This is new yarn, Boohoo."

Aunt Verdella took the ball from me and gave it a high toss. Boohoo caught it on the first bounce. "Who did she ask for? Me, or Uncle Rudy?"

"Not you or him. Somebody else."

I rolled my eyes. "Just tell them, 'Sorry, you have the wrong number,' next time."

"No. I'm just gonna tell Crackpot to stop calling us all the time."

Boohoo came downstairs a few minutes later, with Monkey and a couple of Matchbox cars and asked Aunt Verdella if they could go "home" now.

I made my voice sound as fun as it could. "You could stay here tonight, Boohoo."

Boohoo walked past me, without even a pause in his step. "No. I'm gonna go home."

CHAPTER 4

> BRIGHT IDEA #17: If you don't give your ma a hug before you go to school because you're mad at her for not letting you wear your good dress, she might die while you're at recess. Then you ain't going to be able to give her that hug ever.

The next morning, bright sunshine pried my eyes open. I startled, thinking, just for a sleepy second, that I'd missed the bus. I flopped back down, wondering how many days it would take before my mind caught on that I didn't have to go to school anymore. A fact for which I'd be eternally grateful, since my love for school died shortly after Ma did.

I'd returned three days after her funeral, feeling foggy, achy, and weak—like I had the flu. There was a group of freshman boys standing inside the door when I walked in, and I knew by the way they suddenly hushed and bowed their heads, that just seconds ago they were simulating Ma's death the moment the lightning struck her.

Every group of girls that passed me that morning, glanced

at me with pity-eyes that made my skin flush. A few of them stopped and awkwardly told me they were sorry, then flew off like flocks of starlings. All except Lydia Marks, who had tears in her eyes when she hugged me. Tears swelled in mine then, too. Her older brother had died in a car crash the year before, and I hadn't said a word to her because I hardly knew her.

Most of the teachers gave me their condolences. A couple of them offered to help me catch up on the work I'd missed—as if the issue at that point was simply that my grades shouldn't suffer.

And then there was Jesse. He came up to me first thing when I got to school and told me he had something for me. I followed him, while his new girlfriend Karen waited nearby with her best friend.

Jesse pulled an oblong envelope from his messy locker. One corner was bent over like a terrier's ear. "Here," he said. He handed me the card, then stood there like he expected me to open it right then. So I did. Inside was a rhyming verse with the word *sympathy* written in delicate, scrolling letters, as if that's how words are written in Heaven. We'd gotten the same card from two others: Ben Franklin and the drugstore were the only places in town that sold greeting cards.

"Thank you," I said, feeling close to tears for a couple of reasons.

Jesse looked me directly in the eye—unlike most others—and he didn't cower when he said, "I wish I knew what to say besides I'm sorry, Evy, but I don't." He gave me a hug. A firm one. No pat of platitude to my back, or shuffling of the feet when he let go. Karen looked impatient, so I thanked him and walked away, the card pressed against my chest. I was glad he didn't ask me to let him know if there was anything he could do, as so many others had: *What did that even mean?*

. . .

I rolled to my side and ran my fingers slowly through my hair. Once upon a time, Ma and I talked about which college I'd attend—Ma sure that with my 4.0 I could get into any school I wanted to, and she hoped I'd choose U-W Madison. There seemed to be too many choices. But not anymore.

I nuzzled my face into my pillow, remembering Mrs. Hanson, my math teacher's face contorting with *Sympathy* as she talked to me about my grades, two or three weeks before the end of the semester. "I'd like you to go see Mr. Schnell," she said. "I think he could help you get back on track." Mrs. Hanson said this as though *I* had derailed, rather than my life. She took my hand like I was a toddler and walked me to the guidance counselor's office. They'd obviously spoken beforehand, because Mrs. Hanson led me inside and left without a word.

Mr. Schnell told me that Mrs. Hanson remembered how my ma beamed at the last conference when she saw my grades and was told what a delightful girl I was. He asked me how my mother would feel if she could see how my grades had plummeted. I didn't hear much else of what he said because I was watching a fly walk in circles on the desk near his clasped hands, and wondering how it was that God could choose to let a measly fly live, but decide that my mother should die. Suddenly I wanted to smash that fly with my fists until it was black pulp. I'd never felt rage like that before, or since, and it made me feel like a monster. On the bus ride home that day, I scratched so hard that my ankle bled through my sock.

The next day, Mr. White, the science teacher, stood before the class, his rubbery lips the color of chalk and contorting as he reviewed facts about cloud-to-cloud lightning, cloud-to-ground lightning, ball lightning—oblivious to the storm brewing in my head and swirling in my stomach. I bolted from my desk and raced to the restroom without asking for permission because my mouth was full of vomit. Jennifer Martin was standing at the mirror ratting the crown of her hair when I rushed into a stall to retch and she called to me that she'd had stomach flu the week before, but that it was only a twenty-four-hour bug.

My grades may have nose-dived, but I *did* learn something that year. I learned that people have short attention spans. After report cards that semester, I became an apparition who drew less attention than the ghost of Dauber's old grave digger, Hiram Fossard. Except to Jesse, who talked to me some every day—sometimes on the phone, if he and Karen were fighting—but he eventually stopped asking how I was doing, too.

Sometimes I felt bad, though, thinking of Ma looking down on me with disappointment that I wasn't in college—she'd wanted that for me so badly—but when I felt bad about that, I'd remember that most girls from my class weren't going. Some, like Jo Laski, Karen's friend, were getting married, and the rest would take jobs at the paper mill where Dad worked if they were lucky enough to get in, or else they'd just check groceries at IGA, or wait tables. I hoped, though, that if Ma was watching me, I was bringing her at least some happiness, because I was sewing for Jewel's Bridal Boutique and doing my best to help Aunt Verdella raise Boohoo. I didn't know what the future held, but for now, I'd go on believing that something more powerful than time would come along and pull our family out of this emotional dormancy.

I breathed in determination and pulled myself out of bed. I'd shower, then go pick up the gowns Linda had for me—Jo wanted beading on the bodice, and her gown needed fifty-one pearl buttons. And I'd be sewing one of the bridesmaid's dresses, so I'd bring that home, too. I had a stack of alterations to do, as well (neighbors were always asking me to hem, and patch; sometimes they paid me, sometimes they didn't) and then I'd pick up some clothesline because the ropes hanging in the back were rotted and frayed. I'd stop at Dad's if his truck was gone and dust Ma's bells. And I'd write to Jesse.

I threw on a T-shirt and a pair of bell-bottoms, slipped into my sandals, and headed across the road to tell Aunt Verdella what I was up to. Uncle Rudy was sitting in his red metal lawn chair, his eyes closed, a cup of coffee resting on his knee. Knucklehead was lying like a bag of bones at his feet. "Mornin' Button," Uncle Rudy said, without opening his eyes.

I had planned to hurry so I could get into town and get back to sew, but the empty blue chair next to Uncle Rudy looked inviting. I sat down, reaching over to give Knucklehead a few poor-thing-pats.

"Whatcha doing, Uncle Rudy?" I asked, saying it exactly how I used to.

"Just sitting here being with the breeze," he said.

Other than a glance up to make sure the sky was clear as I hurried down the steps, I hadn't noticed anything about the day's weather. I paused, feeling the air, then asked, "What breeze?"

"Close your eyes," Uncle Rudy said. "You gotta be still, though, or you won't feel it."

I sat up straight and did as he instructed, turning my palms up.

At first all I felt was the sun warm on my skin, but then I felt it. A breeze so soft it was like an echo from a whisper.

"See?" Uncle Rudy said quietly.

We sat in silence, feeling the ever so placid breeze that occasionally rose enough to puff a faint whisper through the trees and flutter a few single strands of my hair. Maybe life was like the breeze, I thought. Moving so slowly at times that it seemed it wasn't moving at all, even if it was. Uncle Rudy reached over and cupped his hand over mine, giving it a pat.

Behind us, the screen door squealed, then slammed shut. "Here comes our little whirlwind now," Uncle Rudy said, cocking one eye open. Boohoo streaked across the yard, towel flapping at his shoulders. He dove at me, jumping up on my back, his scrawny arms choking my neck. He smelled like maple syrup and Mr. Bubbles. "I've got you, Dr. *Octeropus*," he shouted as we toppled to the ground.

I loosened his arms. "Oh yeah? Well take this, Spidey-man!" I said, flipping him onto his back and tickling him until his makeshift cape fell off and he turned into a rolling ball of giggles.

CHAPTER 5

BRIGHT IDEA #99: If your best friend goes away and you miss her, you don't need to cry and carry on forever, because she'll be back. And who knows? When she comes back, she might even bring you something so special that your heart almost bursts.

Linda and Hazel and Marge were off to lunch (they went at eleven, so local brides-to-be could pop in on their lunch hours), the sign on the door saying they'd be back at noon. I used my key and found my work boxed and waiting on the desk. A note was taped to the lid with instructions and a clumsily drawn illustration showing me where the beadwork should go. I'd worked at this shop after school and during summer vacation since I was twelve years old, and every few months Ma used to give me another responsibility. I felt so grown-up each time I walked in the door back then, but for some reason, in the handful of days since graduation especially, coming here made me want to curl up in the fetal position and cry like a baby. I grabbed the oblong white dress box, the bolt of apricot chiffon, and the bag of sewing essentials packed for me like a school lunch, and left.

Across the road, Aunt Verdella was hanging laundry, and Boohoo ran in circles around her, his arms outstretched. I tossed her a wave, then started unloading my work. I was on my second trip, pulling the plastic-covered bolt of fabric out of the backseat, when Tommy Smithy's pickup pulled in behind my Rambler.

When Tommy was Uncle Rudy's farmhand, I'd hated him because he teased me. Now he was just a pest.

"Hey there, Button," Tommy said with a grin. His eyeteeth still came to vampire points, and his brown hair was still Toni perm-curly—especially on days like this, with the night's gentle rain moisting the air—but at twenty-three, Tommy wasn't nearly as ugly as he'd once been. In fact, he had a build that made me hate myself for wanting to stare.

"Evy," I corrected.

"Need a hand?" he asked.

"Nope."

"Look what I just got," he said, pulling a piece of paper out of his wallet and holding it out for me to see. "I did it," he grinned. "I'm officially a pilot now."

I slammed the car door and positioned the long bolt of fabric under my arm.

"As soon as my Piper's inspected, I can take to the skies. If you're lucky, I'll be taking you up soon."

"Yeah, right," I said. "I'd have to be in a coma before you'd get me in a plane with you. You can't even keep your truck on course—as the Ford graveyard on your back forty proves." That was the one good thing about having Tommy around—if there *was* something good about that: I wasn't shy around him like I was with other guys. I didn't care what he thought of me.

"I'm still in one piece, aren't I?" he said with a grin.

"Yeah, well you won't be for long, flying in that old wreck that's got to be from about World War I times."

"Hey, that 'wreck' is a Piper PA-12 Super Cruiser!" Tommy looked boyishly defensive, and suddenly I felt bad, remembering him at about twelve, walking on the other side of Uncle Rudy, his skinny strides long, his dirt-smudged face filled with exhilaration as he talked about how he was going to join the Air Force when he was eighteen, and fly a Boeing B-29 Superfortress, like his uncle. But when he was a junior, their tractor tipped over and pinned his dad underneath, crushing his pelvis and doing heavy damage to his spine. Mr. Smithy only lasted a year after that, and I can't say for sure, but I think Tommy was disappointed that he wasn't drafted, because with his mother and the farm needing him, he couldn't enlist in the Air Force as he wanted to. Maybe I didn't have a dream, but Tommy did, and I knew what it felt like to try to take the place of a parent. Besides, I knew Tommy had worked hard to finagle enough time and money to get his pilot's license and to buy that plane.

"I was just giving you guff," I said. "I'm sure it's a fine plane."

"You damn bet it is! It's been modified, it's got a big-ass engine, new wing flaps . . . metal-skin fuselage . . ."

"Well I don't care what's been done with it, I'm still not getting in it. Even looking at planes in the sky and thinking about people being in them is enough to give me the heebie-jeebies."

"Ah, you don't know what you're missing, Button," Tommy said, lifting his eyes toward the sky. "Cruising up there, above all the hassle down here. You become a part of the sky, and feel freedom you just can't feel down here."

The roar of a vehicle sounded down Peters Road, and I groaned inwardly when Brody Bishop's dusty red Mustang sped by, then jammed to a stop and zigzagged backward to block the driveway.

"Hey buddy," Brody called from his car, his bronzed arm hanging out the window.

Brody and Tommy had been friends since childhood. They both liked to fish and hunt, suck beer and drive like bullets. But that's where the similarities ended. Tommy was hardworking, while Brody was as lazy as a newborn. Brody also thought he was God's gift to girls. I could never look at Brody—well built, though short, with dimples—and not think of how strange it was that someone so good-looking could start looking ugly to you when you figured out that what was beneath their looks was so unattractive.

I wanted to flee to the house before Brody reached us, but he was already slamming his car door shut. I knew the second I turned around, he'd be staring at my butt.

"What you up to today?" he called to Tommy. "Wanna do a little fishin'?"

Dad claimed that the Army made men out of boys. If that was true, then it was a pity for Brody's wife, Marlene (everyone called her Marls), that the pin in his leg from a car accident six years ago wouldn't allow him to pass an Army physical. Especially since he was going to become a dad in four months. Brody and Marls lived with his folks, and he used his bum leg as an excuse to quit every job he started. But his leg didn't keep him from hopping from rock to rock down at Dauber Falls when he wanted to fish, or hiking miles over the Smithys' eighty acres to hunt deer or birds. Nor did it stop him from hitting the dance floor on nights when there was live music in town, old and young women alike begging him for a dance so he never got to sit—or so Brody bragged.

Poor Marls, sick from her pregnancy as she was, her ankles bloated bigger than my knees, waited on him like a personal servant because she worshiped the ground he walked on. I had no idea if she knew that Brody gawked at every girl over fifteen that crossed his path. Like he was staring at my chest at the moment. I moved the bolt of chiffon to hang in the crook of my arms to hide my boobs.

"Nah, I can't. I've got too much shit to do." Tommy spat on the grass like he was laying a period on his sentence. I didn't know why men spit on the ground like dogs peed on tires, but I knew that after Tommy spit, Brody would, too. And he did.

"How's Marls?" I asked, forcing myself to say anything at all to Brody, since guys like him made me jumpy. But I was concerned. "Aunt Verdella said she was sick." I didn't know Marls well since she was three years older than me and from Eagle River. I knew enough, though, just by looking at her, to know that she didn't feel attractive enough to be with Brody. Just as I didn't really feel attractive enough to be a match for Jesse.

"Ah, she's always sick," Brody said, talking to my chest, even if it was hidden. "Getting big as a heifer, too."

"That was mean," I said.

"What?" Brody said with a cocky grin. "It's the truth."

"See you guys around," I said, backing up.

"Yep, and you'll be seeing plenty of me, too," Tommy said.

"So I heard."

"At least you'll have something to brighten up your dull days," he teased.

I rolled my eyes.

"I knew she'd be thrilled," he said to Brody. "As thrilled as she was to hear that she's gonna be my copilot."

"Hey, you got it?" Brody asked.

"Yesterday.

Brody pounded Tommy's back, and as they headed to the field so Tommy could check the fences before he brought his cows over, Brody childishly spouted plans for their first flying adventure, hardly a limp in his stride.

It was fun, working with my stereo cranked to ten, chiffon gliding softly under my fingertips in a rhythm as soothing as a heartbeat, Jo's bridal gown spread out behind me on the big, square butcher-block table Aunt Verdella found at the Community Sale last summer and helped me refinish. The morning ticked on and the bridesmaid's dress took shape and I thought of how amazing it was to see a pattern come to life under my hands.

I would have stayed content that day, happy even, had it not been for Boohoo.

I was stitching a wide cuff when Boohoo came in for the umpteenth time. I didn't look up, or listen as he chattered about what he'd found. I was too busy sewing and grooving to my Creedence Clearwater Revival album. "Evy, look. Look!"

"Just a minute," I told him when he got louder than the stereo. I circled the fabric under the bobbing needle to finish the sleeve, keeping my eye on the seam I was stitching.

And then Boohoo started yelling loud enough to cut through the chorus of "Proud Mary." "Get back here, Hoppy! You're gonna fall and break your neck!"

I turned, and there was Boohoo, his muddy knee hooked on the edge of my worktable, one leg teetering on a footstool. "Boohoo!" I screeched. He was on the table by the time I got to my feet, his grubby hands reaching for the fat toad tangled with orange yarn that hopped over Jo's gown.

"What are you doing?" I shouted when I saw the snow-white skirt folding like an accordion under Boohoo's grubby knees, tiny clumps of damp soil dropping from his mitts as the toad leapt out of his hand and he reached for him again.

"Don't worry, Evy, I got him! I got him!" Boohoo stood up on the dress, and when I screamed, he quickly leapt to the floor. He held up his hand, his fingers squishing the toad's pale green potbelly, its legs dangling.

I looked down at the trail of dirt over the lace bodice, and the smudged, crumpled skirt. I clutched my head. "Boohoo, look what you've done!"

Boohoo's smile faded and he looked at the table. "I'm sorry, Evy," he said. And before I could stop him, he reached out and brushed the dirt into one long, dark streak, grinding it into the lace covered fabric. "Stop!" I screamed.

Boohoo tilted his wrist and looked at his palm. Then he moved the toad so he could see the dress, too. "You peed," he told him.

I sent Boohoo back to Aunt Verdella's, then sat down, my arms going limp between my knees. I'd never get our gummy, clay soil out of that dress without leaving a stain. Not in a million years. I could only hope that Linda had enough of the same fabrics on hand and didn't need to run to Porter to replace them, if spot cleaning didn't work. The wedding was in four weeks and the beading alone would take me forever.

I'd finish the second sleeve of the bridesmaid's gown, then go across the street and call Linda. I'd tell her to take the new fabric out of my salary, if it needed to be resewn. I'd offer to remake the gown myself, and assure her that I *could* sew a wedding dress from start to finish. I'd apologize profusely to Marge, since she, not Linda, had sewn the dress, because Linda couldn't sew even as well as me. She was simply a businesswoman who loved the glitz of weddings, and wanted to keep Ma's vision alive since they'd been such close friends. She'd hired Marge and Hazel, sisters who worked out of their homes for years, sewing for family and neighbors who couldn't afford the time or money for a trip to the Twin Cities, or down to the southern part of the state, yet needed something special to wear to a wedding or prom and didn't want to show up at the event in a dress from the Montgomery Ward catalog, that at least five other women would be wearing. I sighed again. Even if the stains could be worked out of the gown, I'd be giving everyone extra work and worry.

The record was finished, the needle making *chh-it, chh-it* sounds as the turntable spun past the last track. Downstairs, Tommy's truck started. I leaned back in my chair and reached for the lever to play the album again, but before my hand hit its mark, I heard Tommy shout, "Boohoo!" And then Aunt Verdella's voice screaming the same. I hurried to the window to see what my brother had done this time.

Brody's car was gone, and I couldn't see more than the bed of Tommy's truck from either window, so I raced downstairs.

Tommy, red-faced from running, reached into the opened window and grabbed the keys. "Damn it, Boohoo, you could have smashed my truck, and you, both!" He yanked the door open and pulled Boohoo out of the front seat, as Aunt Verdella charged into the yard.

"Don't yell at him like that, Tommy," I snapped, to which he told me that *somebody* had better start yelling at him. "What he did was dangerous!" Tommy had genuine fear in his eyes, and I closed my mouth and swallowed the rest of the rant that was about to come.

"I wasn't gonna drive it," Boohoo said. "I was just gonna move it so I could get Hoppy." He looked at Aunt Verdella, then pointed under the truck. "Hoppy's under there and Tommy drives bad."

We were all talking at once then. Tommy lecturing Boohoo—and defending his driving—me tattling to Aunt Verdella about what he'd done to Jo's gown, and Aunt Verdella calling to Boohoo, who had slipped underneath the truck to find the toad.

When Boohoo came out, he was clutching Hoppy without mercy and grinning. That is, until he saw our faces. "I just wanted to get my toad," he said.

"Oh, Boohoo," Aunt Verdella said, still huffing from her hop over. "I know you don't mean to be naughty, but . . . well honey, you go back home now," she said. "And up to your room and stay there for a half an hour until you figure out what you did wrong."

"One hour!" I snapped, because I was still shaking, even though I knew full well that Aunt Verdella would let him out in ten minutes if he cried, which he was already doing.

After Aunt Verdella marched Boohoo back to her house, Tommy left, and I trudged back upstairs to stare at the ruined gown. Then—partially because I dreaded telling Linda what happened, and partially because I was determined to get at least *something* accomplished by the end of the day—I flipped on Simon & Garfunkel and sat down to finish the whole bridesmaid's dress.

It was about twenty minutes after the truck fiasco when I felt someone in the room. I turned, and there he was. Boohoo. Standing in the doorway. "What are you doing over here? You're supposed to be in your room. I heard Aunt Verdella yell at you a few seconds ago, now get back there. You have to listen when—"

"She wasn't yellin' at *me,*" he said. "She was yellin' at *you.*"

"Boohoo, please. Go. I'll come get you when I'm done here." I didn't look him straight in the face, because I'd calmed down and knew that if he looked sad, I'd be pampering him every bit as much as Aunt Verdella.

"She was," he said. "Because somebody's here." He mumbled a name, but his chin was tucked as he struggled to tuck the line of yarn dangling from his pocket back in.

"*Vinny?* I don't know any Vinny," I said.

I reached over to the stereo, lowering the volume, just as he was saying, "No. *Winnie*—not Vinnie. Winnie. Like Winnie the Pooh."

My body went taut, and my heart started thumping in my ears. I put my hand over my chest, just like Aunt Verdella always did. "Winnalee? Was that the name, Boohoo? *Winnalee?*"

"I dunno. But she's peeing and Aunt Verdella is crying."

I hurried to the window and leaned into it so fast that I bumped my forehead on the glass.

There was a van in the driveway, painted with wild psychedelic colors and shapes I couldn't make out except for the purple peace symbol on the roof.

Aunt Verdella was in the middle of her yard, one hand over her heart and the other working as though she was trying to scoop me from my house. She stopped and ran-hopped to the front steps, her arms flailing, then ran back to the center of the yard to gesture again. Back and forth she went, her arms scooping, clutching her chest, her mouth, the sides of her head. Everywhere! She must have seen me in the window, because she yelled, "Button, hurry! *Hurry!* She's here! Our Winnalee has come home!"

Then there she was. My very first, forever best friend. Coming down the front steps with a green army bag slung around her neck and resting below the opposite hip. Her dishwater blond, hip-long loopy hair and bright peasant dress billowing in a wind that must have blown in with her.

CHAPTER 6

BRIGHT IDEA #12: All the best things in life are worth waiting for. Like Saturday morning cartoons, and summer vacation, and Christmas cookies with candy sprinkles.

I sped down the stairs—glossing my lips and smoothing down my hair as I went—Boohoo thumping behind me, asking, "Who is that Winnie girl, Evy? Who is she?"

I was mumbling, "Oh my God . . . oh my God," as I shoved open the screen door. They were just coming across the road, Aunt Verdella laughing and crying and waving her arms like an excited grade school crossing guard, and Winnalee wincing as she ran across the graveled road on bare feet, her face lit with joy as she screamed, "Button! Button!"

The air filled with happy shrieks as we hugged and leapt in circles and squealed about how we couldn't believe we were together again. I caught Aunt Verdella's blurred image with every rotation we made, her head tipped to the side, her hand on her cheek, one arm around Boohoo's shoulder.

When we exhausted ourselves, we stopped, and, winded and holding hands, we backed up so we could see who the other had become. "Oh my God! Look at you, Button! You're so pretty!" Winnalee's voice was almost as high-pitched as when she was nine. She pulled her hands free and lifted handfuls of my hair, parted in the middle like hers. "And you've got long hair now! Straight, too!"

"Only when I roll it in juice cans, or iron it. Otherwise it's frizzy," I confessed. I tucked my hair behind my ears, hoping Winnalee would notice that I'd finally grown into them.

Winnalee set my hair free, then reached out and gave my boobs a quick bounce. "And look at your knockers!"

"Knockers?" Boohoo asked, giggling, as my face heated.

I licked my index fingers and wiped under my eyes where I knew mascara was smeared. Winnalee didn't go for the "natural look" by wearing foundation, pale blue eye shadow, and gloss to give her lips that just-licked look like I did—but then she didn't need to. She was beautiful as she was, with fair skin that showed no signs of ever having been invaded by zits, and lashes that were naturally brown-black and curled to her eyebrows in a feather-soft arc, not mascara-crunchy and creased like the letter *L* from an eyelash curler, like mine. Her sun-streaked loops flowed in the wind, brushing across petite boobs that actually fit her body—and were obviously not strapped into a bra, judging by the fact that her nipples were showing through her dress like pencil erasers. She was curvy like Freeda, but smaller, and she had hips, unlike yours truly. Nice hips, too, not too wide, not too narrow. She was cute and pretty at the same time, like Goldie Hawn, on *Laugh-In*, but I didn't get to say that out loud because Winnalee was hugging me, saying, "You're still my best friend. I can already tell," and I was smudging my mascara all over again. Aunt Verdella came forward and wrapped her arms around us both, and the three of us laughed as if we'd found fairies.

We were all talking at once then, bombarding one another with questions we were too excited to answer, when Winnalee stopped and looked down at Boohoo, who was twisting two strands of her hair together at her hip. "Okay . . . this *has* to be your little brother, Button. He looks just like Uncle Reece!" She bent over so that her face was level with Boohoo's.

Aunt Verdella went up behind Boohoo and gently pulled his hands free from Winnalee's hair. "This is our little Robert Reece, but we call him Boohoo. He's six years old," Aunt Verdella said proudly.

Boohoo was staring at the braided hemp Winnalee wore around her wrist, two turquoise beads dangling from the tied strings. "I like your *wristlet*," he said.

"He likes yarn," I added quietly, embarrassed because his fixation with strings and tying was starting to slip over to the weird side.

"Are you Crackpot?" Boohoo asked. Winnalee laughed as though his question made sense.

"Maybe. Nice to meet you, Boohoo," she said, giggling, either over his name, his question, or because Boohoo himself was giggably cute. Boohoo didn't answer. He was too busy staring at her long hair again.

The next couple of hours rushed by like playful winds. Winnalee ran through the downstairs of Grandma Mae's house like a sugar-injected kid, pointing out all the things she remembered. She crawled up on the counter and sat propped on her knees, just because she remembered doing that when she was little, then she rushed to the bathroom, where she hiked her dress to her thighs and stepped into the claw-footed tub and sat down, just so she could see if it was as huge as she remembered. (It wasn't.) When we got upstairs, Winnalee lifted the strap of her army bag and tossed it onto my bed, then turned in circles as she looked at the room that used to be hers, hurrying to the window seat and bouncing on it, even though it had no give.

Aunt Verdella tugged Boohoo by the hand and announced that she was going home to cook Winnalee a nice homecoming meal.

"Oh, oh! Would you make bunny pancakes?" Winnalee asked, referring to the rabbit-face, raisin-eyed pancakes she remembered. The ones Aunt Verdella still made for Boohoo, by dropping batter onto the griddle in three blobs, rounding the rabbit's face with the back of her spoon and stretching the two blobs on top into long ears.

That evening when Uncle Rudy came home, Winnalee grabbed my hand and tugged me outside. "Well, lookie who's back!" he said. His face went purple from Winnalee's tight squeeze, and she patted Knucklehead until his back legs buckled. "Wow, this old dog isn't long for this world, is he?" she commented. Aunt Verdella and I winced because Boohoo was standing right there.

"That's quite the Volkswagen Camper you've got there," Uncle Rudy said. "What is it? About a '61, '62?"

"It's a 1962," Winnalee recited, proudly. "It's my hippie mobile. It runs good, too." While they talked, Boohoo combed over the murals on the side of the van like it was a "find the hidden picture" page in *Highlights* magazine, shouting out a number every time he found another delicate fairy peeking from behind a bold flower, sliding down an arched rainbow, or dancing over bright swirls.

Things didn't calm down until we settled at the table to eat our pancakes, eggs, fried potatoes, and ham. Winnalee dipped down and kissed her pancake when Aunt Verdella set down her plate. "I've missed you, Bunny!" she said. I started laughing and Winnalee looked up and grinned. "What? I did!" She looked at Aunt Verdella, who was ha-ha'ing, and suddenly Winnalee's eyes narrowed and her lips parted, as though she just realized it wasn't 1961 anymore, and, in spite of still having the oomph of a shaken can of soda pop, Aunt Verdella had aged to old.

Aunt Verdella passed out plates to the rest of us and sat down. "How's Freeda?" she asked, talking with her mouth full. "Oh, I miss that girl! I wish she had come with you."

Winnalee dipped the maple syrup jug upside down and drowned her plate—eggs and ham and fried potatoes and all. "She got her hairdresser's license and opened a beauty shop a couple of years ago," Winnalee said, while licking two fingers. I don't think Aunt Verdella noticed how Winnalee's face hardened when Freeda's name came up, but I did—it morphed just how I imagine my face did when folks asked me about Dad.

"A beauty shop?" Aunt Verdella slapped the table hard enough that the silverware jingled. "Now if that ain't just perfect for Freeda! Remember when she fixed me and your ma up, Button?" Of course I remembered. They had raced to the mirror and laughed themselves silly. Then later, Aunt Verdella had strutted in front of the TV so Uncle Rudy could see the new her, and he asked who that "looker" was and joked that Verdie was sure going to be mad when he saw that Winnalee and I had brought him home a glamour girl. But Dad only grumbled when he saw Ma's new look, and asked where the Phillips screwdriver was. I hated the way my mind kept a record of every one of my Ma's hurts, and mourned them when I remembered, wishing only that every single hour Ma had on this earth had been happy.

"Freeda was a fairy godmother when it came to helping women gussie up and feel good about themselves, that's for sure," Aunt Verdella said.

"She's always giving them tips on their hair, clothes,

makeup . . . filling them up on psychobabble bullshit." Boohoo covered his mouth and giggled over Winnalee's cussword. "She likes telling people who they should be."

Aunt Verdella missed the sarcasm in Winnalee's voice. "Oh, isn't that wonderful!" she said. "Where's her shop?"

"Northville. A little place outside of Detroit."

"You always wanted to go to Detroit," I said.

"Yeah," she said, her elbow coming up to rest on the table, her hand curling against her cheek. "But then, I wanted a lot of things back then."

Aunt Verdella gave a feeble smile. "At least you got to Detroit," she said.

"Yeah, except that Freeda decided it was a dive once we got there, so we pulled out in less than a year."

Winnalee's face brightened. "Hey, right after we eat, let's go to your place, Button. Your old place. So I can see Aunt Jewel and Uncle Reece."

Everything stopped.

Time.

Forks.

Mouths.

Breath.

Everything.

Well, except for Boohoo, who was making bomb-dropping sounds and little screams as he dropped forkfuls of scrambled eggs over his bunny's remains.

I set my fork down. I didn't want to say what happened. I looked at Aunt Verdella for help, and she looked at Uncle Rudy. He grabbed a couple of strings of ham fat off his plate and got to his feet. "Hey, little buddy, what do you say you and me take Knucklehead out to do his duty?"

Boohoo leapt to his feet and snatched the flubber out of Uncle Rudy's hand. "I wanna give it to him," he said. He hurried over to Knucklehead's mat. "You wanna go do your poopy duty?" Knucklehead struggled to get to his feet. "Hoppy's going out, too." He tossed Knucklehead the ham, then ran to get his toad, who was now living in a secondhand aquarium Aunt Verdella bought last summer when she was going to set up a fish tank for Uncle Rudy, but never got around to it.

After they were gone, Aunt Verdella reached over the corner of the table with both arms, one hand coming down over Winnalee's and the other gently touching her elbow. "Jewel isn't with us anymore, honey," she said, stroking Winnalee's arm. "She was killed in a storm four years ago this August."

"What?" Winnalee asked, in a small voice that made her sound as if she was nine again, and someone had just confirmed that fairies don't exist.

"She'd gone down into the basement to level the clothes in her new washing machine because it was thumping, like they do when they get out of balance. She was standing in a couple inches of water, because the sump pump hadn't tripped on, and lightning struck the house." Aunt Verdella's voice was shaking, and so were my insides. I knew why her eyes were closed, and she rubbed her temples. I'd overheard her tell Ada once that she couldn't think of that day without remembering my frantic phone call (the one I didn't remember), and the sight of me running down Peters Road toward her house, Boohoo in my arms, both of us soaking wet and sobbing.

"Oh God," Winnalee said, shock pooling in her eyes. Then she turned to me, as if she needed confirmation that it was true.

Winnalee reached for me just as Aunt Verdella did, and the three of us held hands across the table like we were praying.

"Button's daddy isn't the same anymore. After Freeda helped Jewel feel better about herself, those two were happy for maybe the first time in their marriage. Oh sure, they bickered now and then about the money she spent, and the messes he left, but there was real tenderness between them, wasn't there, Button?" I nodded as I thought of how sometimes when Dad passed Ma in the kitchen, he'd lean over and whisper something in her ear, and she'd blush and slap his arm as she giggled, and, how sometimes when I got up at night to pee, Ma would be watching the Johnny Carson show, Dad stretched out on the couch, his head on her lap.

We were silent for a time, then Winnalee looked at me and asked, "Did you see her get struck?"

I didn't know what to say, so I looked to Aunt Verdella again.

"She doesn't remember anything about that day," Aunt Verdella told her.

That wasn't exactly true, though. I did remember some things: earsplitting lightning and thunder that rumbled the windows, and the whooshing of heavy rains. I remembered Ma, bent over Boohoo's high chair wiping tomato sauce from his pudgy hands, then her straightening up and asking, "Is that wash machine thumping again?" I remembered her opening the basement door to listen, then sighing hard and talking to Dad as if he was home, saying, "Dang it, Reece. When are you going to level that washer?" Then, when she was partway down the stairs, adding, "About the same time you build a decent platform so the sump pump doesn't keep tipping over, I suppose." I was pulling Boohoo out of his high chair when she cried out, "Oh no! The floor's soaked clear to the boxes of our winter things!"

That's all I remembered. Well, except for one more thing I wished I could forget: that her death was Dad's fault.

"Oh, Button," Winnalee said, tears flowing now. She got up and came to me, leaning over my chair and putting her arms around my neck, her hair spilling down over me like a lemon-scented waterfall. And then she did something that would have dropped me to my knees, had I not already been sitting. She recited the last few lines of the poem—by Yeats, I believe—that Aunt Verdella had recited to us right here in this room, when we were little:

Come away, O human child!
To the waters and the wild.
With a fairy, hand in hand,
For the world's more full of weeping
than you can understand.

CHAPTER 7

BRIGHT IDEA #33: If you decide to wear your new underwear on the outside of your pants because you think they're pretty and nobody will see them if you wear them right, old people and kids who get A's are probably going to stare.

I didn't want our first night together to be sad, and luckily, it wasn't.

We hugged Aunt Verdella and Uncle Rudy and Boohoo good night, then headed out the back door, laughing as we ran.

Winnalee moved her van into my driveway, then yanked open the double side doors. "Come on in," she said, as she hoisted herself inside. "I had the seats ripped out back here to make more living space."

There was a string of hippie beads hanging from a suspension rod behind the front seat, the strands pinned to the floor by two droopy potted plants. Winnalee kicked the thin mattress with tangled sheets against the wall, and shoved a Styrofoam cooler out of the way.

"It's a mess, I know," she said. And it was. Crumpled potato chip bags and candy wrappers sat in nests of wadded clothes that were everywhere but in the white laundry basket propped beside the plants. A cardboard box was buckled against the wall, a sketch pad curved to fit inside. Winnalee reached down to pick up a half-crushed blue pastel and tossed it in a box.

"Oh! Oh! I've got something to show you!" she said as she grabbed a fat duffel bag off the floor. She made like she was going to unzip it, then stopped. "I'll wait until we're inside." She pulled a few record albums out of the collapsed stack and shoved them in my arms, then muttered, "shoes . . . shoes." She found a pair of sandals with frayed straps under the rubble, then rescued a pair of flattened moccasins from under the mattress, holes in each sole the size of quarters.

I grabbed the laundry basket. "Here," I said. "Let's fill this with your dirty clothes and take them inside. We'll wash them at Aunt Verdella's in the morning. That's where I do my laundry."

"I don't think all of them are dirty," Winnalee said, as I scooped them off the sand-pocked floor. "I'll come back for my plants."

Loaded with her things, we headed to the house, the sunset spinning our hair to gold.

Winnalee spilled the contents of her duffel bag over my bed. Deodorant, a bar of soap, a bottle of Breck shampoo, a toothbrush, toothpaste, a fistful of hemp chokers and bracelets, a tangle of beaded earrings, and, a package of *Trojans*! I looked away.

Winnalee started shaking wrinkles out of her clothes, sniffing them when she wasn't sure if they were clean or dirty: granny dresses in bold patterns, prairie dresses with tiered skirts in fairy-floating fabrics, a few mini-length dresses, empire-style, with big bell-shaped angel sleeves, or elastic gathered-at-the-wrist cuffs. A couple of faded tie-dyed T-shirts, the necklines haphazardly expanded with scissors, a couple of pairs of denim cutoffs with frayed hems, and two pairs of blue jeans, the bottoms of the bells ragged and brown from walking on them, just like mine. She picked up a fringed leather jacket and tossed it aside. "Won't need this until fall," she said. She gathered a bunch of dirty underwear, rolled like socks, and tossed them on our heap for washing. I didn't see any bras, but then I'd already guessed I wouldn't.

Winnalee rummaged through the army bag that apparently served as her purse and grabbed a rubber band, slipping it onto her wrist, then continued to dig. "I must have left my brush somewhere," she said. "Shit."

I opened my drawer and took out the hairbrush Winnalee had left behind that magical summer. The one I once grabbed out of Penny's hand and put back on my vanity, telling her it was not for using, but for remembering. "Do you recognize it?" I asked. "It was yours."

"Oh. My. God! I can't believe you kept this thing!" I glanced at the scuffed blue plastic cup on my nightstand, the cup Jesse drank from the first time he stopped at my house, and the gum wrapper chain, yards long, that was looped over the curtain rod above the window seat, and made from the silver foil wrappers of every piece of gum Jesse gave me, or chewed himself when I was around him in the last three years. "I keep everything the people I love leave behind," I said. But that was only partially true. Ma's things—every last thing she owned—was still in Dad's house, untouched. Even her Kenmore sewing machine, though it was better than the old Singer Aunt Verdella picked up for me after the motor burned out in my first one. Aunt Verdella believed I should have all of Ma's personal belongings, but I wasn't sure Dad agreed, so I left them where they were.

Winnalee laughed as she unwound a tangle of blond hair

from the bristles. "Wow, this is nine-year-old hair." She grinned, then stopped. "Okay, that's kind of gross," she said, flicking the snarl of hair into the air.

Winnalee brushed, then swirled her long loops over to one side and cinched them at the shoulder with the rubber band. "I like keepsakes, too. That's what I want to show you." She rooted around in her duffel bag until she found a sandwich bag. "Don't look! Don't look!" she said, turning her back to me.

She tossed the empty plastic bag on the bed and spun around, holding out what I thought was a movie ticket. "Ta-da—my prized possession!"

I stared down at the ticket in my hand. "A three-day pass to Woodstock? You were going to go to Woodstock?"

"I *did* go!"

"But this is your ticket."

Winnalee's eyes were close to bursting—as if she'd gone to the festival yesterday, rather than over nine months ago. "They weren't taking tickets by the time I got there. The mob had flattened the fences, so I poured in with everybody else. I drove there myself, too. All the way from Northville, Michigan, to Bethel, New York, even if I'd just gotten my license the day before and couldn't drive worth a shit. It wasn't hard finding my way once I got to Route 71—you just followed the caravan. The traffic stalled miles from Yasgur's farm, so I just left my van parked on the road like everybody else and walked. Blistered the hell out of my feet—I didn't think to grab my sandals—because the pavement was hot as hell. But it was worth it!"

"Freeda let you go to a rock festival? And by yourself?" The minute the question was out, I realized how stupid it was. Freeda was every bit as loose with her parenting skills as she was with her body. I, on the other hand, didn't even dare ask to go see the Woodstock movie with Penny, because Aunt

Verdella heard the movie had nudity and drugs in it, so she said I had to ask Dad. Which I didn't. "You're so lucky to have Freeda," I said.

Winnalee rolled her eyes. "Yeah. Right. Freeda turned into a regular Carol Brady after we left here—all but for the cussing part. She got weird first. Staring off into space a lot, and crying without making a sound. Then I think she started seeing a shrink, because when school let out for summer vacation that year, she dragged me to this office once a week and left me in the waiting room for a good hour at a pop. Not that I minded. They had markers and big sheets of paper sitting on this kiddy table, and I'd make pictures for the lady at the desk until Freeda came out, wearing red eyes and this fake, ain't-it-all-good smile.

"She turned into a real drag then. After I went to Woodstock, I came home one morning and found her digging through my room. I don't know what she was looking for, but I went off on her. She was ready to go off on me, too, then stopped, claiming she had to pee. She told me to stay put. Like I didn't know she'd gotten a library card and was into this let's-read-how-to-be-the-perfect-parent-so-your-kid-forgives-you-for-leaving-her-and-lying-to-her kick! I'd seen that dorky *Between Parent & Teenager* book she had stuffed below the vanity when I was looking for ass-wipe. What a joke. She shut and locked the bathroom door—like *that* in itself wasn't suspicious? Freeda would pee with the door open, even if the whole congregation of the First Baptist Church was sitting outside it. *That* didn't change because she got her head shrunk.

"She came out and delivered her lines like some seventh grader in a bad school play, telling me how it wasn't *me*, it was my *actions* that were bad. It was so stupid I couldn't even take her seriously." Winnalee rolled her eyes again, then busied herself putting her ticket carefully back in the plastic bag. I didn't say so, but I felt sad for Freeda, who obviously had realized that her parenting skills were lacking, and wanted to do better. I knew from handling Boohoo just how hard it was to raise a kid.

"So no," Winnalee said as she tucked the Baggie back in her duffel bag. "I didn't ask her if I could go to Woodstock. I just went. And I'm glad I did it, too. It was the most mind-blowing experience of my life, Button. Hundreds of thousands of people crashing under the stars to peace and love, sharing food and drugs and sex, and getting down to some of the best music you could ever hope to hear. I got this close to Janis Joplin. This close!" she said, holding her hands a foot apart. "It was so frikken cool, Button. We were all brothers and sisters—no judging, no greed, no meanness—just peace and love. Acid was being passed out like Halloween candy, and the air was so thick with pot smoke that you could get high just breathing. Even the pigs just let us be."

I was holding on to the frame of the window seat like it was the edge of a cliff. "Did *you* do those things?"

"Which things? The acid, the weed, or the sex?"

"Any of them."

"I didn't drop any acid. Tried it once before Woodstock and had a bad trip. Who needs *that* shit? I smoked a lot of joints, though. And had a lot of sex."

"You didn't," I whispered, horrified, yet intrigued.

Winnalee laughed. "Everybody did!"

I could hear Ma's voice saying, "If everybody jumped off a cliff, would you do it, too?"

"Freeda had a shit fit when I got back and told her where I'd been, but I didn't care. I'd gone, and that's all that mattered."

Winnalee picked up her stack of albums and asked where my stereo was. I took her into my sewing room, where Jo's soiled wedding gown and the near-finished bridesmaid's dress hung. "Holy shit, what's all this? You aren't getting married, are you?" She looked relieved when I told her no.

I explained the bridal shop and how I worked for Linda now, as Winnalee pulled a few vinyl records from their covers. "No kidding? Cool! I couldn't do something like that. Look at this . . ." She pulled the bottom of her dress up and flopped the hem over to show me the gnarled zigzag of black thread. "I did this myself. Looks like a squished tarantula, doesn't it?"

Winnalee dropped her skirt and lifted the stack of 45s sitting near my stereo, swishing through them like a card player looking for an ace. One of the red snap-in inserts necessary to fit the 45s on the skinny turntable spindle fell out of the hole and rolled under the table. Winnalee didn't seem to notice. "Simon and Garfunkel . . . The Carpenters . . . Three Dog Night . . . The Bee Gees . . ." She glanced up, giving me the kind of smile people gave Boohoo when they thought his babyness was cute. But she gave me a real smile when she came across John Lennon's "Give Peace a Chance." Winnalee set down my 45s and picked up one of the few albums I owned. "Creedence Clearwater. Cool," she said. "They were awesome at Woodstock." I didn't even know they *were* at Woodstock, but I was glad to hear it. I didn't want Winnalee thinking I only listened to bubblegum music—even if I mostly did.

Winnalee stacked a couple of her albums on the turntable, cranking the volume up high so we could hear the music in the bedroom. Then it was my turn to grin, because Winnalee sounded like Boohoo mimicking a cartoon bad guy as she sang along with husky-voiced Joplin with her still-little-Winnalee voice.

Winnalee paused at my vanity and pulled Jesse's picture from the edge of the mirror. "Is this your boyfriend?" she asked, flipping the picture over, seeing the back was empty, then turning it back to his face again.

"No. That's Jesse," I said. "We're just friends."

"You sounded sorry when you said that. Course, can't say I blame you. He's cute. Well, if the Army hadn't butchered his hair . . . which is a far cry from what will end up getting butchered in the end. I hate that goddamn war."

Winnalee flopped on the bed, her legs bent, her dress falling away from knees that were round and smooth and small. I turned away, because if she wasn't wearing underwear, I didn't want to know.

"I can't believe you had sex," I said aloud, even though I'd meant to only think it.

"Haven't *you?*" she asked, her face going into shock mode.

I felt myself blush and I looked down. Up until that moment, I hadn't known it was possible for a girl to be embarrassed because you *hadn't* had sex yet. In my school, there were only a handful of girls who'd lost their virginity, and that was to boys they planned to marry after they graduated. I only knew two girls who had sex with pretty much anybody, and the raunchy nicknames their behavior earned them was enough to scorch a person's eardrums. But Winnalee? When Uncle Rudy let out a cussword when he whacked his thumb with a hammer, Aunt Verdella scolded him because I was standing nearby. "Kids don't do what they're told, they do what they see," she said to him: I knew what Winnalee had seen.

"Weren't you afraid of picking up VD?"

"That's what antibiotics and these are for," she said, giving the packet of rubbers a toss back into her bag.

As uneasy as I was over hearing that Winnalee wasn't a virgin anymore, I wished I wasn't too embarrassed to ask her if it hurt bad the first time, because I was worried that I'd cry on my wedding night if it hurt. And I'd ask her how much she bled, because I thought it would be embarrassing and scary to turn into a bloody mess. I wanted to ask her, too, if she was embarrassed to show her naked body to guys she didn't even know, much less love (though I could pretty much guess what her answer to *that* would be) and if sex was as fun as guys made it sound.

Winnalee watched me as she rooted through the army bag she used for a purse, her eyes narrowing to slits, her smile widening. "I can't believe you've never done it."

"I came close, but no," I said, even though I knew that letting a twenty-year-old feel me up a little and giving Dougie Beemer a few tight-lipped kisses on prom night didn't exactly meet the criteria of "coming close."

"Man, Button. You gotta ease up a little. Get with the groove."

I guess she wanted me to learn how to loosen up quickly, too, because when her hand came out of her bag, she was holding a pack of Kools. She flipped the lid and pulled out a stubby homemade cigarette. The paper was twisted, the ends pinched—just how Penny had described the rolled joint she'd seen once. I blinked in horror.

I wanted to beg her not to light it in the house (or anywhere on our property, for that matter) because Boohoo or Aunt Verdella could pop over at any time. But I was already looking like a nerd, so instead I just sat stiff and quiet as Winnalee tucked her legs Indian-style on the bed and ignited a match. She sucked hard and held her breath until her face turned red, then blew out a small puff of smoke that smelled like molding hay. Not exactly an unpleasant odor, but still I yanked the window behind me open, and cleared my throat as I wondered just how much a person had to inhale before they got high.

"You want a toke?" she asked, holding it out. I shook my head in tight little jerks. Winnalee just shrugged, took another drag, and stacked the bed pillows behind her and leaned back.

"You're a lot like your ma," she said lazily. I instantly felt a stab of guilt for cringing at her words. "You're prettier, though," she added, which gave me a moment's relief, then another layer of guilt.

"You're a lot like yours, too," I said.

Winnalee's eyes, pink as Bazooka, spit open. "You're crazy. I'm *nothing* like that holier-than-thou hypocrite! You remember her, Button. She was fun-lovin' and free. Didn't let anyone rip her up or tell her how to live. Now she acts like a frikken nun! She's always harping about 'kids these days,' and she says she's not sleeping with another guy until she's in love and there's a ring on her finger. Can you believe it?"

Of course I could believe it. I was waiting for the same things.

"Like what? It's a prize to be somebody's *Mrs.*? I mean, think about it. *You're* Mrs. So-and-so . . . what about the guy? You don't see him having to give up his identity when he gets married, do you? It's bullshit."

I looked down at my fingers, tangled on legs that didn't look so bad when I was sitting and they were spread out to the normal width of a thigh. Every bridal gown I worked on made me want to be a bride. One Sunday a few months ago, when I ran to the shop for more needles, I slipped on a finished gown, veil and all, just to see if I'd make a pretty bride. Hazel came into the shop unexpectedly, and I tripped all over myself, explaining that I was suspicious that the darts didn't line up evenly so I was checking them out, since the bride and I had the same bust size (which obviously wasn't true, since my boobs were flattened and bulged almost to my neck, making me look more like a Victorian queen than a bride). And like I'd have needed to try on the veil if any of that was true anyway. God! How embarrassing!

I glanced up at Winnalee and wondered if she could read my thoughts. Then I realized that about now, she was high enough that she probably couldn't even read *her own* thoughts.

Winnalee was hungry, so we made grape Kool-Aid and Jiffy Pop popcorn, and brought them upstairs.

"Hey, remember when we usedta eat Kool-Aid powder straight from the package?" Winnalee asked, as she swirled her glass in front of the light and watched the Kool-Aid crawl up the side of the glass, smiling as if she was playing with a rainbow. "Mmmm, that was good."

When Winnalee was talking about drugs and sex, my stomach had felt tight and my heart felt a bit sorry. But right now, at this moment, with her giddy about the fun things we'd done, her giggles washed away those feelings of unease. Once, after the Malones left, and Dad made some snide remark about Freeda being so promiscuous, Ma said, "It's none of our business, Reece. Freeda's ways aren't hurting you, they're hurting her." I decided I would remember Ma's words, no matter what Winnalee told me. And I'd remember what Aunt Verdella always said when people gossiped about how others lived: that it wasn't our place to judge others, only to love them.

Winnalee imitated herself as a child, licking Kool-Aid from her finger, and I giggled. Then, in a burst of pure joy, I said, "I just can't believe you're back!"

"I know it. It kicks ass, doesn't it?" Her eyes were glazed, her laughter slow and happy.

Winnalee popped a fistful of popcorn into her mouth, stood, and stripped naked as she chewed, not caring that her pubic hair and bare boobs were facing me (which I suppose made sense, considering that she'd let hundreds of thousands of strangers see them already). She still wore the faint memory of her girlhood potbelly below her navel, but otherwise she had the perfect body. Her armpits were fuzzy, though, and I wondered if that was because she'd been on the road for days or if it was some sort of hippie thing.

Winnalee tugged a too-big T-shirt over her head and

flopped back on the bed. She grabbed the foil popcorn pan and set it on her stomach. I grabbed my nightie, turned off Country Joe and the Fish, and went downstairs to brush and change. When I got back up, the popcorn tin was on the floor and Winnalee was almost asleep. "Button?" she said, her voice slow and drowsy. "Is Aunt Verdella raising Boohoo then?"

My stomach tensed. "I guess you could say that."

"Nice," she said slowly.

"Not exactly. Aunt Verdella's too old to be chasing after a kid. So as soon as I'm settled . . ."

Winnalee came back to life with frazzled energy. "Button, don't say that. Aunt Verdella's not too old to raise a kid! She'll *never* be too old to raise a kid!"

Winnalee wore the same look she wore at the table, and I understood. Aunt Verdella's ways made her seem forever young. But every now and then, like when she'd lift her arm and I'd see skin hanging like soggy crepe paper, or when she'd struggle to get out of her chair after crocheting for a couple of hours and move stiffly for a few steps, I'd get scared and wonder how many years she'd still be around, and how I could ever face life without her.

I took Winnalee's things off the bed and hung the peasant dress, then stuffed the rest of her clothes in my laundry basket. I folded her denim shorts and pairs of jeans that felt clean, and took them to the closet to stack them on the shelf. I scooted my clothes over, and picked up the urn to tuck it in the corner down by my shoes.

"This picture here on your nightstand," Winnalee called. "Is this for real?"

"The tree?" I asked, as I hurriedly used my foot to bare a spot in the corner of the closet. "Yeah. Uncle Rudy took it."

"Wow," she said. And then she was standing there, in the closet doorway, any additonal comment she was going to make about the photo forgotten at the sight of the urn. She handed me the tree picture and took the urn, rotating it in her hands and staring. I didn't know what to say, so I just stood there biting my cheek and wishing I'd thrown the thing away years ago.

"Who would give a kid an urn filled with fireplace ashes—or whatever they were—and tell them that it was their dead ma? Who would do something like that?"

"I'm sorry," I whispered.

She shoved it back in my arms, took the tree photo back, and left the closet. "Hey, speaking of trees," she said, after a bit. "Did you ever find our Book of Bright Ideas that I left for you in our magic tree?"

"Of course I did, it's *my* prized possession." I rushed back into the bedroom, pulled the drawer on my nightstand open, and plucked out our book. Winnalee snatched it and moved over so I could flop down on my belly beside her. She opened the book at random:

"Bright Idea number fifty-six," she read: *"If a girl asks if she can have a sleepover at your house, ask her if she pees the bed first. Otherwise you're going to have a big spot on your mattress and your sister is going to cuss when she has to scrub it and flip it over and make you take a bath."*

Her head dropped to the book and she laughed, "God, I was such a dork."

"No you weren't," I said, laughing only because her laugh was contagious. "You were fun and sassy and believed in magical things. I wanted to be you when I was little."

Winnalee cocked her head to look at me, lumps of loopy curls falling over her face, so I brushed them behind her ear. "You're kidding," she said.

"No."

She studied me for a bit, then smiled, but almost sadly. "You wouldn't think like that now."

"Why would you say—"

"You're just how I knew you'd be," she said, interrupting my question.

"Nerdish?" I asked, looking down.

"No. Serious and quiet. Soft, like cotton."

I smiled, then looked at our Bright Ideas book. "We never did get the hundredth idea written."

Suddenly Winnalee bolted up to her knees. And before I knew what was happening, she had me pinned on my back, grabbing for my mouth with fingers that stunk like marijuana smoke. I drew my knees up, rocking side to side, batting at her hands as I giggled. "What . . . are you . . . doing?"

I was horrified when Winnalee pried my mouth open and cocked my head toward the lamp. She leaned in and examined the inside of my mouth. "Yep, I knew it," she said, letting go, and not bothering to wipe my spit from her fingers. "The insides of your cheeks are still chewed to shit." She grabbed my arms to examine them for scratch marks.

"Don't," I said, tugging them free and tucking them against me. I wasn't laughing anymore.

I guess I needn't have worried that Winnalee would make a big deal out of my scarred mouth or the fine jagged lines scratched into my skin after Boohoo ruined Jo's dress. She just looked at me for a few seconds, her face seeped with empathy, then she leapt to her feet as if the last bit of her lazy fog had suddenly lifted. "Hey, let's go climb the magic tree! Come on!"

"You serious? Right now?"

"Sure! Why not?"

So across the moonlit lawns we ran, holding hands like we did when we were kids, our giggles shooting like stars through the nippy night air.

The living room light was on at Aunt Verdella's, the TV flickering, which meant she was snoring in her chair, her crochet needle limp in her hand.

Winnalee went up the tree first, me hesitating only a second as I thought of the last time I'd climbed it. "Come on," Winnalee called, as she stepped long and lodged her foot into the small center between the fork. "Man, what happened to our floor? It shrunk."

"No, our feet grew," I said, even though Winnalee couldn't be more than a size six.

Seconds later, we were in the tree, our bare feet pinching each other's, our backs braced on the rough limbs behind us. The sky was smeared with stars that sparkled as brightly as my hope, that this might be a summer every bit as magical as the one of '61.

"Where you wanna go?" Winnalee asked.

I shrugged. "I don't know. A city someday . . . I don't know which one. Someplace bigger than Dauber. Just to see it, if nothing else."

"No," Winnalee said, slapping my arm gently as she laughed. "I mean, where do you want our magic tree to take us?"

I looked around, as if anyone was nearby to see us behaving like children. "Anywhere. You decide."

Winnalee bubbled her cheeks with breath as she thought. "To the best place there will ever be. To Woodstock!" she shouted, lifting her fist into the air.

So off our magic tree spun us, me giggling as Winnalee made rocket sounds.

Winnalee was as exuberant as if our game was real. She jumped down, dancing in circles, her T-shirt lifted up over her head, swinging her swaddled arms side to side, her body doll white as she danced across the moonlight-splotched grass, singing out, "'Scuze me while I kiss the sky . . . dar dar dar dar, dar dar dar, dar dar dar," until I would join her.

After we exhausted ourselves, we climbed back into our tree, our bare legs dangling over a thick branch, and we stared up at the sky and wondered out loud how nine years had passed, and how we'd gone from being little girls to women.

Winnalee was sleepy from pot and too many hours on the road, so we crawled into bed before midnight, me lying on my right side, she on her left, our arms bent into pillows. "I'm so glad you're here," I told her.

I loved all the things Winnalee was—gutsy, impulsive, high-spirited—so when her free arm, cooled from the early summer night air, came down to wrap around me, I wished for all of those traits to seep from her skin into me.

"I missed you guys so much, Button. Especially you." Winnalee sounded like she might cry, even as she smiled, but she quickly recovered. And then, as if we were in the middle of a game, she asked, "Okay, after I left . . . best moment ever . . ."

She waited as I struggled to find something. "When I got my driver's license," I said. "And Dad handed me keys to a car. I was so excited at the thought of having my own wheels! Well, until I saw the Rambler—it's so ugly! And, until I drove to Penny's house, my friend after you left. She lived in town. I was *so* scared without Aunt Verdella in the car to help me watch for deer and to tell me when to signal, that I shook all the way there. And when I pulled into Penny's driveway, I banged into her mom's car, knocking out a taillight."

"You didn't!" Winnalee giggled.

"I did. Dad had a fit and told Aunt Verdella that if I was going to drive like a speed demon, he was yanking my keys. Speed demon? I didn't drive over thirty-five miles an hour the whole way to Dauber, and was crawling when I pulled into Penny's drive. But I stomped on the gas instead of the clutch." Winnalee giggled. "Yours?" I asked.

"Woodstock. Of course. But I already told you about that. You ask one."

"Most embarrassing moment?"

Winnalee laughed. "I don't think I've had one. You?"

"I've had so many I can't even keep track of them. But one of them would have to be Mardi Gras, 1963, when I was eleven. We were having a picnic down at the park and everybody was there . . . the Smithys, the Thompsons . . . about twenty of us. Us kids swam until it was time to eat, and when we got to the picnic table, Aunt Verdella looked at my bathing suit, plastered to my skin, and she said to Ada—but loud enough so everyone heard—'Oh my goodness, look at that! Our little Button's sprouting breasts!' God, I thought I'd die right on the spot. I hadn't even noticed, except that my chest had been hurting. But sure enough, there they were, sitting under my sailor suit like two plums."

Winnalee laughed. "Bet Tommy had fun with that one," she said, and I nodded and rolled my eyes.

"But I don't know if that was more embarrassing, or, when Penny and I used her mom's Kirby vacuum cleaner hose to give ourselves hickeys."

"You *what?*" Winnalee rolled onto her belly and slapped the mattress as she laughed. "Why?"

"It was Penny's idea. She thought it would make us look cool. She practiced on me first. She didn't know how long to hold the hose, so was experimenting. I ended up with a row of perfectly round, big 'hickeys' from under my jaw down to my collarbone. Even one above my jawbone. Right here!" I poked my skin to show her. "Who gets a hickey on their *face*? I thought I'd croak when Benji Tyler ripped the cover off the ketchup bottle in the cafeteria and shouted, 'Hey Evy, your boyfriend's looking for you.'"

Winnalee giggled. "I hope you got her back and put one right on her forehead."

"I didn't get the chance to. She saw how stupid I looked and decided it wasn't a good idea after all."

Winnalee was still laughing. "I woulda taken her down and plastered her with them!"

"Best kiss ever," I said when she stopped laughing, because remembering that humiliation wasn't exactly fun.

Winnalee shrugged. "I don't kiss," she said, which totally threw me, because obviously, she'd gone all the way plenty of times.

"You're kidding? Why not?"

"I don't know. Different question . . . saddest mo—never mind. Sorry," she said.

"Your saddest moment?" I asked carefully.

Winnalee hesitated, then her voice fell to almost a whisper. "When I stopped believing in fairies."

I wanted to protest. To insist that she could never stop believing in enchanted becks filled with fairies, and other magical things. But Winnalee rolled to her back, her wrist coming down over her forehead, so I didn't say it.

We lay there for a time, the game over, each of us lost in our own thoughts. And then I asked the question I wanted answered the most. "Winnalee, how long are you staying?"

"I don't know," she mumbled, her eyes closed. "There any jobs around here?"

I grinned. "We'll find you one."

"Button?" she asked, turning back to me and peering out from half-closed lids. "Was your life good? I mean, after we left? Between you and your ma especially?"

"Yes," I said, blinking against the bittersweetness that suddenly stung my eyes. I scanned my mind to find a memory to share with Winnalee. Something that would show her that it got easier, better, after that summer. But I couldn't think of any major ancedote, because the truth of the matter was, Ma, like me, wasn't the kind to do outrageous things. All I had was memories of quiet, everyday moments. Like after Aunt Verdella's comment about my boobs, when Ma found me in the park's restroom, huddled against the cement wall crying, and hugged me. Then her teasing me into smiling by telling me that if anyone should be crying, it should be *her*, because she had boobs the same size as an eleven-year-old.

Then there were the hours in the kitchen, trying new recipes that never looked like the photos in the magazines we pulled them from. And meandering through sewing stores looking for fabric for our latest projects. Some Sunday afternoons, when Ma was backed up with work, we'd drop Boohoo off at Aunt Verdella's and go to the boutique and leave the "closed" sign up, and sew together. Ma would catch me up on the week's episodes of *General Hospital* and *Days of Our Lives*—she kept a little TV on in the sewing room at the store—and while we sewed, we'd fret over the villains' latest antics and pity the victims as if they were real people. But I didn't tell Winnalee any of this, because how could someone who went to Woodstock find any of that ordinary stuff interesting?

"I'm glad things got better," Winnalee said, and her eyes fluttered closed.

I lay watching her sleep in moonlight that crawled over my shoulder and lit her like a princess. Kissed by the soft glow, the bends in Winnalee's curls glistened like they were dusted with freshly fallen snowflakes, and suddenly I was ten again. Sitting in the Bel Air with Uncle Rudy, while Aunt Verdella ran into the IGA for a few things.

It was early November, and a wintery mix was falling. Uncle Rudy must have gotten tired of listening to the *whump, whump* of the windshield wipers, because he shut them off and stared ahead. I thought he was watching people push carts to their cars, but he wasn't. "Lookie this, Button," he finally said. He pointed to a snowflake that had just touched down on the glass. "Watch what this little guy does."

I stared hard at the snowflake, which quickly started to

melt. "See? There he goes. Slippin' right across the windshield to join up with this other partially melted snowflake that's hurryin' to meet him. Now watch . . ." I scooted to the edge of the car seat as Uncle Rudy's finger followed the wobbly trail of water gliding down the glass. "See that? They're picking up more snowflakes as they go."

Then he told me to watch a raindrop. I folded my arms on the dashboard and leaned closer. When a fresh raindrop landed where I stared, I got excited. "It's doing the same thing, Uncle Rudy. Look, right here," I said, yanking my mitten off and bending my fingertip against the glass. "And here's a raindrop going to meet him." And sure enough, as they made a little stream and traveled down the glass, they converged with nearby raindrops. I watched another raindrop. Then another snowflake. Then another raindrop and snowflake. And not once did a raindrop join with a snowflake, or vice versa. I shared this marvel with Uncle Rudy, as if it wasn't his observation in the first place.

"Yep, that's what I'm seeing, too," he said.

We were still watching the glass when Aunt Verdella opened the door, letting the cold air in. She prattled about the good sale on Maxwell House coffee as she shoved her bag into the backseat and slipped in next to me, *brrrrrrr*ing. She took off her crocheted hat, shaking it, sprinkling my skin. "Oh, I'm sorry, Button." She giggled as she dabbed at my cheek with the cuff of her wool coat. When I went back to staring at the windshield and she saw that Uncle Rudy was doing the same, she leaned forward and looked out, asking what we were looking at. I told her, and she sat back. "Hmm, I always thought opposites attract. That's what they always say anyway."

Ever since that day, when I met somebody new, they'd be talking, or smiling at me, or someone else, and I'd quickly determine if they were a raindrop or a snowflake. Because if they were a raindrop like me—colorless and soft, so ordinary that no one could pick them out of a crowd—then that could mean that maybe we'd join together and slip down the halls, two drops in the same stream.

I stared at Winnalee as she rolled on her side and curled her legs up. She was a snowflake for sure. Intricate and sharp, sparklingly beautiful. So unique you'd never mistake somebody else for her. So I was confused. How was it that we—a snowflake and a raindrop—could defy nature as we were doing, melding together—twice—to slip down the same path?

"It feels the same, you and me," I whispered, and Winnalee stirred, and murmured, "Yeah . . . but I'm not the same, Button. Maybe I seem like it, because being back here is making me feel little again, but I'm not the same anymore. Not at all."

I tugged my pillow down, folding it over to tuck under my head, and stared at the dark smudges of vines on the wallpaper. Winnalee was half sleeping. High. And wrong.

I was dangling on the verge of sleep when Winnalee flipped onto her back. "Shit," she mumbled.

"What is it?" I asked.

"I forgot to bring my plants in. They need water."

The plants that were in her van. Herbs perhaps. Or maybe some variety of flowers that, when they bloomed, would look so magical that you could believe fairies danced on them while you slept. "I'll get them," I told her, and she murmured a thank-you.

I grabbed my new stationery to bring downstairs, knowing I was still too excited to sleep, then went out and grabbed the two heavy plants from the van. I lugged them into the spare room downstairs, the one with the bed that sunk in the middle, and put them under the window, alongside Aunt Verdella's tomato starter plants. I watered them, then fingered the wilty long leaves in apology. I'd always pitied neglected plants. They were like children nobody bothered to pour milk for.

Maybe it was the surprise and joy of having Winnalee back in my life, and the night of pulsing rock music and climbing our magic tree, that made me so bold. Or maybe it was just hearing about a world I wasn't brave enough to enter, where people gave away their love without embarrassment or fear. Whatever it was, I wrote to Jesse—a snowflake for sure—without second-guessing every word I put down. I told him about the dress Boohoo ruined, and about Winnalee and her return. I told him about what loving a friend meant to me, and that, yes, I'd love to (pen) pal around with him. I even signed the letter, "Love, Evy."

CHAPTER 8

BRIGHT IDEA #6: If a little kid named Elroy tells you he bites people when he gets mad, believe him. If you don't, you're going to end up with tooth marks on your hand.

When morning came, Boohoo was the one who announced it, bouncing on his knees at the foot of our bed and crowing like a rooster.

I grabbed him and pulled him down between us, whispering my best rendition of Foghorn Leghorn—one of Boohoo's favorite cartoon characters—into his ear. "Hey boy, I say, I say, quiet down, Winnalee's still sleeping." Boohoo giggled and squirmed in protest as I popped kisses on his cheek.

Boohoo pushed my head back to stop me. "Aunt Verdella says to get up and come eat because she made a big breakfast . . .'cause she's here," Boohoo said, jabbing his thumb toward Winnalee. "She's downstairs."

"Aunt Verdella is?"

Boohoo nodded. I made the shush sign and lifted Boohoo out of bed. I closed the door almost shut and we headed downstairs.

Aunt Verdella was standing in the spare bedroom, the door ajar. "Good morning, honey," she said, giving me an affectionate hug. "I'll bet you girls were up half the night, talking."

"Yeah," I said, and Aunt Verdella beamed.

She bent and peered down at Winnalee's now-perky plants. "What on earth are these?"

"I don't know. They're Winnalee's."

"Some kind of hybrid tomato, maybe?" Aunt Verdella said.

"Yeah, that's what they are. Hybrid tomato plants." We turned to see Winnalee shuffling into the room, yawning.

"Morning, sweetie," Aunt Verdella said, giving her a morning hug. "That's what I thought." She sized up the plants. "Boy, you sure do have a green thumb. These tomatoes are a good four inches taller than ours.

"Uncle Rudy wants to plant this week. Yours can go in our garden, too, Winnalee. Rudy will mark them so you know which ones are yours."

"That's okay," Winnalee said. She turned her back to Aunt Verdella. "This variety does better indoors."

"Really? I never heard of keeping tomato plants indoors the whole time."

"Well, these are *special*," Winnalee said, giving me a sly wink.

And then I got it.

I widened my eyes at Winnalee, then herded Aunt Verdella out of the room.

. . .

That morning, Winnalee tagged along to the bridal shop with me. I didn't say anything about the marijuana plants, even if maybe I should have.

I carried the apricot bridesmaid's dress, sheathed in a clear garment bag, holding it high so it wouldn't drag, while Winnalee carried in the box with Jo's ruined dress. Linda was sitting at the desk, taking an appointment over the phone. I could hear Hazel talking with a customer in the big back room where the sewing machines and fabric were kept, and the gowns hung and the girls got measured. Winnalee plunked the dress box on the counter, then wandered off to inspect the front room. When Linda finished her call, I introduced her to Winnalee, who by this time was at the metal cabinet where the patterns were kept in neat rows, sliding the drawer back and forth as if the smooth glide itself made her happy.

"Oh," Linda said, "I heard Jewel talk about you and Freeda so often, I feel as if I know you already."

"Yeah, well in spite of what you heard, I hope you'll like me anyway."

Linda laughed lightheartedly, though I wasn't sure Winnalee was kidding.

When I had no reason left to stall, I sheepishly told her what happened to Jo's dress. Poor Linda already looked like she hadn't slept in a week, which she probably hadn't. This was a busy time for the boutique, with dozens of dresses waiting for final fittings, and more orders coming in. And that meant having to deal with nervous brides who insisted that the waist that suddenly needed to be taken in or let out had nothing to do with nerves that either kept them from eating, or caused them to eat too much. Plus, Linda's husband, Al, had gotten laid off indefinitely and she was worried about how they'd make ends meet once the store quieted in the fall. "I'm sorry. I'm so sorry," I kept repeating.

Linda's face contorted with panic, but she instantly tried to hide it behind a tight smile. I opened the lid so we could examine the damage together. "Oh no," she said. "I was hoping the dirt would be contained to the overlay. Still, Hazel is a wiz at removing stains. She got blood off of satin once."

The bell on the door chimed and Linda looked up. Her face went wedding dress white, and she hurriedly folded the bodice lengthwise. "Jo," she said. I grabbed the length of the smudged skirt that was hanging over the front of the desk, and folded it. But it was too late. "Is that my dress?" The excited giggles gave way to *oooo*s. I turned to see Jo Lanski and three of her friends rushing toward the desk. "It *is* my dress. I can tell by the sleeves!"

"Oh, no peeking yet," Linda said. But it was too late. Jo grabbed the shoulder of the gown and unfolded it.

"My God, what happened?"

Linda and Jo were talking at once then, the bridesmaids gasping. Jo was horribly upset, and Linda was pretending she wasn't. "We'll get the stains out, honey, and no one will be the wiser. Don't you worry. It was an accident."

"Get them out? How? Stick it in the washing machine?"

"No, no, we'll spot-clean it."

Jo was livid, and she turned to me as if I could rescue her, maybe because I was her peer. "I don't want an already-washed wedding dress. If I wanted that, I would have worn my mom's dress like she wanted!"

What choice did Linda have but to promise Jo that we'd sew the gown from scratch again? (At least after she asked to use the phone to call her mother.)

"Oh honey, don't cry," Linda said after Jo and the girls left, and Winnalee called Jo a "rag." "Marge is back from Vegas, so—"

"I'll do it," I said, blinking. Embarrassed about my watery eyes. "Marge shouldn't have to do it. I'm the one who ruined it. Well, Boohoo did, but you know what I mean."

"That's okay, dear. It wasn't your fault. I'm sure Marge won't mind."

Everything in me was screaming, *I want to do it! Please let me sew it!* but I knew Linda wouldn't give me the job. She'd known me since I was nine, and to her I was still a kid, even though I'd moved past "easy" patterns by my twelfth birthday.

"Honey, I think we'll let Marge handle it. But you'll have to be on call to get the beading done stat, as soon as she has it finished."

I couldn't say a thing. Linda was every bit as old to me as I was young to her, and the thought of pushing for the job made my whole body itch. Plus, I knew Linda thought I worked too slowly. And I *did* when it came to the finishing work that needed precision, so that the long row of buttons lined properly and wouldn't bunch, and the appliqués would lie smoothly. But I didn't work slowly when I was cutting a pattern or sewing seams. And Ma herself said that I could hand-stitch a hem faster than she could, and just as neatly. Not that Linda would know this since I worked at home. Sometimes I just wished that Linda—sweet as she was—knew more about sewing. Then she could take one look at the bridesmaids' dresses I produced and see how perfectly they draped, and how polished the seams were. Then she'd *know* that I was ready to take on the most important gown in the ensemble.

"Did you have any problems with that one?" she asked, nodding toward the apricot dress.

"No," I said. "It was a cinch."

"Then maybe you could give us a jump-start on our next project." She nodded toward the counter to our right, where she had stacks of bridesmaid dress "kits" put together in four stacks (gathering together the pattern, fabric, notions needed for each dress was Linda's favorite task). "I was going to give this one to Marge, but she'll be busy now."

"I could take all four of them—the flower girl's, too."

"Well, let's just start with two for now. The others are going to need adjustments, but these two—the two size eights—don't need any."

As she bagged the kit for me, she asked if I had the pattern for Jo's dress, or if Marge still had it.

"Marge must have it. But it's a Simplicity pattern, number 9218. The bride's dress is a size seven."

Linda shoved past Winnalee, pulled out the pattern, then went in the back room to hunt for the same fabric.

I went to stand beside Winnalee, who had now climbed up inside the display window and was circling the mannequins who were bent in romantic poses, heads tilted sweetly, virginal smiles on their plastic faces. She scrinched her nose as she pulled out the yellowed skirt of the bride's dress, then tugged at the boat neckline and boinged the small, stiff bow set at the fitted waist as if she expected it to twirl. "What's *this* in the window for? It's butt-ugly and old. Why don't you guys put a dress in here that at least looks like it came from this century?"

"It's Ma's wedding dress," I said. "The first bridal gown she sewed. She put it in the display window when she opened this place."

"Well why's it still here?"

I fidgeted. "Well, because it's Ma's."

Winnalee shook her head. "Your ma had a good sense of fashion, Button. And if she was marrying Uncle Reece today, you can bet your right boob she wouldn't be wearing *this* outdated thing. She's probably rolling over in her grave. And who wears elbow-length gloves anymore?"

Hazel came out of the fitting room with a tousle-haired bride-to-be, their chatter interrupting our conversation—not that Winnalee's comments themselves wouldn't have ended it, because to us she might as well have suggested that someone change the way we depict Jesus hanging on the cross.

After the bride left, I introduced Hazel to Winnalee, then had to explain all over again what happened to Jo Laski's dress. Hazel, tall and bony, gasped, then patted my arm with fingers cool to the touch. "I was wondering what the ruckus out here was," she said. "But these things happen, dear."

When we got outside, Winnalee said, "At least you got out of having to make that dress over."

"But I *wanted* to make it," I told her. "It's my fault it got ruined in the first place, so I should *have* to." In some ways, I suppose it was odd that I felt comfortable telling Winnalee about the vacuum cleaner hickeys, yet couldn't make myself tell her that the primary reason I wanted to sew it was that Ma always talked about the day I'd sew an entire wedding gown, as if it would be my initiation into womanhood. I wanted that initiation.

"Really?" Winnalee asked, as we opened the doors to my Rambler. "Then why didn't you tell her you wanted to sew it?"

"I did."

"It sounded more like an offer to me. And a half-assed one, at that. Come on, let's go back in there and you insist on doing it." Winnalee came around the car and grabbed my arm. She tried dragging me back to the cement step, but I dug my heels in tight. "I can't do that," I told her. "It's her store. Her decision."

Winnalee frowned. "Well, that's fucked-up," she said. "It was your ma's place."

"But it's Linda's now."

I was glad to get out of there, and eager to get home to start working on the bridesmaids' dresses. But Winnalee was hungry and wanted to stop at the A&W first. After we parked, she leaned over and honked the horn—as if that would get the carhops to us any sooner, it being the noon hour and every space in the lot taken.

"Oh my God!" Winnalee shouted, leaning over and looking around me. "Is that Tommy Smithy in that car? Second one over . . ." I turned and squinted, and saw Tommy's arm crooked in the passenger window of Brody's Mustang.

Winnalee jumped out of the car and hurried to theirs. She opened the door and tugged Tommy out, wrapping her arms around his chest for a quick hug. "I knew that was you, you dumb son of a bitch," she said, so loud that I could hear her—and so could just about everybody else in the lot. "How in the hell are you?"

Tommy's cheeks might have been pink from his sunburn, but he wore that bloated look guys always get when a girl who looks out of their league gives them the time of day in public.

Brody slipped out of the car and gawked at Winnalee over the roof. She was still staring up at Tommy, asking him if he knew who she was, so Brody took the time to dab at his golden hair. "Course I know who you are," Tommy said. "You still cuss the same, sound the same, and you're still a shrimp." Winnalee socked him playfully in the arm, and Tommy added, "And you still can't hit hard enough to leave a mark."

Tommy quieted down some then, so I couldn't hear his words, but his tone was pretty much the same as when he spoke to Winnalee back in '61. Like she was a stupid little kid. But he sure was looking at her differently, his eyes dipping for quick peeks at her boobs, which, as he obviously noticed, were naked under her T-shirt, and her tanned legs that were bare under a miniskirt.

"Hey, buddy. You gonna hog all the good-looking girls for yourself, or are you gonna introduce me?" Brody came around the Mustang, grinning, his thumbs dipped in his jean pockets.

The way Winnalee's body moved as she took a few steps toward Brody made it obvious that she'd inherited more from Freeda than her penchant for cussing. "Hi. I'm Winnalee Malone."

Brody introduced himself, then eyed Winnalee from head to toe, his tongue jutting out the side of his cheek. "Now aren't you a sight for Dauber's sore eyes," he said. He glanced at Tommy like they had a secret.

That's when the carhop came to the Rambler. Winnalee called over her order, then yelled at me to join them.

I groaned inside because I was wearing a too-small knitted shirt that Aunt Verdella bought me on a closeout sale so I couldn't exchange it for a bigger size—she always thought I was smaller than I was—and it was clinging to me like Saran Wrap. Brody would notice, too. I gave the shirt a quick tug, but it just sucked right back to my bra, so I kept my shoulders curled forward.

"Hi, Button," Tommy said.

"Evy," I reminded him.

"Hey, you just let Winnalee call you Button."

"That's different," I said, and I hoped he wouldn't ask why, since I didn't know.

"So is your friend," Brody said with a grin.

I wanted to grab Winnalee and whisper in her ear that Brody was married. Instead I just stood there, arms crossed, gawking at the line of cars, hoods glistening in the sun, so I didn't have to watch the guys watching Winnalee's boobs—or mine.

Winnalee asked them if they knew of any places that were hiring bartenders or waitresses.

"I know of a place," Brody said, with a grin that made me want to bite my cheek.

"Seriously?"

"Yeah. The new bar down past Evy's old man's place.

Used to be Marty's Place. Some dude from Chicago bought it and I guess he's looking for a couple girls yet." His gaze brushed over Winnalee and me, and I tugged at my shirt some more. "You two might want to look into it." Tommy looked down and shook his head.

The carhop came and latched our tray on to the window of my car, calling over to us so we could pay her. I made a move to head back to my Rambler, and Winnalee grabbed my arm, clamping me beside her. "Why don't you boys come by one of these nights," she said. "Bring a little beer, and we'll have a smoke and a little fun."

I suppose Winnalee didn't realize that in Dauber, beer and marijuana were horses of a different color, and that guys like Tommy (the jury was still out on Brody), who didn't think anything of getting smashed on beer, were appalled by pot. I'm sure Tommy would have let Winnalee know this, too, but he thought she meant cigarettes.

The guys left, and while Winnalee and I ate our burgers and had our root beer, I told her that Brody was married. "Your point?" she asked.

"His wife is pregnant, too."

Winnalee turned to me. She had a splotch of ketchup on the corner of her mouth. "What? You think I make a habit of stealing other women's husbands?" She sounded indignant.

I sighed with relief, then tripped over myself trying to take the insinuation back. "I should have known better." And I should have. Even Freeda didn't sleep with married men.

Winnalee's eyes narrowed. "Look, Button. I don't have any use for husbands."

I almost felt sick to my stomach. "I'm sorry. *Sorry.* Forget I said it, please."

Winnalee snapped her last french fry between her teeth as she watched me. "Button, you're a beautiful piece of work, you know that?" She downed the last of her root beer and thumped the mug back on the tray propped on the window. She honked for the carhop.

"Nope," she said. "I don't steal husbands. I just ball 'em, and give 'em back."

My mouth probably dropped open big enough to drop a root beer mug in without chipping my teeth, and Winnalee laughed. Hard. And so I laughed, too, even though I was embarrassed that I'd taken her seriously.

CHAPTER 9

BRIGHT IDEA #55: Just because your friend talks to somebody you don't like, doesn't mean they can't be your friend anymore. Maybe runny noses don't bother them.

We were on Highway 8 when Winnalee shouted, "Wait, stop! There's your dad!"

Dad was in the driveway, hunched over the hood of his car. He craned his head around, saw it was my Rambler, then turned back again.

Winnalee didn't wait for me to put the car in park before she leapt out, shouting, "Uncle Reece! Uncle Reece!" Dad turned and squinted into the sun. "It's me," she called. "Winnalee!" Dad tossed the empty oil can he was holding onto the mound of empty plastic containers piled at the corner of the house.

I shut the car off and gingerly stepped out, watching, as Winnalee leapt up to wrap her arms around Dad's neck, her feet dangling above the ground. I looked down, feeling every bit as confused as I'd been as a child over the ease with which Winnalee could cozy up to Dad—and him to her—while I chewed my cheek when I *had* to talk to him. I stepped back, my foot leaving the drive and sinking into grass that was as scraggly as his hair.

"Man, Uncle Reece. You look like a dog-chewed bone," Winnalee said after she dropped back to the ground.

"It must be the same dog who chewed off the bottom half of your skirt," Dad said, his brows bunching with fatherly disapproval.

Winnalee looked offended, then slapped him on the arm, right over the tattoo of a knife jabbed through a heart. "It's a miniskirt, Uncle Reece. And stop changing the subject." Dad was wearing work pants, the thighs smeared with greasy handprints, and a gray T-shirt that looked as dusty as his skin. Winnalee gave his concave stomach a whack. "What the hell . . . you give up eating?"

"What? I eat," he said, sheepishly.

"It sure as hell don't look like it," Winnalee said. Then she half smiled, half frowned. "It's good to see you again, Uncle Reece. But I'm so sorry about Aunt Jewel. Christ, who gets struck by lightning?" She wrapped her arm around his middle, leaned in, and gave him a hug.

Dad didn't say anything, but he gave her shoulder a comfort squeeze. I lifted my foot and scratched at my ankle.

Dad had to wash the oil from his hands, so we tagged along inside . . . or should I say, I tagged along inside after *them*.

Apparently Winnalee didn't notice that the house had fallen to ruins, because she didn't say anything. She just followed Dad into the kitchen, while I wandered off into the living room to check Ma's bells. I could hear water running in the sink, and Winnalee's voice chattering. Woodstock . . . a job . . .

her van . . . random words peaked above the murmurs, along with an occasional "Hmm" or chuckle from Dad.

I ran my finger over the shelf that Ma's bell collection sat on and the dust made a gray smudge. I glanced toward the kitchen, wondering if I could dust them without getting caught. I decided not, so merely blew and dabbed at the grime the best I could.

"Button?" Winnalee called. "Where are you?"

"I need something from my room," I called, then hurried off. I dug around the near-empty drawers and closet to find something I could grab to support my excuse, and ended up taking a summer nightgown that I hadn't worn in two years.

I was hoping to drag Winnalee out of there right away, but she wouldn't budge. As they talked—mostly Winnalee—I watched Dad as he opened a beer. I knew his profile so well that if I was artistic like Winnalee, I could draw him to a T. I knew every bend of his ears, and the precise spot alongside his nose that glossed when he was overheated. I knew the exact outline of his beard when the stubble built, and the spot near his jawbone where a twitch would crop up when he got irritated. And I knew, by the stiffening in his neck, the exact moment when he'd feel me staring and glance up and we'd both turn away.

Dad walked us to the car. "You'd better come see us, too!" Winnalee warned, her voice scolding, yet playful. "We'll cook you something yummy so you can beef up and get your hunky body back. Won't we, Button?"

"Sure," I mumbled.

"You been checking the oil?" Dad asked as he thumped the hood of my car, probably because he felt he had to say *something* to me.

"Yeah," I said, and he reminded me—again—that I could crack the engine block if I ran out of oil.

"You and your dad are weird together," Winnalee said as I backed us out of the drive. "Like strangers."

I didn't comment.

"But then," Winnalee said, "I guess you two were always like that with each other."

But we weren't. Not for that stretch in between when you left and when Ma died. We weren't so much during that time.

I watched Winnalee from the corner of my eye, wishing I could say those words out loud, because keeping them to myself made me feel like the tree in the picture Uncle Rudy gave me, only with my roots dangling loose in midair.

"It's kinda weird, isn't it?" Winnalee said, as we rumbled down Peters Road, the ruts bumping our ride, the wind thumping through the windows tossing our hair. "They *made* us . . . we share half of their genes . . . seems like it should be easier getting along with them, doesn't it?"

"Yeah," I said, and the roots of my sadness reached over to twine with hers.

CHAPTER 10

BRIGHT IDEA #11: If somebody says you missed the boat, they're probably not talking about a ride in a canoe.

Winnalee and I headed to Aunt Verdella's early, two mornings later, carrying a basket of dirty laundry between us. Boohoo was in the yard, his pants pulled down enough to show the tops of his butt cheeks, humming as he swirled urine in loops over the grass. "Boohoo, what are you doing?" I shouted.

"Taking a leak, by the looks of it," Winnalee mumbled under her breath.

"I'm doing what you told me . . . ," Boohoo replied.

"You told him to piss in the grass? Why, Button, you surprise me."

We were close enough now for Boohoo to hear that one, so he responded, "No. She said to practice so I wouldn't forget my letters in the summer. That's what I'm doin'. I'm writing my name."

"I didn't tell you to do it with *pee*," I said. "Pencils, Boohoo. Peeing is private. Not something—"

Winnalee interrupted. "So how far did you get before your pee pencil ran dry?"

Boohoo's stream slowed to a stop, and he shook himself off, hiked up his pants, and beamed. "I got to the *h*, this time."

"Cool," Winnalee said, giving his head a pat as we passed.

Uncle Rudy was just coming out the door when we reached the porch, Knucklehead hobbling behind him. "Mornin' girls," he said.

"Where you off to so early?" Winnalee asked.

"Well, Tommy's bringing the cows over in a bit, so I thought I'd give him a hand unloading them."

"I wanna help, too," Boohoo said, bopping up and down.

"Boohoo, don't get too close to the cows," I warned, and Uncle Rudy assured me he'd keep a close eye on him. He reached down and patted Boohoo's head. "He's a good helper, this one. He's gonna help me with my garden today, too, aren't you?"

"Yep." Boohoo beamed, as he pulled a wad of yarn from his pocket. "Uncle Rudy, can cows wear leashes?"

Aunt Verdella was at the kitchen window when we got inside, her belly strained against the sink as she watched Uncle Rudy circle the house. She was wearing a smile when she turned. "You two want some breakfast? I could make some more French toast."

"No. We have cereal and milk at home," I told her, because judging by the pyramid of new yarn on the counter and the stack of crocheted items waiting beside a box on the dining room table, she was planning to get right to work after she got the dishes done.

"Hey, where are you going with that?" Winnalee asked,

when Aunt Verdella opened the basement door to take our basket down. She shot me a look, then hurried to take the basket. "Why would *you* run this down? It's *our* dirty laundry."

Aunt Verdella glanced at me, then leaned closer to Winnalee, as if in doing so I couldn't hear her. "Button doesn't like basements. They scare her."

Winnalee looked confused at first, then her mouth formed just a hint of a circle. "Exactly why *I'm* doing it," she said.

Aunt Verdella cleared the table, gobbling up the cold wedges of French toast glued with syrup as she carried Boohoo's plate to the sink. "And I weighed myself, too. One week of dieting, and I haven't even lost a pound!"

"Dieting? Aunt Verdella, why you dieting?" Winnalee asked as she stepped up into the kitchen. "I love you just the way you are . . ." She wrapped her arms around Aunt Verdella and gave her a squeeze. ". . . all pillow-squishy and warm." Aunt Verdella gave a sickly moan.

"Well, opening Saturday is only two weeks away. You all set, Aunt Verdella?" I asked.

"The Community Sale?" Winnalee guessed, smiling, no doubt because she remembered how we'd gone along once and bought things for our adventure bag with the money we earned from selling homemade pot holders.

Aunt Verdella nodded. "I'm going to make a few more baby sweater sets and a couple of ponchos, then I'll be good to go."

She poured me a cup of coffee and Winnalee a cup of juice, then began rummaging through the clutter on the counter, pulling out a strip of cream-colored crocheted lace. "Look at this pattern," she said, handing it to me. "I thought this would be pretty for the edge of a tablecloth. What do you think?"

Winnalee grabbed the lace to admire it, then looked up, her eyes wide. "Hey," she said, holding it against her denim cutoffs. "Wouldn't this look cool on jeans?" She turned around and held the lace between the waistband and her butt. "Here maybe? Or," and she spun back around, "here," she said, running it down the outside seam.

It did look cool, and I told her so. Aunt Verdella laughed. "I never saw that before, but I guess if they can make dresses out of paper, why not put tablecloth lace on jeans? I'll make you up some lace and Button can sew it on for you. I wouldn't quite know where to place it."

"Far out," Winnalee said. "Thanks."

"Oh! Speaking of baby sweater sets," Aunt Verdella piped—as if that's what we were talking about—"I ran into Nancy Bishop and her daughter-in-law, Marls, yesterday, and I was thinking . . . Button, we should give Marls a baby shower. She hasn't made any girlfriends here yet, so I can't see that anybody else is going to give her one. It would be a nice gesture, don't you think?"

"Sure," I said, while Winnalee stared off with disinterest.

"Good. I'll call Nancy today and see if we can't set up a date. I'll ask them to put together an invitation list. I'll come up with a few games—everyone loves baby shower games—and I'll make up a few little crocheted items for gifts. We'll keep the food simple. I was thinking sandwiches, some chips, a pretty Jell-O mold, a sheet cake. I've got a couple quarts of my homemade pickles left, I think."

"I saw Uncle Reece a couple days ago," Winnalee said, cutting in to change the subject even though Aunt Verdella wasn't finished with the last. "Man, he looks almost as rough as Knucklehead."

Aunt Verdella forgot all about the baby shower once *that* comment was made. "He's not sick, is he?"

"No. It's just that Winnalee hasn't seen him since . . . well, 1961," I said.

Aunt Verdella's face wrinkled with worry. "I should make up some beef stew today and bring it over. He likes beef stew."

Winnalee's eyes moistened. "I felt bad for him. And that house makes me sad without Aunt Jewel in it."

Her words were like a mirror held up to my own heart, and I puckered my lips together so I wouldn't cry.

"But Uncle Reece was the same in some ways," Winnalee added. "He said a dog must have chewed away half of my skirt." She rolled her eyes, but she was smiling.

"Oh, I think girls look cute in those short skirts," Aunt Verdella said. "I'm always telling Button she should wear them. She'd be a lot cooler in the summertime."

Winnalee looked at my damp face, then at my bell-bottoms, and frowned.

"At least I never had to get sent home from school to change, like Penny did. She was always getting sent in to have the assistant principal measure her skirts."

"They measured skirts at your school?" Winnalee said. *"Huh?"*

"Yeah. They'd have random checks in gym class," I explained. "We had to kneel on the floor and the phys ed teacher would hold up a yardstick. If anyone's skirt measured any more than two inches above their knees, they got sent home to change and got zeros for the day. They'd haul girls out of the hall and send them to the office to get measured in between, too, if they could tell they were too short."

Winnalee shook her head. "See? That's what's wrong with this whole damn country—always pushing to make us conformists to somebody else's ideals. I would have told them where to stick their yardsticks."

She sighed, then looked up wistfully. "Aunt Verdella? Do you think Uncle Reece will find somebody else someday? You know, like Uncle Rudy found you after his first wife died. I don't get into that marriage shit, and I sure don't mean any disrespect for Aunt Jewel, but I feel bad thinking of Uncle Reece living the rest of his life over there all alone."

I looked up, shocked that Winnalee would say such a thing. Aunt Verdella's chair groaned as she shifted her weight. She gave me a quick, nervous glance, and bit at her lip.

Winnalee didn't wait for a reply. "Maybe I can find someone for him," she said. "I'll keep my eyes open at work."

"Work? You found a job?" Aunt Verdella piped, obviously eager to change the subject.

"Yep. The night before last. At that new bar out on Highway 8. The Purple Haze. Marty's old place."

"Oh, where Freeda used to work!"

"Yeah," Winnalee said. "But when Marty had it, it was nothing but a boring bar and dance hall where old people and families with kids went for a fish fry on Fridays, or to hear a country 'n western band some Saturdays. But now it's gonna be cool. They're gonna have live music every weekend—rock bands!—and black lights and fluorescent paint. Brody Bishop tipped us off, and I wanted to apply before the owner ran any help-wanted ads, so after we got home from town, we ran out there. The place isn't opened yet because he's doing some rewiring and stuff, but it's gonna be a fun place to work. He hired me to do the artwork on the walls, too. The owner seems real nice."

I squirmed in my chair. The owner, who introduced himself as "Reefer," didn't seem nice to me. He was older than Dad, judging by the white twined through the thinning hair that hung down his back in skinny strings, and he didn't smile once while we were there. He didn't ask Winnalee if she had any experience serving drinks or waiting tables, either. He just swirled the wrench he was holding in circles, cueing her to spin around.

The Purple Haze was divided into two sections, with the horseshoe-shaped bar in the smaller of the two, with an opened doorway and large cutaway window where drinks and plates were put for the waitresses who worked the back room. Dad and his friend Owen played guitars at Marty's years ago, and I got to go along with Ma for a couple hours. Ma and I didn't dance, but there was a lady with dark hair dancing, and Ma said, "If she was a redhead, she could pass for Freeda." The woman didn't look like Freeda, so I assumed it was how she danced.

Winnalee had wandered into the back, and I followed her. She called to Reefer, her girlish voice echoing in the empty space. "You need black lights and fluorescent psychedelic shit on the walls. Not posters—too ordinary—painted images. Hendrix's head, Joplin's, peace signs, flowers. Maybe some optical illusions. Shit like that. I could paint them for you. I'm an artist, you know."

"That right," Reefer said, drifting over to the doorway and leaning against the frame.

"Yep." She pointed to the small window alongside the wall facing the parking lot. "I painted my van out there." Reefer glanced. "I'd do it cheap, too. Two hundred bucks for the whole job."

"Shit," Reefer said. "My boy can paint the walls for nothing."

"But can he paint the pictures? I'll do the artwork for one-fifty."

"You serious? What do you think, I'm made of money?"

"No. But you might be if you make this place the most kick-ass joint in the county—which is what I'm trying to help you do. One hundred and fifty bucks. That's my bottom price."

"One hundred."

"It's a deal. Now how about—"

I had to pee ever since we left the A&W, so it seemed like a good time to exit: Dickering made me bite myself.

Coming back, I stopped in my tracks. Winnalee was *da, da, da-ing* a sped-up verse of "Proud Mary," her arms lifted above her head, moving as if she was pounding drums, her hips gyrating. "Yep," she said when she stopped. "Just as I thought. You need to resurface this dance floor. How can people dance on a floor as rippled as a potato chip? It's gooey, too. Old varnish, or just plain dirt. I don't know which."

"I suppose you refinish wood floors, too," Reefer said.

"Nah. Just sayin'."

Reefer shrugged, then headed back to the horseshoe bar, Winnalee following. "My friend here can cut loose on the dance floor, too. I've seen her do it." She didn't mention that I was only nine years old at the time.

"So I got the painting job, and when the place opens, I'm gonna wait tables. I'm starting on the artwork this morning," Winnalee said proudly. "Anyway, like I said, I'm going to keep my eye out at work for a woman for Uncle Reece."

"Well, from what I've heard," Aunt Verdella said, "the crowd there is gonna be pretty young and wild. And, well, I don't know if the women there would really be Reece's type."

Winnalee laughed. "He liked them young and wild things once."

Aunt Verdella's lips quivered, then her face folded in worry. "Winnalee, there's a lot of men in places like that who will try to take advantage of a pretty, innocent thing like you. You be careful out there, okay?"

As we headed toward home so Winnalee could get out to the bar, Uncle Rudy and Tommy were standing next to his empty cattle truck. The mailman pulled up to my box and Boohoo made a dash for it. "I'll get it!" I yelled as the mailman pulled away. But Boohoo opened the box anyway, then started waving a single letter in the air. "Evy's got a boyfriend! Evy's got a boyfriend!" I chased him around the yard, my face as red as the flag on the box, or so Tommy pointed out afterward.

CHAPTER 11

BRIGHT IDEA #46: You can tell a scaredy cat 100 times that there's no sharks in a lake, but they'll probably still just stand in the water up to their ankles and shiver like there is.

The next morning I woke with a start, my guts clenching, my breath freezing in my chest. I shot up, bracing myself on my elbows, straining for what had wrenched me from my sleep. I glanced to make sure Winnalee was in bed (she wasn't when I partially woke up and glanced at the clock at 3 A.M.). I was relieved to find her asleep, her long loops and baggy T-shirt spun around her like a cocoon. Her arm dangling over the edge of the bed spotted in fluorescent, primary paint like a psychedelic leopard.

I slipped downstairs and squinted out the front door. Thunderheads were stacking in the southeast, and heavy air squeezed against my skin. There wasn't a sound; even the birds seemed hushed in fear. I closed the screen before a fat bee could swagger in, and took a jagged breath. I had never liked summer storms, but after Ma was killed by one, my unease over them turned into outright terror when lightning exploded in the sky.

Boohoo was across the road playing near the ditch. He waved and I waved back, forcing a carefree smile. I heard him yell to Aunt Verdella or Uncle Rudy, then he headed over. "Stop and look!" I yelled, because my nerves over his— anyone's— safety always frayed when a storm was brewing.

"Boohoo, you have to watch for cars," I scolded, when he reached me.

"I listened for them," he said. I pulled him to me and gave him his morning hug. God, how I hated it when I sounded critical and owly like Ma did when I was his age.

"You must have been planting the garden this morning," I said, forcing a cheerfulness I didn't feel as I brushed the dirt patches off his knees.

"No, we did that yesterday. I was just diggin'. Guess what, Evy?" He grabbed my hand and tugged me to the corner of the porch. He pointed to the field where Tommy's cows stood chewing their cuds. "That one right there, the littler one? The one with the black star on his face? Tommy said I can call him what I want and it can kinda be like he's mine. I named him Licker, because that's what he did to my arm when we put him in the *paster,* 'cause he likes me. Is that a good name? Licker?"

On another morning, I would have laughed like I always did when Boohoo warmed my heart with his ways. But the storm brewing inside me, because of the storm brewing outside, had me too tense to laugh. "It sure is," I said, as I tipped my head back to see how fast the clouds were moving. "But you stay out of the field unless Uncle Rudy is with you, you hear?"

"I know that," he said. "Uncle Rudy told me."

"And don't try peeing on the fence, either. There's current running through that fence now, and you can get zapped that way."

"I know that, too. Tommy told me."

I headed back to the door, Boohoo chattering behind me. Then I stopped. "Was that thunder?" Boohoo listened for a split second, then shrugged. I went inside and he followed me into the kitchen.

"Guess what, Evy? That party you guys are gonna have for that lady with the fat belly because she's got a baby in it? On that day, Uncle Rudy and me and Tommy and Brody, and his dad, and maybe my dad, too, we're goin' fishing. Uncle Rudy said we can't be around you ladies 'cause you'll just be harping at us not to mess things and not to pick at the food."

"Sounds fun, Boohoo."

"Yep. It's gonna be. We're going up to the Willow Flowage. Tommy and Mr. Bishop are bringing their boats. Dad said there's northerns up there as big as me."

"Dad told you that?" I asked hopefully.

"No, he told somebody else. But I heard him. He said he caught one forty-two inches up there, and that's how much I am. Evy? Is it time for *Captain Kangaroo*?"

I glanced up at the clock. "Almost," I said, wishing I had a TV so Boohoo could watch it by me. Outside, thunder groaned like a monster disrupted from his sleep, and I struggled to hold down my fear as I always did around Boohoo—anyone, for that matter. "You wait here until I get dressed, then I'll walk back with you. I want to talk to Aunt Verdella about the baby shower. I'll hurry."

But Boohoo was already heading for the door. "Captain might drop Ping-Pong balls on Bun's head. That's the best part." And out the door he went, the screen door cracking behind him.

I hurried to the door and stood on the porch. Dark-bellied

clouds hung behind Aunt Verdella's house as Boohoo ran, his arms and legs pumping. Lightning snapped from one cloud to another, followed by the groans of distant thunder. Mr. White had said that lightning from a cloud ten miles away could strike a person. I scrutinized the dark clouds, wondering how far away they might be, as I held my breath and waited for the bolt I was sure would stab down to skewer my brother to the ground. *Run, Boohoo, run!* I shouted in my mind.

I didn't start breathing again until Aunt Verdella opened the front door and pulled him safely inside. *It's okay. It's okay,* I told myself. *Aunt Verdella is as vigilant about storms now as I am. She won't let him play outside when it's lightning, or run water, or touch anything electrical.* I repeated these things in my head a few times, while my teeth tore tender skin from my cheek.

I went inside and shut the door, leaning against it and closing my eyes. Reminding myself to breathe. But the second that breath came, fear snatched it away again, because a stranger was standing in my living room, watching me.

His dark hair was hippie-long and hung in dirty clumps. His shirt was hanging open, his chest tangled with black corkscrew curls. He moved like a dazed ghost. "Fuckkkkk," he muttered, as he rubbed his stomach and looked around, obviously trying to figure out where he was.

I yelped, my hand reaching for the doorknob. With a storm outside, and an intruder inside, I felt trapped.

He squinted at me. "Whoa, you look a whole lot different in the light of day," he said, his voice hoarse, the whites of his eyes salmon pink. He looked down at his bare feet and wriggled toes that were long and buckled, then wagged his head as he searched for something on the floor. He muttered an "Oh," then shuffled back into the spare bedroom.

Winnalee! She'd slept with him downstairs, then came upstairs after they did it!

The guy trundled back wearing a pair of huarache sandals, his cracked heels hanging over the flattened backs. I slid away from the door so he could get out, and flinched when he turned and held up his hand, but he was only giving me the peace sign.

I locked the door the second he left, and peered out the window. I didn't see any vehicles but ours in the drive, so unless he parked on the road out of the range of my vision, he had a long, wet walk ahead of him.

The stink of smoke and booze—God knew what else—hovered in the air where he'd stood. I darted into the downstairs bedroom and cringed at a pale stain on the sheets, wondering if it came from the guy. I rolled the whole thing—Winnalee's discarded panties included—and tucked the soiled bedding under my arm.

I stood in the doorway, eyeing the room for any other trace left by the stranger. There was a wad of rolled toilet paper in the bottom of the empty trash can, the milky tip of a used rubber showing. Grossed out though I was, I glanced around, even though I *knew* I was alone, and pulled back a flap of tissue paper to have a look. No wonder girls wanted guys to use them, I decided. Who'd want *that* to get inside of them?

While I was still squinting at the condom, a bolt of lightning struck so close that it startled the hair on my arms. I uttered a quick "I'm sorry" (to who, I'm not sure) then scooped up the trash can. I stood in the doorway, looking the room over for any other "evidence" I didn't want Boohoo or Aunt Verdella finding. That's when I noticed that the plants were missing.

Not just Aunt Verdella's tomato plants, but Winnalee's pot plants! Thunder pounded in my head and in the sky.

I stuffed the sheets in the bathroom hamper, dumped the garbage and put the trash basket in the tub to bleach later, then rushed to the front door. The rain was no longer coming down in sidewinding sheets, but tiny splashes were pocking the walkway and rain was spilling from the eaves. I rocked from foot to foot, wondering how on earth I was going to tell Uncle Rudy that he'd planted dope in his garden. That's when Tommy pulled into the drive.

He jogged to the porch, raindrops splotching the shoulders of his white T-shirt. He opened the door. "Was that Chet Bouman I just saw leaving here?"

"I don't know who it was."

"Chet . . . long haired, greasy-looking bastard? Reefer's son? His Beetle was parked on the road last night. And I mean *on* the road. In front of the barn. I almost hit the damn thing on my way back from the Bishops'. I just saw Chet heading to it."

I sighed. "Well if you knew who it was, then why were you asking me?"

"Evy, those Boumans are dope dealers. What was he doing here?"

I told him to never mind about Chet Bouman because I had a bigger problem on my hands. I told him about the missing marijuana plants.

"Jesus," he said. "Dope? She was growing *dope* in your house? And now it's in Verdella and Rudy's garden?" He shook his head. "You're going to have to tell them."

"I can't do that!"

"Then you'd better tell Winnalee to get her ass over there and dig them up. It's *her* problem, not yours."

"I don't know what time she got to sleep," I told Tommy. "And you can hardly wake her after an early night."

Tommy scratched his stubbly chin, as I strained my ears. "It still lightning?" I asked, embarrassed that I needed to.

"Nah," Tommy said. "It's passed, Evy." He said this with an unusual softness to his voice. He sighed. "Ah, come on. I'll help you dig them up."

"Winnalee told Aunt Verdella they were hybrid tomatoes," I explained as we hurried across the glossy grass. "A new kind that grows best indoors. Aunt Verdella must not have told Uncle Rudy, though. I didn't even know he'd taken them."

"You can't have that shit in your house," Tommy said. "Drug dealers . . . pot. You want to go to jail?"

"I can't get arrested. *I* didn't grow the plants. And *I* don't smoke it."

"Bullshit. If it's in your house, you can get busted." I reminded myself that Tommy didn't know everything, even if he pretended to.

Uncle Rudy's truck was gone, and Aunt Verdella's front door was shut—water always got in and soaked her rug if it wasn't—and I only hoped the back door was shut as well.

The garden was enclosed with snow fence to keep the deer and rabbits out. Tommy unfastened the makeshift gate and we slipped inside. The heavy rain had washed away any prints Uncle Rudy and Boohoo had patted and stomped over narrow rows of seeds, so that if it wasn't for the line of string running from stick to stick along the length of the garden, a seed packet tucked upside down on each, you'd never have known anything was planted. Well, except for the tomato and marijuana plants standing at the south end.

Tommy reached for the shovel wedged into the ground, and I followed him to the spiky-leafed plants. "Hurry," I told him, as I glanced back at the porch.

Tommy had one plant lying on its side in the grass, the dirt clump at its base snarled with roots, when Boohoo came flying out the door. When he reached the snow fence, he peered between the slats and shouted, "Hey, you guys, why you digging up our garden?" And then, without giving me a chance to reach him and explain—as if I *had* an explanation—he raced to the house to tattle.

I clutched the sides of my head and harped at Tommy to hurry.

Aunt Verdella was still in her housecoat, her uncombed hair sporting more cowlicks than a guinea pig's, as she hurried across the yard, her loose boobs wagging as she trotted. "See? I told you. They're digging up me and Uncle Rudy's garden!"

Aunt Verdella stopped at the fence. "Button? What on earth are you doing?" She closed her robe when she saw Tommy.

"Wrecking our garden!" Boohoo said. "That's what they're doin'."

I looked down at my granny-length nightgown, not even covered by a robe, and crossed my arms to cover my own soft mounds.

"Button?" Aunt Verdella, her skin spotted with freckles and liver spots, looked young and old at the same time. Her eyes were filled with the trust of a child on Christmas Eve.

I wanted so badly to lie to protect her—protect Winnalee—yet I couldn't think of one believable fib. I walked to the fence, my body sagging with sorry. "Boohoo, go inside for a minute, please." He started to protest, but I pointed. "Now, Boohoo." I waited until his face smudged the kitchen window, then I told Aunt Verdella the truth.

She looked confused. "Pot?"

"Wacky weed . . . Mary Jane . . . marijuana . . . dope," Tommy said, as he strode along the garden's edge, a plant dangling from each hand. "They smoke the leaves to get high. It's illegal, and you can get busted for growing it."

Aunt Verdella looked at the plants as if they were loaded pistols with no safety lock. She stepped back. "Our little Winnalee is one of those *addicts*?" Her hand came up to cover her heart. "My Lord!"

I tried to tell her that marijuana wasn't addictive in the same way as other drugs, but worry had already crusted over her eyes, and I knew that nothing I said would chip it away.

"That scary man I saw walk out of your place this morning . . . who is he? Is he mixed up in this drug stuff too?"

"Chet Bouman. Drug dealer, ma'am," Tommy said, sounding like a sheriff in a bad Western. I shot him a glare to let him know he *wasn't* helping.

"She had them when she came," I explained.

"Oh dear," Aunt Verdella said. "Our little girl's in trouble." She looked down at the plants, then side to side, as if flashing red and blue lights might suddenly emerge from the woods. "What we gonna do?" she said in a whisper.

"We've gotta get rid of them," Tommy said, nodding over toward the old woodstove sitting on a sheet of asbestos at the edge of the yard, where they burnt their trash.

"Oh my goodness . . . my goodness . . . ," Aunt Verdella muttered from the snow fence as Tommy and I headed toward the stove. "No, wait! Not here! Fanny Tilman's stopping by this morning to drop me off some variegated yarn. She catches wind of this and she'll have it all over Dauber that Verdella and Rudy Peters were growing *marriageawana*."

Tommy looked down at me and murmured, "How in the hell would Fanny Tilman know what burning marijuana smells like? Well, unless she puffs a little loco weed while she knits." I whacked him in the arm for making jokes at a time like this.

Aunt Verdella called to Boohoo to stay put, then hurried us out front. She stopped in the middle of the yard and sent Tommy to hide behind the shade tree near the picnic table—even though a grown man half hidden behind a tree would certainly cause more suspicion than one standing in the middle of the lawn, holding uprooted plants during planting season. She sent me to the road to scout for cars.

"The coast is clear," I said.

"You sure? You sure?" she asked.

I looked again, exaggerating the swivel of my head. "Yes."

She let Tommy come out from hiding. "Hurry, Tommy, hurry!"

We crossed the road, but Aunt Verdella had to check at least ten more times before she'd cross it herself, for fear that someone would catch her in her housecoat.

I ran inside to grab matches and a paper-stuffed grocery bag filled with what Uncle Rudy called "burnabelia," which I kept under the counter, then hurried into the backyard. Tommy crumpled the newspaper and flyers and stuffed them into the old oil barrel poked with bullet holes to let in the air necessary for creating a draft. He shook as much of the dirt off the plants' roots as he could, then stuffed them inside. The smoke hung low in the damp, heavy air, and I backed up as he did, in case I could end up higher than a kite from inhaling the smoke.

"It smells funny, doesn't it?" Aunt Verdella said, wrinkling her nose. "I hope our neighbors don't smell it." To which Tommy responded, "Mrs. Peters, the Thompsons are your closest neighbors, and they're five miles away. So don't you worry."

Aunt Verdella wiped her hand up her sweaty forehead, leaving her two-toned bangs standing on end. She picked at the collar of her robe like she didn't know what to do next. "Oh, Winnalee," she said quietly.

"Don't worry, Aunt Verdella. I'll handle Winnalee." I didn't know how, but I would.

"I know how *I'd* handle her," Tommy said as Aunt Verdella hurried back to Boohoo. "I'd kick her out on her ass."

"She's been my best friend since we were kids, Tommy!"

"I know that. But don't expect that she's the same person she was back then."

"So? I'll bet Brody changed since you guys were kids, too, but he's still your best friend."

Tommy put his hands up, showing his palms. "Friend or not," he said. "Screwing drug dealers in your house? Growing dope? She's nothing but trouble. For you, for Verdella and Rudy, *and* for Brody."

"Brody?"

Suddenly Tommy morphed into Dad, judging Ma's friendship with Freeda. The hair on my arms prickled. "Like what? Brody's some innocent bystander? You can bet that when Winnalee starts work at the Purple Haze, he'll be there every night. And not because Winnalee invited him, either."

"He's married," Tommy said flatly.

"Yeah, and he should remember that!" I stomped into the house and slammed the door without thanking Tommy for his help.

I was nervous about telling Winnalee that we destroyed her marijuana plants. I figured she'd have a conniption fit, and she did. "Damn, Button. They were almost ready to bud!"

My arms itched as she scolded me, and I turned away, near tears. Sometimes, it felt like my whole purpose in life was to try to keep everyone happy. To not disappoint them. To keep everyone liking me. And it was exhausting. I loved Winnalee and was so grateful that she was back, yet already it felt like I was trying to subdue a tornado with my bare hands.

Winnalee's rant seized when she saw me scratching. She exhaled hard. "Geez, Button. When you got a beef with someone, say it, don't scratch it."

These words made me tear up, and that made Winnalee sigh. "I guess I should have known weed would make you uptight. Sorry. I shouldn't have brought the plants here in the first place." She put her hand over mine to still it and gave me a hug. I wanted to tell her that a lot of things she did worried me, but she was already turning on the stereo. She started dancing before the vanity mirror like nobody was watching. "You've gotta come to work with me one of these nights," she said. "See my artwork and stuff." Winnalee was looking like a seductive stripper one minute and a kid cutting loose on a wedding reception dance floor the next. Suddenly I didn't know whether to laugh or cry. She glanced up, then grabbed my arm. "Come on, Button. Dance with me!" So I did.

CHAPTER 12

BRIGHT IDEA #94: If you always ride on the slow rides that don't lift far off of the ground, just because you're afraid of falling, you won't fall far, that's true, but you won't get many thrills, either. And you won't be proud of yourself when the carnival's over.

The day of Jo Lanski's wedding, I was holding down the fort at Jewel's Bridal Boutique because Linda and Hazel and Marge were at the First Methodist Church helping Jo and her bridesmaids—including Amy, Jesse's former girlfriend—get dressed. Winnalee came in to keep me company once she woke up.

A bride-to-be, Cindy Jamison, one year older than I and dressed in bell-bottoms and a tie-dyed shirt, huffed with irritation as her mother plucked pattern after pattern from the cabinet and showed her yet another dress that looked like something Audrey Hepburn would wear. "M-om," Cindy whined, stretching the title into two syllables. "I don't want an old-lady fifties-looking dress. And I hate lace."

Mrs. Jamison held up a pattern of a sleeveless dress, fitted waist, lace overlay from neckline to hem, and a long train. "But this is beautiful, honey. With your small waist and—"

Cindy threw up her hands. "Mom, this is *my* wedding!"

"Would it help if we omitted the lace?" I asked.

Mrs. Jamison looked at me like I'd lost my mind. "But it would look like an ordinary dress then," she said. "Maybe if it had some ruffles."

"I hate ruffles worse than lace!"

Winnalee was sitting behind the desk drinking a Tab, her feet hooked on the ledge, her naked legs showing. She got up. "What kind of a dress do you want?"

Cindy looked at Winnalee, who was wearing a flowing rayon minidress with tiny flowers and angel sleeves that belled in layers from the elbow down. "Something like you're wearing," she said. "Well, not just like that, but you know what I mean . . . something flowy. Sorta like something a hippie angel would wear."

Mrs. Jamison gasped. "You can't wear a hippie dress to your wedding!"

"But that's what I want. Why do you insist on making me look a wedding cake?"

I stood off to the side, chewing my cheek and hardly breathing—Linda was trusting me to please any customer who came through the door while she was gone, and if Cindy didn't find a dress that made her happy, I'd fail miserably. Yet if her mother—who was footing the bill—wasn't happy, then we'd lose a customer. I could tell Linda was still upset with me over Jo's dress, so it's not like I needed more trouble.

I stepped forward and rummaged for a Simplicity pattern I knew was there. A simple, empire-style dress with full sheer sleeves gathered into a cuff. I pulled it and held it out. "Maybe something like this?"

Cindy took the pattern and wrinkles lifted her nose. "This

still looks too *weddingy.* The sleeves. I don't like sleeves with cuffs. That's something a pirate would wear. I want ones like hers."

"But this *is* a wedding," Cindy's mother said. She looked at me, and huffed. "First she insists on carrying her grandma's Bible instead of a bouquet, now this."

Winnalee snatched the pattern, then tossed it on the desk. "Hold on a sec," she said. She headed outside, while Mrs. Jamison and Cindy argued under their breaths. Through the gauzy curtains, I saw Winnalee leap out of her van with an oblong pouch and her curled sketch pad. When she came back in, she started drawing a gown with a thick leaded pencil, the skirt of the dress swirling as if the faceless model was in the middle of a spin. The angel-sleeves were rather wide and fluttering like wings over naked arms. The bodice was softly gathered and cinched underneath the bust, empire-style. "Like this?" she asked. And Cindy cried, "Yes!"

Winnalee ran her pencil softly across the high waist. "And this could be a wide, ivory ribbon, or a ribbon the same color as the bridesmaids' dresses."

"It's so plain," Mrs. Jamison complained.

"You could have crystal doohickeys glued on the ribbon to make it look more *bridal* if you wanted to," Winnalee said.

"I don't know . . . ," Mrs. Jamison said. "It just doesn't look like something a bride—"

"Oh, but wait!" Winnalee flipped the paper over and started sketching the back of the dress. "Check this out," she said, as if the dress were already made in her mind, even though I knew she was making this all up as she went along.

She swirled her pencil into who knew what, but something big and bunched like a bouquet at the middle of the bride's back. Then she drew wide strands of ribbons hanging down the length of the dress and spilling over a slight train.

"Chiffon would be beautiful for this dress," I said. "Very

flowy." And Winnalee added, "Yeah, and if you let your hair hang loose, curl it maybe, you could wear a crown of flowers, with those . . . those . . . little sprigs of tiny white flowers . . . what's that shit called?"

"Baby's breath," I said, cringing because she'd cursed in front of customers.

"Yeah, baby's breath," Winnalee said. "It would beat having to wear one of those geeky veils, wouldn't it?"

Cindy was grinning from ear to ear, but her mother was not. "No veil?"

"You could have a narrow band of tulle hanging from the back of the crown," I suggested.

"Look, Mrs. Jamison," Winnalee said. "If you want a wedding disaster on your hands, stuff Cindy in a dress that looks like a wedding cake. She'd make the whole wedding a living hell for everybody. Trust me, I know her type. I'm one of them."

I stiffened. You don't say things like *that* to customers you're trying to please!

"I would, too," said Cindy, her chin jutting as she tried to look like a true rebel, though I doubted she was anything more than a spoiled whiner.

"But what about the bridesmaids' dresses?" Mrs. Jamison asked.

"Same style," Winnalee said. "But maybe midi-length. And just a plain bow at the back of their dresses. All in some far-out material, maybe tie-dyed. Pale, soft colors, I suppose, because it *is* still a wedding. Wait . . ."

Winnalee dug in her pouch and pulled out a handful of pastels, some used down to stubs. She tossed her hair to her back and started drafting a less dramatic version of Cindy's dress. Then she used her pastels to color it, blending pinks and turquoises and yellows into a muted tie-dyed pattern. Cindy watched over her shoulder, muttering excited little *ooooh*s.

"Winnalee," I said quietly, "I don't know how we'd find material just like that, or even similar. Flower prints and Swiss dots are what's in."

Winnalee finished the dress, handed the pad to Cindy, and said, "Then we'll dye it ourselves."

I'd never dyed anything, but for a pair of old kitchen curtains that I was determined to take from a yellowed white to bright pink. When I was through with them, they were the color of spawning salmon with jaundice.

Everything happened in a rush then. Cindy insisted that I sew the dresses—even though Mrs. Jamison pointed out that Hazel had sewn *her* wedding dress and she trusted her. Winnalee jumped right in, then, like she was doing me a favor, saying, "Button here's been sewing since she was old enough to sit up. She'll nail these dresses." Winnalee got up and ran to the fitting room and came back with the bridesmaid's dress we just brought in. "Look at this," she said, lifting the plastic. "Look at the . . . the . . . well, look how good it looks. Better than store-bought."

"But have you sewn a bridal gown before?" Mrs. Jamison asked.

"What does that matter?" Winnalee asked. "A dress is a dress, no matter what color the material is."

So the Jamisons placed their orders—Mrs. Jamison looking only slightly sick at this point—and set up a time for Cindy and her three bridesmaids to come in to be measured. "I'm having Hazel sew *my* dress," Mrs. Jamison said, and out the door they went.

"There," Winnalee said. "You just got your first wedding dress order!" She sat back down and took a slow slug of her soda, looking pleased with herself.

"Winnalee, I can't dye fabric! And that glob on the back of the bride's dress . . . what is that supposed to be, anyway? A clump of bows? A bouquet of flowers? How can I make something when I don't even know what it is?"

Winnalee yawned. "Relax, Button. I'll help you dye the material if you can't find anything close. I've tie-dyed T-shirts before. How hard can it be?"

"Oh my God," I groaned.

"As for the thingy on the back of the dress, well, you're on your own there."

CHAPTER 13

BRIGHT IDEA #18: If the kid sitting behind you got a bruised knee because somebody pushed her down on the playground, you might feel bad, even if you're not the one who did the pushing.

In so many ways, I envied Winnalee. She was liberated, and free from the burden of trying not to upset or offend anyone. She didn't obsess about things the way I did—tugging her shirts to hide her boobs, biting her cheek to keep from saying things that might upset someone. She wasn't afraid of new challenges, and didn't worry about if she was good enough. She'd driven to New York and attended Woodstock all by herself, and she was brave enough to go braless in public. But me? I had trouble taking off my bra just to sleep, and I still hadn't undressed in front of Winnalee. Nor had I found the courage to go to the Purple Haze, even though Winnalee was starting to get hurt feelings because I was blowing her off every time she asked.

I lay awake much of the night trying to figure out how I'd construct the wedding dress Winnalee sketched for Cindy. In the dead of night, with the room pitch dark and void of any sound but the soft puffs of Winnalee's breath, I could see Ma clearly. Not the face that had been softened by Freeda's rough touch, but her face as it was when I was small. Two worry gouges carved between her eyebrows, lips whitened with perpetual disapproval. That's the face I saw when I closed my eyes to try to sleep, warning me not to screw up this project.

It was Saturday morning, so I hiked over to Aunt Verdella's while the grass was still wet with dew, to help her load her things for the Community Sale, and to get Boohoo. "Hey, Evy," Boohoo said. "Can we stay here until Cap'n Kangaroo's over?"

I loved Boohoo in the morning when he just woke up. When his body and voice were still drowsy and he was squishy to hug. "Sure," I told him. "*If* you'll go with me to Porter and be a good boy all day."

"What do we gotta go there for?" he asked, as I nudged him out of the way so I could slip a box of afghans onto the bed of Uncle Rudy's truck.

"Fabric," I said, and Boohoo scrinched his nose. Aunt Verdella ha-ha'd and added, "Ain't he the cutest little thing when he makes that face?" He was, but he wasn't the cutest little thing when you got him in a fabric store.

"Can we go somewhere good afterwards?" he asked, and I promised him we could go to McDonald's afterward, *if* he was good while I shopped.

I cleaned off the breakfast table where Uncle Rudy and Aunt Verdella's plates, and Boohoo's half-filled bowl of Quisp were still sitting, and I did the dishes while Boohoo watched TV. He wouldn't leave until the show ended, even if after the commercial all Cap'n was going to do was say goodbye.

The Trix commercial was on when the phone rang, and

Boohoo was laughing because, for whatever reason, he loved the Trix bunny. I picked it up.

"Button, is that you?"

"Yes?" I said, as I tugged the phone chord as far as it would go to get away from the blaring TV, in the hopes I'd hear the voice enough to recognize it.

"It's Ada," she said.

Tommy's mom sounded upset, and instantly my stomach tightened, thinking maybe something had happened to Uncle Rudy or Tommy while they were haying. "What's wrong?" I asked.

"Well, Mrs. Bishop just called here—I'm at work. Max and her are in Ironwood, Michigan, for her uncle's funeral, and Marls just called her because she didn't know what to do. She's got some bleeding, and she can't find Brody. I wasn't thinking until after I dialed, that, of course, Verdella would be at the sale—which explains why I couldn't reach anybody else I tried, either. I sure am glad I got you, though. Button, could you go over to the Bishops' and bring that poor girl to the hospital? It's far too early for that baby to come now. I tried to talk Marls into calling an ambulance, but she doesn't have health insurance and was afraid her in-laws would get upset if she rang up that expense."

"Yes, of course I will," I said. I was pacing, and caught sight of Boohoo, already coming to life and hopping in place, yarn twirling down over him.

"Thank you, honey. Let me know, okay?"

I hung up the phone. "Boohoo, shut the TV off. Now. Hurry."

"What's the matter, Evy?"

I didn't know what to say to him—or what to do with him. Certainly I couldn't bring him with me. "I have to run somebody to the hospital and—"

"Is somebody sick?" he asked, his yarn going limp against the floor.

"Yes. Hurry now."

"Do I gotta go, too? I don't like hospitals, I don't think."

"No, Winnalee will watch you," I said, hoping it was true.

"Goody. I like Winnalee."

"You want me to what? Watch Boohoo? What am *I* going to do with a little kid?" Winnalee mumbled when I told her.

"Just watch him."

Winnalee propped on her elbows and forced her sleepy eyes open. "I never babysat before, Button."

I blinked. I'd babysat the Thompson kids all through high school, and helped take care of Boohoo since his birth. Every girl I knew babysat. "There's nothing to it," I said as I dug through the rubble for my purse. "Just make sure he doesn't start anything on fire, break anything, or get run over. Past that, just feed him if he gets hungry. Winnalee, I have to hurry. Marls could lose her baby. I've got to get her into town."

"Lose her baby? Who?"

Winnalee must have been too groggy to absorb the opening part of the story, so I repeated it quickly.

"Okay," she said. She sat up. "I hope she's all right. And I hope I don't do anything stupid."

"You say that like you don't have any control over what you do," I said as I slipped on my sandals.

"Well lots of times, I *don't*!"

I warned Boohoo to be good, and flew out the door.

Marls was in tears when I got there—but to my relief, blood wasn't oozing down her legs and pooling to the floor. I helped her to the car, telling her over and over again that everything would be okay, and hoping it was the truth.

I didn't know if I should drive slow—Tanner Road, where

the Bishops lived, being heaved and rough, and the Rambler didn't have a smooth ride on the best of roads—or fast, so I could get her there more quickly. So I drove in-between. I was glad when we got on Highway 8 and I could speed up. "Are you in pain?" I asked Marls more than once, because her whimpering rose and fell like someone having pangs, but each time she told me (or shook her head) no.

"Here's the Smithys," I said. "So we've only got sixteen miles to go now." We both cocked our heads toward the farm. "He said he was going to help hay," Marls said, as we scoped the field. Uncle Rudy was on the green baler, and Tommy hunched over a hay bale. Uncle Rudy's and Tommy's trucks were the only vehicles in the driveway.

I glanced over at Marls, then watched the Smithys' farm fade in my rearview mirror. *Brody should be with her*, rolled in my mind, and no doubt, in hers.

Marls was almost giddy with relief when the hospital came into view. "Thank you so much for bringing me," she said. "Brody can give you some money for gas later."

I reached over and squeezed her hand. "Don't give that another thought. It's what anyone would do for their neighbor."

I left Marls in the car and hurried inside to tell the lady at the desk the situation. Then I followed two nurses and a wheelchair out. They helped Marls out of the car, and I shut the door behind her and started walking alongside them. Marls looked up, her face blotchy, her gray eyes almost colorless underneath the tears. "You don't have to stay," she said, but I told her I would. I didn't want her there feeling left alone when she was so scared. I reached down and touched her hair while she answered questions at the desk, then took a seat when they wheeled her into the examining room.

After what seemed forever, I saw a gurney leave the examining room, Marls lying on her back. I was relieved to see the mound of her belly under the green blanket, even though I knew the baby still had to be there, since births were supposed to take a long time. After they hauled her away, I waited, then went up to the desk to ask what was happening. "They've taken Mrs. Bishop to a room and will keep her overnight for observations. After they get her settled, you can see her."

I paged through magazines while I waited, but I only looked at the pictures. I was too worried about Marls—and how Winnalee was doing with Boohoo—to actually read.

Another half an hour passed before the lady at the desk told me I could go up. She gave me Marls's room number and told me where I could find the elevator. There was a nurse inside her room, the door partially shut, so I waited.

Marls looked as pale as the sheets, but she looked more peaceful, too. "They said I'm not dilated at least, and they gave me something to help me not go into labor."

I stood by her bed, looking down, and my chest swelled with pity for her. I was practically a stranger, yet at the moment, I was all she had.

"They think everything's going to be okay," she said, as she gently massaged her belly.

"Good," I said.

"I'm so tired now."

"I could sit with you while you sleep," I offered.

"No, you go. I've taken enough of your time. But could you please hand me the phone first?"

I was in the hall, contemplating if I should really leave, when Marls placed a collect call. Her voice floated out a childish, scared whisper as she said, "Mom?"

Dad was in the yard shoving the lawn mower over grass so long that it had to be bending under the machine, when I slowed to turn down Peters Road. He glanced up when he heard my Rambler and his arm came up to give me a slow, half-mast wave. Still, that was better than what greeted me when I pulled into my drive.

Winnalee's screams reached me before she did, rushing into my window as if they were looking for a place to hide. She came flying around the side of the house, arms bouncing, hair wild. I rammed the car into park and yanked the key. "Winnalee?" I shouted.

Boohoo appeared from the backyard then, wearing the devil's grin and holding an upside-down broom poised in the air.

Winnalee raced to the driveway and wedged herself between me and the car, her scream so shrill that it pinched my eardrums.

"Boohoo!" I shouted, as he reached us, dancing side to side like a boxer as he sought a better aim at Winnalee.

I reached out and grabbed the broom as it was coming down, and yanked it from his arm. "What are you doing?" I shouted, my palm stinging. Boohoo took off like the Tasmanian Devil, laughing as he ran. I stared at Winnalee in disbelief. "Why were you letting him chase you with a broom?"

"Because it seemed like a hell of a lot better idea than letting him *hit* me with it!" She held up her arm to show me two strips of red welts. One of them was already tinged with blue.

"Boohoo, get back here right now!" I shouted.

He didn't stop, so I dropped the broom and chased after him. I snagged his wrist and held him as I delivered every threat I could think of. He wouldn't watch cartoons for three Saturdays! He couldn't wear his Spider-Man cape for a month! He wouldn't get candy for the whole rest of the summer!

I expected Boohoo to plead his case, beg for forgiveness, or cry when I plunked him on the steps. Instead he just smiled up at me and said, "Can Winnalee watch me next time you guys are gone, Evy? She's fun!"

Winnalee looked down at his sweaty head as she thumped up the porch steps on bare feet. "I'm never watching you again, you little shit."

I told Boohoo if he got off the steps he'd get a spanking—I'd never spanked him in his life—then followed Winnalee inside. "Please don't talk to him like that," I said. "We don't swear at him."

"Well I don't know how in the hell you can help it," she huffed.

I wanted to swear at him, and her, when I saw the mess inside, though. Drawing paper ripped to confetti was scattered over the floor and furniture, and even the swag lamp was tangled with yarn. "You think *this* is bad, you should see the kitchen," Winnalee said.

I snapped a loose crayon under my sandal as I headed there, then stood in the doorway, my hand over my mouth. Cocoa Puffs dotted the floor, and the table was covered by at least two-thirds of a loaf of peanut-butter-smeared broken bread. A fly was busy drinking Kool-Aid from a capsized cup, and his cousin was perched on the still-opened jelly jar. "Man, Winnalee."

"I know, I know. I tried to make him clean up the mess before you got home, but when I handed him the broom, he started swinging it at me!"

Winnalee threw her hands into the air and slapped them down on her thighs. "Bright Idea number ninety-nine point five," she said. "Never ask Winnalee Malone to watch a kid, because she'll only mess things up." She turned and headed out of the room, her thumps soon sounding above my head.

I screwed the lids back on the jars and headed to the sink for a washcloth. "Hi, Tommy. Evy? Can I get up now?" Boohoo yelled from the steps.

"No!" I shouted, cereal crunching under my feet as I sidestepped to sop up the Kool-Aid still dripping off the table. I stared down at the floor, then slapped the washcloth in the sink even if the table was still a mess, and headed outside for the broom. I almost ran into Tommy, who was coming up the steps, carrying it. "You looking for this?" I yanked the broom from him.

"Hey, Evy. Can I go by Aunt Verdella now? She's coming." Boohoo pointed down the road.

"No. You were very naughty when Winnalee watched you. You chased her with this," I said holding up the broom, "and turned the house into a pigsty. You are going to stay right there until I say you can move. And I mean it, Boohoo."

Boohoo started to get up. "Yeah, but—"

Tommy cut in, giving him a glare. "Didn't your sister just tell you to stay put?" Boohoo sat back down.

"I don't need your help, Tommy Smithy," I snapped.

"Seems to me you do."

"Did you want something, because I've kind of got my hands full here right now. And it hasn't exactly been a good morning. I just got back from the hospital. I drove Marls there."

"Marls?"

Granted, Tommy delivered cows all the time, so he probably knew more about bleeding vaginas and birth than most women, but those were cows, and I couldn't get myself to say that Marls was hemorrhaging. "She was having some problems," is all I could say.

"Jesus," Tommy said.

"Brody was nowhere to be found, of course."

"He never showed up this morning. He's probably fishing. Is she gonna be okay?"

"I think so, but they're keeping her overnight. Anyway, what did you want?"

"I came to see if you were home. I had something to show you."

As Tommy headed for his truck, he glanced to the field, where a couple of cows were slopping water at the stock tank. "I'm not even gonna ask why Boohoo's cow is wearing yarn around his neck," he said, shaking his head.

I expected Tommy to grab whatever he wanted to show me from his truck, but he didn't. He just jumped in and drove off, leaving me wearing a thin film of guilt for being so short with him. I headed for the house, giving Boohoo yet another warning to stay put, *and* to stop throwing rocks at ants.

Winnalee was in the kitchen, smearing peanut butter on the table with the dishcloth. "Is Marls okay?" she asked.

I repeated what little I knew, and Winnalee didn't say anything. She just kept cleaning.

"Winnalee?" Boohoo shouted. "I can't get up, so could you come out here so I can say some sorrys?"

"Man," Winnalee mumbled. "Now he's gonna be all sweet and I'm gonna have to forgive him." She dumped a dustpan full of confetti into the trash can, then headed outside. A few minutes later, I heard the two of them, their shouts nothing but excited gibberish.

Boohoo was in the middle of the yard, bopping up and down and screaming as he jabbed toward the sky. Winnalee was beside him, her hands cupped above her eyes to shield them from the sun.

"Holy shit!" Winnalee cried. "It *is* Tommy's plane!"

"I told you!" Boohoo shouted. "It's Tommy's Piper! I could tell!

"Tommyyyyyyyy!" Boohoo screamed, as I spotted the moving dot that had to be Tommy's red-winged, white bellied plane. I squinted, my insides jumping every bit as frantically as Boohoo's and Winnalee's outsides were, but out of fear, not excitement.

Boohoo and Winnalee kept clutching each other as they

laughed and shouted, Winnalee completely forgetting that minutes ago, Boohoo was her mortal enemy.

The Piper made a wide arc then headed toward us.

"What's that lunatic doing?" I screamed, as Tommy's plane skimmed above the treetops, so close Tommy could have probably reached out and grabbed a pinecone. When the plane got close, the nose dipped as if it was sniffing us out. "Here he comes!" Boohoo shouted.

Winnalee's head fell back, her hair wavering, as the Piper's shadow spilled into the yard. "What does his plane say? What does it say? Lady Godiva? Cooooooooool! Hi, Tommy!"

I clamped my eyes shut, and crouched down, my arms instinctively wrapping around my head as Tommy's plane buzzed over the house, whirring like a table saw.

When the pitch of the plane's engine rose, I peeked up with only my eyes to see if the plane was lifting. It was. But it was also circling. I pressed my knuckles against my mouth, silently pleading with Tommy not to dive at the house again.

But he did. Twice more. I cursed him under my breath and promised myself I'd punch him when I saw him again.

"I want a ride, Tommy!" Boohoo shouted as the Lady Godiva headed toward home, "Take me! Take *me*!" When the Piper was nothing but a faint buzz and a speck, Winnalee, breathless from shouting the same, turned to me and said, "Oh my God, Button, were you *ducking*?"

CHAPTER 14

BRIGHT IDEA #16: If your babysitter tells you that the best place to hide things is right out in the open, don't believe her.

The whole ordeal of Winnalee's marijuana plants might have been over for me and Winnalee, but it wasn't over for Aunt Verdella. "I'm worried about that girl," she told me a couple of nights later, when, restless while Winnalee was at work, and still obsessing because Jesse's last letter ended with *Okay, gotta go. I got a letter from Amy—sort of an apology—and I suppose I should answer it before it's lights out,* I hiked over with a basket of dirty laundry.

I startled Aunt Verdella when I came through the door. She dropped the paper she had in her hand into the opened kitchen drawer and shoved it shut, leaving a fringe of envelopes peeking out. "Sorry," I told her. "I didn't want to wake Uncle Rudy or Boohoo by knocking."

"Button, since when does family need to knock?" she said. "Come on in. I dozed off late this afternoon and now I'm wide awake, so I was just catching up on your dad's laundry."

I looked down at the basket I'd just brought in and cringed. "I wasn't going to bring ours over, but . . ."

"It's okay, honey," she said. "Running downstairs is good exercise for me." She grabbed the basket and made an exaggerated *phew* face. "With as much beer as our little Winnalee spills on her clothes, the customers must go home stone sober. I'll just presoak these in the washer tonight and get them whirling in the morning.

"Oh," she told me, stopping halfway across the dining room. "I called over to the Bishops this evening and talked to Marls herself. She's got placenta previa and that's why she was spotting." I must have looked confused, because she explained how that means the placenta was down by the cervix, instead of above it, and the pressure of the baby caused some tearing. If the truth be known, pregnancy scared me, and I was creeped out by all those parts inside, which seemed as foreign to me as Japan, so I just nodded like I was listening and understood.

"Is she going to be okay?" I asked.

"Well, the doctors think her placenta will move, but she's got to take it easy for a while."

"I'm glad the baby's okay," I said.

Aunt Verdella's eyes, like her bladder, weren't what they used to be, so when she worked in the evenings she kept the room well lit. I examined her freshly cut and colored hair in the stark light as she prattled more about Marls's pregnancy. The old growth was a medium auburn, but the inches of roots were more of a Pepto Bismol pink. Aunt Verdella noticed me staring. "Does it look all right?" she asked, patting the side of her head. "Fanny said it's two-toned."

I told her it looked real pretty and she said, "Maybe it was just the lighting at The Corner Store. I told Fanny; Claire knows what she's doing."

Aunt Verdella headed my basket downstairs—still talking, though I couldn't hear what she was saying—while I stared at Dad's clothes—pants as worn and limp as him, shirts with arms too lifeless to pick up a six-year-old boy. Brody would be a dad just like him, and it made me sad for the baby Marls was carrying.

Aunt Verdella's voice stopped, the house going dead silent, but for the soft hum of a fan upstairs. I cocked my head and listened harder, then went to the basement door, fear gripping me. "Aunt Verdella?" I called. "You okay?"

"Oh my goodness, my goodness," she uttered.

"You okay?" I asked again.

Aunt Verdella started up the stairs. Her arm was stretched in front of her, something dangling from her hand. I couldn't see what in the dim light, but I was prepared to wince, sure it was a dead mouse.

I moved back to let her step into the kitchen, and glanced even if I didn't want to. Then I all-out stared with disbelief and horror when I saw that it was something *worse* than a dead mouse. It was a used rubber, pinched and half crumpled.

"It, it was wrapped up in the sheets," she told me, heading to the trash can, where she stopped to grab a paper towel to wrap it in first.

"It wasn't mine," I said quickly.

Aunt Verdella waved off my declaration. "Oh, I know that, honey."

She turned to me, her face sagging with disappointment. "You know," she said. "I've been thinking about Winnalee, as it is. This whole dope thing . . . and now this." She took a gulp of air, held it a second, then blurted out, "Button, *you're* not on dope now, too, are you?"

Her worry was so absurd that I couldn't help laughing. "Aunt Verdella, you know that if I was even tempted—which I'm not—Ma would reach down and whack me in the head. Besides, life itself should be enough of a high, shouldn't it?" And for me, it *was*. At least on days when I heard from Jesse (and he didn't talk about old girlfriends). He was writing once or twice a week now, and I was writing him every day—except for the day neither Winnalee or I could scrounge up a lousy six cents to leave in the mailbox for a stamp. Jesse noticed I hadn't written that day, too. "It just didn't seem right when roll call came and your letter wasn't there." He signed that letter, *Love, Jesse*.

"Maybe we should take her to a doctor," Aunt Verdella said, her voice chasing off my daydreams. "Ellie Connor's boy was addicted to drugs and that's what they had to do with him. The doctor put him in the hospital and gave him medicine until he was done with the shakes and vomiting."

"Marijuana isn't like that, Aunt Verdella."

"And that strange man she had over to the house . . ." Chet Bouman. A creep according to Tommy. A cool cat who was into Transcendental Meditation and played the bongo drums, according to Winnalee. Aunt Verdella's sentence stopped mid-stitch, and I didn't encourage her to continue.

Aunt Verdella sprayed another pair of Dad's work pants with water, then rolled them. "I'm worried about her, Button. And I feel responsible, since Freeda isn't here to look out for her."

Aunt Verdella smacked her tongue against her gums. "I love that girl, you know I do, but she's like a grown-up Boohoo. *So* lovable, yet so prone to trouble. I sure do wish Freeda was here. She had a way of snapping people back in line."

"Winnalee isn't doing anything that Freeda herself didn't

do," I reminded her, then corrected myself. "Okay, except smoke pot, but she stopped doing that now." I didn't add the "in the house" part.

Aunt Verdella went to the ironing board. She licked her finger and tapped it to the bottom of the iron, then unrolled a damp shirt and stretched out the collar. "Button, you notice how whenever we bring up Freeda, Winnalee changes the subject?"

"I know."

Aunt Verdella's iron, when pressed against line-dried cotton, emitted a warm smell that reminded me of sunny Saturday afternoons. Ma's laundry day.

Aunt Verdella shook her head. "Freeda was only sixteen when she had Winnalee. Just a baby . . ." I'd known this fact as a child, but sixteen sounded pretty old then. Now the thought of someone being a mother at that age was almost enough to make me hyperventilate. Marls was twenty-one, and she looked like a scared kid when I drove her to the hospital. "She had reasons for leaving Winnalee as she did, just as she had reasons for taking her from Hannah. I wish Winnalee could see this," Aunt Verdella added.

"Me too," I said.

Aunt Verdella sighed. "I was thinking, the other day, how it don't seem to matter how someone's parent turned out in the end. What has the most impact, seems to me, is how that parent was when that child was little." Aunt Verdella glanced at my arms, as if every scratch I'd ever cut into them was still showing. "Our Jewel changed over time, yet you seem more influenced by her mommying when you were little, than by her mommying after you were more grown." She smoothed a sleeve over the ironing board and pressed the iron to the cuff. "I guess the same is true for Winnalee."

Aunt Verdella looked up and the harsh light magnified her weariness. "Oh, I'm just being a worrywart about most everything these days. I went over to your dad's earlier tonight, and that stew I made him was still in the fridge, dried, and fuzzy with mold—your dad loves beef stew. He had a stick of summer sausage in there, tooth marks on the end like he just picks it out and takes a chomp when he's hungry. That's no way to eat."

It was always the same when the topic of Dad came up. Aunt Verdella fretted, and the whole time she did, pity and scorn wrestled inside me. "Dad will be okay," I said without conviction.

Aunt Verdella hung dad's shirt and reached for another. She worked quietly for a minute, then said, "I don't know if we should say anything to Winnalee about what we found."

I looked down, my cheeks burning.

"Oh, honey, don't *you* be ashamed."

I fidgeted. "I was hoping you wouldn't know what it was."

Aunt Verdella chuckled a bit. "Oh, Button, those things have been around since Adam and Eve. Well, not that long ago, or none of us would be here"—she paused to giggle—"but practically since they invented latex. Course, in my day, they were mostly used by married couples . . . or cheating men. You remember that couple that lived above the drugstore? The Johnsons, Beulah and George?"

I shook my head.

"I don't suppose you would. That was a long time ago. Anyway, Beulah always feared George was cheatin' on her. She was sterile, so they had no reason to use, you know . . . but Fanny Tilman put a bug in Beulah's ear that she'd seen George in the pharmacy when she went there for Epsom salt, and that she was sure he was buying some. Beulah asked the pharmacist if he had, and he told her that he couldn't discuss what his patrons bought, even to a spouse, and she figured he was covering for George.

"Beulah had this dog named Willa, so bony, that I swear,

she clinked when she ran like a set of keys. Anyway, don't know how she did it but she trained that little thing to sniff out the scent of a woman—*and*"—Aunt Verdella paused and lowered her voice, as if to make it too small to climb the stairs where Boohoo slept—"the smell of *latex*."

I couldn't help but giggle. Half because of the story, and half because Aunt Verdella was telling it so earnestly. That's when Winnalee came in, giggling, too, because apparently she'd caught at least the last part of the story. Winnalee passed out quick hugs, kicked off her sandals and sat down, drawing up her knees and planting her heels on the seat. "Oh my God. Latex? As in *rubbers?*" Winnalee asked, oblivious, of course, to what led to the story in the first place.

Aunt Verdella dipped her head, and her chin bubbled under her pinkened face.

"We know what rubbers are, Aunt Verdella," Winnalee said, rolling her eyes as she squeezed a "geez" out of her giggles.

"Yes, I *know* you know what they are.

"Anyway, that part of the story about Willa is true, because Beulah ordered an afghan from me once, and when I delivered it, that little dog wouldn't stop sniffing my legs and yapping, hopping in circles. That's what she'd do if she smelled a woman. Hop in circles, going clockwise. But if she smelled latex, then she'd hop counterclockwise." Winnalee and I were in stitches by then, Winnalee was in such hysterics she was snorting.

But Aunt Verdella wasn't even cracking a smile.

She made the shush sign, while glancing toward the ceiling, and we clamped our hands over our mouths so we wouldn't wake Uncle Rudy and Boohoo.

My breath was hot against my hand, my cheeks billowed, as Aunt Verdella continued her story.

"George was taking out the trash one day, Willa at his

heels, and he ended up across the alley, at this young widow's place, helping her change the inner tube on her boy's bike tire. Course, Willa went nuts, and when Beulah heard her and rushed to the window to see her standing outside the garage hopping counterclockwise, she ran for George's twenty-two. Good thing she didn't know how to load a gun—she was trying to put the shells down the barrel!—or George and the widow would have been deader than doornails."

Winnalee and I wiped our tears after the story was over, but kept bursting into fresh giggles every time we looked at each other. "Poor woman," Aunt Verdella said. "To be that scared of losing her man."

"Poor *woman*?" Winnalee said. "Poor *man*, is more like it. With a wife like that he'd be stupid *not* to cheat. I mean seriously, to be that jealous? How dumb. Why would anyone be jealous because her man slept with another woman, anyway?" she asked.

"You serious?" I asked.

"Of course I am. Nobody owns someone else's body. We should all be free to share them with whoever we want. Besides, just because two people sleep together, it doesn't mean they love each other. It's just sex."

Aunt Verdella startled. "Oh, Winnalee, I hope you don't mean that, honey."

"Times have changed, Aunt Verdella. At least for women. Men, they've been doing that shit for centuries, but with the Pill especially, now women have the same perks as guys. It's no big deal."

"But it *is* a big deal, Winnalee. And *times* might have changed, with all this women's liberation stuff, and the Pill and all, but I'll tell you one thing that will never change—men. No matter what they say, or how sweet they talk to get what they want, in the end, they aren't gonna want a woman who's been with every Tom, Dick, and Harry."

Oh boy!

"Well, women might end up with Tom, or Dick," Winnalee said, "but I think Beulah will see to it that they can't be with *George*." Winnalee laughed at her joke, but Aunt Verdella and I didn't.

"Why does everything have to be about right or *wrong*, anyway?" Winnalee huffed when she got done laughing.

"It's not about being wrong, Winnalee. It's about what hurts."

"*Hurts?* Hell, unless the guy's *really* hung, what's there to hurt?" Winnalee cracked up all over again.

"Hearts, Winnalee," Aunt Verdella said. "I was talking about hurting hearts. Somebody else's if you're cheating, and your own, if you're waking up next to a stranger who's treating you like one the next morning."

I stood up abruptly, and picked through the box of items for the Community Sale. I put my hand inside a crocheted-rooster toaster cozy to make him stand up. "Oh, this is cute, Aunt Verdella."

"Isn't it? I just found that pattern. If you like it, Button, you take it. I've got plenty for the sale." She was speaking to me, but her eyes were on Winnalee.

I turned my back to Aunt Verdella, and stretched my eyes at Winnalee until my forehead hurt. "We'd better go. It's late, and I've got a dress to finish in the morning."

Aunt Verdella looked at me and muttered a quick "Oh, that's good, honey," but she kept glancing at Winnalee, her wrinkles sunk deep with worry.

"*What?*" Winnalee whined, as I yanked her to her feet.

"Okay . . . okay . . . ," Winnalee said as we headed across the dark yard. "I guess I should have shut up about that stuff. Aunt Verdella's a little old-fashioned."

"What do you expect, Winnalee? She's sixty-eight years old! Who makes a joke about men who are 'well hung' to a sweet old woman who crochets and makes bunny pancakes?"

"Well, she doesn't seem old to me. In fact, *you* seem more like an old lady than she does. Aunt Verdella has *sex,* Button. S-E-X! It's not like she was going to fall over dead because I said something *she* didn't know."

Suddenly it felt like there were a hundred anthills trapped under my skin, but I was determined not to scratch in front of Winnalee. My jaw tightened. "What? *Unlike someone else you know?* Is that what you're implying?"

"You said it, not me," Winnalee said as she crossed the porch.

We headed straight upstairs, me following Winnalee, and the whole way I was telling myself that no matter how insulted I felt, I would *not* humiliate Winnalee back by telling her what Aunt Verdella found.

Winnalee pulled down her hot pants and gave them a toss with her toe, then stripped off her shirt—she wasn't wearing a bra, of course. She started digging through the heap of her clothes that were tangled on top of the dresser.

I turned away and grabbed my nightgown from the window seat.

"Bet you can't change up here, in front of me," Winnalee taunted.

"I have to brush," I said.

"Man, Button, why you always have to act like such a prude? We're two girls, for crissakes."

I wasn't about to defend myself, just because I didn't want thousands of people looking at my nipples, or because I didn't want to show her my ugly, bulky, lumpy knees and stilt-skinny legs!

Winnalee found her sleeping shirt and pulled it over her head, her head popping up from the neck hole. "All you want to do is sit around the house, cleaning and sewing, chasing after Boohoo, and sweating in your long pants. You might as well be ninety!"

"I do not!" I said, my eyes stinging.

"You do too. I've asked you how many times since I started working at the Purple Haze to come with me to see my artwork, but you haven't. Even if *I* went to your job with *you*. You just stay home every night and write to some guy who isn't even your boyfriend, because you're too uptight to party. *That's* being an old lady!"

The invisible ants scampered along the length of my arms. "It's not that I'm too uptight to party. I told you, I don't want to sit in some bar and choke on smoke and be hit on by potheads and junkies. But I want to see your artwork. I really do. I told you I'd go in the morning sometime if we could get in."

"And *I* told you that it doesn't look cool unless it's dark and the black lights are on." Winnalee's hands were on her hips, the back of her hair still stuffed in her shirt. She opened her mouth to say more, then stomped to the closet instead. I could hear hangers clanking and I wondered what kind of mess she was making.

She came out with the urn and marched over, ramming it against me and letting go, so that I had to take it or let it crash to my bare toes. "There!" she said. "Since you're lugging your dead mom around with you every day anyway, you might as well have something pretty to carry her in. Your turn!"

Winnalee dived to the bed and pulled the sheet over her head, snapping the light off and leaving me standing there holding the urn, a tear—one—slipping down a cheek that had gone as cold as window glass in winter.

"I can't believe you'd be so mean," I said. My legs felt as hollow as empty pant legs, so instead of returning the urn to the closet, I reached behind me and set it down on the window seat. I must not have scooted it far enough back, though, because it caught on the edge and capsized. A tinny, rippling sound carried it across the floor, and I didn't bother to retrieve it. Winnalee and I had had our first fight ever, and all I could do was stand there, helpless to stop crying.

I guess our argument bothered Winnalee, too, because after a moment she called softly, "Button? I'm sorry."

She slipped out of bed, her white T-shirt and skin glowing in the moonlight. She came and wrapped her arms around me. She led me to the bed and sat me down beside her. "You're a good person, Button. Better than me for sure. Maybe that's why I got so nasty. But I'm sorry, okay?"

We were quiet for a while, then Winnalee said, "Way to say it, and not scratch it, Button. I'm proud of you."

I ran my hand over the arm that was curved across my stomach. There wasn't a hint of itching left under my skin. "Winnalee? I'll go to the Purple Haze to see your artwork," I said. "Not this weekend—it's Marls's shower—but next. Friday night. Even if I have to sit alone."

"Cool," Winnalee said. "You'll have a good time. Promise. And you won't have to sit alone, either, because Brody's been comin' around most nights."

CHAPTER 15

BRIGHT IDEA #71: When people say don't feed a stray dog because then they won't go away, they're telling the truth. Then your sister is gonna get mad because all the bologna is gone.

One thing good about Dauber was the way people pulled together for their neighbors. Like when Ada set the donations jar on the counter at The Corner Store, a slit cut in the plastic lid so patrons could help out by dropping spare change or a dollar or two into it, to help families after someone died, or their house burnt down, or they were injured badly in an accident. Ma thought the whole ritual was cheesy. Especially the way people wrote their names and the amount they gave on notebook paper that sat beside the jug. I agreed with Ma at the time, yet when a check came to our house after Ma died, I looked over that notepaper carefully. Not to see how much anyone gave, but to see who cared about Ma.

People came together for parties, too, whether it was a

fund-raiser for someone who was sick or strapped, or a shower for a new bride or a new baby. It didn't matter if they knew the person well. If they lived within a ten-mile radius, they joined the festivities simply because it was the neighborly thing to do. So I knew we'd have a good turnout for Marls's shower.

Aunt Verdella was rattled when Mrs. Bishop insisted on having Marls's shower on a Saturday instead of a weeknight as she'd hoped for, since she reserved Saturdays for the Community Sale. "But that's the week with the longest day in the year," I reminded her. "The sale gets done at four, and the shower's at five. There will be plenty of time before dusk."

"But I won't be here to prepare," she fussed.

"We'll get most things done the night before," I said. "And I'll see that everything's done by the time you get home."

So I baked a double layer cake while she was at the sale, frosted it mint green, then sat staring at it like it was an empty lawn in need of ornaments. Winnalee shuffled into the kitchen then, half asleep from her long night at work, and headed to the bathroom. "I don't know what to do with this thing," I said. "I should have just picked up some of those hard candy cake decorations. But I hate how, no matter how well you dampen the backs, you never can get all the paper off."

Winnalee held up her finger as she yawned, then grabbed her army purse from the counter. She pulled out two red stir sticks—why she'd saved them, who knew—and stuck them into the cake, one on each end. "There. Now run a string between them for a clothesline, and cut out little baby clothes. You must have some babyish-looking material laying around here somewhere." Then Winnalee wandered into the living room, leaving me to marvel at her ingenious idea.

An hour later, I asked Winnalee if she'd keep Boohoo occupied so I could peel eggs for potato salad and make sandwiches. After that first babysitting calamity, she hadn't watched Boohoo in our absence once, but she had started playing with him now and then. She'd spot him through the window and drop what she was doing to dart outside and corkscrew the tire swing until it lifted a good two feet, then leap up to stand in the center, opposite of Boohoo and *weeeee* right with along with him. She drew Boohoo pictures with his color crayons now and then, too. Her hand whooshing over the paper to draw him in authentic Spider-Man costumes and heroic poses. She told outlandish stories about his adventures as she drew, until he was immersed in the fantasy as if it was as real to him as fairies had once been to her. Not that Boohoo never got on her nerves—he did—but when that happened, she'd stomp off and cuss a little, but a few minutes later, she'd be loving him up again. But not on the day of the shower. The day I needed her to play with him the most. So Boohoo continually trailed off and I had to go looking for him and drag him back into the kitchen, where he poked at the tiny clothes with grubby hands, smashed eggshells on the table, and asked me a million times if it was ten o'clock yet, because that's when they were leaving for the Willow Flowage.

Sixteen women showed up, most of them strangers to Marls. When Aunt Verdella saw the sweat glistening on Marls's upper lip, she dragged the only reclining lawn chair we had away from the picnic table and stretched it out under the tree. "Come on, honey," she said. "You'll be more comfortable in the shade." Aunt Verdella lifted Marls's swollen legs and propped them on the plaid plastic. "Come on, some of you bring your chairs over here so Marls won't be sitting alone." So Mrs. Bishop sat beside her, her knees and feet pressed together. Two older Bishop relatives whose names I kept forgetting sat alongside of them, and Tammy, Marls's best friend, a girl the same age as Marls from Eagle River, squeezed her lawn chair between Marls's chair and her mother-in-law's.

June Thompson squealed with delight to see Winnalee again, and Ada hugged her warmly, then helped us carry out the food. Rita Dayne—a flutter of apologies for being late—showed up while we were eating.

Rita was striking-looking and outgoing, just like her son. A true snowflake. She laughed good-naturedly when Verdella handed out pieces of Bazooka gum and asked the ladies to chew it, then form it into the shape of a new baby. And she celebrated as though she'd won a new car when Marls chose her gum-baby as the best, and she won one of Aunt Verdella's rooster toaster cozies.

"Your boy Jesse and Button are close," Aunt Verdella told Rita after the games were over. "She writes to him every day, and waits for his letters." I could feel my cheeks flush, and I hoped Rita thought it was from *the* sun, not *her* son.

"That's so nice of you, Evy," Jesse's mom said. "He doesn't admit it, but I think he's homesick since he left the country. But it won't be all that long before he's on leave again." Ada asked about Jesse then, and Rita proudly told everyone how he was a part of a special division that assembled and kept track of missile parts. So high on the security list that they couldn't travel into Berlin during their three-day passes. "They can go into the place where the nuclear heads are kept, but only in pairs. If a single soldier goes in himself, the guards are ordered to shoot." The ladies gasped, and I swelled with pride for Jesse's importance. Winnalee mumbled something sarcastic under her breath, and Rita said, "I'm just grateful that he didn't get sent to Vietnam."

"My grandson wasn't as lucky," a woman I didn't know named Mary said, and Winnalee sidled up next to her to discuss the horrors of the unjust war in 'Nam.

Paper plates, weightless as dragonflies, fluttered in my hand. Last time Jesse'd written, he'd said, *Maybe we can take in a movie when I'm in Dauber. But I warn you, I throw M&M's in the popcorn box while the butter's still hot. Amy used to hate that because they melted on the popcorn, but I love it. If that will bug you too, I'll get you your own box.* He'd asked me for a date—*a date!*—and in the handful of days since he'd mentioned it, I admitted to myself that although I'd always called Jesse my friend to others, in my heart I had been in love with him since the day we met. We were getting closer with each letter I wrote him—I could feel it—and while Winnalee was at work, I started playing "Make It with You" by Bread, sure that would end up being our song and we'd have it sung at our wedding.

As if Mrs. Dayne might read my thoughts, I hurried to stuff the used plates into the paper bag brought out for that purpose. I carried the bag back to the burning stove, and stood with my head bent to the sun, my eyes pressed closed, and smiled because I loved how I felt when I thought of Jesse putting his arm around me at the theater, of us kissing while little kids giggled behind us.

When I got back to the front yard, Marls was explaining placenta previa, and how the doctor believed that her placenta would be moved completely aside by her next visit. The conversation slipped into an exchange of personal stories of morning sickness, ruptured navels, and childbirth. Stories that made the women nod and laugh, but made Marls's smile quiver and my stomach feel a little nauseous. Winnalee was stocking the tub with fresh ice so I made my way over to her. "I think I'm gonna have a beer," she said. She bent down and cranked her head toward me. "You want one?" Winnalee and I were eighteen now, old enough to legally drink, but I didn't like the smell of beer, much less the taste. I shook my head, even though I worried that refusing would make me look like an old lady again.

Winnalee straightened up, water from the can of Pabst

dripping on her bare feet. "What are you all doey-eyed about?" she asked, grinning.

"Nothing," I said—even if I was thinking about what a great mother-in-law Rita would make.

"You've been like this since the topic of Jesse came up. So . . . ," she said, cocking her head. "He *isn't* just your friend, is he?"

Winnalee was always asleep when the mailman came, so she never saw the way I slipped outside at ten minutes to ten, staring through the porch screen so I wouldn't waste time running downstairs. She wasn't there to see my disappointment when the mailman left nothing but flyers, or my elation when a letter actually came.

"Button? Winnalee?" Aunt Verdella shouted. "Could you girls bring over a few more cans of pop when you're done with the ice?"

We were carrying them over to the table when Fanny Tilman pulled in at the end of the drive—the only place left to park but for the road. "Speaking of ice," Winnalee said, and I dipped my head to giggle.

Fanny was digging in her backseat when Tommy's and Mr. Bishop's pickups came along, boats bouncing behind them, Brody's Mustang following like a caboose. They parked alongside the road, and as soon as Mr. Bishop's truck stopped, Boohoo crawled out over Uncle Rudy's lap and tumbled into the ditch. Dad slid out of the truck after Uncle Rudy. "I can't believe Dad actually went," I said to Winnalee.

"I told him he *had* to . . . beats sitting on his ass alone all day," she said.

"Aunt Verdella! Evy! Winnalee! Look what I got!" Boohoo shouted, popping up from the ditch, lifting his arm in the air. He ran in zigzags behind Fanny, his towel cape tied under his chin. Winnalee leaned against me and whispered,

"Oh look, is it a bird? Is it a plane? No, it's Spideyman and *Spikey*woman." I tipped my head against hers and puffed giggles into her hair. Boohoo stopped, concentrating on the tiny fish in his hand.

"I'm late," Fanny said, no *sorry* in front of it. "I had a headache most of the day, and had to lay down after I got back from the sale."

"Probably heatstroke," Winnalee whispered, and I jabbed her and told her to shut up or we'd get caught being rude. Fanny scanned the crowd as she crossed the yard in a dark brown dress with gray flowers, a heavy sweater draped over her shoulders, even though the sun was hot enough to dry horseflies to jerky.

Why Fanny Tilman ever dropped a quarter into the donations jar at The Corner Store was a mystery to me, but there was no mystery as to why she came to parties given for people she didn't know: free food, and a chance to latch on to some gossip.

"See? See?" Boohoo said, holding up his hand. He had the tip of his index finger jammed into the tiny gill of a four-inch perch—so he could carry it like men did a big catch, no doubt. He brought it to the table, stopping beside each woman and not budging until they raved, then he ran off to tag the guys who were lugging two buckets of dead fish into the backyard.

"You men be sure and wash good with the hose after you clean those fish, or you're not coming near this table," Aunt Verdella called. She grabbed a plate to hand to Fanny, who stood clutching her purse in front of her, as if she expected someone to dish up for her. As Aunt Verdella did, Fanny harped. "No, that's too much ham on that bun . . . I don't care much for potato salad without a lot of mustard . . . no, no chips. Lands-sake, Verdella, what you trying to do, make me as fat as you?" She squinted at the crowd after her fat comment. Either to see if anyone was giggling, or maybe just to see who was there. "She's a bitch," Winnalee whispered, and I stiffened because I could tell June Thompson heard. June just rolled her eyes and said quietly, "Tell me about it."

Aunt Verdella made the guys stand in line, school lunchroom-style, then scooped food onto their plates. "Go wash," I told Boohoo, who stunk like sweat and bug spray, and was poking at the poor dead fish's eye. "Go on, little buddy," Tommy said. "Then come over and sit by us guys over at the beer tub. That's where the fishermen sit."

Marls's friend Tammy helped when it was time to open the gifts, jotting down the name of the item and the gift bearer as Tammy held up each little sleeper, or blanket, or toy, so we could admire it. There wasn't much oohing and ahing over Fanny's gift, however—a dozen cloth diapers, unused, but yellowed with time.

Marls called to Brody to show him the froggy-patterned infant seat Rita had gotten them, but he didn't glance over. Even though she called his name three times. Tammy was in my line of vision, glaring over to where Brody sat on the grass with Tommy, while the older men sat on lawn chairs. Brody had ignored Marls since they pulled in, though he had made the point of going up to Winnalee to flirt a little before he joined the guys.

Tammy's eyes shrunk to squints when Winnalee got up and headed back to the beer tub, and Brody jumped to his feet, making a federal case about how he was "so thirsty he was farting dust." Then laughing like it was a coincidence that he and Winnalee should both be fishing for an icy can at the same time.

Marls looked crushed under the weight of her belly, and Tammy looked ready to explode when Brody picked Winnalee up by the waist, acting as though he was intending to tip her upside down into the tub of melting ice. Her short empire-style dress crept even higher up her thighs as she kicked, and I hoped she was wearing underwear.

"Put me down, you stupid son of a bitch," Winnalee screamed, but she was laughing. Brody's dad made a joke only the guys could hear and a couple of them chuckled—even Dad. Mrs. Bishop glanced over at them with dead fish-eyes.

"Brody, you be careful. She's just a little bit of a thing!" Aunt Verdella called. And Fanny Tilman grumbled, "That girl should cover up."

Poor Marls, with her body bloated so that she hardly looked like herself, and her face water-balloon-puffy. All the ladies clucked about how "cute" she looked pregnant, but obviously, Marls—and Brody for that matter—didn't think so. My heart hurt for her as she watched Winnalee, a girl far prettier, far thinner, far sexier than she, squirm out of Brody's arms, then grab a fistful of ice and start chasing him in circles across the yard.

Tommy shot me a do-something look, and while I was scrambling to think of some way to interrupt them, Tammy rose from her chair and marched over to where Brody was pinned up against the tree laughing as though he was being tickled, sloshing beer down the front of Winnalee's dress as she struggled to stuff the dripping cubes down his shirt. "Your wife could use something to drink, Brody," Tammy snapped, loud enough for everyone to hear. Marvin Thompson and Max Bishop busted out in now-you're-in-trouble chuckles. Brody looked up, like it was the first he realized that anyone was watching them.

Winnalee backed away. "Yeah, get your wife something to drink," she said.

Brody looked irritated for the interruption. "What kind does she want?" He didn't wait for an answer. He reached into the tub at random and pulled out a 7 Up. He was about to toss the can to Tammy, when Winnalee yanked open the neck of his shirt and sent the ice sledding down his back. The can popped into the air and dropped to the ground with a thud, the pop-top splitting and sending a sizzling spray onto the grass.

Tammy bent to pick it up. "You're such a jerk," she said.

"*What?* It was Winnalee's fault!" Brody protested. Max Bishop snickered again, which made my jaw tighten. That was his daughter-in-law sitting under the tree, humiliated and hurt and trying not to cry.

Aunt Verdella leapt to her feet, her smile jumpy. "Button, why don't you bring out the cake now?"

I carried it out and set it on the table. The women stood for a better look, and cooed over it like *it* was a baby.

"Bring it over to show Marls before we cut it, so she doesn't have to get up," Aunt Verdella said. "Poor thing."

"Oh, Evy, that's darling," Marls said. I was happy to see her smile, though her smile stretched as tight as her stomach when Aunt Verdella announced that the clothesline idea came from Winnalee.

While we ate cake—Winnalee beside me, thank God—the party relaxed and conversation flowed until the gnats and mosquitoes came to claim the yard.

It was Tommy who made Brody help carry the gifts to the Mustang, and while they did, Marls came up to me and Aunt Verdella to thank us. She looked pale and too tired to be upset anymore. "You come visit us girls anytime, Marls," Aunt Verdella told her as she patted her arm.

Fifteen minutes later, there was no one left but us and Tommy—and surprisingly, Dad. The guys were sitting by the beer tub, talking about fishing, and Winnalee ran to the house to get a bag for the torn wrapping paper and cake plates.

Aunt Verdella was chattering like a squirrel, all happy because the party had been a success and she'd done well at the sale. But then she stopped abruptly. "Button, what's wrong?"

I was staring over by the guys. At Dad, whose legs were stretched, his eyelids soggy from beer. He was oblivious to the fact that Boohoo was standing beside him, patting his arm saying, "Dad . . . Dad . . . Dad . . ." Boohoo's fish was in a bread tin with icy water now, because Uncle Rudy had told him it wouldn't be good to eat if it wasn't kept cold. Dad was oblivious to Boohoo, but he noticed the splot of water that sloshed from the tin. He moved his arm to keep the water from dousing his cigarette.

Aunt Verdella gave me a troubled glance, then called out, "Reece?" She pointed down at Boohoo. But Boohoo was already setting the bread tin down by Uncle Rudy, asking him to watch his fish while he went to get Hoppy.

CHAPTER 16

BRIGHT IDEA #95: When you sing, sing rowdy like Elvis. And when you dance, dance like you're at Marty Graw.

"Where's my new hot pants?" Winnalee called from the top of the stairs.

"On your dresser!" I called back. Her "new" hot pants were really a pair of white hip-hugger bell-bottoms with an impossible stain on the thigh, which she had asked me to make into short shorts because she knew white would look great under black lights. She'd run a strip of red Magic Marker on the fabric under the butt to show me where to hem them, not realizing that I had to go shorter or the marker would show. Then she had me tack a crocheted lace yolk on the back of the waistband. "I love the way you ran the patch of lace around one hip, too! Cool!" Winnalee called from the bedroom.

Winnalee clomped down the stairs in chunky-heeled

white boots that laced to her knees. Her hair was hanging in still-damp ringlets, and her lips were glossed. She turned around and bent slightly. "Can you see my undies in these things?"

"Yeah," I told her.

Winnalee sighed and pulled her hot pants off. Then, right there in the living room, she stripped off her panties. "I know. I know . . . the cheeks of my ass are gonna be sticking out, but it will look stupider if my underwear is showing. Reefer wants them short, anyway."

Winnalee grabbed her purse and headed to the door. "Tommy and Brody will be by to pick you up at nine-thirty. The music starts at ten, but I want to show you my art first. See you later, Button!"

It was Winnalee's idea that Tommy go to the Purple Haze with Brody, so I wouldn't have to sit alone, or with Brody (which might have been *worse* than sitting alone). The guys showed up, honking while I was trying on the third outfit Winnalee had left on the bed for my consideration. It was nine-fifteen. Winnalee had wanted me to wear either a mini-skirt or shorts, claiming I'd melt to death in pants, but I'd told her I wouldn't get caught dead in public with my darning needle legs and cauliflower knees. Winnalee didn't have time to argue, so she picked out my best pair of bell-bottom hip-huggers, and three tops she thought would look great with them. "Whatever shirt you wear, tuck it in, too, and wear the thick belt I left on your bed." I'd tried on all three of the light-weight knits, but all of them clung to my boobs like skin.

"Evy, come on!" Brody called from the front yard.

"I'll be right down!" I shouted. The truck honked again, and Brody shouted that if I didn't hurry, they'd leave without me. Out of options, and out of courage, I settled on the black shirt—I wasn't about to wear white and have my boobs glowing like two bright harvest moons.

I'd changed so many times, and so fast, that my face and scalp were sweating, and I knew that in ten minutes I'd look like I was wearing an Afro, in spite of the juice cans I'd left wound in my hair all day, and the half of a jar of Dippity-do.

"Evyyyyyyy, for crissakes, what are you doing up there?" Brody bellered. He'd probably paced the grass bald already, as anxious as he was to get to the Purple Haze to see Winnalee.

I brushed my hair, and patted so much powder over the shiny spots that I feared my cheeks would look like floured bread dough, then strapped one of Winnalee's hemp chokers around my neck. I stuffed a tube of New London lip gloss into my purse and was about to fly out the door, when I realized that I hadn't switched sandals with the last outfit change. I hurried to the other side of the bed, and swiped underneath with my foot. The urn came rolling out. It had vanished the morning after Winnalee and I argued, so I assumed she'd picked it up and put it away. But there it was, bumping against the floorboard without its lid.

I dropped to my knees to look for my sandal—this time it was Tommy who was bellowing—and saw the urn lid butted up beside my shoe. I grabbed them both, screwed the lid back on the urn, and rolled it like a bowling ball into the closet.

The parking lot was already crowded when we pulled in, about twenty minutes after ten. "Right there!" Brody bitched as Tommy passed yet another space.

"Chill, you dumb son of a bitch. A full-sized truck wouldn't fit in those spots. Crissakes, why can't people learn to park?"

"I told you we should have taken my Mustang."

Tommy wasn't happy to be here, that much was apparent. Even though he'd taken the effort to buy a new shirt (navy and white; wide, horizontal stripes), judging by the fold creases.

He circled the second row of cars while Brody complained some more. I looked over at Brody and asked innocently, "Why didn't you bring Marls along?"

"And ruin all my fun?" Brody said. Tommy called him a "dick-weed."

Brody was out of the truck the second it stopped, but Tommy just sat there, his hand hanging over the steering wheel. "What a piss hole Bouman's turned this place into," he said.

I slid over to the passenger door. "I thought you said you haven't been here yet."

"No. But you can tell just by looking at the scuzballs going in."

Fat-bodied moths circled the bare bulb above the front door, and mayflies clung to the screen. "It's the jukebox," Tommy told me, as we neared the front door. I suppose because I looked impressed that a local band could play "In-A-Gadda-Da-Vida" just like Iron Butterfly.

Tommy jerked open the door so I could step inside, but I made him go in first. Not that anyone would have noticed our entrance: The place was that packed. People stood shoulder to shoulder around the bar, waving bills to get a drink. From what little I could see through the archway, the dance hall was even fuller. "What do you want to drink?" Tommy yelled over the music and chatter. "Anything," I said, as I strained to spot Winnalee.

We might have stood there forever waiting for drinks, but for Brody, who came up and snatched the bill out of Tommy's hand. He joked his way to the bar, then whistled to the cute bartender, calling her by name.

Tommy was tallest, so I asked him to spot Winnalee. "She's in the back," Brody said, handing me a Pabst. "Come on."

The lit stage, two feet off the floor, was filled with beat-up-looking speakers, a drum set, propped guitars, but no band members. Girls were clustered nearby anyway. There were two tall cage-like constructions made of pipes built on tall platforms on both sides of the stage—for what purpose, who knew.

It wasn't easy examining Winnalee's artwork, since people—mostly guys—hung near the walls, their dark silhouettes blotting out so much of the fluorescent forms that you could hardly make out what they were. Tommy found a bit of wall space to the right of the stage to lean against, and I followed to stand beside him. There was a group of guys sucking beer beside us, and Brody butted them out of the way. "Check this one out, guys," he said to me and Tommy. He pointed to a series of pink fluorescent rectangles, boxes within boxes, that in the black lighting had such dimension it looked like a hallway you could walk down to reach forever. "Far out, huh?" Near the "hallway" was the image of a dark-haired woman screaming into a microphone. "Grace Slick," Brody shouted. He pointed to the colorful swirls of music bursting from her mouth and said, "How cool is that?"

Tommy didn't talk, and neither did I, since it was so noisy you'd have to shout. He watched the place like a police officer, while I stared at white clothing, made brilliant purple white in the black lights, moving as if the forms were empty. The room was stuffy and hot, thick with the smells of cigarette smoke, beer, and musk perfume. I took a sip of my beer, cringing at the taste, but thirsty all the same.

"Evy? Evy Peters?" I turned and saw Amy and a few more girls from my class. "Oh my God, it *is* you! Stacy said it was, but I said 'no way.'" Amy glanced up at Tommy and her left eyebrow lifted as if she thought he was cute—and my date.

"Jo's dress was so pretty," she said, still watching Tommy. I thanked her, as though I'd made it myself. Amy glanced at the stage while the girls she was with gawked and gossiped beside her, then Amy turned back to me. "I got a letter from Jesse," she yelled, in an effort to be heard over Eric Burdon and War's "Spill the Wine."

"Yeah, I know. He told me he was going to write you back." I knew it was childish to feel the need to let her know Jesse and I were writing each other, *and* that I knew she'd written to him first, but I couldn't help it.

"I think he's forgiven me for being so stupid," she said, her smile dazzling in the black lights. She leaned closer and shouted beer breath into my already frizzing hair. "It was my mom's idea to break up with him. She said I was too young to tie myself down while he was in the service." I only nodded, because really, what could I say?

"I know you guys are friends . . . Has he said anything to you about me?"

My stomach clenched, and I took a long swallow of beer to soften it. "No. Only that you'd written and he *supposed* that he should be polite and write back." Amy looked disappointed. "Well, put in a good word for me, will you?" she said. She gave me a pathetic smile, than scuttled off to catch up with her friends. I took a long chug from my sweaty bottle, and wished for Winnalee to appear so I could gush over her psychedelic paint job and leave.

The band came out the back door and found their places onstage. The drummer tested his sticks against the drums, while the guy at center stage tuned his guitar. The band members were skinny and homely, but the girls still gravitated to the stage to oogle them. Ma was right: Women loved musicians.

Brody left the three girls he was flirting with and hurried back to Tommy and me. "This way. She'll be coming out now."

Brody tugged us through the crowd. And there she was.

Winnalee emerging from the same door the band members had come from, her shorts and tight white shirt and boots a purply white blaze. Another girl, almost as pretty, also dressed in white, was beside her, and Chet was behind them. Winnalee stepped over tangles of cords and disappeared. I rocked side to side on tiptoes to see where she'd gone. The jukebox went dead mid-song, and Brody started jabbing Tommy and laughing like a buffoon. "There!" he shouted, pointing. Apparently there was a set of steps leading up to the metal cages and Winnalee came up them, the outline of her hair luminous like the edges of a cloud lit by the sun at its back. She stepped inside the cage and struck a mannequin pose (but not of the virginal bride variety) and held it—same as the girl in the cage on the opposite side of the stage did. The lead singer shouted behind him, "One, two, three . . ." and the band lit into an earsplitting version of "Honky Tonk Women." That's when Winnalee came to life. Her body pulsing to the beat of the drums, her long, loopy hair writhing along with her. Brody stuffed two fingers into his mouth and whistled.

I turned to Tommy, dumbstruck.

"What? You didn't know Winnalee cage-danced on weekends?" Tommy shouted, as he leaned over me.

I couldn't even speak. I couldn't do anything but bend my head back and stare up at Winnalee as she danced, the cheeks of her butt a soft, shimmying bulge under her shorts, her breasts jiggling.

The song was half over when she spotted me. She waved proudly, and I lifted my hand timidly to wave back.

I curled my finger at Tommy and he bent over. "She doesn't take her clothes off, does she?" I asked him. He shrugged.

I looked back at the stage, just as Brody was handing a beer bottle through the pole slots. Winnalee squatted, her legs spread, and took it—turning so he could tuck a dollar bill in the waistband of her shorts. She shook the beer bottle while the crowd—the guys anyway—hooted. Winnalee clamped her thumb over the lip of the bottle and shook it vigorously. Lurid catcalls filled the room when she lifted her thumb and sent a spray of foam above her head. She tossed her wet hair and droplets sparkled in the stage lights. She bent to grab another bottle. She shook that one more vigorously, and sprayed the front of her flimsy white shirt. I stared in disbelief as guys formed a line in front of her cage, extra beer bottles and dollar bills in their hands.

Winnalee set bottles of beer off until by the end of the set, she was soaking wet, and beer was dripping down through the bars to darken the dusty floor beneath the cage. I tipped my own bottle back, my second, and chugged.

By the time the band took its second break, Winnalee's hot pants were filled with dollar bills that drooped over her waistband like a limp tutu, and I'd had three drinks and was feeling tipsy. She freed herself from the cage and, bumping aside the guys who swarmed her, hurried to me. "Did you see my art?" she asked, as she handed me an opened beer.

"Some of it. It's so crowded."

"Come on, I want to show you my favorite!" She led me across the room, and through a group of girls who eyed her with envy—or contempt, I wasn't sure which. "This one!" she shouted above the jukebox, pointing to a big peace sign with the images of Jesus and Buddha painted inside. The symbol was made of arms sleeved in paisley print. It was beautiful and I told Winnalee so.

"It's my favorite, too." I didn't need to turn to know that it was Brody who'd claimed this.

Winnalee rolled her eyes. "You probably don't even know who Buddha is, Bishop. Or Jesus, for that matter." She yanked some bills from her shorts and shoved them in Brody's hand. "Here, shut up and go get us some drinks. Pabst. Five of them."

"Hey," she told me. "Jezebel—I don't think that's her real name, though—the other dancer? She wants you to sew some of this lace on her shorts, too. Some other girls—that group right over there, talking to the lead singer—they asked me where I got them, too. I told them you probably wouldn't mind adding some to their bell-bottoms or shorts—for a price, that is, so they're going to drop them off here. I hope you don't mind." She didn't wait for my answer. She just grabbed me with a beer-sticky hand and said, "Come on, let's go outside. It's hotter than a bitch under those lights. If I didn't take a beer shower now and then, I'd frikken melt up there." She grabbed Chet's hand and tugged him outside with us, and Tommy followed like a conscientious bouncer.

I was finishing my fourth beer (Tommy his fifth), and my legs were so wobbly that Tommy had to catch me from tripping on the cracked pavement just outside the back door. "You're gonna get sick, Evy," Tommy warned when Brody brought back another round. But at that moment, I didn't care. I'd drunk away my shock and nothing much seemed like a big deal anymore. I didn't even mind that my hair was hanging in bushy clumps over my boobs, or that my shirt had lifted out of the waistband of my hip-huggers and I could feel Tommy's calloused hand on my bare hip when he steadied me.

Winnalee took a joint from Chet and lit it. She held the smoke until her billowed cheeks darkened, then danced across the gravel, moving in slow motion, singing, circling Chet while the jukebox inside played "Spirit in the Sky." In minutes, I knew, her face would morph into the little girl's face it had been—the one that saw rainbows in shadows and beauty in raindrops.

I don't know what we talked about, or why we laughed. I

didn't care. All I cared about was that I felt carefree and young, and that I wasn't worrying about saying the right things.

Winnalee crooked her arm around mine, forcing me to dance with her. I giggled as we moved between the guys like square dancers, singing: *When I die and they lay me to rest, I'm gonna go to the place that's the best.*

But when I heard—really heard—the lyrics we were singing, I stopped, my mostly empty beer bottle swaying from my hand like a pendulum winding down. I let go of Winnalee and looked up—even the stars were swaying.

Ma was up there. Looking down. Seeing beer slopped down my too-tight shirt—even if it wasn't spilled intentionally—and me drunk and dancing "sexy" with Winnalee, who *had* purposely soaked her shirt in beer. I could almost feel her horror over Winnalee's butt cheeks peeking from her pants as she bent to pick up a shiny pop-top that suddenly fascinated her, my naked hip bones showing above my too-low waistband. My head was spinning like I was on a carnival ride from the beer and the thoughts, and suddenly I felt sick.

I tried to make it to a clump of brush before I vomited, but I didn't. "Jesus Christ!" Brody bellered as he leapt back, then looked down to see my vomit splattered on the bell of his jeans. Winnalee hurried to me, and in between my heaves, I slurred, "It's a good friend . . . who will . . . hold your hair back . . . while you puke."

I struggled for my breath and balance when I stood back up, and stared down at the splotch of vomit over my sandal. My toes wriggled to crawl out of the stenchy mess.

Tommy crouched down and yanked the strap off my heel and pulled the sandal from my foot. Then he picked me up. "You either come with us now, Bishop, or you catch your own ride home. It's midnight, and Cinderella just spit her pumpkin seeds. Time to go."

"She's gonna barf on you, man," Brody said.

I could feel Tommy's chest and belly, hard and warm through his shirt. I wrapped my arms around his neck and tipped my head toward him to keep it from falling backward. His neck was soft against my face and smelled like Hai Karate aftershave. Suddenly I wondered what it would be like to have his skin in my mouth, giving him a hickey. Or to feel his mouth on mine as he gave me one. A real hickey, not a vacuum cleaner one. Like the ones that were as permanent as tattoos on Winnalee these days. I heard the soft murmur of my moan, and wondered if it was the heated thought, or the sick swirling in my belly that had caused it.

Tommy insisted I sleep on the couch, so I'd be near the bathroom in case I needed to throw up again. I argued with him that I was done, but fifteen minutes later I was hanging over the toilet with dry heaves. When I came out, Tommy had a pillow from the downstairs bedroom on the arm of the couch, along with one of Aunt Verdella's afghans. He led me to them. "I told you you were going to get sick if you drank any more," he said. I told him to shut up. He shook his head and sat down on the chair across from the couch, saying nothing, as I ranted about Amy, and God knows what else, while the room whooshed in wide circles around me. Tommy didn't comment, best I can recall. He just opened a pack of gum and reminded me to keep one foot on the floor.

I woke once in the night, my head still spinning, and sharp pains in my stomach. I opened my eyes a crack and saw that the chair was empty, then closed them again. That's when I heard Winnalee's giggle in the distance, and Chet Bouman telling her to "Shhhhh" so she wouldn't wake me. I tried to open my mouth to tell them to empty the trash can themselves this time, but I didn't have the energy.

The morning sun woke me, stabbing at my eyelids. It felt like woodpeckers were pounding on the sides of my head, and my mouth tasted like one had died in it. I could feel someone staring at me, and believed for a second that it was Tommy. I forced my lids open and there was Boohoo, lying stretched across the back of the couch, staring down at me. "You sick, Evy?"

I groaned a yes, and asked him to leave and come back later.

"You got stomach flu? You smell like you got stomach flu."

"Yeah. Now go away for a while. Please?"

I flinched as the screen door screeched, then slammed. I wanted to fall back to sleep, but I wanted to brush my teeth and get a drink of water even more.

I shuffled into the bathroom and grabbed my toothbrush. I looked like hell. My hair was matted like Boohoo yarn, and my skin was the color of soured milk. I was embarrassed to think of even Tommy seeing me looking like this. Yet in some strange way, I felt happy, too. Almost proud. I'd gotten drunk. Stepped out of my old lady mold and acted just like everybody else my age. And I wasn't sorry, in spite of getting sick.

I was lathering my mouth with toothpaste when I heard the front door open. I sighed. *Why couldn't Boohoo ever listen?*

"No, she was sleeping downstairs," I heard him say. "She stunk like puke."

He was talking to Aunt Verdella! They couldn't be here *now*! Not with Winnalee and Chet cozied up in the same bed! I spit, and wiped my mouth on a bunched towel.

Boohoo was at the end table when I scaled the kitchen

doorway, grabbing the pack of Dentyne Tommy had left on the living room end table. I jetted through the dining room just as Aunt Verdella was reaching for the bedroom doorknob. "Button?" she called, as she leaned into the doorway.

Oh my God!

"Aunt Ver—" I stopped shouting. It was too late. The bedroom door was wide open, and over her shoulder, I saw what had stopped her in her tracks. Winnalee naked under a spill of hair, straddled over naked hips and hairy legs. Her head was tossed back, and the room was filled with groans and panting and the smell of body heat. Chet's hands were cupped over her butt as she grinded herself against him. *Oh. My. God!*

Aunt Verdella let out a high-pitched gasp, and Winnalee froze.

Chet's head lifted up from the pillow and I gasped. Because the man under Winnalee wasn't Chet. It was Brody. "Oh, shit!" he sputtered. I darted around my stunned aunt, grabbed the doorknob, and slammed the door shut.

Behind the door, the bed squeaked and feet thumped the floor. Aunt Verdella and I stood in place, too shocked and embarrassed to move. "Evy?" Boohoo called. "Can I have this gum?"

"Take it outside," I said, without looking.

"Why? Gum ain't messy. How come you didn't get a good kind? This stuff burns your tongue."

Aunt Verdella backed away from the door, one hand over her heart, the other clamped over her mouth. She looked at me with shock-shattered eyes, and I turned away, feeling as ashamed as if it was *me* having sex with a married man right before her eyes.

Aunt Verdella walked stiffly but quickly to Boohoo. "Come on, honey," she said, taking his shoulders with shaky hands. Boohoo snatched the gum off the table and babbled, "Why we gotta go already?" as she led him out.

I just stood there. Not knowing what to do, my stomach feeling sick all over again.

The bedroom door opened and Brody peeked out. He looked at me, then cocked his head both ways. "She gone?" he whispered.

I turned my back to him, and itches devoured my skin.

Brody went out the back door, then darted across the field, his shirt whipping from his hand, no trace of a limp in his stride. He was hurrying to get to Tommy's house, no doubt. To get a lift home—and an alibi.

We weren't supposed to judge people, only love them. That's what Aunt Verdella taught me. And I'd tried not to judge Winnalee when she smoked pot. I even forced myself not to judge her when I saw her spill beer on her shirt for the boys. And hadn't I stopped myself from judging her when used rubbers showed up twice? But *this*? I struggled to remember to only love her, but at the moment I was feeling every bit as judgmental as Fanny Tilman.

Winnalee sat down on the other end of the couch, and fidgeted some, then got up. "You want something to drink?" she asked as she headed to the kitchen. I was thirsty and my head felt like a ball of yarn, yet I shook my head.

Winnalee went into the kitchen, her bare feet padding the floor softly, like she was walking on tiptoes. I knew that if she spilled on the counter, she'd wipe it up this time. Maybe she'd even pause to put the dish she'd left on the table last night into the sink, and pick up the couple of stray potato chips she'd dropped on the floor. She'd try to be helpful and good—as if *I* was the one she had to make amends to. I knew this. I don't know how, but I knew.

By the time she came back from the kitchen, I was both chewing my cheek and scratching. She set her glass of Kool-

Aid on the coffee table, then busied herself picking up the tiny gum wrappers left on the couch cushion. She hurried to take her boots that were lying prostrate in front of the bedroom door and sat them upright alongside the front door, and she gathered her colored pencils from the end table. And when I still hadn't said a word, she went into the bedroom and came back with the dirty sheets bunched in her arms and went in search of the laundry basket.

I heard her ice cubes tinkle like wind chimes when she picked up her glass, and the whoosh of the cushion as she fell into the chair across from me.

"You're mad at me, aren't you?" she finally said.

I turned and stared at her in disbelief.

"Not so much mad," I said, "as disappointed. How could you, Winnalee? How could you do that to Marls . . . to yourself? Brody doesn't care about you. He doesn't care about anyone but himself. And you don't care about him, either. Why would you do something like that?"

"It's not my fault he doesn't care about Marls," she said defensively. "And I don't even know her."

I blinked at her. "And that somehow makes it okay? You've met her. You know she's pregnant . . . You know she loves him. You know Brody and you couldn't care less about each other. Isn't that enough? Marls is just like you, Winnalee. And me. And everyone else. She's just trying to find something good in life." My mouth started quivering. "I'm looking at you right now, Winnalee, and I can't even believe you're the same person I used to know. You were mesmerized by the rainbowy shadows coming through the window at The Corner Store, and the thought of finding fairies." I shook my head. "I would have never thought that you'd grow up into somebody who had to get high to get by. Or somebody who would slop beer on her boobs to get a buck, and sleep with some married guy who is just using her. You thought something of yourself back then, Winnalee. And I wanted to be just like you."

Winnalee's nostrils worked like fish gills as her eyes gathered tears. "I told you I wasn't the same person, but you wouldn't listen!" Winnalee set her glass on the floor and dropped her forehead into her cupped hands.

My head was pounding, and I felt like I might throw up again when Winnalee started sobbing. "Don't hate me, please?" she begged.

I sighed. "I don't hate you, Winnalee. You're my best friend. But I'm . . . I'm just so disappointed in you. I always wanted to be just like you. A snowflake."

Winnalee continued to cry, and I started, too. "I don't even know why I do those things," she said. "I just don't want to feel bad, and those things make the bad shit go away. But then afterwards, I feel worse."

"Then stop doing them!" I said.

Winnalee looked up at me, torment twisting her features. "Don't make me leave. Please."

The anger and disappointment seeped out of me, and I went and squeezed into the chair beside her. I wrapped my arms around her. "I'd never ask you to leave."

"I told you I'd changed, Button. I warned you. But please don't stop being my best friend. No matter how disappointed you get in me. Please don't stop being my best friend."

"I won't," I told her, and she melted against me like snow that had turned to rain.

CHAPTER 17

> BRIGHT IDEA #44: If your sister tells you she's going to give you a swat on the behind if you try running off to play without cleaning up the mess you made in your bedroom first, don't think you can outrun her if she has longer legs than you.

When I was kid, I once sat on the cement casing of the basement window so I could overhear Ma having it out with Aunt Verdella. But I didn't do the same when Winnalee went inside to talk to Aunt Verdella, three days after. Instead I sat at the picnic table and strained to hear Boohoo's occasional excited shouts floating from the backyard, where he and Uncle Rudy were scouting for new sprouts in the garden.

I felt sorry for Winnalee, who, as she headed for the front door, turned and said, "You want to ask me that question about my most embarrassing moment now? I think I have an answer."

I chewed my cheek and chipped frayed barn-red paint off the table with my fingernail as I waited.

. . .

When Winnalee finally came out, she was carrying a plate of watermelon wedges. She sat down on the front steps and set the plate down between her bare feet. She crouched forward, her face disappearing behind her hair. I got up and went to sit beside her on the cool cement. "You okay?" I asked, trying to get a peek at her face. She sniffled and wiped her cheek with the back of her hand, and nodded.

"Aunt Verdella is the best person in the whole world," she said. She shoved her hair over one shoulder, exposing a grouping of fading hickeys on her neck.

"I know she is," I said.

Winnalee sniffled. "I wish she had raised me."

I shooed a fly away from the watermelon, which was glistening wet, and red like spilled blood.

The screen door in the back squealed and Boohoo's voice sounded through the windows. "You have to wash first, Boohoo," Aunt Verdella called. And then "I cut the last of the watermelon, honey. The girls have it outside. I'll bet there's a piece left for you."

Winnalee looked over at me and smiled sadly. Her eyelids were swollen and looked sore. I took her hand. "I'm proud of you for talking to her, Winnalee. That took courage," I said, and fresh tears bubbled from her eyes.

The door burst open, the edge whacking me between the shoulder blades. Boohoo shimmied himself between us. "Can I have some?"

I handed him a slice, then grabbed one for Winnalee and me. "Spit out the seeds, Boohoo," I reminded him.

"Yeah," Winnalee said. "Or else you'll grow a watermelon in your belly."

Boohoo leapt off the steps and pulled out the front of his

shirt. "Look at me. I got a watermelon growing in my belly. And now my belly's fat like the Bishop lady's." He shook his hips and laughed, then squirmed back between us. I spit out a seed and Boohoo watched it arc and drop. He took a bite. "Watch mine," he said, and he spit a seed. "Mine went farther than yours, Evy."

"Bet I can whip you both," Winnalee said. She spit, and we soon had a game going: longest spit out of three tries wins.

I guess I must have heard the motor, but with the relief that came after Winnalee's talk with Aunt Verdella, it was easy to dive into the challenge of our silly seed-spitting game, and I, like Boohoo, like Winnalee, didn't pay the approaching car any mind. That is, until it pulled into the drive.

"No way, Boohoo!" Winnalee shouted, getting up and going to the edge of the half-moon patch of bald ground to stand beside Boohoo, facing the steps. She pointed at a seed lying in the dirt. "This is mine. Yours is way back there." Boohoo protested, and their arms playfully wrestled as they bickered about whose seed was whose.

The car pulled in—a Ford Galaxie, dusty white, with a dent in its front fender. I expected to see some old codger looking for Uncle Rudy sitting behind the wheel, but instead, it was a woman. She wore dark sunglasses, and her hair was gleaming like a pot of melted pennies. The chunk of watermelon in my mouth suddenly felt as dry as old toast. I stood up, my heart pounding. Boohoo and Winnalee were still arguing.

"Winnalee," I whispered.

Winnalee, still bent over, stopped chattering and turned her head toward the drive when I said it again. "Jesus Christ," she muttered.

The car door squealed as it opened, and Freeda stepped out. She was dressed in a pair of white shorts, her sleeveless blouse tied at her waist as it had been the day I first laid eyes on her. She was tanned, and shorter than I remembered, and her hair wasn't long anymore. It was parted on the side, the bangs falling down over the side of her face to the bottom of her ear. The crown was ratted high and formed a bubbled arch down to the nape of her neck.

"Who's that?" Boohoo asked.

I kept my voice low and even. "Go get Aunt Verdella. Now."

Freeda stood looking at us for a moment, her car door hanging open, her hand on her hip. She pulled off her sunglasses and poked them into her fiery hair. Her eyes narrowed to two black-lined slits.

"Winnalee," she said. "You forgot one of your little mementos from Woodstock, so I thought I'd bring it by." Freeda ducked into the backseat. Winnalee straightened and went stiff as a colored pencil. I glanced at the door, hoping for Aunt Verdella to appear, then turned back to Freeda. Just as she was lifting a tiny baby out of the car.

CHAPTER 18

BRIGHT IDEA #40: If you bring a kitten home from the box outside the Piggly Wiggly, somebody's gotta clean the litter box.

Fear looked foreign on Winnalee's face, but there it was, freezing her eyes so they couldn't blink, and stretching her neck taut so she couldn't speak.

The front door opened and Aunt Verdella stepped out. I took one look at her face—joyful, flooded with relief and love—and knew, just as Winnalee had to know, that it was no coincidence that Freeda was here. I stared at the baby girl, dressed in a pink sundress and a white bonnet that was too big for her head, and grappled to make sense of it all.

That's when Winnalee bolted, the half-eaten slice of watermelon spinning from her hand like a loose wheel as she raced toward home. "Winnalee! Goddamn it, you get your ass back here! You hear me?" Freeda screamed.

But Winnalee didn't stop. She jumped in her van and rammed it into reverse. Backing out with such force that she couldn't spin the steering wheel quickly enough, and the rear end dipped into the ditch. "Oh dear, I knew she'd be upset!" Aunt Verdella said as the back tires of Winnalee's van kicked up grass.

Who knew which direction Winnalee intended to go—probably west, toward town. The Purple Haze maybe, or maybe straight out of Dauber—but when she jerked the van into first gear, her wheels ended up pointing her south, proving that escape doesn't care which way it goes, as long as it's someplace else.

I didn't think. I just reacted. Running across the yard as fast as I could to get to my Rambler and go after Winnalee, Aunt Verdella fretting behind me to not speed and to find her.

Winnalee's van, cumbersome as it was, sped down the dirt road, the colors of peace and love lost in a swirl of dirt. I tried to keep up with her, but the only thing that could race at that speed was my thoughts. A memento from Woodstock? A baby? Winnalee had *a baby*? How could she not have told me? I racked my brain, searching for any clues that I'd missed. The small pouch below her navel? Her withdrawing before and during Marls's baby shower? Her insisting that she had changed? None of these, even added together, were enough to make me suspect she had a kid. *Why hadn't she told me? And how could she have left it?*

As Winnalee's van neared the end of Peters Road, I begged her to slow down, then held my breath, fearful that she'd miss the turn and smash into the woods. One of her taillights lit and she made a precarious wide turn down Marsh Road.

I didn't need to think long or hard about where Winnalee was headed then. She was headed for the one place she might believe could take her back to the magical land of fairies and make-believe. The place where things like reality and responsibility didn't exist: Dauber Falls.

In the summer in 1961, Winnalee was convinced that we'd find fairies at the falls, after reading a book called *The Coming of Fairies,* which claimed that two girls had found them down near a beck. We spent our summer making plans to sneak off to find them. And the day that Hannah showed up and Winnalee learned the truth, she'd run off to the falls herself. I'd followed, and when I couldn't find her, I hid from Fossard's ghost in an old bomb shelter, quaking under a cot until I was found.

Dauber Falls might have held the power to soothe and comfort Winnalee, but I'd been terrified of the old Fossard homestead you had to cross in order to get to the water, ever since I was a child. Mainly because of Tommy, who pulled out the ghost story of Hiram Fossard, the humpbacked grave digger who'd lived there, whenever he wanted to antagonize me. Fossard had carved a bomb shelter into the hill near his home because he believed the Russians were going to nuke us. But Fossard was equally afraid of going underground, and one day, when his fears proved too much for him, he went berserk and shot his dog, his wife, and then hung himself. When Winnalee and I were nine, Tommy told us that folks claimed Fossard's ghost—still afraid of going into the ground—walked the property at night, his shovel scraping behind him. When I was a kid, I used to duck on the rare occasions we passed the Fossard place, the hair on my arms standing on end, my teeth gnawing at my cheek. Granted, maybe the story of Fossard's ghost was nothing but a scary story to tell around the campfire, but just being on his property made it feel real and gave me the heebie-jeebies all over again.

I reached the dead-end sign and slipped down the driveway that once took Fossard to and from the cemetery (about the only place he ever went). I leaned close to the windshield and focused on the two ruts that provided local fishermen or partying teens with the shortest route to the water, and tried hard not to look at the old house slumped to my right, with its peeled paint and busted windows. Or toward the patch of red pine to my left where the bomb shelter sat. I tried to keep my mind on Winnalee as my Rambler rattled over the ruts, but with the tall blades of grass scraping the bottom of my car like a shovel over dirt, it wasn't easy.

Near the end of the drive, there was a gap in the woods where a pickup or two could wait in the shade for its owner. Winnalee's van was parked there, under a canopy of leafy limbs. I butted the Rambler up close to her vehicle and got out, pressing the door shut behind me. I hurried to reach the clearing (as if ghosts were more likely to linger in the shade). Once in the open, the sun turned the skittering insects into metal-shiny streaks, and I felt safer as I headed toward the sound of rushing water.

I spotted Winnalee at the water's edge, sitting on a gray boulder, her back rounded, the wind ruffling her hair. Below her, water foamed like root beer as it whooshed over boulders deposited like stepping-stones. I didn't call out to Winnalee, but pecked my way down the steep bank, careful to not lose my footing on the coating of loose rocks.

She must have sensed me behind her, because she drew her legs up and bowed her head against her knees.

"Winnalee?" I said, speaking only as loud as the rushing water dictated I needed to.

She didn't say anything, but the tightening of her back told me she'd heard me.

I took a few careful steps forward and sat down on the boulder beside her. Her hip was soft against mine.

"You must think I'm terrible," she finally said. "Sleeping with Brody, getting high, . . . cuttin' out on my kid."

"I don't think you're terrible," I said, hoping I was telling the truth.

"I'm not like Freeda, though." She turned her face toward mine and her eyes were wet and pleading. "I love my kid, Button. That's why I came. To find you guys and see if you'd raise her."

Wind swirled into my mouth, drying my tongue.

Fresh tears, clear as rain, glossed Winnalee's eyelashes. "It's true," she said. "You've gotta believe me. I'm not like Freeda, but I'm no better for a kid than she was for me. I know that. Look at how messed-up I am, Button. You saw what happened when you left Boohoo alone with me. Shit, I'd be cussin' at her in no time, and draggin' her ass all over the country. She'd grow up just like I did, and she'd turn out just like me, not making a damn thing out of herself. I don't want that for her, Button. Not for *my* kid. So I thought maybe Aunt Verdella could raise her. Teach her how to be more like you."

I put my arm around Winnalee and she leaned into me. "I swear, I was only coming here to ask, then I was going to go back to get her. But when I got here and learned about your ma, and saw that Aunt Verdella had all she could do to keep up with Boohoo, I didn't know what to do. So I just smoked up, screwed, and danced . . . you know?"

"I'll help you raise her, Winnalee. Aunt Verdella will, too."

Winnalee shook her head. "No. I can't raise her, Button. I'd be no good for her. You know it's true. Freeda said she'd help me, too, but we'd only be at each other's throats. Shit, it started the minute we got home from the hospital. I was still hurting bad from the stitches they sewed into my crotch, and my boobs were hard as rocks and leaking all over the place, and there was Freeda, stuffing my lap full of books on how to introduce solids to your kid, and how to potty train. Shit like that. Now why'd we need to know that right then? Hell, I didn't even know how to hold her yet! And I was so tired I could have died, and Freeda was waking me up in the night every time that baby cried. So there we were, fightin' like always. A kid shouldn't have to listen to that shit, you know?"

I wrung my hands. "Freeda left you for the same reasons," I said in a scared whisper.

"Bullshit! She left me because she didn't give a shit about anybody but herself."

I tucked my head down, wanting with everything I had to tell her that I'd once overheard Freeda tell my ma her reasons for leaving Winnalee. And those reasons *were* almost word for word the same as Winnalee's. But Winnalee was too upset to hear me, and I knew it.

Winnalee sighed. "I thought it was just the weed making me gag—like an allergy or something. So I quit smoking and drinking, and my stomach settled down. But I started getting fat. And then I felt her, like a flutter of fairy wings inside me. I couldn't stay with the thought, Button. Does that make sense? I put on baggy granny dresses and I didn't look down. I stopped lying on my stomach. And I took my bath in the dark.

"I never did tell Freeda. She just figured it out when my gut got so big it would have been like trying to hide a watermelon under your clothes. Even then, I denied it."

I took Winnalee's hand and the breeze tickled her hair across my wrist. "I would have been scared, too."

"I *was* scared. Scared half to death. Especially when Freeda started talking to me about giving birth. I didn't want to hear that shit! So I kept telling myself that later, later I'd deal with it and figure something out. I said that until I didn't have any time left, and Freeda finally yelled at me, 'Listen kid. That baby's in there, and like it or not, one way or another, it's coming out.'

"Freeda said we'd do okay with her, but I knew that wasn't

true. I knew she'd be tryin' to raise her like she tried raising me after she saw that shrink. Knockin' down any spirit that girl was born with, and tryin' to raise her like some Brady kid, when that's something we Malones are *not*. That's what I was afraid of. You gotta believe me, Button."

"Of course I believe you," I said.

We sat quietly, watching the water swirling with the same chaotic intensity that swirled in Winnalee's eyes.

"It's bad enough," she said, "that my kid, like me, won't have a father. I don't know who her dad is, any more than Freeda knows who mine is. A kid should have a dad. Just like you and Boohoo do. But if she can't have that, then she can at least have a good mommy, and that's not me. And that's not Freeda."

I looked down, suddenly wanting to draw up my knees, too, but not having enough room to do so. *Not like ours, Winnalee. Your baby shouldn't have a dad like ours.*

One thing I learned from grieving over Ma is that people can't cry forever. Even if they think they might. Sooner or later the weeping stops, leaving your eyes scratchy and as dry as your heart. And even if you want to cry again because you remember getting the tears out giving you at least some temporary relief, you can't. Winnalee cried until the sun dropped to scrape against the backsides of the trees. And when no more tears would come, I tugged Winnalee's hand, coaxing her up, and we climbed the bank. It was almost dark, the sunset faded to a muddy gray. Clouds of gnats hung in the weak rays of sunlight loitering between trees, and I swatted at them as I kept my eyes peeled to what might be lurking in the dark patches. "You're crushing my hand," Winnalee said. "You're not still afraid of Fossard's ghost, are you?" She gave a tired laugh when I didn't answer. "Button, you're a piece of work."

. . .

Winnalee wouldn't go over to Aunt Verdella's, where Freeda and her baby were. Instead she headed upstairs and dropped into bed, bunching the pillow in her arms as if it was her baby, then curling herself around it as if *she* was the baby.

"You want me to go call Reefer and tell him you won't be in?" I asked, mainly because I knew Freeda and Aunt Verdella were waiting for some word.

Winnalee glanced at the clock. "Yeah, call him, though if he hasn't figured out yet that I'm not coming in, he's a total idiot."

I paused at the bedroom door. "Should I bring the baby back so you can see her?"

"Tomorrow," she said.

I nodded and stepped out of the room.

"Button?" she called.

I stepped back. "Yeah?"

"Her name is Evalee. That's your name and my name put together. E-v, *Ev,* like the beginning of Evelyn, and a-l-e-e, like the end of Winnalee."

I smiled. "What's her middle name?"

"Woodstock," she said.

CHAPTER 19

BRIGHT IDEA #41: If you try to help your new friend write a *G* in cursive, when you aren't sure how to write one yourself, you're probably both going to get the letter circled on your paper.

"Button, that you?" Aunt Verdella called from the kitchen, when I came through the front door. I could hear Uncle Rudy and Freeda talking.

"It's her!" Boohoo yelled back. He was sitting on his knees next to a playpen, winding a ball of yarn while he watched Evalee.

"*Shhhhh,*" I told him.

"It's okay, Evy. She don't wake up for nothin' when she's sleeping. That's what Freeda said."

I smiled. Just like her mommy.

"Tomorrow's her birthday," Boohoo said. "Guess how old she's going to be? Six weeks old. That's how many. She was born two weeks early. Freeda said that's why she's such a peanut."

The lamp shade had a sheet of Reynolds Wrap capped over it to mute the light, so I crouched down by the playpen to get a better look. Evalee's legs were tucked under her bottom, her mouth sucking. Her face was round, her skin sugar-cookie white. Eyelashes the color of milk chocolate were curled against her full cheeks. Her tiny mouth was squished to one side in a cute pout, and her bottom lip was making sucking movements. I reached down and fingered the wispy blond hair that I was sure would grow into loops like Winnalee's. She was beautiful, just as I knew she'd be, and I wanted so badly to pick her up and sniff her baby smell.

"Guess how much long she is?"

"Um . . ."

"Twenty-one inches! So small that if she was a musky, you'd have to throw her back."

My cheeks bulged with a laugh, and I gave Boohoo a hug.

"Was I ever that little, Evy?"

"You were exactly that long when you were born," I told him, my heart swelling for them both.

"When I was zero old, I was that long? I don't think so," he said.

"Sure you were. I'll dig up a picture and prove it," I said, hoping I could find one in the album at Dad's without Ma in it, so as not to hurt him with that sad story.

Aunt Verdella peeked into the room. "She's cute as a cupcake, ain't she?"

"She is," I said with a smile.

"Button? Get your ass in here and say hello!" Freeda hollered.

"Come on," Aunt Verdella said. "And Boohoo, you go upstairs and get your jammies on now, okay? It's late."

Boohoo started to protest, but Uncle Rudy stepped into the dining room. "Hey Spider-Man, how about coming upstairs and givin' your old uncle Rudy a hand finding his slippers. I go crouching down to look under my bed, and I might get stuck on all fours for good."

"In which case you'd be wearing a leash forever, too," I said. Uncle Rudy's grizzly face folded into a smile.

Boohoo scooped up his yarn balls and got up. "I'll bet Chameleon took them," he said. "I'll find them for you, Uncle Rudy, and wrap them in my web so he can't steal them again."

I headed to the kitchen, but stopped by the stairwell, looking up at Boohoo as he thumped up the stairs behind Uncle Rudy. "Boohoo? Don't go trying to make a web around the baby, though, okay?"

Boohoo stopped and peered over the banister. "I know that, Evy. Aunt Verdella already told me."

Freeda was standing at the counter, measuring formula powder into a line of baby bottles, and Aunt Verdella was filling the coffee pot. Freeda turned when I came in, and spread her arms. "My God," she said. "I couldn't believe my eyes when I saw you today. All grown up, and pretty as a goddamn model. Come here, kid."

Freeda hugged me hard, then backed away. She jabbered about my long hair, my flat ears—she insisted they needed to be pierced—and my big "knockers," while my face heated. "Where's Winnalee?" she asked when she was done marveling at me.

"Home. She's exhausted."

"I suppose she is," Freeda said. "With the life she's been living since she pulled into Dauber."

Aunt Verdella's head dipped sheepishly. "Button, you understand why I had to find Freeda, don't you?"

I nodded.

Aunt Verdella tilted her head. "I knew she'd be worried. And I was worried, too."

"Good thing you found me, too," Freeda said, "since Reece doesn't pick up his goddamn phone. I finally got smart and asked for Rudy's number—Rudolf, who knew—but when I called here all I kept getting was a little boy calling me Crackpot and hanging up."

"That was *you?*" I said, and we all laughed.

Freeda leaned her butt against the counter and propped her hands behind her, her eyes softening and saddening at the same time. "Button, I'm so sorry about your ma. I couldn't believe it when Verdella told me. Jewel was too young to die, and you kids were too young to lose her."

Freeda shook her head slowly, her green eyes dampening. "Jewel was the first female friend I ever had. I could kick my own ass for not lookin' back after I left here, but hell, all I knew how to do back then was run without looking over my shoulder. Especially from anything that looked like love. I just didn't trust it. And with Hannah on my trail, well . . . It's just the best I could do at the time. But oh, I missed you guys."

Freeda looked up, her milky neck swan-pretty. "It's going to take me a while to realize Jewel's gone."

"I still forget sometimes," Aunt Verdella confessed. She started crying then, and as always, her tears broke my heart.

"Evalee is so cute," I said, to steer her—to steer us all—to something joyful. "I'll bet Winnalee looked just like that when she was a baby." I cringed after I'd said it. Freeda left Winnalee when she was a newborn. How would she know?

Freeda turned back to the sink and started filling the bottles. "I love that little baby in there with everything I've got," she said. "*And* I love Winnalee. That's why I don't want her making the same mistake I made. She takes Evalee back now, and that little one never needs to know her mommy left her in the first place. She doesn't, and Evalee will never forgive her, just as Winnalee will never forgive me. I don't want that for Winnalee. It's hell."

Aunt Verdella's head snapped up. "Oh, Freeda. Winnalee will forgive you in time. You're her mama. And she's got a kind heart. You watch. In no time, she'll be calling you 'Ma.' "

I guess Aunt Verdella didn't see the absurdity in that comment. Winnalee had refused to call Freeda "Ma" for all the nine years since she learned that's who she was. It was doubtful that she'd start calling her it now.

Thinking the word *call* startled me into remembering that I was supposed to make one. Aunt Verdella helped me dig through cluttered drawers for the phone book. I had to shout so the bartender on the other end could hear me over the jukebox. "At least she's working," Freeda said after I hung up. "Though I can't imagine her waiting tables—hand her a plate or a cup and she's as klutzy as a fawn on roller skates."

"Well, she *does* seem to come home wearing more beer than she probably serves," Aunt Verdella said. They laughed, and I cringed. I busied myself carrying the filled bottles to the refrigerator, grateful that neither of them knew that on weekends, Winnalee set down her order pad and climbed into a cage to dance for dollar bills.

Aunt Verdella poured three cups of coffee, and we sat down at the table. "Verdella told me about your dad," Freeda said, as she tucked the short side of her hair behind her ear. "How he's checked out of life. Out of you kids' lives."

"Well, I didn't exactly say it like that," Aunt Verdella said.

Of course she didn't. Aunt Verdella always used her love for Dad to smooth over the sharp edge of the truth.

Boohoo came barreling down the stairs then, marching into the kitchen proudly. "I found his slippers," he said. "And I tied them right to the bed legs so Chameleon can't run off with them again."

"Oh dear. Freeda, remind me to take my sewing shears

upstairs when I turn in." She looked at Boohoo. "Honey, didn't Auntie tell you to get your jammies on and get to bed?"

"I'm hungry," Boohoo said.

Freeda looked at him. "For a kid with an imagination like yours, I would have thought you could come up with a more original excuse than *that*?"

Aunt Verdella hurried to dab a baking powder biscuit with jelly. "Oh, he's a bottomless pit, this one," she said, while Boohoo studied Freeda under tucked brows.

Freeda watched him, too. "He sure looks like Reece."

Boohoo took two bites of his biscuit, then tossed it on the rug for Knucklehead. Freeda looked at the poor dog and shook her head. "And that old thing looks ready to kick the bucket."

Aunt Verdella stiffened, the same as I did. Knucklehead had slept with Boohoo up until climbing the stairs became too much for him, yet feeble as he was, when Uncle Rudy and Boohoo settled down to watch TV at night, Knucklehead always stretched out on the floor alongside Boohoo. Aunt Verdella and I often shared a secret smile when Boohoo unconsciously rubbed the dog's floppy ear against his cheek as if it was the silky edge of a blanket. Whether Boohoo found Knucklehead dead, or we did, we both dreaded the day we had to explain to him why Knucklehead wasn't getting up.

Boohoo looked at Freeda, and crinkled his nose. "Buckets? You and Winnalee sure do talk funny."

"Boohoo, you'd better brush your teeth and get upstairs. Go on now," Aunt Verdella said.

Boohoo headed for Freeda's chair, probably to grab a stray ball of yarn from underneath it. But Freeda stopped his head with her hand. "Didn't your auntie tell you it was bedtime? Go on now. Mind."

Boohoo looked up, his chin jutting out. "You ain't the boss of me."

"He's got his daddy's bullheadedness, too, I see." Freeda

peered down at Boohoo. "You got a lot of gall, talking to me like that, kid."

"Oh yeah?" Boohoo said (though I doubt he knew what gall even meant). "Well *you* got big knockers!"

Aunt Verdella gasped. "Boohoo!"

Freeda laughed, and tugged Boohoo into her arms. She kissed him hard enough to flatten his cheek, even as he wriggled to get free.

"I don't think I like you," Boohoo said after he broke loose.

Aunt Verdella and I scolded him in unison, but Freeda only laughed and swatted him playfully on the behind. "I'll grow on you. Now get to bed."

After Boohoo went upstairs, Freeda looked at Aunt Verdella with intense eyes. "We've got a few family messes on our hands, don't we?" She shook her head. "It's goddamn crazy, what's happening in both of our families. We all oughta know better."

Aunt Verdella touched the side of her face and nodded. I looked down. "But I'm back now," Freeda said. "So is my attitude. And shit's gonna hit the fan in Dauber now. You can count on it."

CHAPTER 20

BRIGHT IDEA #64: Sometimes your eyes tell the truth even when your mouth doesn't.

I wrote to Jesse after I got home that night. A long letter about all that had transpired. Guilt kept my pen scrawling, because even if Jesse and I weren't officially a couple yet, I felt bad about that drunken moment when Tommy carried me to the car and I had wondered how his skin would taste.

I fell asleep late, and slept until a knock at the door woke me the next day.

I didn't bother tossing a bra under my T-shirt, because I was sure it was Freeda (though I would have guessed her to just barge in). Instead, it was Marls Bishop.

"Marls," I said. *Oh please,* I begged in silence. *Please, be here only because Aunt Verdella told you to stop in to visit anytime!*

"Can I come in?" she asked. Even through the rusty haze of screen, I could see the anguish in her eyes.

I looked over my shoulder. Winnalee had been sleeping like dead weight when I'd left the bedroom, but there was no guarantee she'd stay that way. "Or we can just talk out here," she said, as if she understood.

"Can I get you anything first?" I asked, still through the screen.

She shook her head, so I stepped out onto the porch and closed the door behind me.

Three of Uncle Rudy's old lawn chairs were on the porch, and a small table that Aunt Verdella had picked up at the Community Sale. Winnalee had plucked yellow daffodils from the flower bed and propped them in a jelly jar. Marls waddled to the lawn chairs and sat down. I joined her.

"You look good," I told her, even if it wasn't true. Her face was even blotchier than it had been at the shower, and her navel strained against her shirt like a giant nipple. I wondered if she was scared, thinking about how that baby had to come out.

"When's the baby due again? I know I should remember, but . . ."

"August twelfth," she said.

"Oh. Nice. Is your . . . has your medical problem corrected itself?" I couldn't get myself to say "placenta."

"Yeah," she said.

I was racking my brain, thinking of any other question someone might ask a pregnant woman they hardly knew. My left leg crossed over my right, then they switched places again, as if they were as unsure and uncomfortable as the rest of me. "Do you have names picked out?" Marls was picking at a hangnail on her pointy finger and didn't say anything, so I quickly added, "It's okay if you don't want to say. I suppose—"

"Evy?" she said abruptly, looking me right in my eye. "Is Brody having an affair with Winnalee?"

The air in my lungs snagged in my throat, and I gripped the armrest.

"I'd ask her, but I don't know if she'd be honest with me." Marls's puffy eyes were pleading. I looked down, and brushed at a loose thread squiggled on the leg of my pajama bottoms.

"Brody lied to me Friday night. He told me he was hanging out with Tommy, and gotten too drunk to get himself home. He claimed he crashed at the Smithys'. But that wasn't true. I went there at three in the morning—his car was in the driveway—and Ada woke up when I knocked. She told me that Tommy was sleeping, and that Brody wasn't there. Was he here?"

I could feel her next to me, her muscles tense, her body heavier with dread than with baby. I didn't know what to say. I had no desire to protect Brody. But Winnalee?

Seconds ticked by painfully, as I bit my cheek, and begged for someone, *something*, to interrupt this conversation.

Marls hoisted herself up. "It's okay, Evy," she said. There were tears in her voice, but they didn't reach her eyes. "Your silence is all the answer I need." She headed for the steps, and held on to the porch door frame as she lowered herself down.

"I'm . . . I'm sorry," I whispered.

If Marls heard me, she didn't react. She just lumbered to the old Chevy that Brody used before he got his Mustang, and drove off.

I didn't know what to do after she left. I went back inside and looked for something to clean—which wasn't exactly like looking for Easter eggs, since Winnalee tended to drop everything right where she used it.

I caught my reflection in the living room window, and noticed how I moved like Ma when I cleaned. Quick. No wasted movements. It made me wonder if that wasn't why she cleaned so often and so hard; because the messes we made in our house were a lot easier to clean up than the messes we had made in our lives.

CHAPTER 21

BRIGHT IDEA #66: It doesn't matter if you stop thinking about your math assignment over the weekend because you didn't do long division in your last school and you don't know how to do it. That assignment is still going to be due on Monday.

Aunt Verdella was feeding Evalee on the couch when I got inside. I leaned over and the baby looked up at me with round eyes that would probably be the same shade as Winnalee's when they lost their newborn murkiness. Her hair was still damp from a bath, and darkened with baby oil. Someone had tried making a curl on top of her head, but it wouldn't bend and so stood straight up like a baby porcupine's quills.

"Good morning, pretty baby," I cooed. The stream of milky bubbles crawling up the glass paused as Evalee's lips pulled away from the nipple to smile. I giggled, my distress over Marls's visit and my hope to get Aunt Verdella alone to tell her about it shoved aside by that sweet baby's smile.

Freeda was in the kitchen rattling dishes and harping,

"Boohoo, pour that stuff carefully. Look at the mess you're making. You've got cereal bouncing all the way over to the fridge."

"Knucklehead will eat it," Boohoo said.

"By the looks of things, that dog wouldn't be able to get on his feet if you'd dropped a steak."

"Yeah he could. Watch. Here, Knucklehead. Here, boy."

A chair scraped against the floor, and water ran in the sink, then Boohoo yelled, "Aunt Verdella, Knucklehead just peed on the floor!"

"Oh dear," Aunt Verdella said. "He's been doing that." She turned to me. "You want to give our little cupcake her bottle? I should get in there."

"Sure." I reached for the baby and Aunt Verdella wriggled to her feet. "I'm coming!" she yelled.

There was the whack of the screen door, and Freeda shouted, "You little shit! Get back here and pick up these Sugar Pops!" I looked down at Evalee, who was staring at me intently.

Just as Aunt Verdella only went higher, not faster when she ran, when she was trying to hush her voice, it didn't get any quieter, only deeper. "Freeda, we don't talk about Knucklehead dying in front of Boohoo."

"Why not?" Evalee squirmed and I took her almost empty bottle from her mouth and lifted her to my shoulder to burp her. Fearful that the back door was open and Boohoo would hear the conversation, I headed into the kitchen.

"We just don't." Aunt Verdella was pushing at the door with the toe of her canvas shoe when I got into the kitchen.

"That's crazy, Verdella. What in the hell you gonna tell him when the old dog croaks? That he went off to the store to buy doggie biscuits and got lost on his way home? Crissakes, Verdella."

My stomach tightened and I rocked Evalee side to side.

"Well, I don't really know what we'll tell him. That dog's older than he is, and Boohoo loves him so."

"All the more reason to prepare him a bit, don't you think?"

"We don't want to upset him," Aunt Verdella said.

Freeda paused for a second. "Wait a second here . . . Boohoo couldn't have been more than a baby when Jewel died. What have you told him about her?"

For a second, there was silence (but for Evalee's milk-scented belch).

"Verdella?" Freeda said slowly, while cocking her head. "What have you told him about Jewel?"

"Nothing," Aunt Verdella confessed.

"Verdella, look at me. What do you mean 'nothing'? Are you saying you haven't told him *how* she died? Or do you mean that you haven't told him about her, period?"

"We don't really talk about Jewel in front of Boohoo, Freeda."

Knowing we did this was one thing, but hearing the admission spoken out loud made it sound crazy.

"What the hell, Verdella. So that boy doesn't even know he *had* a mother?"

My insides clenched, and I cocked my jaw to the side to find a spot of skin that didn't feel raw and sore.

"Well, after Jewel died, that baby was missing her so badly that if anyone even said her name, he'd toddle to the door and cry for her. It was pitiful. Just pitiful. So we stopped saying 'Jewel' or 'Ma' in front of him. I guess it just got to be habit."

"Well, where in the hell does he think he came from? A cabbage patch?"

"He's never asked, Freeda."

I dipped my head. No, Boohoo had never asked about his mother, or about death, period, for that matter. But then, what would have prompted him to wonder? We kept all pictures of Ma hidden away, we made an effort to scoop dead birds out of the yard before he could find them, and we'd never driven past the cemetery with Boohoo before, much less taken him with us on Memorial Day. Not once.

"That's not the point! He should know who his mother was."

Freeda must have realized how absurd that sounded, coming from someone who had kept Winnalee in the dark about who *her* mother was for nine years, because she—we—went silent. Aunt Verdella and I exchanged nervous glances as Freeda grabbed a coffee cup from the mug tree. "No good comes out of keeping secrets like *that*, Verdella. Ask me. Ask Winnalee."

I looked down. Evalee's face was pressed against my heart, her closed lids so thin that the tiny veins colored them like lavender eye shadow. As I carried her carefully into the living room and lowered her into the playpen, I felt like crying, though I wasn't sure why.

The back door opened and Uncle Rudy's and Boohoo's voices filled the kitchen. Freeda wouldn't let this topic drop for good, but she would for now.

I reached down and pulled a summer-light blanket, busy with ducks, over Evalee's bare legs, and paused at the sound of a vehicle. I leaned over the playpen and pulled back the sheer curtains. Winnalee's van was peeling out of the driveway.

Winnalee never woke before noon. Eleven, at the earliest. Fear slammed into my stomach. I should have had the foresight to know she'd bolt when Freeda showed up, just as Freeda had bolted when Hannah showed up in Dauber.

"I'm running home for a second," I called into the kitchen. "I'll be back in a bit."

I hurried inside and thumped up the stairs. The bedroom looked trashed, but then it had looked that way since Winnalee's arrival. I searched frantically for her duffel bag, knowing that while she might leave clothes behind, she would never leave that. Not with her prized possession inside.

I yanked open drawers to find them half full—which told me nothing. I grabbed at any mounds on the floor that looked even high enough to be concealing a duffel bag, but found nothing but more clothes and the occasional shoe underneath. Under the bed I found Winnalee's flattened moccasins and a couple of romance novels given to me by June Thompson. Winnalee never kept her duffel bag in the closet, but maybe, just maybe. "Oh, please," I whispered, tears blurring my vision when I came out empty-handed.

My steps were slow and heavy on the stairs. I shoved open the screen door and sat on the porch—anything to delay having to walk across the street and tell Aunt Verdella and Freeda that Winnalee had left.

"How you doing over there?"

I looked up and saw Tommy heading toward me, a hammer swinging from his hand.

"Your hangover gone?" Tommy called, his voice full of tease.

"Shut up. That was days ago."

"I've recovered, too, thanks for asking," he said.

"You didn't even have a hangover," I reminded him, as I looked wistfully down the road.

"I wasn't talking about my stomach. I was talking about my neck." He cocked his head to the side and pulled down the neckline of his shirt to show me a small bruise faded to yellow-gray. He grinned. "You could have told me you were a vampire."

I turned away. *My God!*

I heard a car coming. I stood on my tiptoes, as if I could see over the treetops if I was only an inch taller. I hurried to the road, and looked down. "Tommy, come here. Is that Winnalee's van?"

Tommy jogged over and studied the emerging dust ball. "Yeah, that's her."

I reached the van before Winnalee had the key out of the ignition, Tommy alongside of me. "You came home. I thought . . ."

Winnalee rooted around on the passenger side floor for her army bag. "Thought what?"

"That . . . that you'd gone to do something fun without me."

Winnalee rolled her eyes. "Fat chance of that. I had to call to find out what time I work today. Reefer, the dumb ass, never posts a schedule for the week like a normal boss, and he wasn't around when I left last night. I ran over to your dad's to use the phone. It's not like I was going to use Aunt Verdella's with *her* there."

"Oh," I said.

There was something in the way Tommy was watching Winnalee that was unnerving me. She didn't seem to notice, though. She pulled a frozen pizza wrapped in sweating clear plastic from the seat. "I thought I was going to get lucky when the bartender said we're having music tonight—I'd rather dance than wait tables any day—but it's not a band. Just some hippie with a guitar who's been hanging around. Reefer finally said he could play, but he's not paying him.

"I've got to hurry. The bastard wants me there in an hour and I haven't even hit the tub yet. Would you put the pizza in, Button? I'm starving."

"Sure," I said.

She handed me the pizza, started to walk away, then

stopped. "Oh. I ran into Linda at The Corner Store. She told me to give you this." She pulled a folded note from her pocket:

Button, Mrs. Jamison came in. She told me about Cindy's dresses. She was concerned. You really should have asked me first, honey, but Cindy's a pretty headstrong girl. Come in tomorrow and we'll talk. Bring the sketches. L.

"What a bitch," Winnalee said, then headed toward the house.

"Hey, Winnalee," Tommy called, taking a step after her.

"Save it, Smithy. I'm in a hurry."

Winnalee went inside and Tommy snagged my arm when I went to follow her. "Tell your friend there, Bishop's all hers now if she wants him—though I doubt she does. He called me right before I left the house and said that Marls pulled out a bit ago. She's going back home to her folks."

I stuffed Linda's note into my pocket and sighed. "Marls was here this morning."

"She was at my place, too. I didn't know where Brody was Friday night, so I didn't have anything to tell her."

"Lucky you," I said. Then I headed inside to turn on the oven.

I made the pizza and called to Winnalee that it was done.

"Thanks!" she yelled down the vent.

Winnalee grabbed a slice of pizza and ate it where she stood. "You should see the hot guy I ran into at the store," she said, fanning her mouth. "He's working at the mill during his summer break. Some program the mill does for college kids, I guess. Anyway, he's kinda shy and slouchy, but *so* cute. Ada introduced him to me—Craig something or other—a goofy last name. I asked your dad about him, but he said he never sees the daytime crew."

I blinked at Winnalee. She hadn't seen her baby in weeks, and Evalee was right across the road, yet all she could think about was some cute guy? "I fed Evalee her bottle this morning," I said carefully, yet purposely. "She's really pretty, and so, so sweet. She smiles and mimics you if you make baby sounds. Boohoo says she sounds just like Pebbles Flintstone."

Winnalee stared at me for a second, her whole being frozen, the slice of pizza drooping in her hand. "Button. I can't do this right now. I'm sorry, but I just can't." She set down her half-eaten pizza slice and went out the back door.

CHAPTER 22

BRIGHT IDEA #67: If it seems like somebody doesn't like you, don't go thinking that it's because they think you dress funny or stink at dodgeball. Maybe they're just ignoring you because they're just shy about talking to strangers.

"Guess what, Evy?" Boohoo said, when he interrupted me an hour or so later. "Dad's coming over for supper tonight. You and Winnalee, too."

I looked up. "Dad's coming?"

"Yeah. That Freeda lady said he has to, or she's gonna kick his ass."

I set down my seam ripper. "Boohoo, you can't swear like that."

"It's what she said."

"Well, *you* can't say it."

"Okay." Boohoo's mouth tugged to one side. "I don't like that Freeda. Just the baby. She smells poopy right now, though, and I don't like her when she smells like that. We're gonna have *baskettee*. Freeda's making it."

"Nice," I said. "Why don't you like Freeda?"

"Because she's bossy."

"I'm bossy sometimes."

"Yeah, but I don't have to listen to you when you're bossy. Freeda says if I don't listen to her, she's gonna sit on me."

I laughed, and Boohoo told me, "Getting sit on isn't funny, Evy."

I tucked my lips tight and kept my head down.

"I'm going now. Cupcake should be done stinkin' by now 'cause Aunt Verdella said she'd take care of it. Anyway, tell Winnalee about supper."

"Winnalee's working tonight," I said. "Tell Freeda that, okay?"

"I ain't telling her nothing," he said, and off he went.

Uncle Rudy was in the backyard, dropping an armful of boards in a heap when I got there. "What're you making?" I asked.

"A lean-to for Knucklehead," he said.

Boohoo turned, the long board he was carrying teetering and clipping Uncle Rudy on the chin. "That's what a doghouse without walls is called. A lean-to." He frowned. "Knucklehead's gotta stay outside now because he's a pee-pants."

I gave Uncle Rudy a private, sad smile, then I went inside.

Freeda was in the kitchen, her eyes watering over the mound of onions she was chopping. Her long bangs clung to one cheek, and she gave them a quick blow. "Hi, kiddo," she said.

"Hi. Did Boohoo tell you that Winnalee's working?"

"He did. Crissakes. We've been here twenty-four hours and she's still not seen her kid."

Aunt Verdella was in the living room singing "Patty Cake" and working Evalee's hands to roll 'em, roll 'em. She stopped, looking confused. "I can never figure out which way to roll their hands. I mean, I want to roll 'em clockwise for me, but then it's counterclockwise to them, and that ain't right, is it?"

I grinned and told her I didn't think it mattered.

"Poor Knucklehead. And poor Rudy and Boohoo. They sure love that old dog."

She didn't mention the conversation Knucklehead's accident had led to, and neither did I.

Her face brightened with a new thought, and she started rolling Evalee's arms again, even though the song had stopped. "I'm making pineapple upside-down cake for dessert. You know how your dad likes that."

I nodded.

"Button, would you take this little one so I can get started?"

"Sure," I said, reaching for the baby.

The whole house was engulfed in steam from boiling pasta and the smells of garlic and warm cake when Dad pulled in. I carried Evalee into the kitchen, because I wanted to see Dad and Freeda's reunion—seriously, I couldn't imagine it. When the Malones came in '61, Dad quickly developed a love-hate relationship with Freeda. Laughing with her and defending her at first, then getting all judgmental and uncomfortable when she developed a friendship with Ma. Freeda may have ultimately been the driving force behind Ma and him getting along better, but before that, she was the source of many of their fights.

Dad was wearing a short-sleeved, Aunt Verdella–pressed shirt, and his face was shaved smooth. He looked awkward when he stepped inside, a six-pack of beer in the crook of his arm, and Aunt Verdella hurried to bring him a hug. Freeda was standing at the stove, her head tipped back as she dropped a string of spaghetti into her mouth. She turned while chewing. "Reece!" she dropped her fork and scooted around the table to get to him.

I never thought of Dad as anything but a dad up until that moment when he saw Freeda for the first time in nine years. His eyes flicked over her tanned limbs and the yellow summer dress that leaned against her skin, the cotton limp from age and humidity. But then, as if he'd been scolded, he looked away.

Freeda wrapped her arms around Dad and tugged his head down so she could press her cheek against his. She whispered a couple of sentences into his ear—no doubt about Ma, judging by the way Dad's eyes stayed closed longer than a blink. Dad patted Freeda clumsily between the shoulder blades and she let go. "Glad you came, Reece," she said, giving his chest a quick tap.

"You didn't give me much of a choice," Dad said.

Freeda laughed as she headed back to the stove. "I didn't give you *any* choice."

"Look, Reece," Aunt Verdella said, pulling me to Dad so he could see Evalee in my arms. "This is Winnalee's little one. Evalee.

"We were shocked, too," Aunt Verdella said, in response to his expression. "Even Button didn't know." Dad gave Evalee a little smile and jiggled her hand.

"Boohoo, aren't you gonna say hi to your dad?"

"Hi," Boohoo said, without looking at him. He came to me and took Evalee's bare foot to bounce it. "Hi, Cupcake. It's me. Uncle Boohoo." Dad looked into the pot on the stove, and Boohoo looked up at me. "Aunt Verdella said I'm like her uncle, so that's what she can call me. Uncle Boohoo. I'm gonna call her Cupcake."

Aunt Verdella shut the fridge and gave Uncle Rudy's arm a squeeze. "You boys go in the other room and watch TV so we can get this meal finished," she told them. "Boohoo, you too."

It was unnerving sitting at the dining table, my arms tight to my side so Dad could prop his elbow or stretch his arm alongside his plate. Dad's knee budged up against my leg twice, so I crossed my legs at the knees, then again at the ankles to keep them out of his way.

I didn't have anything to add as they updated Freeda on the local news, so I ate in silence and occasionally harped at Boohoo to stop wrapping his milk glass in spaghetti "yarn" and making a mess on Aunt Verdella's crocheted lace tablecloth. Boohoo didn't stop, though, until Freeda snatched up his glass and took it into the kitchen. "Crissakes, Reece," she said as she was coming back. "You don't step up to the plate and knock your son in line soon, I'm gonna have to do it for you. This kid is as adorable as a puppy, and listens about as good as one."

Aunt Verdella laughed nervously, and I squirmed.

"So, Reece," Freeda said after the chewing slowed, "I see you don't keep up your place anymore—it looks like a shack—and I doubt you pick up your guitar any more often than you pick up your phone. Your kids obviously don't know you from beans, and you rarely come over here . . . so, what *do* you do these days?"

I could have snapped in half like an uncooked spaghetti noodle.

"Oh, Freeda," Aunt Verdella piped. "Reece works hard. The graveyard shift. And somebody or other is always calling him for help with their vehicle or when they need an extra hand on their farm. He's tired all the time, aren't you, Reece?"

Dad stabbed his fork into his salad. "Tact never was your talent, was it, Freeda?"

Freeda tossed her head back and laughed. "Nope. But I've got other talents to make up for it." Freeda nudged Dad playfully, then rolled her eyes when he swayed without even the hint of a smile. "Ah, Reece, loosen up already, will ya? I'm not picking on you. Seriously, I just want to know how you spend your days. I mean, crissakes, it's been four years."

Aunt Verdella and I lifted from our chairs in unison. "I'm gonna bring in the cake. Pineapple upside-down, Reece."

"I'll get the plates," I said.

Aunt Verdella and I didn't talk when we were in the kitchen. We only listened, and hurried.

"Button? Aren't you going to have any cake?" Aunt Verdella called when I delivered four plates, then retreated to the kitchen again.

"I'm full," I called.

"Land sakes, what's *that* got to do with it?" Aunt Verdella asked, then added, "I've been full since 1950, but I'm still having cake."

"Yeah," Boohoo said. "That's why you're fat as Fred, too."

I was swabbing at splotches of tomato sauce on the stove top when Aunt Verdella came back in to get the coffeepot. "Oh, look how nice you cleaned up. Thank you, honey. But you didn't need to do that."

It was obvious they'd be visiting for a while, since Dad looked relaxed by the time the beer was gone, so I excused myself as though I was going home to work, then slipped into the Rambler and drove to Dad's while I had the chance. I took my time, tenderly taking down Ma's bells, one by one, and washing them like they were fragile babies.

CHAPTER

23

BRIGHT IDEA #74: Just because you feed a stray dog doesn't mean he's gonna lick you nice and be your friend forever. He might just walk away when the bologna is gone.

That night Winnalee startled me awake with a jab of light and a curt "That bastard!" My eyelids quivered in protest, so I kept them closed as I asked, "Who?"

"Brody Bishop, that's who! He's telling everybody at the Purple Haze how I got him drunk and practically raped him. How I'd been chasing him for weeks even though he kept telling me that he was married and loved his wife. That slimewad!"

I rubbed the sleep from my eyes.

"It's not fair! He's the one who was chasing my ass around and wouldn't give up until I gave in. It happened, and I'm not excusing it—I don't have to—but I'm pissed that he lied."

Winnalee was unlacing her boots. "That girl you knew from school, Amy *Slutface*? She was gossiping about me in the can, saying I was the reason Marls left. What a joke. She left because he treats her like crap, and because he doesn't bring in a damn dime. Good thing I was smoked up and mellow, or I'd have scratched her eyes out.

"But smoked up or not, I would have beat the crap out of her if I'd been there when she said what she said next—what Jeanie, the bartender overheard—that I'd ditched out on my kid. So my *'sister'*—a 'slut' just like me, came to Dauber to dump her back in my lap."

"Oh, Winnalee . . . ," I said. "I'm sorry."

"Not half as sorry as that bitch is gonna be the next time I see her!"

Winnalee kicked off her boots and dug for one of her oversized T-shirts. "I'm sick of creeps like Brody, and Chet—he's on my shit list now, too. He didn't even care that I was cryin' about what they said about Evalee!" Winnalee tugged her T-shirt over her head roughly. "Man, this place is *so* backwards."

She crawled into bed and I rolled to my other side to face her. "Maybe it's not that it's so backwards, Winnalee. Maybe it's just that it's not Woodstock."

"Well I wish it was. Nobody judged anybody there."

I didn't say it out loud but I wondered if they'd have judged *me* if I'd been there and kept my cauliflower knees clamped together, and my lips squeezed shut when the joints were passed.

Winnalee blew out her anger, then quietly said, "Button? Will you bring Evalee over here sometime tomorrow?"

"Sure. I'm going to buy fabric for Cindy's dresses in the morning, then I've got to go to the shop to talk to Linda. I should be home by mid-afternoon."

"Okay."

"Winnalee?" I said carefully. "You know, you have to face Freeda at some point or other."

"Like hell I do. I just wanna see my kid. That's all. Screw everybody else. Well, except you. And Aunt Verdella. And Uncle Rudy. And Boohoo. And maybe . . ."

CHAPTER 24

BRIGHT IDEA #27: If your teacher makes you work in a group and a snotty girl who thinks she can draw good, but she can't, tells you she'll draw the pictures and you can write the report, just grab the paper and start drawing.

Linda and Hazel were both at the desk when I got to the boutique after my trip to Porter for material. "Evy," Linda said, stopping mid-sentence on whatever she was saying when I came through the door.

I felt awkward, and I could tell that Linda did, too. I stumbled all over myself as I explained how it came to be that Cindy Jamison hired me to make the original wedding gown Winnalee had drawn. Linda listened, her smile shaky. "I figured that, after I bumped into Winnalee. But it'll be okay. We'll see that it is." She fumbled for her notepad. "Hazel measured Cindy and her bridesmaids last night. I've got their measurements here. Did you bring the sketches?"

I felt itchy. Hazel and Marge always measured the customers they were sewing for themselves.

I handed Linda the sketches, while Hazel leaned over her shoulder. "What's this here?" Linda asked, smearing her finger in tight circles over the glob at the back of the dress.

"Roses made out of chiffon," I said, because by now that's what I decided they would be. "You know, like a bouquet. I already figured out how to make them." (It would have been more honest to say that I was *trying* to figure out how to make them, since my three attempts so far looked like nothing but clumps of snow left on the edge of the road by a snowplow.)

Linda looked up at Hazel. "What do you think? Can you make a pattern for this?"

"Well, I don't see why not. Most everything I made for the first twenty years I sewed, I made from my own patterns."

What could I say to that? I forced a smile and thanked Hazel for offering to help, and Linda for being understanding.

Linda gave a nervous laugh. "Well there, I feel better. I have to admit, when I first heard that your little friend came up with the design, I was a tad worried. I didn't know what she'd come up with. A see-through gown maybe?"

Obviously, she'd heard the gossip. I stared at Linda's tight, painted smile, and wondered if *I* looked that fake when I used a smile like a shield over what I was *really* feeling and thinking.

"Okay, then," Linda said with maybe too much enthusiasm. "I'll find some pretty fabric and some . . . is this ribbon under the bust?"

"I bought everything I'll need already. For the bridesmaids' dresses, too. It's out in the car." Linda sat up tall, her arched brows rising so high they disappeared under her bangs.

"You bought it already?"

Linda went to the car with me to haul everything in. She fanned her hand over the bridal fabric and nodded with relief, but she was not so relieved when she saw the bridesmaids' fabrics. "I see you didn't find any tie-dyed pastels—Mrs. Jamison will be relieved—but why are there four different shades of the material here? Were you unsure which color to get? If so, you should have brought back a small sample . . . this had to be costly."

"I figured if Cindy couldn't have tie-dyed material, she'd at least want something different," I said as I fingered the rainbowy print, each bolt of the design a different color. One in peach tones, one in soft shades of turquoise, one in buttery yellows, and one in lavender colors. "Doing a garden variety of colors is in for bridesmaids' gowns. That's what the clerk at JoAnn Fabrics told me."

"They're lovely," Hazel said.

"But if Cindy Jamison will think so is another matter. It's not what she asked for," Linda said.

I didn't tell her that it was the closest to tie-dyed as I could get, but there wasn't enough of any of the colors for four dresses. Instead I said, "She'll like them when she learns that Winnalee thought this idea was cooler than tie-dyed." (I didn't see any point in telling Linda that Winnalee hadn't even seen the fabric yet.)

I was glad when Hazel invited me into the work room to show me how she goes about making patterns. Hazel was as dull as oatmeal, but she minded her own beeswax and stuck to business.

It was early afternoon when I got home, carrying the wedding gown fabric and the bag of sewing notions. I was about to call to Winnalee to tell her that I was heading over to grab Evalee as soon as I'd brought in the rest of the fabric, when I heard the shouting coming from upstairs.

"Maybe so, but I never slept with a married man! Messed-up as I was, I had *some* scruples!"

"I don't even know what *scruples* are!" Winnalee screamed back at Freeda.

"Obviously not!" Freeda snapped.

"And like hell, anyway! You're such a hypocrite."

I couldn't move. I just stood there, inside the door, holding my breath.

"I was messed-up, Winnalee. I've been over it with you a million times. And although I don't expect you to understand, because you were never hurt the way I was, I at least hoped that you wouldn't see my wild ways as about having fun. I at least hoped you wouldn't mimic me!"

"Yeah, yeah . . . do what I say, not what I did. You're a joke, Freeda. Now get out of here, and leave me alone."

"I'm not going anywhere, Winnalee. I've had Terri managing the shop for six weeks now, because dragging Evalee there wasn't working out so good—the kid was starting to stink like perming solution and peroxide! That baby needs some stability in her life, damn it!"

"I know that! You think I'm stupid? And that's exactly why you're *not* gonna be the one raising her. You don't know a damn thing about giving a kid a stable life—hauling me around from school to school, dump to dump."

"We've been in the same place for seven years now, Winnalee, so don't give me that crap. Let the past stay there, already. Evalee is your baby. She needs her mother."

"Yeah, well. I needed mine once, too, and all you did was stuff a vase with ashes and tell me that it *was* her. I was coming back to get my kid, Freeda. I wasn't gonna wait until she was five."

Winnalee came flying down the stairs in bare feet, while Freeda screamed, "Winnalee, where in the hell do you think you're going? Get back here! We are *not* finished!"

In her fury, I don't think Winnalee even noticed me standing there. Or if she did, she didn't care. She dashed out the door, and before I could set down my things, her van was spitting gravel.

It took Freeda a while to come downstairs. When she did, she walked with heavy, sad steps. She reached the bottom of the stairwell and paused, one hand on the banister. "Damn it," she said. "I told myself I wouldn't yell."

Freeda sat down on the landing, her feet on the floor, her elbows propped on her knees. She mumbled fractured sentences as she sobbed, "Evalee needs . . . we can do this . . . no life . . . my God, what a mess." I swayed from foot to foot and wished Aunt Verdella was there.

"She'll come around when she cools down," I told Freeda, and Freeda huffed, "I've been telling myself that for nine years—I don't believe it anymore."

Freeda shook her head. "Look at the mess I made, Button. She's like a lost sheep. Always looking for someplace that feels like home. Sleeping with anybody who will have her. I just want the running to stop. Here. With her. I want them to be like a *real* mother and daughter—whatever the hell that is. It might be too late for me and her, but it doesn't have to be too late for her and Evalee."

Freeda dried her eyes and sighed. She stood and shuffled to the door and peered out absentmindedly. "It's gonna be a scorcher today," she said with a tired sigh. "You'd better get something cooler on."

Winnalee came home around eight-thirty the next morning. The butt of her cutoffs was damp, and she smelled like marijuana. Small flecks of debris were tangled in her hair—the tip of a twig, crumpled bits of last year's leaves—telling me I was right when I guessed she'd gone to Dauber Falls. "My van's acting up," she said in a tired voice as she headed up the stairs. "Can you give me a lift to work? I've gotta be there by three today, and wait tables till the music starts."

"Sure," I said. "We'll have to leave a little early, though. I need to get gas. You okay?"

She didn't answer. She only said she needed a nap before work.

I went to the stairs and looked up. "Winnalee? Bright Idea number ninety-nine and one half: *When it seems the whole world is on your case, just remember that your best friend is on your side.*"

Winnalee nodded. "Thanks."

We were only about a mile down Peters Road when Winnalee asked, "What does Evalee look like? The last time I saw her, she looked like a raisin, only red and peely."

I smiled. "She doesn't look like a raisin anymore. Her skin is fair, like yours—the color of sugar cookies. She's got the cutest little mouth, and right before she smiles, she blinks two or three times, real fast, like she's startled. Her eyes are perfect circles. Darker than yours, but they'll probably lighten in a month or two. She doesn't have much hair, and it's too soon to tell if it's going to be curly, but you'd think so, since it's blond like yours. Aunt Verdella says she's a good-natured baby."

"She doesn't look like she's gonna be a gray person, does she?" Winnalee asked.

I still didn't know what a gray person was exactly, but I did know that Evalee wasn't one. "Winnalee," I said. "She's your daughter. How *could* she be?"

Neither of us commented when we reached the end of Peters Road and Freeda's car was parked in Dad's drive. Ma had always kept the drapes pulled on the windows facing the road after it got dark, but Dad kept them shut even when the sun was shining. They were opened now, but I couldn't see inside.

When we reached The Corner Store, Winnalee said, "Oh, look who's here. The Grim Reaper." I glanced at the building. Fanny Tilman was peeking out of the door in her winter-wool sweater.

Fanny moved out of the way to let me in when I went in to pay for my gas, and as usual, she didn't acknowledge me. Ada did, though. She was all smiles as she glanced out at my car, then back at me. "Where you girls off to today?" she asked, not because she was nosy, but because she was friendly.

"I'm running Winnalee to work," I said.

Ada smiled. "Where's your aunt been? I haven't seen her in a few days."

"That's because the Malones are back in Dauber, wreaking their havoc," Fanny said. She had a quart of milk sweating on the counter—it would probably curdle before she decided she had enough gossip to take home along with it.

"Fanny," Ada scolded.

I wanted to shout at that heartless, judgmental old bag, and defend the Malones, but instead I ignored her, just as Ada was doing.

"Freeda was in here buying diapers a couple days ago, though. She sure is an outgoing gal, isn't she? And pretty as ever. She showed me a picture of the little one. Such a little dolly."

"Just what this world needs. Another illegitimate child," Fanny said.

I gouged at my arms as I went to fetch two pops from the cooler and clunked them down on the counter. Ada looked out between the paper signs tacked on the window to see Winnalee heading toward us. "Fanny, that's enough now. I like those girls and I won't have anyone bad-mouthing them." I kept my head down to dig in my purse for change, hating myself because *I* wasn't the one who said those words.

I said goodbye to Ada—ignored Fanny—and had just slipped back into the car when Tommy pulled in.

"He's got Craig with him," Winnalee said.

"Craig?"

"Yeah, that new guy Ada introduced me to. Come on!" She got out of the car, peeking in through the window to say "Come on" again.

"Hey, Tommy," Winnalee said. ". . . Craig."

"I'm taking Craig up in the Piper," Tommy said, more to me than Winnalee.

Craig *was* cute, but short. So short that I found myself slouching even more than I normally did as I stood across from him. He kept his head half down, a shy, close-mouthed smile playing on his lips. A raindrop, it seemed, making me wonder why Winnalee was interested in him.

She whacked Tommy. "You still haven't taken *me* up yet. How many times do I gotta ask?"

"Well, I start haying tomorrow, so it won't be for a while. I'll be busy from sunup to sundown for at least three weeks—five if that dipstick Bishop doesn't show up to help."

"Does that mean Button will actually get some work done, then?" Winnalee asked, giving me a nudge.

"She'll be crying her eyes out, she'll be missing me so much," Tommy teased. I rolled my eyes.

"I could give you a hand haying after work," Craig said. "I get off at four."

"Cool," Tommy said. "Rudy's gonna run the bailer, so that'll help."

"Hey, maybe we could swap some of my help haying, for time in the air."

"I'm not licensed to teach, you know."

"I know. But just being up there with you, you telling me things, would help."

"Sure," Tommy said.

"We'd better get going, Winnalee," I said.

"Yeah, we've gotta burn out, too," Tommy said. Craig said goodbye, while giving us each an instant's worth of eye contact, then they headed to the store, and I headed to the van.

"Wait up!" Winnalee called. I stopped and turned. But Winnalee wasn't talking to me. She was calling to Craig. I slipped into the Rambler, and Tommy headed inside the store. The vinyl seat felt scorching hot even through my jeans, as I worried about if she'd be late for work and watched Winnalee playing with her hair as she talked to Craig. The breeze was plastering her dress to her naked body, and she didn't tug at the material even once.

"What did you say to him?" I asked, when Winnalee got back.

"I asked him if he wanted to go out sometime."

"You're kidding."

I cranked the key. "Hell no," Winnalee said. "It's a new era, Button. We don't have to sit on our asses *hoping* a guy will ask us out. We can be the ones asking."

"What did he say?"

"He said *sure*."

"Man, Winnalee. How did you even know if he likes you enough to want to take you out? Weren't you afraid he'd say no, and then you'd have to feel stupid?"

She looked at me like I'd just asked her how she knows she's a girl. "I suppose you would ask that. You still haven't figured out that Tommy has a crush on you."

I squirmed.

She opened her soda pop and took a chug. "You've got a broken radar, Button. Which means that this guy you write to could either be madly in love with you, or just be stringing you along. Not like you'd know the difference. And let me guess. You haven't figured out yet that your dad and Freeda are getting it on, either."

First the comment about Jesse and my broken radar, and now *this*? I kept my face turned to the side window. "She's just lending him a hand, Winnalee, that's all."

"Yeah, I don't doubt she's *lending him a hand*," she said with a sarcastic laugh.

When we reached the Purple Haze, Winnalee opened the car door and kicked it wider with her boot.

"I pick you up at two, right?"

"I can probably get a lift."

"No. I'll pick you up. Two?"

"Two-thirty," she said.

I drove home slowly, watching the sunset brighten with pinks and lavenders through my dusty windshield, and trying hard not to wonder if Winnalee's assessment of me with guys was true.

CHAPTER 25

BRIGHT IDEA #72: When you can't find a bright idea for three weeks, but you need one or you'll never get to 100, ask a big person for one and write it down. Even if it's something stupid like "If you lay down with dogs, you're gonna get fleas," at least you're one closer to 100.

When I got home, I dragged the alarm clock into my sewing room so I wouldn't have to keep getting up to check the time. I'd have to wait another day or two before Hazel got me the pattern for Cindy's dresses, but I took out the fabric and pattern I'd picked up when I bought the rainbowy material, and had kept hidden in the sewing room for a night like this.

It must have been near midnight when I saw the two beams of light swing across the yard. When I lived with Dad, there were lots of evenings when someone came to the house while I was alone, and I never got scared. And when I moved into Grandma Mae's house, I knew I would never suffer a moment's fear of intruders, not with Aunt Verdella and Uncle Rudy right across the road. But that was before Winnalee started bringing scary guys home from the Purple Haze—five since Chet. I stayed to the side of the window and peered out through a small gap in the curtain, hoping it wouldn't be somebody scary.

I sighed with relief when I recognized the outline of Tommy's truck. That is, until he opened his door and the interior light came on. Brody was with him.

I headed downstairs and yanked the door open. "What are *you* doing here?" I snapped at Brody as he was getting out of the truck. In a million years, I would have never guessed I could use that tone with Brody Bishop, but just the sight of him made me angry, and that made me brave. Brody blinked at me, so I turned to Tommy. "I can't believe you'd bring him here."

"Never mind that," Tommy said. "We were heading out for a beer and saw three squad cars heading down 8. We waited a bit, then followed to see what was going down."

"Man," Brody said. "The Purple Haze is lit like the Fourth of July. Pigs squealin' all over the place. This whole county can't have more than four cruisers, so they must have pulled in some pigs from other counties. They had the road blocked off and made us turn around."

My chest tightened. "Why? What happened?"

Brody's eyeballs lifted. "Duh."

"A drug bust, no doubt," Tommy said.

"A drug bust?"

Brody's eyeballs lifted. "What? You didn't know Reefer's a pusher? Everybody and their cousin knows that."

"I was coming to tell you," Tommy said, "thinking Winnalee was there. But I see she's off tonight."

I shook my head. "Winnalee's not here. She's working. I dropped her off myself. Something's wrong with her van."

"Man, she's screwed," Brody said.

Fear swirled in my stomach. "Can she get in trouble for

just being there as an employee?" I asked Tommy, as if he was supposed to know.

"Depends, I suppose, on what she's been doing."

"Yeah, well I can tell you what at least some of the girls there are doin'," Brody said with a chuckle. "At least the ones he's been bringing up from Chicago."

"What?" I asked.

"Christ, how dumb are you? Screwing for money, that's what."

"Winnalee wouldn't do something like that!"

"You don't think so, huh? She took her shirt off while she was in the cage a couple weeks ago," Brody tattled. "Reefer's been encouraging the girls to do that. You know, turning the place into a tittie bar."

"Shut up, Brody." I turned to Tommy. "I wonder what the cops will do?"

"Search the place," Tommy said. "Question Reefer and his slimy son, probably the staff, too. Maybe even the customers."

"Shit, I'm almost glad your cows got out and we had to go chase them all over hell, or we would have been there, too," Brody said, thinking only of himself, as usual.

I bit my cheek so hard that I winced. "What should I do?" I asked Tommy.

"Wait around until you hear something. Nothing else you can do."

I was pacing, wringing my hands, blood on my tongue.

"Man, oh man," Brody said. "Action in Dauber. About time!" He guffawed, like he was watching a TV sitcom.

Tommy could tell that I wanted to rip Brody in two. "Hey, buddy," he said. "Why don't you take my truck back to my place, get your car, and head out?"

"I can hang around," Brody said. "Thanks to Winnalee, I don't have any reason to go home."

"You are such an asshole," I snarled, surprising myself with the swear. Brody was about to smart-off back at me, but he stopped. Tommy could act like a goofy teenage boy when he was horsing around, but when things got tense or there was trouble, he clicked into man mode and authority engulfed him so that only an idiot wouldn't back down when he glared at them. "Beat it, Brody. I mean it."

"Shit," Tommy said after his truck pulled out. "I should have grabbed my flashlight from the truck before he took off. You got one?"

"What for?" I asked.

"Because we'd better start poking around her van before the fuzz do. Make sure Winnalee doesn't have any dope stashed for them to find."

My insides clenched. "You mean they'll come here and search her van?"

"I don't know, but I don't think we should take any chances."

I hurried into the kitchen, grateful that when I flicked on the flashlight, a ring of light, faint as it was, lit the counter. Tommy took it and I followed him out to Winnalee's van.

"Jesus!" Tommy said. He tossed a wad of Kleenex, a bunched rubber dangling from it into a semi-crushed box (did she *ever* throw those things out?). I looked away, my eyes painfully stretched, my cheeks hot.

We found a plastic bag under the front seat, crumbs of dried leaves tucked in one corner, and another bag under the passenger's side with two pills inside. The bag was stained where red food coloring had bled. Tommy took both bags and the Kleenex wad to the burning barrel and lit them on fire, then we sat on the front steps, the light from the porch patting our backs.

"Thanks for helping, Tommy. I know you don't like Winnalee."

"It's not that I don't like *her.* It's that I don't like the things she does. I know she's messed up, though." He nodded toward Aunt Verdella and Uncle Rudy's house. "Freeda's back, huh?"

"Yes. With Winnalee's baby."

"I thought maybe that was just a rumor."

Tommy stretched out his long legs and crossed them at the ankle, twining his fingers over his stomach. I looked up at the sky, smeared with stars and a bright three-quarter moon.

"So Winnalee isn't going to raise her kid, Freeda is?"

"I don't know," I said.

We sat quiet for a time, then Tommy asked, "Do you ever envy her?"

I blinked at him. "Because she has a baby?"

"No. Because she can let herself do whatever she wants. I envy Brody sometimes for that," he said. "Even though I'd despise myself if I did the things he did."

I drew my feet in until my heels bumped up against the steps, and wrapped my arms around my legs. I wasn't about to tell him that as much as I worried about Winnalee, there *were* times when I wished I had her same freedoms.

"You can bet," Tommy said, "that if Winnalee or Brody lost a parent and had a brother to raise, or a farm to run, they wouldn't do it."

Tommy slapped a mosquito on the back of his neck, then slouched over and pinned his elbows against his knees.

"What would you do if you could do anything?" I asked him.

Tommy shrugged. "Fly commercial planes," he said. "You?"

"I don't know. I like to sew, and Dauber feels like home, but maybe I'd like to visit other places."

"I just want to fly over them," he said.

Tommy was staring out over the darkened yard, and I was watching him, thinking about how little I knew about him, really. He had the same girlfriend all through high school, but I couldn't recall her name. Aunt Verdella thought she was sweet and Ada believed they'd marry someday. But then Mr. Smithy had his accident, and a year after graduation, she left Dauber to go off to school to become a nurse. Nobody talked about her after that.

Tommy settled back against the door and we sat quietly. "Owl," Tommy said after a hoot broke the silence.

"Button? That you?" I startled, and saw nothing but darkness, even though I knew my eyes were open. I could feel cement cold and hard under my butt, and damp cotton cool against my cheek. I lifted my head from Tommy's shoulder. *God!*

Tommy startled; he had dozed off, too.

I stood up and strained to see across the road. "Aunt Verdella?"

"Winnalee's on the phone, honey," she called.

"They always get one call," Tommy said.

We hurried across the yard. "What am I going to tell Aunt Verdella and Freeda?" I asked, my breath coming in scared huffs.

"Just wait and see what Winnalee has to say."

Winnalee hardly sounded rattled when I got to the phone, though she was almost whispering. "Can you come get me?"

"Where?" I asked, trying to sound casual, because Aunt Verdella was watching me, her hair standing on end like a toaster cozy rooster.

"At the Purple Haze," she said. "I'll explain later. Just hurry. I'll meet you on the road. Don't pull in, okay?"

I hung up the phone and tried to look as casual as possible. "Winnalee needs a ride home from work," I said. "Something's wrong with her van so I drove her there."

Aunt Verdella glanced up at the clock. "It's four in the morning. She works *this* late?"

"Tommy was keeping me company until I had to pick her up at two-thirty, but we dozed off on the steps," I said. Tommy looked down at his shoes.

Aunt Verdella clicked her tongue against her teeth. "Oh, that poor thing. She waited this long before calling? She probably didn't want to wake me, then decided she'd better, or she'd never get home."

"She's turning you into a liar," Tommy said as we headed for my place.

"And you've always been nosy," I said, making things between us feel normal again.

Tommy drove because I was too shook up to drive, but we took the Rambler because I was afraid Winnalee wouldn't recognize his truck in the dark. He started slowing down about a quarter mile short of the Purple Haze, when Winnalee stepped into the road.

She climbed into the backseat, reeking of beer.

I cranked around in my seat. "My God, Winnalee. What happened?"

"We got busted," she said. "I was on break, so I went out back to take a pee. I wasn't gonna go in the can when *those* bitches were in there. I was crouched down behind the bushes you puked on when it happened. The back door was open, and I heard the pigs shouting. Girls were screaming. A couple guys ditched out the back door. I just stayed down while those idiots searched the place. It took them forever, too."

"You must have been so scared," I said.

"No. I was pissed. That guy who was playing guitar now and then on weeknights? He was right with them—I'll bet he was undercover the whole time. Anyway, I climbed through the window in the guys' john after they hauled Reefer and Chet off to jail."

I reached back and clamped her knee. "You okay, though?"

"Yeah. My legs are scratched up a little from the brush, but that's about it. I'm tired as shit, though. Man, I hope those girls who wanted lace on their pants are smart enough to drop them off at the bridal shop, since that's where I told them you work."

I blinked, shocked that Winnalee would think of sewing at a time like this.

Tommy peered in the rearview mirror, even though it was too dark to see into the backseat. "You got anything stashed at Button's?" he asked, no sympathy in his voice.

"Course I don't. I don't do that shit in her house anymore, and Button knows it."

"You sure about that?" Tommy asked. "We found a nickel bag in your van with weed flakes in it, and another with a couple downers, too. That's about all they'd need."

"They were uppers, stupid. And they were old."

"It doesn't matter," I said. "We burned the evidence."

Winnalee sighed, and after a bit, said, "Shit. That was a good place to work, too."

CHAPTER

26

BRIGHT IDEA #35: If a kid says somebody blew the whistle, it could mean somebody tattled, or else it could mean that it's just time to come in from recess.

An officer came to the house mid-morning to question Winnalee. Boohoo was in his sandbox when they pulled in, so of course he had to run straight over—which, I suppose, was better than running inside to tattle.

While the officer drilled Winnalee about the Boumans—had she ever seen them exchange drugs for money? Had she ever had a customer hand her money to pass to the owner or his son, saying he "owed" it to them?—I held her hand and squeezed it now and then. Not because she was afraid, but because she was being mouthy. "Look, you *know* they were selling dope there because you found it, right? So why you asking me?"

"That your vehicle?" The officer asked, jerking his chin

toward her hippie mobile. Winnalee nodded. "You mind if we take a peek inside?"

Winnalee looked annoyed. "Don't you need a search warrant or something to do that?"

"We're asking nicely, not forcing entry into your van," the officer said, as he glanced at Boohoo, who was circling the squad car.

"Then no, you can't."

"Does this car make sirens like on TV?" Boohoo asked. The policeman nodded, then turned his attention back to Winnalee. I turned mine to Aunt Verdella's house, hoping the officer would leave before she or Freeda happened to glance outside.

He asked a couple more questions, then gave Winnalee a card, telling her to call him if she remembered anything else.

"I might be a cop when I grow up," Boohoo said as he tailed the officer to his car. "Else Spider-Man."

The officer patted Boohoo's head, then slid behind the wheel. Boohoo hung at the window and pointed from one gadget to another to ask what they did. "I'm sure the officer has work to do, Boohoo," I said, as I pulled him back.

"*Officer?* Is that another name for *cop*? Like *pig*?"

I couldn't tell if the cop was amused or insulted by Boohoo's question, but Winnalee sure thought it was funny. She cracked up as she headed back to the house, while my whole body cooked with embarrassment.

"Hey, officer, can you make the sirens go when you leave, like a real cop car? I like that sound."

"Boo . . ."

But it was too late. The cop was pulling out, his siren screeching *and* his lights flashing. Boohoo raced to the road to watch him leave, his skinny arm waving.

Out in the country, any time you heard a police siren it meant there was an accident or a fire, and you usually knew who the victims were by the direction of the noise. In a flash, Aunt Verdella's door opened and she flew out, holding her chest.

"Look at Aunt Verdella," Boohoo called to me. "She's hopping high as a kangaroo!" Freeda came out on the steps, her face full of questions.

I hurried to meet Aunt Verdella. "It was nothing. Nothing," I told her. "There was a drug bust at the Purple Haze last night, that's all, and he wanted to talk to Winnalee. He put on his siren for Boohoo."

"Oh dear, I knew we should have put her in the hospital!" Aunt Verdella said.

"Winnalee didn't do anything wrong," I told her. "The creeps running the place did. They arrested the Boumans, but are questioning everybody who worked there to see what they know. That's all."

I walked Aunt Verdella back to her yard, knowing if I didn't, Freeda would be over—and probably yelling—within seconds.

I explained everything all over again when we got to Freeda. I expected her to rant and rave, but she didn't. She only marched back into the house and got on the phone. She tapped her foot as she waited, then said, "Darla, put Terri on." And when she had her on the line, she said, "Terri, you're going to have to hold down the fort a bit longer, because I'm stuck on another battlefield."

I ditched out the door, and later, when Boohoo came back, I asked him what else Freeda had said on the phone. His answer was "Nothin' much. Just that if all this keeps up, they're gonna be hauling her to the *lunasylm*."

Two days later, on Dad's day off, he brought his toolbox over to my place to look at Winnalee's van. We were outside at the time and I checked the mailbox while Winnalee gave Dad her van's symptoms.

I was closing the mailbox—nothing from Jesse yesterday—when Freeda opened the front door, her hand shielding her eyes from the sun so she could see across the road. She came down the steps. "My cue to split," Winnalee said. "Yell if you need anything, Uncle Reece."

I waved to Freeda, who paused, then spun around and went back into the house. I followed Winnalee inside.

"She's putting the moves on your old man," Winnalee said as she flopped onto the couch.

"You're crazy," I said.

"No I'm not. She probably went back inside to put on some lipstick and perfume, then she'll be heading over here so she can get Uncle Reece all hot and bothered. You just watch. She'll be trying to get him to smile five seconds after she gets in the yard."

I went to grab a Tab and came back. "See what I mean?" Winnalee said, when Freeda's laughter filtered through the screens like a playful breeze. I sidled up to a window and peered through the lace curtain. Freeda wasn't *trying* to make Dad laugh. She *was* making him laugh. She was also holding Evalee.

Winnalee had her bare feet propped on the coffee table, her arms crossed. "Told ya," she said.

I didn't mean for Freeda to see me, but apparently she did, because she waved for me to come out.

"Take this kid inside before the sun cooks her, will you? Introduce her to her mommy while you're at it." I knew Winnalee wouldn't understand that I didn't have any choice.

Evalee's head mashed against my chest as she tried to hide from the bright sun. I didn't know about taking her inside without asking Winnalee first, but Evalee's head felt too warm already, and it's not like I wanted to stay standing outside with Dad there.

I patted Evalee's back and carried her up the steps.

"We, uh . . . have company," I said.

Winnalee, no doubt thinking I meant Freeda, shot up from the couch like she was going to raise a sword, if she had one. But when she saw I was holding Evalee, she stopped and just stood there, staring, her eyes pained even as a faint smile tugged at her mouth. She walked to us slowly, her eyes tearing. "Ohhhhhhh," she said. She took Evalee's hand.

"Do you want to hold her?" I asked, carefully.

Winnalee's eyes went round with fear, and her hands came up to crisscross each other. "I don't know how to hold a baby. She was eight days old when I split, and I didn't even know how to hold her then. I don't think Freeda really did, either."

"I'll show you. Sit down. Now put your feet back on the coffee table, and your knees together." I set Evalee down on her lap. "See? Your legs make a little La-Z-Boy for her."

"But she's gonna fall," Winnalee said.

"No she won't. Just keep your legs together."

"If you haven't noticed, I'm not exactly good at that." Winnalee didn't laugh at her joke, but I did. A little.

Winnalee kept her legs stiff, but the rest of her softened. "Awww, she *is* pretty," she said. "Real pretty. I'm glad, because that's one of the things I worried about when I was pregnant. You know, because maybe her dad's sperm was all junked up from drugs. I was afraid she'd be born with feet where her hands should be, or have a head as tiny as a pea, and her eyes cocked funny . . . something awful like that. Not that I wouldn't have loved her anyway, but man, Button, it's hard enough gettin' picked on at school because you're different in a *good* way."

Winnalee looked down at Evalee, who was kicking gently

against her stomach, while her mouth struggled to find her fist. "Now what do I do?"

I sat down beside them. "Talk to her. Sing to her. Something like that."

Winnalee started belting out a verse of Joplin's "Piece of My Heart" like it was a lullaby. "Look, she likes that song, too! Awww, she smiled at me."

I chuckled. "She doesn't even startle when you or Freeda raise your voices," I noted.

Winnalee turned to me. "Is she supposed to?"

"I don't know. But a lot of babies do that when people get loud. Boohoo did when he was around Aunt Verdella, until he got used to her."

Winnalee looked back at Evalee intently. "I don't want her getting used to people screaming and fighting."

"But you weren't doing . . ."

"Take her, Button."

"Take her?"

"Just take her, damn it," Winnalee ordered. I lifted Evalee from her lap.

Winnalee headed for the door, then stopped, probably because she remembered that Freeda was out there and that her van was broken. She turned and ran up the stairs.

CHAPTER 27

BRIGHT IDEA #96: When you go on a trip to buy a special surprise for your best friend, sing "You Are My Sunshine" and think of all the big people and the little people who are your sunshines. Then look at the old houses you pass, and think about the people who lived in them, and hope that they were somebody's sunshine, too.

One thing I liked about sewing was that it made sense. You had a pattern—even if someone else cut it out for you—and you followed it. You sewed seams together, keeping your eyes close to where you were stitching, and there was no worrying, no guesswork about how it would turn out.

For the next few days, Winnalee was quiet. A couple of times, she said she was going out for a while, and didn't say where she was headed. Maybe looking for work. Or maybe sitting down at Dauber Falls, thinking. I missed her. Even when she was right beside me at night, I missed her. But mostly, I worried.

. . .

Before Freeda came, Aunt Verdella was over at my place almost more than she was home. But not so much anymore. So she startled me when she suddenly appeared in my sewing room, so early that the dew was still on the grass. I hurried to shut my stereo off, but Aunt Verdella stopped me. "I like this song," she said, doing a little dance to the last chorus of "I Want You Back." She ha-ha'd when the song was over, then leaned and peered into the hallway. "Uh-oh, I probably woke Winnalee."

"No, she's not here."

Aunt Verdella cocked her head. "I didn't think she got up this early."

"She normally doesn't. She usually sleeps until nine or ten."

"Where'd she go?"

"I don't know. I was sleeping when she left. I'm sure she'll be back soon," I said, hoping I was right.

"Okay," she said, giving me a hug and cooing over the hardly made dress. "Your ma would be so proud of you, making your first wedding gown." I smiled, knowing this was true.

I moved some folded fabric off the only spare chair I had in the room and Aunt Verdella sat down. "Freeda's giving Cupcake her bath, and Boohoo and Rudy are out in the garden, so I thought I'd come see my favorite girl."

"Cupcake." I repeated the nickname that was starting to stick, and giggled.

Aunt Verdella tapped the bolt of fabric. "Oh, this is pretty. What's it for?"

"One of Cindy Jamison's bridesmaids' dresses. It isn't exactly what she wanted, but when I told her it was Winnalee's idea to do the dresses in the same fabric, only different colors, she decided it was cool."

Aunt Verdella smiled, then she tapped my arm excitedly. "You aren't gonna believe it, but I weighed myself this morning, and I lost four pounds since Freeda got here. In just one week!"

"Way to go, Aunt Verdella!"

"Freeda's helping me. She makes me eat my meals on a dessert plate—whatever I want, but not sweets—as long as I eat it on that plate. And if I try snitchin' anything from the pan or Boohoo's dish, she slaps my fingers like I'm a baby puttin' a fork in a light socket. Good thing, too, because I don't even notice I'm doin' it until she taps me."

I didn't know if people were supposed to notice a four-pound weight loss, but I pretended I did. "Your uncle Rudy couldn't tell. But that's a man for you. Freeda's going to color my hair tonight, too. She said it's two-toned. I didn't think it looked two-toned, did you?"

"I don't know . . . ," I said.

"Well, Fanny and Freeda sure did."

Aunt Verdella picked up a spool of thread and snagged the loose end back onto the groove along the rim. "She's sure got your dad coming out of his shell."

"Who? Fanny Tilman?" I joked.

Aunt Verdella laughed. "Oh, Button, you know who I meant. We drove over there last night to bring him some supper, and I couldn't believe how she got him laughin'. She decided his house better get fixed up before it crumbles, and like it or not, she's going to see that it does. I'm gonna watch Cupcake and she's going over there tonight after she does my hair and he heads to work, and she's gonna start ripping up that water-ruined linoleum in the kitchen." Aunt Verdella's laugh had the jitters. "He's probably gonna have a conniption fit, but Freeda said she'll deal with him."

"I wish she'd find a way to deal with Winnalee," I said.

The corners of Aunt Verdella's eyes drooped, and I was sorry I'd let those words pop out. "Oh, Button, she's trying, but those two . . . sometimes I think Freeda and Winnalee are just too much alike for their own good. Both are headstrong and set in their ways. But they love each other."

I nodded.

"Button, do you talk to Winnalee about Freeda?"

"I can't, Aunt Verdella. She just gets mad." I didn't mention that the last time I tried to, Winnalee cut me off, saying, "I'll cozy up to Freeda about the time you cozy up to your dad." Winnalee didn't realize that my situation was different: Freeda actually *loved* her. But she shut me up on that one, all the same.

Aunt Verdella shrugged. "I guess it's just harder to fix things with your blood relatives than it is to fix things with the family you choose."

Aunt Verdella stood up and peered out the window, pulling back the curtain. "What on earth is that boy doing now?" she said. "He was in the garden with Rudy when I left."

I stood up and squeezed beside her to take a look. Boohoo was by the lean-to, crouched over Knucklehead.

"He's probably wrapping him in yarn," I said.

"Well, he's up to something. That little dickens. Come on, walk me home."

Aunt Verdella must have noticed me staring longingly at the mailbox. "You must be waiting for some mail from that boy."

"He's taking me to a movie when he gets home on leave," I told her.

"Oh, boy." She giggled a little, then said, "My little Button, getting popular with the boys. But then I'd expect that, you being such a pretty, sweet thing. Tommy's gonna be jealous," she said in a singsong voice. I rolled my eyes. Aunt

Verdella *would* say that—even if *I'd* been born with feet where my hands should be, and a head the size of a pea. She always assumed that everyone loved me just as much as she did.

When we reached her yard, Knucklehead was standing on spindly legs drinking from his water dish, a Pampers strapped around his hindquarter and his tail poking out of a raggedy hole. Aunt Verdella laughed so hard that she had to cross her legs and hop to the house. "Good heavens, maybe *I'd* better start wearing Pampers!"

Winnalee came barreling down the road while we were still outside, and relief dropped my shoulders. Aunt Verdella was just about to tell me "one more thing," but a loud crash in the house interrupted her. "Oh dear, I'd better get inside and see what that boy did now."

Before I even reached the sandbox, Winnalee was coming out of our house—her duffel bag and army purse slung over her shoulder.

Panic slammed me in the stomach and I started running, shouting, "Winnalee! Where you going?"

Winnalee didn't look at me, she just hurried to her van all the faster. She yanked open the passenger door and tossed her bags in. "Winnalee!" I screamed. "What are you doing? Where are you going?"

She was already behind the steering wheel, and the metal door was hot to the touch when I hung my hands over the door frame.

"Crissakes, announce it to the whole world, will you?" she said. She glanced in her rearview mirror.

I was almost panting and near tears. "You've got your duffel bag."

Winnalee didn't look upset. She looked almost happy.

"I'm not leaving for good, Button," she said. "Just for a couple of days."

"Where are you going?"

"To Hopested, Minnesota, to see Hannah," she said. "To ask her if she'll raise my kid."

CHAPTER 28

BRIGHT IDEA #5: If your sister tells you that nine times seven is sixty-three, but you think it's sixty-seven, don't bother drawing nine dots and counting them seven times. You'll miss *Bewitched,* and be wrong anyway.

I stared at Winnalee in disbelief. Was this what she'd been contemplating when she slipped away? And did she *really* believe Hannah should raise Evalee? I'd heard Freeda confront Hannah with my own ears. I wanted to shout, "Are you crazy?" but instead, I said as calmly as I could, "Winnalee, you do know what happened to Freeda when she was little, right?" Winnalee's grip on the steering wheel whitened her knuckles. "Winnalee . . . look at me. You *do* know that your uncle Dewey was molesting Freeda when she was little, don't you? And when Freeda told, Hannah slapped her and called her a liar."

"Freeda *does* lie," Winnalee snapped.

"About little things maybe, but not about something like

this. Are you forgetting that I was there when Hannah showed up at Aunt Verdella's? That I saw Freeda confront her? Freeda brought up specific instances, Winnalee, and she was not lying. If you'd been there, you'd know it, too. It's why she rushed back to Hopested to get you. She'd learned that Dewey was back living with Hannah, and she wasn't about to let him hurt you. Yeah, maybe she was wrong in *how* she did it, but she wasn't wrong in getting you out of there."

"Yeah? Well, I'll tell you this much. After I leave Evalee, I'm never, ever gonna take her back. I wouldn't do that to her."

She glanced in the mirror again. "I've gotta go," she said.

Winnalee let the van roll backward, but I didn't let go of the door. "Wait!" I shouted. "I'm going with you."

"Why?" she asked, suspicion squinting her eyes.

Because I don't want you facing Dewey, Hannah, the truth, alone.

"Because I'm your best friend," I said. "And I could stand to get out of Dauber and go on a little adventure."

"Cool. Jump in," she said.

"I have to grab my purse," I told her. I glanced across the road. Our pens were always strung around the house, except for the one I always kept tucked in my stationery box. But it was upstairs, along with Winnalee's sketching pencils. But if I hurried, I could scratch Aunt Verdella a—

Winnalee interrupted my thoughts as if she'd heard them. "It should take you five seconds to run inside and grab it from the hook inside the door. You aren't back in that time, I'm pulling out without you."

So I got my purse and hurried back to the van, feeling every bit like I did at nine, and tagging along after Winnalee searching for beings that didn't exist.

Winnalee jutted out her chin to blow air into her face. "Roll your window down, will you?" She shook her head. "I don't know how you can stand wearing jeans in summer. You make me sweat just looking at you." Winnalee flicked on the radio then, and turned it up until the dashboard pulsed. She bounced with the music, and sang with carefree abandonment, as though we were two hippies going off to Woodstock.

CHAPTER

29

BRIGHT IDEA #10: Never eat cotton candy in the rain.

When we got to Hopested, Winnalee started pointing out the stores she remembered, and I had to reach over and grab the wheel a few times, or we would have rammed into the cars parallel-parked on Main Street. "Oh, oh, Ma got her prescriptions filled at that drugstore right there! I always got Pixy Stix." And "Oh, oh, there's the Laundromat where we used to go. I liked climbing in the dryer and pretending it was my spaceship. And that restaurant, right next to it? Right there? A lady named Doris worked there. She always gave me extra pickles." Winnalee spotted the flag waving above the rooftops a few blocks ahead. "My school! I didn't know it was *this* close to town!"

When the one-story brick building came into sight, Winnalee swerved to the curb rather than pulling into the empty parking lot, and jumped out. "Oh my God, look at how small it is! Come on," she said. She took off running.

I tagged her into the school yard, where she stopped and spun in slow, starstruck circles. "Isn't it cool?" It looked like most every other school building to me: one story, brick, windows lined in rows like desks, with a blacktopped playground filled with the usual assortment of equipment: swings, a slide, a jungle gym, a merry-go-round.

There was something heartbreaking about watching Winnalee cupping her hands over the sides of her face to peer in the windows. "My kindergarten room!" she shouted. "They still have the little playhouse! Come see, Button. Come see!" She pointed out where they lined up to get their milk, and where the napping mats were kept. "And there's the table I fell against when I tripped over my shoelace. I split my lip open. Ma thought it would scar, but it didn't."

Winnalee took off for the playground toys, giggling like she was five again, while I tried to subdue the unease I felt when I heard Winnalee call Hannah *Ma*. She insisted that I get on the merry-go-round with her, then spun us until the horizon smeared, and leapt off before the spinning stopped. "Come on!" she yelled. I dragged my foot in the dirt until the merry-go-round stopped and staggered after Winnalee.

Winnalee hiked up her long dress and tied it in a knot at her thigh, then climbed up the monkey bars. She braced her feet on the two opposing poles near the top and elevated herself up above the highest tower. She lifted her arms above her head, and shouted, "Winnalee Malone! Maker of Magic! Fairy of Fun! Princess of the Playground!" She peered down and giggled. "Debbie Rutherford used to get *so* mad at me when I'd say that. So I'd do this . . ." She stepped down one wrung and clutched the bars. Then, using her whole body, she jerked side to side so that the jungle gym wobbled. Winnalee stopped.

"She'd scream then, because she thought I was using magic to make the bars shake. Like I could make the whole thing crumble and crash to the blacktop and bury her alive if I wanted to."

Winnalee didn't climb down until her cheeks were flushed, then she stood quietly, blinking against the breeze as she looked over the playground and building. "Freeda didn't have any right taking me away," she said slowly. "I was happy here. I could have stayed in the same school for all my grades."

We stopped at a gas station I was sure I remembered from my trip to Hopested with Aunt Verdella when I was nine. I used the restroom first, then Winnalee. While she was gone, I dug in my purse for change. I wasn't sure how much a three-minute call home would cost, but certainly more than the few cents I managed to scrounge up. There were two customers waiting in line, and the old clerk was so putzy that I knew I wouldn't have time to cash a couple of dollars before Winnalee stepped out. I dialed O for the operator and told her I wanted to make a collect call.

Boohoo answered.

"Collect call from Evelyn Peters. Will you accept the charges?" the operator asked.

"You ain't Evy. Who is this?" Boohoo asked.

"Operator, he's only six years old. He doesn't understand," I hurriedly explained.

"Collect call from Evelyn Peters. Will you accept the charges?" she repeated, as if I hadn't spoken.

Say yes, Boohoo. Say yes!

"Boohoo? Who's on the phone?" Aunt Verdella's voice sounded far away, like maybe she was talking from the living room, or even out on the porch. *Give her the phone, Boohoo. Please!*

"It's Crackpot again," Boohoo groaned, and the line went dead.

"I'm sorry, Miss. The party you dialed did not accept charges. Please try again another time." She hung up.

The restroom door opened, just as I was hurrying to press down the receiver so I could try again. "You called them, didn't you?" Winnalee barked from across the room. The elderly clerk leaned around a customer to gawk. Winnalee marched down an aisle lined with motor oil and antifreeze, her eyes pinched.

"I tried to," I said when she reached me. "Aunt Verdella will be worried sick tonight when we don't show up and she doesn't know where we are."

"What did you tell her? I don't want Freeda knowing my business."

"Nothing. I didn't get to talk to her. I called collect and Boohoo answered."

The clerk grabbed a pen and peered out at Winnalee's van. When Winnalee noticed, she snapped, "Geez, we're eighteen. Legal adults. Not a couple of stupid-assed runaway kids!"

Hannah's house was small and dirty white. A section of the roof on the nearby barn was caved in, and broken farm equipment was scattered across the overgrown yard. A stack of windows, some broken, were leaned up against the house, and chickens were feeding near the front door.

Winnalee stopped the van and pointed. "I remember them," she said, as if the chickens could possibly be the same birds that had been there when she was a kid.

A face appeared in a window, the head too small to belong to someone the size of Hannah. Winnalee grabbed her fatigue-green purse off the seat and we got out. "I'm nervous," she whispered. I took her hand.

A man opened the door before we cleared the chipped cement steps. He was short and had narrow shoulders. His eyes were bright blue, like Winnalee's, and his boyishly round face looked at odds with the Uncle Rudy–deep wrinkles. He reached up and scratched his grizzly cheek.

"Uncle Dewey?" Winnalee asked.

"Who is it, Dew?" came a wheezy voice from inside.

Winnalee started crying then, and brushed past Dewey. He backed up and let me in, tipping an imaginary hat. I stepped over the ladies' flats with sides stretched wide like boats and an array of work boots that cluttered the doorway, and followed Winnalee into the kitchen. Hannah—every bit as big as I remembered—was sitting at the table, a sheet of notebook paper pinned under her forearm. She had to be at least fifty—Freeda was thirty-three—but any lines that had tried crinkling her face had obviously been stretched to lie flat. She still wore a crucifix around her neck, but either a different one than the one she wore to Dauber, or the same one on a longer chain, because it was no longer embedded in the folds of her neck.

"Maaaaaaaaaaa," Winnalee cried, as if she'd just jumped out of our magic tree and landed in yesteryear.

Hannah looked confused for a moment, then a cry escaped from a round mouth that looked as small as a Cheerio on a face that size. Her hand came up to pat over her chest, as if she was feeling for her heart. "Winnalee?" she whimpered. She didn't get up, but swiveled herself to the side. I tried hard not to stare at her belly, which filled her lap to her knees.

Winnalee rushed forward, wrapping her arms around Hannah. "Ma, Ma," she kept repeating, as she sobbed like a baby. Hannah was wheezing tears every bit as heartfelt as Winnalee's, as she patted her back. I felt overwhelmed as I watched. Up until she was five, Winnalee'd believed that Hannah was her ma. And for the next four years, she'd believed that Hannah was dead. Now here she was, crying in her arms. I dabbed at my eyes, happy for Winnalee, but wishing that it could be me hugging Ma, four years later, because her death had all been one big, fat lie.

"Dewey, Dewey," Hannah said, her double chin smashed against Winnalee's arm. "It's Winnalee. Praise the Lord, it's Winnalee."

Dewey stood near the wall, watching them.

Winnalee sniffled hard as she sobbed and laughed at the same time. The bathroom door was open, so I slipped inside to look for Kleenex. The room was bare, but for two limp towels, and it smelled like urine. Mottled dirt huddled near the floorboards, and a gummy film edged the tub. I couldn't find any Kleenex, so I unrolled two lengths of toilet paper and brought them into the kitchen. Winnalee and Hannah paused in their hugging to take the toilet paper wads, and I backed up, looking away to give them their privacy.

The kitchen, like the bathroom, was void of any clutter. There wasn't even a set of canisters on the counter, or a spoon rest on the stove. No rugs were scattered on the linoleum, and the sink and dish drainer were empty. The bareness of the room gave the illusion of cleanliness at first, but a closer look revealed black crud gumming the base of the faucet, and scum outlining the ridges on the dish drainer. Spatters of food were dried on the stove top and splotched the floor. I remembered how our already clean house had to become spotless after Boohoo got mobile, and I flinched to think of Evalee crawling around this mess.

"This is Button," Winnalee told Hannah as she straightened, nodding toward me. "She's been my best friend since I was nine."

If Hannah realized that I was the big-eared kid who'd let her into Aunt Verdella's house once, she didn't show it. Her arms loosened from Winnalee and dropped to the table, as if exhausted. "And this is your uncle Dewey," she told Winnalee. "You wouldn't remember him because the last time you saw him you were still in diapers."

Dewey gave a tobacco-speckled grin. "Give your uncle a hug," Hannah said as she sniffled.

"Ain't she pretty, Dew? Prettier than Freeda ever was." I tried to imagine Aunt Verdella comparing me and Boohoo like that, but I couldn't.

"But not as pretty as me," Dewey joked. The three of them laughed.

"I never thought I'd see you again, Winnalee," Hannah said. "Praise the Lord for bringing you back to me." She broke into fresh tears, and they continued to leak as she explained that she was making up a grocery list for Dewey to take to the store. "Dewey's been on the road for two weeks, and I'm down to nothing," she said. "I should make something special tonight. Anything you want, honey."

Winnalee's eyes cocked to the side. "Spaghetti! The kind you always made that comes in a box, with that little can of sauce and packet of powdered cheese."

"Dew, look up there," Hannah said, nodding toward the cupboard above the stove. "It should be a red box."

Dewey fumbled around, not even checking behind other boxes and cans, so Hannah asked me to look. My too-short shirt rode up my belly as I reached, and I paused to tug it back down, glancing at Dewey as I did so.

I found one box, but Hannah decided we needed another.

"Oh, oh!" Winnalee said. "And doughnuts! Can you make doughnuts? I never got doughnuts after I left here. Not even store-bought ones." She turned to me. "Ma makes the best raised doughnuts in the whole world. They melt on your tongue like snowflakes, only they taste a whole lot better."

Hannah laughed, then directed me and Winnalee around

the kitchen with her finger, having us check her lard supply—lard made better pastry than shortening, she said—and dig in the bottom cupboard to see how much flour she had. I flinched at the tiny white worms that were curled around the bottom of the crumpled flour bag. "Just throw that out," Hannah said. "It looks almost empty."

Dewey stuffed Hannah's list in his shirt pocket, but dawdled near the door, grinning and listening. "Dewey," Hannah said, "are you gonna stand there all day gawking at these pretty girls, or are you gonna get to the store? Go on now!" I glanced at Winnalee to see if that comment made her squirm, too. But she was crouched down, digging in the cupboard for the big yellow glass bowl that she remembered them making doughnuts in.

After Dewey left, Hannah broke out in tears again. "I just can't believe you're here." I wondered if she cried a lot on regular days, too. "I thought it would kill me when Freeda took you away. You were my baby girl. You cuddled with me and loved me no matter what I looked like." Winnalee set the bowl on the counter and melted against Hannah like butter. I cringed with shame. *I'd* noticed what Hannah looked like.

Hannah yanked the chair next to hers. "Sit down, honey," she told Winnalee. "You too," she said to me.

Hannah talked about her bad knees, her bad hips, her high blood pressure, and a host of other ailments. "I can't even get to church anymore with these knees," she said. "Not even with my walker. Janis Marshall used to take me. She still stops on Sundays, at least, and drops off the program."

"Awww, Ma," Winnalee said. I waited for Hannah to ask Winnalee about her life since she'd left. She hadn't yet, and that didn't seem right somehow.

"I was so worried about you . . . ," Hannah said, shaking her head, and I breathed out a relieved sigh. "So scared that Freeda would lead you down the same bad path she'd taken. I prayed every day that that wouldn't happen, and hoped my prayers would work just as well here, as in church." She shook her head. "I don't know what went wrong with that girl. Lord knows I tried to teach her the difference between right and wrong." Hannah half patted, half squeezed Winnalee's arm, which looked as tiny as Evalee's in Hannah's meaty grip. "Just tell me that *you're* still my good girl. That you didn't turn out like Freeda. I couldn't bear it if you told me anything differently."

Winnalee winced, and I knew it wasn't from the pressure of Hannah's hand.

"Winnalee is as good as they come," I said, surprising Winnalee and myself for speaking up. "She's caring and loving, and tries to do the right thing."

Hannah looked pleased, so I forced myself to smile at her. I wanted to *mean* that smile, but my lips felt tight against my teeth. I looked down, frustrated with myself. Hannah was being Aunt Verdella–affectionate, and was going out of her way to see that Winnalee's homecoming was a true celebration. Shouldn't a grandmother every bit as affectionate as a loving, devoted aunt deserve a smile that opened like a friendly hug? And maybe she'd handled things with Freeda horribly, but people changed. Ma changed. Still, in spite of the pep talk I gave myself, there was something that kept me from giving her a genuine smile. Something as sharp as my bones against the wooden seat beneath me. Something that made me feel as shaky as the uneven legs that swayed my chair when I rose.

Hannah looked up at me. "Did you need something, dear?"

"No. No," I said. "I'm just getting a little sore from sitting."

Hannah laughed. "No wonder. You don't have an ounce

of meat on that rump. We'll change that when Dewey gets back, though."

"I think I'll go outside and stretch my legs for a little bit. Give you two a chance to catch up." They didn't try to stop me.

The chickens scattered when I got outside. I stood a few feet from the steps and tucked my hair behind my ears. This was where Freeda had played when she was little. Winnalee, too, for the first five years of her life. I tried to picture them here—Freeda running free, the sun coloring her skin to copper. Winnalee, her loopy hair dancing as she unearthed treasures—but I couldn't. Not in this yard, scattered with rusty metal sharp enough to cut and poison tender skin. Not in this house, dripped with stains like dirty brown tears on the outside, filthy on the inside.

There was really no place to walk. I feared stepping on something sharp, and the wood ticks that had to be thick in a lawn as tall as a field. Walking close to the house didn't appear to be an option, either: Thistle clumps circled the house, and shards of busted glass were jabbed into the yellowed grass beneath the leaning windows. I went to the stubby driveway and shuffled in tight, restless circles. I was thinking of Winnalee's desperate cry when she first saw Hannah, and how she had called her "Ma." And I was wondering how on earth Winnalee had found a way to remember this house, this home, this family, as every bit as magical as fairies.

I stood for a time, kicking at the pebbles on the dirt, wondering what Boohoo was doing at the moment, and whether Uncle Rudy was still in the garden, or settled in for the local news. I wondered what Aunt Verdella was cooking for supper. I could almost see her glancing out the window as she cooked, and again after the dishes were done. Then once night settled in, realizing our lights weren't on and fussing to Uncle Rudy and Freeda that we should have been home by now, and wearing herself ragged trying to guess where we'd gone. I stared at Hannah's house, and longed for my own.

"Button? Button!" Winnalee called as she busted out of the door and leapt down the front steps.

"Come on," she said. "I've got something to show you."

Winnalee disappeared behind the house, and I followed.

She was jumping up and down in front of an oak tree, her face turned up. "She said she didn't think anybody took it down. That it should be here."

"What are you looking for?" I asked, so I could help her find it.

"The wind chime I made. Right before Freeda took me. I found these copper pipes in a bucket in the barn, all different sizes, and I strung them from an old hubcap. I used a fat branch in the center for the pipes to clang against. It was really pretty cool, and it made cool sounds, too. Like a real wind chime." She cocked her head to listen. "Why can't I hear it? You'd think I could at least hear it."

She hoisted up the hem of her dress and stepped high to circle the tree. "Button, if I hung something on a low branch thirteen years ago, how far up would that branch be now?"

I smiled. I had thought that trees grew from the trunk up, too, until Uncle Rudy set me straight. "Trees don't grow taller from the bottom, Winnalee. The branches get longer, the trunk thickens, but the growth happens at the top so it would be hanging at the same height."

And then I spotted it, tethered to a branch by a long loop of plastic-coated wire, the kind Aunt Verdella made Christmas wreaths with. The wood hanging in the center of the chime was gray and pocked and rotted to a stub. "It's right here."

Winnalee squealed. "Where? Where?"

She bounced with excitement when I reached out and whacked the copper pipes against one another so they'd jangle.

Winnalee batted at the chime again, giggled, then stopped when the sound of a vehicle joined the chimes. "Come on. I think Uncle Dewey's back. Let's go make doughnuts!" She headed toward the house.

I didn't want to go help Dewey carry in groceries, or eat spaghetti that came from a box, or make doughnuts. Revulsion churned in my stomach, and I was stiff with fear. All I wanted to do was leave.

But I followed Winnalee anyway.

Winnalee was scooping flour straight from the bag into a sifter. "You always let me sift the flour, remember?" she said to Hannah, twirling the green-capped handle, and bent to watch the flour float into the bowl like a snowfall.

"And you always made a mess," Hannah said, then gave a wheezy laugh.

"I'm not kidding, Button. These doughnuts are the best you'll ever taste."

I thought of the story Freeda told when she confronted her mother. How Dewey had held her on his lap, right across the table filled with cut doughnuts, his hand in her underwear. Hannah had sat across from them as though nothing horrible was happening, even while tears ran silently down Freeda's cheeks. I wondered if Freeda was being held on this side of the table, in this very chair when it happened, and the thought made me feel sick to my stomach.

Hannah instructed Winnalee from her stool, and Dewey teased her that she had more flour on her dress than in the bowl. I scrubbed the table good, and took a turn helping Winnalee knead the dough. Hannah greased the bowl, rubbed the mound of dough until it was shiny, then flipped it and covered the bowl with a towel. She set it in front of the window so the sun could plump it.

I felt like a bad person, the way I kept noticing Hannah's fat. Like the way her short hair—the silver strands straight and thick like the handles on Fourth of July sparklers—bent over the rolls at the base of her neck, so that when she looked down and the roll smoothed some, the hem of her hair stayed bent in a downward curl. And try as I might, I couldn't stop staring at the way her upper arms were made of bulges, and pocked like rotted wood. It wasn't nice to notice those things, so I turned away so I couldn't. God and Ma were catching me, I reminded myself. Probably wanting me to remember that my scrawniness wasn't exactly pretty, either.

While the dough was rising, Hannah moved to a stool propped at the stove and made spaghetti and heated two cans of corn. After we ate, Hannah instructed us to go upstairs to strip the bedding in the guest room. "You can't sleep on dirty sheets," she said. "I got a washer and dryer downstairs now, though I wish Dewey would move them up here so I could get to them."

"Which room used to be yours?" I asked, as Winnalee led me past two closed doors.

"I had a crib in Ma's room downstairs. After I got too big for that, she tried to move me up here. But I didn't like being upstairs alone—Dewey lived in Colorado then—so she ended up letting me sleep downstairs by her."

Winnalee stopped before the last room at the end of the hall. The only one with the door hanging open. "This is the guest room. I think it used to be Freeda's."

The room was small, the walls the color of brown mustard. It was empty, but for a bed and a small nightstand. The sheets smelled musty as we tugged them off the mattress. "Winnalee, did you tell Hannah why you're here? You know . . . about Evalee?"

"Button, we just got here."

I bit my cheek. "Winnalee, I hope you'll reconsider this whole thing. Hannah . . . she's not, well, in good enough health to take care of a kid. Maybe she could handle it while Evalee's this young, but she'll be crawling and walking soon. Think of how much running around Aunt Verdella has to do with Boohoo."

"She's always had bad knees and bad hips and stuff," Winnalee said, her chin set. "And she took good care of me."

I looked down and yanked the corner of the fitted sheet free. "How long are we staying?" I blurted out. "I have sewing to do." *And this house is a hellhole!*

Winnalee went still, the pillow she was holding dangling half in and half out of its case. "Button, I haven't seen her in thirteen years. Would it hurt you to stay a night or two for my sake?" Winnalee jerked the pillowcase free, wadded it up, and tossed it toward the hallway.

"No," I said quietly, as the pillowcase drifted behind the half-opened door. "I'm sorry."

I rolled the sheets and kicked the door closed with my foot so I could grab the pillowcase. I bent and paused, shocked by the childish graffiti that covered the inside of the door.

I straightened up, still staring. At my eye level, the words *Fuck You* were carved into the thick paint in angular letters, clear down to the wood. A trail of triangles—tears? blood?—ran from the words. Drawings in faded black marker filled the bottom third of the door. It was the picture in the center, drawn with skill no greater than that of a kindergartner, that held my attention, though. A rectangle formed the body, and straight lines made the limbs. A round head floated above it, and a wide smile stretched across the circular face. Two dots formed the eyes, and from the bottom of each ran an unbroken line, all the way to her L-shaped feet. Red marker was scribbled across the floating, smiling, crying face.

My insides went cold, even as my skin was damp from the stuffy, upstairs air. The dirty sheets turned slimy in my fists and I dropped them. I stepped back.

Winnalee scooped up the bedding—she was humming "Who'll Stop the Rain"—and kicked the door open so wide that it banged against the wall. She stopped in the hall and looked at me. "You coming?"

I started after her. "I want to go home," I murmured.

She turned around so fast that the toes of her sandals butted up against mine. "Why?"

The skin on the inside of my elbows quivered and I clawed at them. "I just do," I said, not wanting to lie, yet not knowing how to tell her the truth, either.

Winnalee shook her head. "I shouldn't have brought you here. You never stayed overnight at my place when we lived in Dauber the first time. I'll bet you never stayed at Penny's, either, even after you were older."

No amount of scratching was quieting my skin. "It's not that," I said.

"Why then? Because you don't like Hannah? I saw the way you were staring at her, Button. Like she's some kind of circus freak."

"No, no." I tried to keep my voice hushed so they wouldn't hear us downstairs, even though I doubted they could over their playful banter. "It's him," I said. "He gives me the creeps."

"Uncle Dewey?" She rolled her eyes. "Why? Because Freeda told you bad things about him?" She didn't mention the drawings on the door. "Well, she's a liar. I've told you that a hundred times already, even though I shouldn't have to. She told me Ma was dead. Isn't that proof enough to make you question the things she said about Uncle Dewey?"

The air felt too thick to breathe, and my legs felt weak.

Say it, don't scratch it.

Say it, don't scratch it.

"He was staring at my boobs," I told her.

"Guys do that, Button. You know that."

"But they don't stare at their niece's butt."

Winnalee's lips puckered. "Why are you doing this?" she asked, her words a pleading whisper.

I didn't know what to say. What to do. So I just stood there, itching.

"Fine. I'll take you home in the morning," she said, spinning around to face the stairs. "When I go to pick up Evalee."

I worked the doughnut cutter, keeping the circles close together and making neat rows, as if everything would be fine as long as I kept the cuts in a perfect line. One. Another one. Then another—putting all my energy into butting the metal doughnut cutter up against the last doughnut without cutting a tiny half-moon into its soft side.

At the counter, Hannah watched the dough sizzle. "You have to watch for the browning edges. And be sure you don't puncture the skin when you flip them, otherwise grease pools inside. I'll tell you when to flip them." I looked up as Hannah was reaching for a cookie sheet lined with paper towels. "Dewey, move," Hannah scolded. "This grease is hot."

Dewey reached across Winnalee and grabbed a handful of doughnut holes from the platter in front of Hannah. She slapped at his hand. "Dewey, those aren't even sugared yet!" Dewey laughed like a naughty little boy.

"Oh, turn those two right there, honey," she told Winnalee. "That's right. That's right."

I should have kept my eyes on my work, I told myself later. If I had, I wouldn't have seen Dewey turn toward me, his cheeks bulging with doughnuts holes, two more cupped in his hands. He grinned, flashing teeth caked with mashed doughnuts, then dropped his hand down so the doughnut holes rested at his crotch.

It was so quick that it was easy to tell myself that maybe he hadn't meant it like *that*.

"Dewey, stop that and get out of the kitchen," Hannah scolded. Dewey raised his eyebrow at me and popped the two holes into his mouth, just as Winnalee was fishing more doughnuts out of the grease. "Get it! Get it! Stab that doughnut right in the hole," Dewey said, then glanced back at me and snickered.

I stared down at the dough, plump and soft and white as Evalee's skin, and I wanted to scoop it from the table, tuck it back in the bowl, and cover it with its dish-towel blanket. There was a telephone hanging on the wall, the cord looped like Winnalee's hair, and I longed to yank it loose and call home. Ask somebody to come get me, like I'd done the night of Penny's slumber party when I was in fourth grade and scared of the Ouija board.

"Dewey, I mean it. You're in the way. Go watch TV or something!"

I stared at the circles of dough, blinking hard, the taste of blood in my mouth. The table jostled, but I didn't look up. Not until Winnalee snapped, "Did you just grab my ass?"

Winnalee was holding the long-handled fork, drops of grease dripping from the tines. She stared at Dewey, her mouth hanging open. Then she turned to Hannah. "Uncle Dewey just grabbed my ass."

"Winnalee!" Hannah said.

"I was just pattin' you out of the way," Dewey said, and Hannah mimicked his words like a parrot.

"He was just pattin' you out of the way, honey."

"No," Winnalee protested. "That isn't what he did. You saw him! You were looking right over here. He patted my ass first, then he rubbed it. Like this." She tossed the fork onto the counter and rubbed her behind hard enough to tug her dress along with her hand.

"Oh, Winnalee. Honey, please don't use that profane language like your mother. It lowers a girl, talking like that."

I was on my feet in a flash, my back to the wall. My purse and Winnalee's were lying on the heap of shoes in the doorway, and I edged over to scoop them up.

Winnalee was staring at Hannah, her eyes so big, so pretty, so hurt. "But he . . ."

Dewey grabbed another handful of doughnut holes and moseyed out of the room. For a moment, there was no sound but the sizzling of hot grease. Then Hannah shouted, "The doughnuts!" She reached for the long fork, and the sizzling grew fainter with each doughnut she plucked from the pan.

A TV in the next room clicked on. The local weather. *A sixty percent chance of rain tonight* . . .

Winnalee was still staring at Hannah. "Maaa . . . ," she whimpered, her voice as weak as a kitten's.

"Come on now, Winnalee. We gotta get more dough in here before this grease burns."

"But he grabbed me," she said to Hannah, who was busy lifting pale white circles of dough from the table and dropping them into the hot grease. "Ma?"

Hannah didn't look up.

Winnalee turned to me. Her cheeks slack, her eyes a muddied blue.

I held out my hand and mouthed the words, "Let's go."

Winnalee circled the table, catching the edge with her hip as she reached for my hand. She moved like a sleepwalker as I pulled her down the stubby hall.

"Winnalee?" Hannah called.

"It's okay. It's okay," I kept saying, because by the time we got down the front steps, she was bawling. I hurried us across the yard, weaving as if the metal scraps were land mines.

I helped her into the passenger side and buckled her in. I shut the door and ran around to the driver's side.

Hannah was in the kitchen window, leaning forward, as if her arms were too weary to prop her up straight. Her hand was over her mouth.

I jerked open the driver's door. Winnalee was staring at the house. She turned to me, her eyes screaming, *I don't understand!*

I looked back at the house. At the scraggly lawn filled with broken things that could cut the flesh of children. I could see Winnalee running with a pail of copper pipes, her long loops floating behind her like strands of Harvest Gold yarn. Her hands working hard and her spirit working even harder to bring some music, some magic to this horrible place. I peered into the van. "I'll be right back," I told Winnalee.

I didn't run. I walked. In long, determined strides. I could feel someone watching me as I passed the front steps, but I didn't look, and I didn't speed up. I wasn't scared that Dewey or Hannah would come outside and try to stop us, because a new awareness had come to me like a Bright Idea: I was armed with the truth, and the truth, for some, was something that could cut far deeper than scrap metal.

At the oak tree, I unwound Winnalee's wind chime, determined not to leave even one tiny part of the little girl Winnalee once was behind. The copper pipes sang out as I carried it to the van.

Winnalee was curled up like a baby when I opened the door. Her legs were tucked under her dress, and her arms were wrapped around her head.

"Get me out of here," she begged, and I assured her that I would. I gently set the wind chime behind my seat and climbed in, and we drove away in rain that glossed the roads to black.

Winnalee cried herself to sleep, and didn't wake but for the brief moment when we reached St. Croix Falls and I smoothed the tangled hair from her face and asked her if she had to pee. She shook her head no. I locked the van, went inside, and made a collect call to Aunt Verdella. I didn't know what Winnalee would think of me telling them where we'd gone and what had happened, but now that it was over, I wasn't feeling so brave anymore, and all I wanted was Aunt Verdella's arms.

"Oh no," Aunt Verdella cried after I told her where we'd gone, and what had happened. "Freeda, they'd gone to see Hannah. Dewey made a pass at Winnalee. No, no, he didn't hurt her . . . Button, did he hurt her?"

I told her how he'd touched her, and Aunt Verdella started to cry. "Oh, that poor baby." She repeated the story to Freeda, who bellowed cusswords about killing "that sick son of a bitch."

Winnalee was awake when I got back to the van, and she talked the rest of the way home, her emotions roller-coasting with hurt, anger, confusion, and grief. "It's like Hannah died to me twice now," she said.

I reached over and held her hand, waiting for her to mention Freeda. She didn't until we were passing through Dauber. "She saved me from getting hurt when I was little, didn't she?" She sounded confused about how on earth she couldn't have known that until now. "I feel so stupid."

I squeezed her hand. "You just wanted to believe something good."

It was after two in the morning when we pulled into Aunt Verdella's driveway. The kitchen light was on, and the door opened before we even got out of the van. Freeda came out first, Aunt Verdella on her heels, their arms opening. I grabbed on to Aunt Verdella, and over her shoulder I saw Freeda hugging Winnalee. Winnalee's arms were straight at her sides, her head facedown against Freeda's shoulder.

They stayed outside talking, while Aunt Verdella and I dozed on the couch, me with my head on her lap. Freeda and Winnalee didn't come in until the sky started brightening and the birds were chirping. They dropped into Uncle Rudy's recliner side by side and slept. Neither of them woke when Evalee and Boohoo did.

CHAPTER 30

BRIGHT IDEA #13: Just because a girl is wearing a raggy dress and ugly brown shoes and doesn't have milk money, doesn't mean you've gotta let her pull your hair.

The summer after Ma died, I was standing in the middle of the living room, watching a storm rage outside the window. Uncle Rudy was lowering himself into his favorite chair with the *Dauber Daily*, and he glanced up. "In a little bit, those storm clouds will have pushed off, leaving nothing behind but blue skies," he said. "Storms never last forever, Button."

I thought of his promise a couple of mornings after our trip to Hopested, when we woke to skies so bright and blue that it stung your eyes when you stepped outside. Sure, questions about the future hovered in the air like rising fog. Yet no one seemed concerned—not even me—because when Freeda and Winnalee woke that morning after Hopested, they were behaving how they had in the past, which meant that their storm had passed.

"Crissakes, Winnalee. It's just a shit diaper. It won't kill you," Freeda said as she shoved a disposable diaper and a cleansing cloth into Winnalee's hands the afternoon of our return.

Winnalee was sitting cross-legged on the floor, Evalee lying on a blanket before her. "I'll gag," she said as she gingerly lifted Evalee's legs. "Maybe even throw up. Freeda, come on, you know I have a weak stomach. Especially when I'm overtired."

"Yeah, well, time to muscle it up," Freeda said.

"Just cross her ankles with one hand, and hold her legs up out of the way," Aunt Verdella called from the kitchen.

"How?" Winnalee asked.

"Like this." Freeda demonstrated, while Boohoo stood nearby reciting, "Cupcake's a poopy pants. A poopy, puppy, poopy pants!" Freeda was crouched down beside Winnalee, giving step-by-step instructions that could hardly be heard above Boohoo's chanting. I told him to quiet down as I checked the window for the mailman, since I thought I'd heard a car.

"Boohoo, come on, knock it off," Winnalee said, as she struggled to undo the diaper tabs while holding Evalee's legs high. "You're getting her all rowdy and she keeps kicking."

Boohoo revved up the tempo of his little song and started hopping in place.

"Boohoo, you're going to jump on her head if you keep that up," Freeda snapped.

He started clapping his hands. "Here, Cupcake. Here, Cupcake!" He followed this with cartoon sounds.

"Boohoo!" Aunt Verdella and I called in unison.

"Damn it, Boohoo. Knock it off right now!" Winnalee snapped.

"Winnalee. Don't cuss at kids," Freeda said.

Evalee wiggled a foot loose from Winnalee's grasp. "She got her heel in it!" Winnalee moaned.

"Okay, that's it!" Freeda said. "You've been acting up for days now, Boohoo. Tying Aunt Verdella up again when she dozed off after lunch . . . swiping more diapers to put on Knucklehead, even after we told you no more because those things cost money. Enough!"

"Cupcake's a poopy heel. A poopy puppy with a poopy heel."

Freeda scrambled to her feet and lunged. Boohoo dropped to his knees and scampered under the table. She grabbed him at the ankles and tugged him out. Then she did what she'd been threatening to do since she came: She sat on him.

"Ow! Ow!" Boohoo screamed. "You're hurting me!"

Aunt Verdella appeared in the doorway, a mixing spoon in her hand. She flashed me a wavering, lopsided smile.

I could tell that Freeda wasn't putting all of her weight on Boohoo, and hoped Aunt Verdella realized this, too. Still, I was fretting for Boohoo, just as Aunt Verdella was.

"Freeda, maybe we should just send him up to his room," she suggested.

Freeda shook her head. "Send him upstairs where there's six hundred toys to play with? *That's* punishment? Nope. I'm not budging until this kid cries uncle."

"Uncle Rudy! Uncle Rudy!" Boohoo called, while Winnalee continued to cuss and gasp over the mess *she* had on her hands. Literally.

"Not *that* uncle," Freeda said, without even cracking a smile. She reminded him that Uncle Rudy was haying at the Smithys—a sensitive issue with Boohoo since he wasn't allowed to go along. "Say you're sorry, and that you'll listen from now on, or I'm not getting up. And trust me, after all the backbreaking work I've been doing over at your dad's the last few days, and with little sleep last night, I could easily sit here all day. Maybe even into tomorrow."

I spotted the mailman pull up to my mailbox, and suddenly I was as eager as Boohoo to have Freeda get off of him, because it didn't feel right to leave in the midst of the drama.

"Boohoo," Aunt Verdella said. "If you mind, I'll let you help frost the cake that's baking."

"He can't just say it, Verdella. He's got to mean it."

Boohoo was crying now.

"Get off of me! Evyyyyyyyyyyyyyyyyyyyyyy, help!"

"Just say you'll mind," I told him, my eyes on Freeda, who wasn't showing even a drop of pity.

"He's gotta mean it," Freeda repeated.

"Okay, okay!" Boohoo shouted.

"Okay what?"

"Okay, I'm sorry."

"What else?"

"You're breaking my back!"

"What else?"

"I'll behave!"

Freeda got up, and offered him her hand. Boohoo knocked it away, and as soon as he was on his feet, he backed up a good six feet and stuck out his chin. "Ha-ha. I was fibbin'!" he said, his fists punching at his sides. "I'm not sorry at all! I was just being behaving to get you off of me."

Freeda propped her hands on her hips and stared at the screen door Boohoo had just slammed. She shook her head. "Verdella, you have *got* to stop babying that boy like you do. Button, you too. You guys are turning him into a little brat. And for what? Because you feel sorry for him? *Why?*" I glanced outside where Boohoo was digging his towel out from under the picnic table. I closed the front door so he wouldn't hear.

Pity flooded Aunt Verdella's face. "He lost his mama, Freeda. When he was just a baby."

"That's right," Freeda said. "When he was just a baby. But he's not lacking for a mother's love. *You're* his mom, Verdella. And between you, and Rudy, and Button, that kid's not lacking for anything—well, except for knowing his father. And knowing who his birth mother was."

Freeda picked up the dirty diaper and paused alongside Aunt Verdella. "And that goes for Reece, too. Your pity for him is only hurting him, too. And it's hurting his kids."

Aunt Verdella's arms moved over her belly, one hand to hold the other wrist, the spoon limp in her hand. "Reece has had it hard," she almost whispered.

"Yeah, and that's a bummer. But life kicks everybody in the ass, sooner or later, Verdella. Come on, you've seen enough of life to know that eventually, *everybody* gets smacked with something so awful that they have every reason to want to roll over and play dead. But it's time for Reece to get back on his feet and start living again. And if you love him, you'll help him do that by knocking off this coddling shit."

"But—"

"No," Freeda said. "No buts.

"*I'm* all for the no *butts* thing, right about now," Winnalee said.

Freeda pointed the rolled diaper at Winnalee. "Stop being a smart-ass. I'm trying to make a serious point here."

"You just swore at your kid," Winnalee said.

"You're a big kid, you can take it. Now shut up."

Freeda turned her attention back to Aunt Verdella. "Take the baby booties off of Reece. He's a man, and he needs to start walking like one."

Freeda went to dispose of the diaper, but Aunt Verdella just stood there, teary-eyed and shaky. I wanted to go to her, to comfort her, but I was afraid if I did, Freeda would jump all over me.

"I did it!" Winnalee said, holding up Evalee, her fresh diaper hanging haphazardly low on her hips, but on all the same.

Freeda came back into the room, patted Evalee's droopy bottom, and said, "Way to go, Mamalee." She looked over at Aunt Verdella and went to hug her. She said something I couldn't hear, and Aunt Verdella nodded. "I know you're right . . . it's just hard, you know?"

"I know. But it's necessary."

I slipped out the front door. Eager for nothing more than to find a letter from Jesse. Something that could lift my spirits up above the problems that still hovered.

But no letter came. Again.

CHAPTER 31

BRIGHT IDEA #65: If you've been wearing a Band-Aid for six days and the edges are starting to curl, don't cry because you're afraid it will fall off and you'll have to look at that bloody mess again. After your sister rips it off and the hair on your arm is done ouching, you're going to see that the owie is healed.

Midweek, the sun woke me early. I rolled over and sighed at the thought of yet another day of weather so hot and humid that your clothes clung to you, and everything you touched felt damp.

I'd been spending my days mainly alone, because Winnalee was afraid of caring for Evalee without Freeda and Aunt Verdella's guidance, and stayed with them throughout the day, coming home only once Evalee was asleep for the night. Then she'd set her alarm—Freeda insisted she be there when Evalee woke—and shuffled across the road at six o'clock each morning. Tommy wasn't even popping in, now that he was haying, and Boohoo was too fascinated with Evalee to break away and come over.

With so much alone time, though, I did get a lot of sewing done on Cindy's dress. It was fun watching a one-of-a-kind dress take form, and doubly fun to show Winnalee my progress each evening. When I finished the first sleeve, Winnalee ran it up her bare arm and made swimming motions to watch the layered angel sleeves flutter. "Oh my God, this is so cool! It's the sleeve I saw in my head, and now here it is, on my arm!"

"Winnalee," I told her, "every piece of clothing you put on started first as a thought in someone's head."

She blinked, then said, "I guess so, but this is the first piece of clothes to come from *my* head."

After about a week of working alone, loneliness started to set in. I pulled out scraps of satin and tried to formulate roses while I waited for the mail. My first flower looked like a squashed baby's ear, and my second, like an overgrown kohlrabi. I was on my third try—better, still not good—watching Freeda hang clothes, and Boohoo dig in his sandbox, through the window. Finally I gave up and went across the road.

"Evy, can you tie this?" Boohoo asked, holding out Monkey, who'd lost his yarn leash. He scratched his mosquito bites as he waited. "I think Knucklehead's gotta stay in the lean-to now, even when it's this hot. I'd put another diaper on him, but I'm afraid Freeda'd sit on me again. That Freeda probably only weighs as much as Wilma, but she's still heavy. Why'd you let her sit on me like that, anyway?"

"Forget about it, already," I said. "Yell when the mailman comes, okay?"

I went inside, where Evalee was squirming in Aunt Verdella's arms and Winnalee was heating her bottle in a tiny pan of water. "Geez, all this kid does is eat and pee and poop and spit up," she huffed.

Freeda was coming up the stairs, carrying yet another load of wet laundry. She glanced at Aunt Verdella. "Why in the hell isn't Reece doing his own laundry?"

Winnalee tipped the bottle upside down and dribbled milk on her wrist. Her lips twisted to the side. "Is this too hot?" she asked, holding the bottle out and waiting for Aunt Verdella to turn over her wrist. "It's just right, honey," Aunt Verdella told her. But Winnalee wanted a third opinion. "Button?"

Freeda rolled her eyes. "Crissakes, Winnalee. I told you. If it doesn't feel hot, and it doesn't feel cold, then it's just right." Freeda dropped the basket. She glanced at Aunt Verdella. "If you even try ironing his shit today in this heat, I'm gonna throw a hissy fit."

"I think the heat's gettin' to everybody," Aunt Verdella whispered to me.

I heard the muted sounds of a car and glanced at the clock. "Evyyyyyyy!" Boohoo shouted.

When I got outside, Boohoo scooted in front of me to get to the mailbox first. He lifted the telltale red, white, and blue airmail envelope and waved it above his head. I held out my hand, not liking the devilish look on his face. "Hand it over, Boohoo." But he ran off, snaking across our yard and then the road, ignoring my pleas, and my threats. I chased him into the house, and into the kitchen where Freeda and Aunt Verdella were going to pause for a cup of coffee, and Winnalee was feeding Evalee. "Evy's got a boyfriend! Evy's got a boyfriend!"

Aunt Verdella turned. "Boohoo, you give Button that letter or *I'm* gonna sit on you!"

"That would *really* hurt. You're two hundred pounds."

"One hundred ninety-two," Aunt Verdella said proudly.

I probably would have had to chase Boohoo through the whole house if he hadn't noticed Uncle Rudy's truck pulling into the drive. "Hey, what's he doin' home?" he asked, letting Jesse's letter sail to the floor as he headed for the door.

Aunt Verdella leaned over the sink. "Rudy?"

I scooped up Jesse's letter and held it against me.

Uncle Rudy didn't come in, but told Aunt Verdella through the window that he came home to grab a blade for Tommy's hacksaw, but he wasn't finding one. "I'm gonna have to run into town," he said. "I'll let the little squirt ride with me."

"Boohoo," Aunt Verdella called. "You come in and wash up first."

I could hear Uncle Rudy's truck door creaking open. "We're just goin' to the hardware store, Verdie. Not to a beauty contest."

"And A&W. We're goin' there, too, right, Uncle Rudy?" I heard Boohoo cheer, so I guessed that meant yes.

I wanted to read Jesse's letter in private, and was about to slip into the bathroom to do just that, when Freeda did.

"That a letter from that Dayne boy?" Aunt Verdella asked, turning away from the window as the truck pulled out. I nodded and tried to look casual, even though my insides were jumping with hope that Jesse would say something to let me know he still thought I was special.

I moved over by the stove and unfolded the letter.

Evy,

Been crazy-busy here. I put in for a three-day pass. Hope it comes through soon so I can go to Ulm. I could use a little fun. I really appreciate your letters, Evy. Busy or not, they're always something to look forward to. You've always been there for me, and I love you for it.

Love, Jesse

The paper shook in my hand. I looked up, blinking, thinking I might cry.

"What is it, Button?" Aunt Verdella asked. I wanted to show the letter to Winnalee so I could ask her if my eyes were tricking me, or if he'd really told me that he *loved* me. But I didn't want Aunt Verdella feeling slighted.

"Nothing," I said.

"Well, Jesse must have said something good to have you glowing like that."

"I think I slept with a Jesse here in Dauber, but doubt it would be the same one," Freeda yelled from the bathroom. "So somebody tell me who in the hell Button's Jesse is."

Aunt Verdella started telling her about his family, where they lived, how Jesse and I had been close since he moved here. "He's cute, too. Even with his hair butchered," Winnalee said. "He writes to her about once a week, and she writes to him every day now." Evalee's bottle made a few squeaks and Winnalee pulled it from her and put Evalee up to her shoulder to burp her.

"They were friends through the last three years of high school," Aunt Verdella told Freeda.

"Friends?" Freeda said, coming out of the bathroom with a teasing glimmer in her eyes. As she headed to her chair, she stopped Winnalee's hand. "You're not banging a drum. Softer." Winnalee sighed and rolled her eyes. *"Friends?"* Freeda asked again.

I wanted to brush the whole thing off, but I was smiling like an idiot. Now that Jesse had used the word *love,* I could finally admit—at least to myself—that I'd always been in love with him.

Freeda's eyes squinted. "You mean you've been carrying this torch for a *friend* all this time?"

I wished I didn't blush so easily. I edged closer to the door, ready to say I had to get home and back to work.

"Sit your butt down. We were talking," Freeda told me, as she reached over the table to whack Aunt Verdella's hand, because she was reaching for one of the leftover bunny pancakes still on the table.

"Oh, ick," Winnalee said, as a geyser of spit-up landed on her chest. She got up to lay Evalee down and to change her shirt.

Freeda stood up. "It's too damn hot for coffee. I'm having ice water. Who wants some? And Button, you're going to tell me all about this guy."

Winnalee pointed the box fan on the dining room table toward the kitchen and came back in as Freeda was bringing our glasses to the table. She lifted her hair off her back, bouncing it. "Damn, it's hot. And it's not even ten o'clock yet." She reached down and gave her cutoffs another roll, bringing them up to her crotch. "I don't know how you can stand it in pants," she said to me.

Freeda peeked under the table. "Jesus," she said. "What's up with *that*?"

"She won't show her legs," Winnalee said. "She doesn't even own a pair of shorts, or a skirt."

That wasn't exactly true. In a box shoved in a downstairs closet, I had a pair of short shorts, and the skirt I sewed and wore when Penny and I went parking with those older guys. I used to wear them around the house sometimes when Dad was working, and Boohoo was with Aunt Verdella. It was humiliating to even think about how I would put them on with a tight shirt and prance around the house while I was cleaning, pretending I was irresistibly sexy.

"No wonder that boy only stayed your *friend* through high school," Freeda said.

"She hates her legs." Winnalee tattled.

Aunt Verdella looked confused. "You hate your legs? Why? You've got cute legs, Button."

Freeda got to her feet, and yanked me to mine. "Okay. Down with those jeans, kid."

I laughed nervously, and Winnalee rolled her eyes. "Good luck with that one. She won't get naked in front of anybody."

"Well, *that's* not necessarily a bad thing," Freeda said, her eyes narrowing at Winnalee.

"I mean not in front of *anybody*. Not even me."

Freeda stood up. "Okay, that's it. Drop your drawers, missy. Let's see what you got goin' on there." She reached for the snap on my jeans, and I wrapped my arms around my hips, covering the zipper and button as I held tight to Jesse's letter. I was laughing, until I realized that she wasn't kidding.

"What do I gotta do, sit on you, too?"

I glanced at the door, and Freeda reminded me that Uncle Rudy and Boohoo had left for town. She grappled to get at the button, backing me against the counter alongside Winnalee, who was fanning her hair again. "Oh, for crissakes," Freeda said. "You'd think I was asking you to strip down to your birthday suit. You got panties on, don't you?"

"Glad she didn't ask *me* that," Winnalee mumbled, and Freeda slapped her with a scowl.

Freeda started tickling me then, making me weak with laughter I didn't feel. I dropped Jesse's letter, and she dropped my jeans.

"Oh, for crying out loud," Freeda said, her hands going to her hips.

"See what I mean?" Aunt Verdella said, all serious. "She's got cute legs."

"You do," Freeda said. "Skinny and pale, but shapely. Damn cute."

I felt near tears, standing there with my ugly, skinny, stilt-long legs showing, my white, bony knees clanking together like cue balls.

Freeda softened, "Honey . . . ," she said. "Are you gonna cry? *Why?* Look at me."

"Oh Button . . . ," Aunt Verdella said, as though *she* might cry.

Freeda lifted my chin off my chest. "Are you *that* ashamed of your legs?"

"They're ugly!" I said, my voice so forceful that I even startled myself.

Freeda shook her head at Aunt Verdella. "No mystery where she got *that* from?"

I nodded. "Yeah. Ma had skinny legs just like mine."

"I didn't mean where you got your *legs* from. I meant, where you got that crappy attitude about your body from."

Freeda bent over so she could look into my face. "They're not perfect, that's true, but they're not ugly, either. Far from it. You think I got perfect legs? Or Winnalee? *Anybody*, short of a *Playboy* model? Well if they got them at all—who knows, the way their legs are always tangled in bedsheets."

Nobody was going to convince me I had good legs. At least somebody with fat legs could lose weight and exercise to get them normal, but there was nothing I could do about mine. Aunt Verdella had been stuffing me since I got my first tooth, but I swear, every ounce of food she fed me only stacked up on my boobs.

Freeda dropped her shorts to her bare feet and kicked them into the bathroom doorway. "Look at this," she said, showing me the outside of her thigh, squeezing it so that the dimples puckered deeper. She let go and put her hands back on her hips again. "We all have things on our body we wish were better, Button. But that doesn't mean we should hate them because they're not perfect."

"I used to have chubby thighs when I was young," Aunt Verdella said. "Can you believe it? But they thinned down, and my middle plumped up. Maybe I whittled them down by all the walking I did over the years." She ha-ha'd.

"Or maybe Rudy rubbed them away." Freeda laughed, and Aunt Verdella blushed.

Winnalee dropped her cutoffs—no underwear, as usual. "Look at my legs, Button. They're almost as short as Evalee's!"

"They're short because you're short," I told her.

"No. They don't even fit with the rest of my body." To

make her point, she whipped off her shirt; it stayed tangled in her hair. She wasn't even embarrassed to be exposing her nipples, pale pink as Evalee's cheeks, right in the kitchen. "Look how long I am here. That's why when we sit side by side, Button, we look the same height. If somebody else hadn't gotten my legs, I'd probably be five foot nine, too.

"And check this out. I look like I have a flat gut, right? Well, watch this." She turned sideways. "This is my gut when I'm not holding it in." Her tiny pouch puffed twice its size. "And look," she said, pointing to the inside edge of her hip bones. "Stretch marks. They creep me out. They look like silver worms."

"Hey, those are your mommy badges. You wear them proudly, little girl. I do mine." Freeda tugged off her panties, and bent back to poke out her hips. "Look at these. I got way more than you. A row on each side, lined up like ribs. Between my boobs and my belly, I looked liked a watermelon patch when I was carrying you." To prove her point, she ripped her short-sleeved white top over her head and snapped her bra off. Her shirt landed on the table over the leftover bunny pancakes, her bra on the floor, over her shorts.

"Wow, you're saggy," Winnalee said.

"Tell me about it. They say you should be able to slip a pencil under your boob and if it doesn't fall out, you're too saggy. Shit, I could stick a whole box of number twos under these girls and keep them there until next semester. I don't know what in the hell happened." Aunt Verdella giggled as Freeda nudged her left boob over and pointed to the stretch marks streaking its side. Then Freeda turned around and grabbed the swell of skin high on her hips. "And get a load of this mess." She shook her hips and shouted, "But ooh-la-la, can these hips swing!"

I envied Freeda as she stood there—a little saggy, a little chubby, a little dimply—because I could tell, *really* tell, that she wasn't ashamed of her body at all. Not even of the patch of dark red hair between her legs, where Dewey had once left his grime.

Winnalee turned, exposing her bare backside. "I got a good ass, I think. Sorta makes up for my stubby legs." Winnalee and Freeda shook their bare bottoms in unison, while me and Aunt Verdella laughed nervously at the absurdity of the four of us standing in the kitchen in broad daylight, three of us in various stages of dress.

Winnalee caught me off guard then, when she grabbed the hem of my shirt in back and yanked it up. "I bet Button's boobs are her best part. Bet you any money."

"What are you doing?" I yelled. I ducked—a bad move, because Winnalee yanked the shirt up over my head with one jerk. She gave my bra hooks a quick snap, then hustled in front of me and yanked it down my arms before I could stop her. "See? See? I knew it! Didn't I tell ya? Ooooo, look at her nips, they're cotton candy pink."

"Nice boobs, kiddo," Freeda hooted. She looked at Aunt Verdella. "Sort of like looking at the ghost of Christmas past, huh, Verdella?" Freeda tossed her head back and laughed.

Freeda blew bangs out of her face. "It's hotter than Hades in here, and even hotter outside, but damn, if it ain't a whole lot cooler when you're naked! Verdella, shed those skins and cool yourself off before you have a heatstroke."

Aunt Verdella brushed away the invitation with a freckled hand. "Oh, I'd scare these girls half to death, showing them this old wreck."

Freeda put her hands on her hips. "Did it ever dawn on you, Verdella Peters, that maybe if girls saw bodies—big and small, old and young, fat and skinny, smooth and lumpy—they just might stop comparing themselves with the perfect bodies they see in magazines and on TV? Young women need to see what regular people look like."

"Freeda's right. I saw all kinds of naked, regular people at Woodstock, and let me clue you, most of them weren't perfect. Not that anybody noticed."

"Yeah, well, somebody noticed yours. Obviously," Freeda said. She turned and nudged Aunt Verdella with her elbow. "Come on, Verdella. Cool off. Show us your wild side. I know it's there!"

Giggles, the kind that fill your mouth when a fat man bends over and you can see the crack of his butt, swelled in my throat. I held my hand over my mouth to keep them in.

Winnalee started dancing like she was back in the cage at the Purple Haze, shouting at Aunt Verdella to take her clothes off. Laughter busted out of my mouth at the thought. I'd never seen Aunt Verdella in less than her big white bloomers and her pointy white bra.

"Damn, I wish it was raining," Freeda said, giving a glance out the window.

Aunt Verdella's face changed after Freeda said that. Maybe because she was remembering the time, long ago, when we—Ma included—danced naked in the rain with the Malones. She lifted her chin and pursed her smile, like she'd suddenly been handed a permission slip from Heaven. Then she peeled her stretchy shorts (and undies!) down, and kicked them behind her. Her legs were skinny for a fat lady, bubbled with veins, and the insides of her thighs looked like wrinkled pockets somebody just emptied.

Freeda started dancing then, dipping at the waist and shimmying, her boobs wagging, then bending backward and shaking with all she had. She circled the table and danced up to Aunt Verdella, who was ha-ha'ing so hard by now, that her whole body wobbled. "Come on, pretty mama. Let it *all* hang out!"

I busted into an outright roar when Aunt Verdella, caught up in the crazy moment, crisscrossed her arms and pulled her white sleeveless shell over her head. And there she was, full-bellied as a just-fed baby, the skin where the waistband of her shorts had been puckered and red circling her middle like a striped hula hoop. Freeda twirled and continued her crazy dips and back bends.

Aunt Verdella broke out in a fresh batch of oh-what-the-hell ha-has and unhooked her big white bra. She tossed it over her head like a wedding bouquet, flipping it into the dining room. "I look like a pinup girl ripped out of the pages of *National Geographic*!" she said, as she looked down at the boobs that had instantly stretched out to recline against her belly. Freeda roared with laughter, then danced her dips and stretches around the table. "Now shake it pretty mama." Aunt Verdella started mimicking Freeda's dance moves.

Winnalee was laughing so hard she couldn't stand up straight. She braced her hands on the table, then started thumping them, her head banging, the tangled shirt flying free from her hair.

I'm guessing that it was Winnalee's rhythmic hand thumps that prompted Freeda to start singing out *da-da-das* in the tune of the guitar opening of Roy Orbison's "Oh, Pretty Woman." Freeda grabbed Evalee's empty bottle from the table, holding it upside down and bringing it close to her mouth like a microphone. She jabbed her hip hard to the side as she pointed first at Aunt Verdella, then at me, while belting out, "I don't believe you, you're not the truth, no one could look as good as you. Mercy!"

Freeda handed the bottle-mic to Winnalee for the rest of the verse, then motioned for Aunt Verdella to take ahold of her hips. Freeda started the train, heading from the kitchen into the dining room, and Winnalee hurried to join them, the pseudo-mic under her chin as she belted out the next verse.

"Come on, Button!" Freeda bellered. "Wiggle what you got!"

I stood there giggling, my arms at my sides, skin touching skin, watching. Each of them was flawed, but none of them cared, as they did their jiggle-dance under the archway and sang off key.

I could see Ma dancing in the rain again. So clearly that it was as if she was in the room with us. Crazy or not, I took down my underpants and hurried to take Winnalee's waist. She passed me the bottle-mic, and I sang as I mocked the crazy dance steps right along with them.

Freeda stopped at the box fan propped on the dining room table, and bent over to offer her shimmying boobs to the whomping air, her voice bouncing back to us as we started the first verse all over again. "Ha cha-cha!" she yelled as she did a spin to move her to the side, leaving Aunt Verdella standing in the rush of air. Aunt Verdella spread her arms and giggled, then turned and shimmied to air her backside. Together, we all shouted out, *"Mercy!"*

We danced into the living room, where Evalee lay awake, blinking up at us. And then she laughed. Not just smiled—laughed!

"Oh my God, she's laughing! Her first laugh!" Winnalee said.

Aunt Verdella was sputtering as she said, "She probably thinks we've all gone crazy."

"No she doesn't! She's thinking about how *she* wants to do the naked lady dance with the big girls! Aren't you, Cupcake?" Winnalee reached down and tore the tabs from Evalee's diaper, then lifted her above her head and danced her to the engine position of our train.

We were laughing so hard by the time we got back into the dining room that we couldn't sing *or* dance anymore—only stand and drape our arms over one another's shoulders to keep ourselves standing as we hooted. "Oh, stop! Stop!" Aunt Verdella begged as she held her legs together so she wouldn't pee.

I swear, my heart crawled right up into my ears, when I saw whose car was parking in the drive. There she was, Fanny Tilman, getting out of the car with a Ben Franklin bag clamped against her sweater.

I pointed, too horrified to speak. "Oh my Lord!" Aunt Verdella shrieked. She hopped in circles, like she didn't know which way to run.

Freeda peeked through the lace curtain and started mimicking the jingle from *The Wizard of Oz*, the one that plays when Almira Gulch is riding her bike to nab Toto.

"Hurry! Get dressed!" Aunt Verdella screamed as she ran-hopped to the kitchen, leaving a trail of *Oh nos* behind her.

We scrambled back to the kitchen, naked hips and shoulders bumping, Evalee's head bobbling, the Malones laughing because they thought the whole situation was hysterical, me laughing out of sheer, nervous horror.

"Hurry! Hurry!" Aunt Verdella cried, as she snatched the white shirt off the table and tugged it over her head. The sleeve wanted to snag on her upper arm, so she pulled all the harder. Winnalee, still naked, her shirt draped over her shoulder like a spit rag, was doubled over Evalee, laughing, unable to say out loud what was obvious to us both: Aunt Verdella had grabbed Freeda's shirt.

I reached for my jeans and fumbled to get my feet in the leg holes. My ears were whooshing, and every little movement appeared to be happening in slow, vivid detail: the porch screen door squealing, Freeda spotting her shorts in the bathroom and shouting out, "Eureka!" Fanny's heel-clacks on the porch. I bent to tug my pants up over my knees, and there were my boobs, jiggling, pulling, hanging like cow udders ten minutes before milking. *God!* I scanned the room for something—*anything*—to hide them from Fanny Tilman's scornful eyes.

"Ver-della?" Fanny called out.

The doorknob was turning and there was nowhere to run,

no chance to finish dressing. I glanced at the table—they wouldn't hide my whole boobs, but at least they'd hide my nipples! I let go of my jeans and they slipped back down my legs, and in a panic, I snatched two leftover bunny pancakes from the platter and clamped one over the peak of each breast.

Freeda was bent over, reaching into the bathroom for her panties and shorts, when Fanny burst into the house, ramming her in the butt and pinning her behind the door.

And there we stood.

Me with my bell-bottoms wrapped around my ankles, pancakes over my breasts. Winnalee gawking at my bunny bra, Evalee grinning in her arms like something was still funny. Aunt Verdella, her face stretched with shock, the sleeves of Freeda's shirt squeezing her upper arms like sausage casings, and the rest of Freeda's shirt strapped around her armpits like a rubber band.

Fanny saw me first, and her head jerked from my face to my bunny-breasts, to my groin. I might as well have been Dewey standing there with food over my privates, because everything in Fanny's expression screamed, "Pervert!"

"Shit," Winnalee said, and I glanced over to see her holding Evalee out, droplets of pee streaking down Winnalee's belly and dripping from Evalee's toes.

Fanny bird-jerked her pointy head to Winnalee and the baby, her eyebrows rising, then dipping when she spotted Aunt Verdella standing by the stove. Fanny's lips, dry and thin as gray yarn, formed a circle of shock. "Verdella! What on earth is going on here?"

I don't know if Fanny heard Freeda thump to the floor, or heard her cuss as she got up, Fanny being in the state of shock that she was. But she sure did jump when Evalee's baby bottle came out from around the door, nipple first. Her head snapped back as Freeda jabbed the bottle near her face. "Honk! Honk!"

Fanny's mouth snapped shut, but her eyes stayed stretched.

She did an about-face and walked out, her heels whacking the porch floor like a ruler over knuckles. In the doorway was the Ben Franklin bag she'd dropped, two skeins of pink yarn peeking out of the top like boobs in a push-up bra.

Freeda slammed the door shut with a *whomp!* and stood in triumph, a saucy grin on her lips. "That's right, Fanny Tilman!" she shouted. "If you can't stand the heat, get out of the kitchen!"

CHAPTER 32

BRIGHT IDEA #37: Sometimes, the only way to shut a person up is by stuffing something in their ear.

Aunt Verdella didn't leave the house for a week after *that* one. And maybe she *never* would have, had a stomach virus not invaded the house, making everyone sick but her, and me, and the baby. There was no one to run for diapers and 7 Up but the two of us, and I wasn't about to show my face alone at The Corner Store.

We waited until Evalee was down for her morning nap, then took off. "She's going to be there. Sure enough, Fanny will be there. Mark my words," Aunt Verdella repeated as we drove. "I wish we could just go to town for them—we'd save a few dollars, too—but we can't be gone that long. Those girls are too sick to care for a baby and a sick little boy. Still, I wish I didn't have to go to The Corner Store. Mark my words, Fanny'll be there."

The store was empty but for Ada. "Oh, that sure is going around," Ada said when I told her everyone at home was sick.

I hurried to grab a couple of jugs of 7 Up and an assortment of Jell-O boxes from the shelves, while Aunt Verdella walked slowly up to the counter, her purse pushed tightly against her belly. "Ada?" she asked slowly. "Has anything *else* been *going around*?"

"What do you mean?" Ada asked, feigned innocence on her face.

"I mean, has Fanny been spreading any gossip?"

Ada laughed. "When *doesn't* Fanny spread gossip, Verdella?"

"I mean about *us*."

Ada gave a soft laugh. "Yes, but don't you worry about it. It's such crazy talk that no one in their right mind would believe it . . . you two and the Malones stark naked in your kitchen, doing some evil, Satan-worshiping dance with Winnalee's baby. . . ." Aunt Verdella covered her gasp with her fingertips, but Ada just laughed. "She's convinced that Winnalee has you all taking drugs now." Ada laughed some more. "That woman must have lost the only two marbles she had left, making up crazy stories like that."

"Oh dear," Aunt Verdella said.

"Don't you worry, Verdella. Like I said, no one will believe such nonsense."

"But . . . ," Aunt Verdella said. Marvin Thompson stepped in the store then, and I touched her arm to hush her.

Ada was getting Marvin a can of Copenhagen while I went to grab Evalee's diapers. He asked about Uncle Rudy, so Aunt Verdella filled him in. "You wouldn't think riding on that baler all day would be good for his back, but it seems to be doing a little better. I think he misses running the farm."

"That boy, Craig Rasmussen, is helping them, too," Ada added. "So that helps."

They talked some about when the hot, humid spell might break, and how their gardens were doing. "Freeda's taken over weeding, and Boohoo's helping, so at least Rudy doesn't have to worry about that."

I set the diapers on the counter.

"Well, I better get going. I'm workin' second shift today." As Marvin was going out the door, he sidestepped to let Fanny Tilman in. Aunt Verdella moaned softly, and Ada gave her a don't-you-worry glance.

Fanny came up and pinned her purse to the counter, standing on the other side of Aunt Verdella.

"What can I do for you today, Fanny?" Ada asked quickly, as if she had really come there to shop.

"I'm just going to get some milk," Fanny said.

"That's it for us today," I told Ada, my voice pleading with her to hurry and ring up our purchases. Aunt Verdella was picking at the zipper on her purse, and I nudged her so she'd open it and get out her wallet.

"Oh," she said, turning to me. "Could you grab one of those little jars of broth? The cubed ones. They go further."

I nodded, then almost ran to the soup aisle.

"So, Verdella," Fanny said, without looking at her. "I see you and the girl are dressed today, at least."

Ada quickly jumped in. "Verdella, have you lost weight? You sure look like it."

"Oh," Aunt Verdella giggled, "as a matter of fact . . ."

"You wouldn't say that if you saw her naked," Fanny said.

Bright patches of red that begged to be scratched instantly sprouted on my arms.

"Fanny," Ada warned, as she took the bouillon and punched in its cost, then gave Aunt Verdella our total.

Pay her. Let's go. Please!

Aunt Verdella opened her purse and grabbed her wallet.

"I believe I owe you for two skeins of pink yarn, too," she said to Fanny.

Fanny rubbed the side of her nose and her big glasses bumped down to the tip. She opened her mouth to say something, but Aunt Verdella took a big breath and said, "Fanny Tilman, I'm not gonna explain what you saw the other day. Not only because you wouldn't understand, but because, frankly, it's none of your business. Now what do I owe you for the yarn?"

Ada gave Aunt Verdella her change, making sure she had the right denominations so she could pay Fanny, and Aunt Verdella set the money on the counter in front of Fanny.

I picked up our bag of groceries while Aunt Verdella closed her purse. "Thank you, Ada," she said. Then she turned to Fanny. "And the next time you come to my house, I'd appreciate it if you knocked. It's rude to barge into other people's homes without knocking. I would have thought you'd know that."

I wanted to shout out loud, I was so proud of Aunt Verdella for leaving Fanny Tilman—*Fanny Tilman!*—insulted and mute. Aunt Verdella laced her purse strap over her arm, stood up straight, and headed for the door. I grabbed the box of diapers and was about to follow, when in a sudden moment of blazing courage, I stopped and leaned over to stand so close to Fanny that I could smell her horehound breath. "And by the way," I told her, "the girl has a name. It's Evelyn."

CHAPTER 33

BRIGHT IDEA #51: Sometimes you have to adjust the rabbit ears nine thousand times before you get a clear picture.

After a good ten days of running to Aunt Verdella's to take care of Evalee, Freeda put her foot down and said Winnalee had to bring her over to our place. Winnalee was a wreck, and I had to assure her over and over again that I *did* know something about taking care of babies.

For three days at least, Winnalee came up to my sewing room several times to get my opinion on something or other. Once even coming in to stick Evalee's butt under my nose to ask if I thought her bottom looked a little red. And she might never have given Evalee a bath for fear of scalding or drowning her, had Freeda not come over to see how things were going and sniffed her. Winnalee acted all nonchalant as she told her she was giving her one before bed. Then, after supper, she insisted I go across the street to quietly lure Aunt Verdella over, while Freeda was at Dad's doing whatever it was she did over there.

"You do it this time and I'll watch," Winnalee told Aunt Verdella, once the tub was filled and everything was laid out.

Aunt Verdella squeezed her hands together, as if to keep them from reaching out for Evalee. "Oh, honey, if I do it for you, you'll only be scared to do it yourself next time. I'll talk you through it."

"Okay, but you check the water first." Aunt Verdella poked her elbow into the water, then gave Winnalee a nod.

"You're doing a wonderful job," Aunt Verdella told Winnalee repeatedly, even though at one point Evalee *did* slip and water filled her ears. "I could have drowned her!" Winnalee cried, and Aunt Verdella had to assure her that a baby couldn't drown in three inches of water, with her mommy holding on to her.

Aunt Verdella left once Evalee was out of tub, and as soon as she went out the door, Winnalee burst into tears. "I don't know what in the hell I'm doing. I love her, Button, don't get me wrong, but this is *hard*. I don't even have a job right now, and still I'm so tired I can't see straight half of the time. When do kids start sleeping through the night, anyway? When they're twelve? I can't even imagine how it's gonna be when I'm working. I'd be flat broke already if Freeda hadn't sprung for the case of formula yesterday. But Freeda's not gonna stick around here forever.

"Come on, Cupcake, bend your arm already." Winnalee was almost crying when she said it.

"Bend it for her," I said. "Just gently."

"I'll break it!" Winnalee said. Before I could counter that comment, Winnalee was tickling her under the armpits trying to make her weak with giggles, but Evalee only started fussing.

I hurried to heat her bottle. "You can take a night job, and I'll watch Evalee. Aunt Verdella will help, too."

When her bottle was ready, Winnalee collapsed on the couch with Evalee. She was jiggling the nipple as they both bawled, and it kept flapping out of Evalee's mouth. I sat down beside them and took Evalee. Her head was damp on my arms and her legs were warm and soft against mine. Her faint eyebrows lifted when she looked up at me, then she started sucking, her tiny hand finding my finger and clutching it.

Winnalee leaned against my shoulder. "Look how nice she calmed down when you took her. She hates me."

"She does not, Winnalee. You were upset and she could feel it and it upset her. She doesn't want her mommy to be upset."

Winnalee sighed. "I love her, Button. Don't think I don't. But I'd give anything if I could just save her for later. For when I'm old. Like thirty or something. Right now, I just want to be a kid. You know? Pick up and go when I feel like it. Party at night. Have sex again, for crissakes. What am I supposed to do about sex? Lasso the mailman when he pulls up?"

"Geez, Winnalee," I said, because I didn't know what to say to *that* one.

"Once you start having it, it's like a drug. You'll see." She sighed. "When the hell is Tommy coming over again, anyway?"

"Tommy?"

"I'm not asking for *that* reason—he doesn't even like me—I just want to ask him about Craig."

"Tommy's haying. Who knows when he'll show up here again."

"You sounded disappointed when you said that," Winnalee told me.

"I did not," I said, even though I suspected Winnalee was

right. But then, people could get attached to anything if they had it around long enough. Hadn't Boohoo cried when he lost Hoppy in the field?

"Maybe I'll call Craig this week and see if he wants to go out. Maybe see a movie. *Catch-22* is playing. That's supposed to be good. I just don't want to sit here and grow old while I'm still a teenager." She sniffled against her hand. "I don't know how you do it, Button. Living like this. No partying. No sex. No pot. I mean, seriously, how do you do it? Never mind," she said. "I know how you do it. You do it by thinking about how happy life will get when Jesse comes back."

I felt defensive, unsure whether I should have felt that way or not. But I didn't say anything. I didn't *have* anything to say.

Evalee fell asleep before her bottle was finished, so we brought her upstairs. Winnalee flopped on the bed. "I've gotta crash. That kid gets up before the birds. Go ahead and leave the light on if you want to read or write to Jesse. I'll be out the second I hit the pillow anyway." She rolled away from me, then after a bit, said, "If I still wrote in our bright ideas book, you know what I'd write? Bright Idea number ninety-nine and three-quarters: *If you go to Woodstock and smoke pot until your brain is higher than ten kites, don't encourage the guy you know you're gonna screw within the hour to blow up his last rubber so you can play volleyball with the crowd. If you do, you're going to end up with a kid you don't even know how to bathe.*"

It was raining by the time Aunt Verdella left for the Community Sale on Saturday. Not a thunderstorm, just rain that kept up for the rest of the day. I put on the new flared skirt I'd been thinking about making since we'd stripped naked in Aunt Verdella's kitchen, and finally had sewn (all but for the hem), and stood in front of Winnalee for at least the sixth time.

"Jesus, Button. I told you. Your legs *don't* look too skinny in it. And like I said, Freeda was right. The flared skirt makes you look like you have hips. But what difference would it make, anyway? We're just sitting around here doing nothing today. And probably every other day for the rest of our lives."

Freeda and Boohoo had gone to the Community Sale last Saturday, just "for the hell of it," and came back with a baby stroller and a Polaroid camera so she could take pictures of Evalee, who was changing every day. I guess Winnalee hadn't heard her say to me, "We'll snap a picture of you in a cute skirt, too, to send to that love-starved soldier of yours."

Love-starved. In Jesse's last letter he'd mentioned that he put in for a three-day pass so he could go to Ulm, and I'd been obsessing about it since, sure that the "fun" he was talking about was sex with a German girl.

Winnalee put her thumb on Evalee's chin and made her mouth move as she said in baby talk, "Ooh-la-la, but you look sexy, Auntie Button. Really!" Then Winnalee said, "You're not going to leave it that long, are you?"

The truth of the matter was, I'd tacked up the hem at least four times, changing the length so often that the hem was filled with pinholes. I started rambling about the different length options, but Winnalee wasn't listening anymore. She was leaning over the armrest of the chair and reaching for the curtain. "Is that Tommy?" she said, straining to see. The day was shifting from dusk to night, and with the living room light on and the sky darkened from rain clouds, it looked dark outside, though it wasn't. I hadn't even heard anyone pull in.

Winnalee raced to the door.

"Just checkin' on the cows," I heard Tommy say.

"Well come in here for a second first, will you?"

"Don't call him in here!" I hissed, pointing to my naked legs.

Winnalee turned. "If Fanny Tilman saw your bare tits and your ass, I think Tommy can see your legs from the knee down. Geez, Button, get a grip. I've got to get the skinny—no pun intended—on Craig. You know, if he likes me."

I was going to run up the stairs, but with Tommy's long strides, I knew he'd catch me halfway up, and be able to see my skinny legs clear up to my undies.

Tommy's skin was dark amber from days spent working in the sun, and glossy from the rain. Even with the room dimly lit and his hair a frizzy smudge, I could see it was sun-bleached.

Tommy stood just inside the door. He looked tired. "Yeah?" He saw me then, and his eyes went straight to my legs and stuck there like two bloodthirsty mosquitoes. "What?" I asked, my armpits going damp.

"Nothing," Tommy said, turning away.

I slid to the chair and sat down, tugging my skirt as close to my knees as I could get it, which wasn't close enough.

Winnalee didn't bother with small talk, like I would have. She just asked him straight-out if he knew if Craig was interested in her. "When we ran into you guys, he said he'd like to go out with me. But when I called his house Saturday night, his mom said he was home first, then said he wasn't."

"He was at my place Saturday night. Him and some of the guys came over and we watched the draft lottery together."

"His number didn't come up, did it?" Winnalee asked.

Tommy gave me a quick glance—my legs, not my face—then looked back at Winnalee.

"Not this time." Tommy gave a couple of names of guys from town who weren't as fortunate, and although I didn't know them well, I worried that they'd be sent to 'Nam.

Winnalee ranted for a bit about the war, then circled back to her original topic. "Well? Is he interested or not?"

Tommy shrugged. "You'll have to ask him."

Winnalee wrinkled her nose. "Guess I know what *that* means." She hoisted Evalee up to her shoulder and headed up the stairs, leaving Tommy shuffling his feet by the door.

Naked legs or not, I went to him and tugged him out onto the porch. "You know something, don't you? You just didn't want to say it."

"Yeah. Craig's not interested anymore. He was, but then Brody started shooting off his mouth. She's just not his type, Evy. Sorry."

I gritted my teeth. "You defended her, didn't you?"

"Defended her? How? By saying it's *not* true that she sleeps with pretty much anybody?"

"Oh yeah, he's probably slept with ten girls just this week, but he's going to judge her?"

"Why would you say that?" Tommy asked.

"Because he's a guy!"

"Not all guys are running around trying to get in the pants of every girl they meet, Evy. Craig's not like that."

I was still steaming as Tommy walked toward the watering trough. "You can just tell that country hick Craig that Winnalee is too good for him anyway. She went to Woodstock, you know!"

Later, Winnalee asked me what I got out of Tommy. "And don't lie, either."

"Who said I was going to lie?" I asked, even if I was. I sighed. "Brody got to him. Craig was interested until then." I expected Winnalee to get angry. Angrier than I was, even. Instead, she just looked hurt.

Winnalee fell into a dead sleep by eight-thirty, and I sat on the bed, a pillow for my table, my good stationery waiting for me to decide what to write to Jesse, when pandemonium broke out. A car was in the drive, the horn honking every bit as intently as an ambulance siren. I barely had my feet on the floor when the door burst open and Boohoo and Freeda yelled up the stairs.

"Evy! Winnalee! Come on!" Freeda yelled. Boohoo was whipping up the stairs. "We're goin' to *Martian* Graw to see the fireworks! You gotta hurry, though, 'cause they're gonna start at nine!" Boohoo was talking about Mardi Gras, which is what Dauber called their Fourth of July celebration, even though nothing past the name resembled the festival in New Orleans. My insides started trembling; we hadn't gone since Ma died.

Winnalee stirred and Evalee whimpered.

Freeda appeared in the bedroom doorway next to Boohoo. She was wearing the shorts she had on earlier that day, the ones that had a stain on one leg. She didn't have any makeup on, and her knees looked dusty. "For crissakes," she said. "How did none of us notice that it's the Fourth of July?"

Winnalee woke, and dazed with sleep or not, mumbled, "It's the Fourth of July?"

"Get your asses out of bed, and grab Cupcake. I don't give a shit if you guys haven't gone to Mardi Gras in four years, Boohoo's gonna at least see the goddamn fireworks. Now come on. Move it! You've got thirty seconds to get down to the car. Thirty!"

Freeda grabbed Boohoo's arm and down the stairs they went.

Winnalee shot out of bed, blinking down at the floor. She ripped off her sleeping shirt and grabbed the clothes she'd taken off. "How'd we not notice it was the Fourth? Man!" I picked up Evalee, who was fussing.

"Shit, Button. Least you're dressed. Can you grab her a bottle from the fridge, just in case?"

"You go," I said, while patting Evalee's back as though she was wailing, though in reality, she was already beginning to doze back off.

"I can't leave you with—"

"Yes you can, go," I said. "I don't want to go. Seriously. I don't want to." She started to protest, but I bent and grabbed her sandals and handed them to her. "Go," I said. "Please."

. . .

Boohoo insisted on coming inside with Winnalee when they dropped her off sometime near midnight. I was still awake, downstairs digging for stamps for Jesse's letter. Boohoo ran to me, wide awake with excitement, even though he was typically in bed long before now. "Hurry and tell her. Freeda and Aunt Verdella are waiting," Winnalee reminded him.

Boohoo had blue cotton candy glued around his lips, and chocolate ice cream dripped on his striped shirt. "Evy, Evy, you won't believe it! There was fireworks—you ever see them? They were so cool. Red ones, green ones, blue ones, going off loud like bombs! The sparkles whistle when they come down, did you know that? It was really neat, Evy. And guess what? Guess what? I rode the *Octerpuss* with Winnalee. It spinned us really high and fast, didn't it, Winnalee? And Aunt Verdella, she went on the *tilterwheel* with Winnalee and Freeda and me, and she screamed so loud she almost busted our ears. You can make it go faster if you lean to one side. I sat on Aunt Verdella's side, 'cause I knew she'd make it spin real good. It was fun, Evy. Really fun!" The horn sounded downstairs and Winnalee told Boohoo he'd better go. "Okay, okay. Next time we're gonna see a parade, too. They throw candy to the kids, right, Winnalee?"

"Go, or Freeda's gonna sit on you again," Winnalee said.

"Night, Evy. I love you. And I love the Fourth of July, too." Boohoo wrapped his arms around my hips and gave me a quick squeeze.

I turned away from Winnalee as she undressed, so she wouldn't see my watering eyes.

"Oh man, Button. You should have been there. It was so funny! They have this guy there who guesses your age and weight. He guessed Aunt Verdella at a hundred and seventy-four, and she got so excited that she jumped up and down and grabbed his face in her hands, and gave him a smackeroo right on the lips!" Winnalee paused to laugh. "She wouldn't get on the scale afterwards, even though she could probably've won a prize. She didn't even care, though. She said his guess *was* her prize. She was still yakking about it on the ride home, saying she must really look like she only weighs that much, him being a *professional* weight guesser and all."

While Winnalee stripped and yammered more about the carnival, I drifted into my sewing room to shut off the lights. Across the road, I saw Freeda and Boohoo's silhouettes in the yard, their arms swirling lit sparklers, dropping sparks upon the grass. I leaned against the windowsill, my arms crossed, my eyes stinging for Boohoo because of all the things he'd been shortchanged on.

CHAPTER 34

BRIGHT IDEA #34: If you tell your new teacher that she's supposed to correct papers with a fat, green crayon because that's what the teacher in your last school used, she's probably going to tell you that you're in a new school now, and in her room, she's using red.

"Oh, Button, you should see how nice your dad's kitchen looks," Aunt Verdella said the next morning (*after* she told me about her looking like she only weighed 174 pounds). "I finally got to go peek at it this morning—Freeda didn't want me seeing it until it was done—and oh my, is it something! So bright and cheery. I can't believe that she got your dad to help, but what was he gonna do? Ripping up those metal strips in the doorways isn't exactly easy work for a woman."

Freeda had just come in from the garden and went straight to the bathroom to wash up. From the kitchen, I could see her lifting first one foot in the sink, then the other, as she said, "Ah, I could have ripped that shit up by myself in ten minutes, but I don't have a problem playing the damsel in distress if I have to. It got Reece off his sorry ass, and he really got into it once we got going." I looked down. Dad never helped Ma with anything around the house. What she couldn't do herself, she asked Uncle Rudy to do.

Aunt Verdella moved into the dining room to go back to her ironing, and I took the bag I was carrying and followed her. Freeda came and leaned against the doorway. "Ah, you're wearing shorts," she said. "Nice!" She spotted Winnalee out the window and leaned sideways to look. "What she doing?" she asked.

I looked. "Showing Evalee the tree where we used to play. And her wind chime, by the looks of it," I said. Aunt Verdella *awww*'d. Then she asked what I had in the plastic bag.

I pulled out the bouquet of flowers for the back of Cindy's dress and held it up. "I had to make them at least a hundred times. Do you think they look like flowers?"

"Yes. And they're beautiful," Aunt Verdella said as she reached for the bouquet. "Look what she did, Freeda."

"Ha-cha-cha!" Freeda said. "Damn, Button, that's gorgeous!"

Boohoo came racing through the house. "What's that?" he asked, reaching for the bouquet with grubby fingers. Aunt Verdella whipped it above her head and handed it to me so I could tuck it back in plastic.

The second Winnalee and Evalee got inside, Aunt Verdella gasped with an idea. "Freeda, why don't you take the girls over to see Reece's kitchen? Cupcake can stay with me while you run. Uncle Boohoo will help me watch her, won't you?"

"Yeah, she likes me. I made her laugh for the first time, didn't I Aunt Verdella?" Aunt Verdella looked up at us with a sly smile. "Yep. You did," she told him.

Boohoo wanted to hold Evalee, so Winnalee went into the living room to get the pillows propped.

"Yeah, you take the girls over, Freeda. Button won't believe it!"

"I, I have to get back to my sewing," I said. "I'm giving Cindy Jamison her final fitting tomorrow and I still have to attach this and stitch on the ribbons."

Freeda redoing Ma's floor was a matter I'd forced myself not to think about, because every time it was mentioned, it felt like someone was taking a seam ripper to my stomach. I didn't want to go, but Winnalee was eager to go *anywhere*, and called a yes into the dining room for us both.

"I'll get my keys," Freeda said. Freeda didn't say anything about me not going to Mardi Gras when Boohoo brought it up again, but I feared if I gave her eye contact, she might. Just as I feared that she might try to get Dad and I to actually say something to each other when we got to his place.

"He's probably sleeping," I said when we pulled in.

Freeda gave the horn three long bleats. "Not anymore," she said.

Winnalee ran ahead, Freeda close behind her. I lagged behind. I didn't want to go into that house—I hadn't even gone to dust Ma's bells since Freeda had started hanging out over there. I didn't want to see Dad, either.

"Hurry, Button!" Winnalee called from the kitchen when I got inside. "This is so cool!"

But I didn't budge. *Couldn't* budge. Because there, inside the door, was a cardboard box stuffed with Ma's old magazines, ready for the burning barrel. There was a wad of coffee grounds sitting on top, and some scrap window trim was wedged in the side.

I reached down and picked up the short stack of magazines sitting on top, shaking out the grounds. I shuffled through them, stopping when I came across a *Redbook* issue I remembered. It was sitting on the coffee table the summer the Malones lived in Dauber. I remembered Ma paging through it one evening, while I was spread out on the floor, coloring in my ballerina book and imagining what fun things Winnalee might find for us to do the next day.

I ran my fingers over the very caption Ma read aloud: *The Delightful World of Caroline Kennedy. First-hand report on the First Family's biggest little problem.* Ma chuckled softly to herself after she read it, which confused me. So when she went to add more ice to her tea, I got up and tiptoed to the ottoman where she'd set it. I wedged my hand on the page she was reading, then closed the magazine so I could see the cover. The picture was of the president of the United States, JFK, holding his daughter up in the air, one hand steadying her at the belly. Caroline was laughing and clutching her dad's hand. I studied the picture carefully, trying to understand the president's pride, and trying to understand why that girl made my ma smile. Everybody went on and on about her like she was Winnalee-pretty, even though she was as ordinary looking as me (only with a nicer hairdo). I could hear Ma banging the metal ice cube tray against the sink, so I didn't have time to read through all those words to find out why Ma thought it was cute that Caroline was a problem, when she didn't like girls who weren't well behaved.

I'd heard the freezer door close, and set the magazine down just the way she'd left it. I scooted back to flop before my coloring book, and with my yellow crayon, I colored Caroline-length wavy hair over the dancing lady's slicked-back bun.

"What's she doing in there?" I heard Freeda ask.

"Probably dusting Jewel's bells," Winnalee said. "She always does that, since Uncle Reece doesn't. Jewel loved those bells." I heard Freeda mumble something, then call out my name. She called out to Dad, too.

I rotated the magazines with shaky fingers and the last one on the stack was *Good Housekeeping*. And another cover photo of the Kennedys. The article was on a book written about the president. I searched for the date to see if it was printed before or after his death, and I pressed my fingers over my mouth when I found it: August 1966. The month and year Ma died.

I wanted to keep those magazines, just as Ma had, but when I heard Dad shuffling down the hallway, I quickly dropped them in the box like a thief who'd been caught red-handed. Dad had jeans on, but no belt or shirt. "Freeda, when the hell do you think I'm supposed to sleep?" he called in a voice I hadn't heard in years, and had forgotten. Light. Teasing. Warm, even. He startled when he saw me.

Freeda poked her nose out of the kitchen doorway. "You can go back to bed in a minute," she said. "I just wanted to show the girls our handiwork." Behind Freeda I could see a portion of the kitchen wall. Not the floor, but the wall. It was covered in wallpaper with big bright, surreal flowers in orange and yellow, with exaggerated stems and leaves. Ma hated wallpaper. And she hated the color orange. *What had they done?*

I shot out the door and ran across the highway. I didn't look back when I heard Winnalee call to me from the front steps. I just kept running, the air swirling my bare legs. Freeda had no business tampering. It was *Ma's* place. *Ma's* things. The things she saved, made, wanted. Even *I* didn't dare move them.

I was about a quarter mile down Peters Road and damp from tears and sweat when Freeda's car came barreling up alongside of me. "Button." Winnalee hung out of the passenger window as the car slowed to a crawl. "Button, what happened? Why'd you leave like that?"

"Get in, Button," Freeda said.

I didn't answer either of them. I just sobbed like a stupid baby and kept walking.

"Button, stop, will you?"

But I didn't.

I could hear Winnalee and Freeda hissing at each other, then the soft squeak of breaks.

Freeda left the car idling, the door hanging open. "Button, you stop right now," she ordered.

"Or what? You going to throw me down and sit on me?" I snapped, without breaking my stride.

"Maybe. If I have to!"

Freeda ran to catch up to me and grabbed my arm. I yanked out of her grasp and wrapped my arms around me like a sweater, pressing against my itchy skin. I kept walking.

"Button, what is it?" she asked, her sandals chomping at the gravel. "Everything was fine. What in the hell was that about?"

I couldn't ignore those words, even though I wanted to.

I stopped. "You're changing everything! Ma's house, the way we raise Boohoo. My clothes. Why are you doing this?"

"Because it *needs* changing, Button."

"But you're getting rid of my ma. The magazines . . . the floor . . . the paint. You're getting rid of *her*! Don't you see that?"

Freeda sighed, then wrapped her fingers around my upper arms. She put her face close to mine. "Honey, *I'm* not the one who got rid of your mom. God did. Or life did—whoever, whatever it is that decides these things. It wasn't me. I loved your Ma. She was my best friend, like Winnalee is yours. You think *I'd* choose to get rid of her? You *really* think that?"

I wanted Freeda to stop talking to me in such a compassionate tone.

"Button, these are only her things. They aren't her. She's gone. And that house is so filled with memories of her that your dad can't wade out of the past. But life is for the living, honey, and he's been living like he's dying for too long. I hope you and your dad remember Jewel forever. She was special enough that you should. And I hope you'll give Boohoo some memories of her, too. But there's a big difference between holding on to your memories, and holding on to the past. Am I making any sense? Probably not, because frankly, I don't know how in the hell to say what I mean.

"I'm not just talking about the family not going to Mardi Gras anymore, or your dad letting the house go to hell. I'm talking about what's at the core of this. The thing I can't put my finger on, but know it's there.

"I saw you and your dad together the night he came over for spaghetti. There's something as spiky and solid as a barbed-wire fence sitting between you two. He won't talk about it. I doubt you will. And I'm not sure Aunt Verdella knows. But whatever it is, it's so sharp that it's keeping both your hearts bleeding. And you may not like it, your dad might not like it, but I'm going to do my best to snap it. For Jewel, for all of you. I'm gonna do it so you can be a family again. So you can all get on with your lives. My friend would have wanted it that way. Do you understand?

"Do you?" she asked again when I didn't answer.

I nodded, my hair tangling in front of my face. Freeda smoothed the strands from my cheeks and her eyes were glossy as wet grass. "Honey, I know this is painful, but it has to be done. Let go, Button, and let me do this. For all of you." Winnalee was beside us then, and she wrapped her arms around our waists, and they led me to the car.

"By the way," Freeda said, when she was behind the wheel again. "Just so you know, . . . your ma hated those bells. She told me so. That sister of hers, Stella, brought her one back from Las Vegas—probably something she got for free—and Jewel made a big deal out of it to be nice. Aunt Verdella was there and thought Jewel was serious. So she gave her one for her birthday. Before long, everybody was giving them to her for gifts and eventually she had that whole shitload of them."

"She did not hate them," I protested. "She dusted them practically every day, until I was old enough to do it."

"Yeah," Freeda said. "But only because she hated dust worse than she hated those damn bells."

CHAPTER 35

BRIGHT IDEA #90: After you play beauty shop, your husband might say you look like a beauty queen, or he might just ask you where the Phillips screwdriver is. Either way, it doesn't matter, as long as your new hair makes you think nice things about yourself.

I suppose Freeda was trying to make amends when she came over the next morning, Boohoo in tow, and told Winnalee and me to be ready in half an hour. I was pressing a seam on one of Cindy's bridesmaids' gowns, but Freeda's eyes warned me that no excuse would do. She squatted down where Evalee was lying peacefully in her playpen and said, "Auntie Verdella is going to watch you."

"And me, Uncle Boohoo. I'm gonna watch you, too." He was about to lean over and pat her, but even at a distance I could smell Knucklehead on him and told him to wash first.

"Where we going?" Winnalee asked, but Freeda told her, "Never mind."

An hour later, Freeda slid her car up in front of the Cut 'n

Curl. "Come on," she said, as she waved to Aunt Verdella's beautician, Claire, who was standing in the window. "Button, you're gettin' a cut and a color. My treat. Then you're putting on that cute skirt you made, and we're sending soldier boy a Polaroid of you." Freeda got out of the car and headed for the door.

"Cool!" Winnalee said, as she nudged me with her hip to get out.

"*Not* cool, Winnalee," I whisper-hissed. "You saw Aunt Verdella's hair. It was Pepto-Bismol pink!"

Winnalee pushed my back until we got inside. Three older ladies were sitting against the wall under dryers, and two were in chairs getting trims, their white, dry curls floating to the floor like paint chips. The whole place stunk like perming solution and hair spray. I leaned down to Winnalee. "There's only old ladies here. What does *that* tell you?" My hands instinctively lifted to clutch my hair.

As it turned out, Aunt Verdella had helped convince Claire to let Freeda borrow her workstation over her lunch hour, since her next appointment wasn't until three (three guesses why!). "I wasn't about to color your hair with that boxed shit, or cut it with sewing shears," Freeda explained as she wrapped me in a plastic cape.

"I don't want my hair cut," I said, fear making me brave enough to say it.

"Well, too bad for your ass," Freeda said. "Because that's what you're gettin'."

Winnalee started giggling behind me. "She just means a trim, Button." She turned to Freeda. "You did just mean a trim, didn't you?"

"Nope, I'm gonna cut it to its last inch, thin it, then give you those little knots you used to love." Freeda shook with laughter. "Sit down, kid. Your ends look like a goddamn rat was chewin' on them. I'm just trimming it, that's all. Then I'm going to frost it. Well, not really frost it—I hate that skunk look—I'm going to use the same technique, but do nice, subtle, golden strands to brighten it up."

As Freeda worked, Winnalee stood beside my chair, lifting one bottle after another from the counter and spraying or dabbing whatever was in them down her curly strands. The beautician working alongside us frowned over the perfumy cloud, then started coughing. "Crissakes, Winnalee. Will you stop? You look like someone shellacked you already."

Freeda patted Winnalee's butt to move her out of the way the first time, but by the third time she had to move her, she snapped, "Winnalee, move your ass!" loud enough that even the old ladies under the dryers frowned.

Freeda stopped and dug in her purse. She pulled out some bills and handed them to Winnalee. "Here. Go buy yourself something pretty." Winnalee gave Freeda's cheek a peck, and off she went.

Freeda spun my chair sideways after she washed the gunk out of my hair and before she trimmed and dried me, so the end result would be a surprise. And when she finally spun me back to face the mirror, I was staring at somebody else, not me. Somebody who belonged on the cover of *Seventeen* magazine. The beauticians fawned over my new look, saying the touch of blond added warmth to my skin, and made my eyes "pop."

"You like it?" Freeda asked hopefully. I nodded dumbly, as I ran my hands down hair so satiny that it didn't even feel like my own.

"You just wait until I'm done with her," Freeda told the skinny beautician Winnalee had almost asphyxiated in that cloud of hair products. "She's got a great little skirt, full and bouncy, that's gonna give her some hips. With her good chest and tiny waist, she's gonna be drooling material."

The beautician's hands went instinctively to her own hips, hidden underneath a smock. "A fuller skirt will help?" she asked. And before you knew it, Freeda was working her magic, telling the whole salon how the "art of distraction" works, and how each of them could bring the eye to their best qualities, and downplay the parts that were "less blessed," or "overly blessed."

Winnalee walked in just as I stood up. She took one look at me and said, "Holy shit!"

Freeda made Winnalee sit down and trimmed the bottom of her hair, as she explained to the ladies what body parts of her own she accentuated, and which parts she was disguising—I was glad she didn't feel inclined to *show* them.

The women might have kept Freeda there forever if she'd let them, but she cut them off, paid Claire for the use of her station, and we left.

When we got home, Boohoo met us at the door. "Guess what, Winnalee? Evalee got all the way up on her elbows. She did! She got up and looked right at me."

Winnalee frowned. "I missed it," she said.

After Aunt Verdella admired my new hair, I ran home to change into my bouncy skirt. Winnalee helped me pick out shoes and a top (a gold one), then Freeda dragged me around the yard and bent me into one "natural" pose after another. Poses, she said, that would best accentuate my "perky knockers" and "long legs."

"Hold that pose," Freeda told me, once she had me sitting on the picnic table, skirt hiked and perfectly fanned, my legs crossed so my thigh would look fuller, my arms behind me and spread, fingers splayed so I wouldn't tip over, and my back so arched that I was sure I'd look like the McDonald's arches. "Hold it, hold it . . . ," Freeda said as she moved to take a few shots. Then we stood behind Boohoo at the picnic table and waited for the snapshots to appear on the paper squares like magic.

After we got home, I snuck peeks at my photograph every time Winnalee wasn't looking. In the morning I tucked my letter, my picture, and my hope into an envelope and sent it off to Jesse.

CHAPTER 36

BRIGHT IDEA #7: If your boyfriend says he doesn't want you going out with other guys, and you tell him you won't, but then do, just tell him that it's a woman's peroggerative to change your mind. If he gets mad, tell him to hit the road. Sound mean when you say it, too, or he might hit you instead of the road.

The day of Cindy Jamison's wedding, Aunt Verdella watched as Winnalee and I loaded the dresses into the van, a smile tickling her lips. She put her arm around Freeda, who was holding Evalee. "I sure am proud of these girls. Thank you, Freeda, for lending me the camera, and watching the little ones so I can tag along and get pictures of Button's first bridal gown."

"Little *ones*?" Boohoo said. He went to stand next to Freeda, and pointed first at himself, then Evalee. "Look at this. Me. Big. Cupcake. Little."

I sat in the back with the gowns, so Aunt Verdella could take the only other seat in the van. Cindy was getting married at the Lutheran church a block off Main Street. We were heading out an extra twenty-five minutes early, because Uncle Rudy had warned us about the detour on Highway 8. "They're redoing that bridge just past the Smithys, and the county's putting in new culverts on a five-mile stretch," he'd said. "You've got to go all the way down Pike's Peak Road, and up Circle Avenue."

Linda was waiting for us, along with Cindy and her bridesmaids, Mrs. Jamison, Marge, and Hazel. The whole dressing room turned into a bouquet of color as the girls slipped into their dresses.

"Look at her dress!" Cindy said to her bridesmaids, when she saw Winnalee. Winnalee had grabbed one of her long granny dresses from her closet, decided it was boring, and shredded the dress from about the knees down with jagged horizontal cuts. She'd done the same with the sleeves, but her cuts were vertical. "I love the way you dress," Cindy told Winnalee. She loved my hair, too, and wanted to know who'd streaked it. She was disappointed to hear it wasn't a local.

I dressed Cindy, and she waved her arms so the petal edges could flutter. "This dress is *so* cool!" Even Mrs. Jamison called the dress "lovely," and bragged to the pastor's wife that Cindy's dress was "one of a kind." Designed just for her.

Linda was pleased, too. After the girls were dressed, she confessed that she had been nervous about me taking on a whole wedding myself, then added, "But like Hazel and Marge just said, they couldn't have done a better job themselves." I smiled, because I knew it was true.

Aunt Verdella took a whole roll of pictures. She gave Cindy and her bridesmaids each one, then handed the rest to me and Winnalee.

I helped the bridesmaids dress, then lined them up so I

could make sure that the hems, when side by side, made a perfectly straight line. While I did this, Aunt Verdella and Linda talked about when or if her husband might get called back to work.

Before we left, Linda held up her finger like she just remembered something, and pulled a paper bag out of her trunk. She handed it to me. "Some girls brought these jeans by. They said you'd know what to do with them. Their phone numbers are pinned to the jeans so you know whose are whose." No doubt Linda thought it was a little mending on the side.

Aunt Verdella insisted we stop for ice-cream floats before going home. She prattled on and on about what a beautiful job we'd done, while we ate. Winnalee shoveled a scoop of ice cream into her mouth and her eyes got huge. She made a couple high pitched grunts, and I thought maybe she'd gotten a brain freeze, but she was even more excited after she swallowed. "Hey, I just thought of something. Aunt Verdella, does anyone ever sell old clothes at the Community Sale?"

She thought. "Well, Aggie usually has some old dresses and hats and things. Most of them come from the forties and the fifties. Some sixties. Just old junk clothes some pack rat like me had boxed away."

"Do they have old buttons and jewelry, belts there, too, like they did when I was a kid?"

"Agnes and Mavis usually carry some. Why?"

Winnalee turned to me, all excited. "Button, you know that wine-colored dress I have that you love? That long one that I wear bunched under the boobs with that big brooch? I got that old dress in a secondhand store. The pin, too. I couldn't do with it what I wanted because I can't sew, but you and I could do that sorta thing together. Let's go to the Community Sale this Saturday and see what we can find. I'll bet we could recycle some old clothes and make some cool hippie dresses. Dresses that Cindy, or those girls at the Purple Haze would buy. Aunt Verdella, will you crochet more of that lace for us? We could do up some old jeans, too."

"Sure, honey."

"This'll be fun. It'll give me something to do when I'm not wiping baby butts and making bottles."

That Saturday, we packed a lunch and took off for the Community Sale. Winnalee and I sang along with the radio as we followed Freeda's car. In the backseat of the Rambler, Boohoo made Evalee's bear dance, and Evalee grinned, her too-big bonnet askew on her head. Through Freeda's back window, I could see her hand gesturing as she talked, and I smiled as I sang. It was one of those moments, one of those days, that I knew I'd remember forever. Not because of its bigness, but because in that simple moment, our hearts were light and happy, and we were twined like roots of the same tree.

The lady named Aggie had a whole rack filled with old-fashioned dresses in tiny prints. I blushed while Winnalee dickered with her until we got the whole lot of them for half of what they'd cost individually. I had no idea how we'd take fifteen outdated dresses and turn them into something girls would buy, but it would be fun to see what Winnalee came up with.

Three hours later, we had the back of Evalee's stroller and my trunk stuffed with old clothes, belts, purses, and bags of gaudy costume jewelry. Evalee was getting fussy, and we were melting, so we went home.

We ate bologna sandwiches stuffed with crushed potato chips, then I lugged Evalee's playpen downstairs because the upstairs was heated like an oven. Winnalee dozed off on the couch while Evalee sat in her infant seat next to me.

I was too eager to wait for bedtime to write to Jesse, so around dusk, I got out my stationery. I started my letter with

It's the little things, the simple times, that we remember, and I told him about the little things in my day that I loved, and about the quiet times I remembered with *him* that I loved. I was on page four when Winnalee woke. Evalee was still sitting contentedly in her chair, watching me, smiling when I paused to talk to her, so Winnalee went off to fill the baby's bathtub.

I was licking the envelope when Winnalee shouted, "Button, come here a minute! Hurry!"

I raced into the kitchen. "What's the matter?"

Winnalee had the baby lying naked on a towel on the table. "Look at this, Button." She pointed at the red, peppery rash that spotted her chest and belly. "I think she's got the measles!"

"They get shots for measles, don't they? I don't think she can have the measles. You got her her shots, right?"

"I didn't get her any shots. I wasn't around. What if Freeda didn't? I think these are measles, Button. Go get Freeda and Aunt Verdella, will you?" Winnalee begged with such desperation, that Evalee could have been wheezing her last breath, rather than making soft little B sounds, her tiny fists punching happily at the air.

"She doesn't look sick to me," I said.

"Just get them. Hurry!"

Uncle Rudy was sitting in his lawn chair. Strands of hay were clinging to his pants and stuck to his shoes. "You're back," I said.

"Yep. Just pulled in." I leaned over and gave his cheek a kiss, then hurried to the house. Boohoo was coming out as I was going in, and slammed into me. "Look what I got at the Community Sale," he said, holding out a ball of twine about a foot in diameter. "Aunt Verdella got something good, too, but I can't tell you what it is. I'm gonna go show Uncle Rudy my binder twine."

"She doesn't have measles," Freeda said when I found her. "Tell her I'll be right over."

Winnalee was almost in tears when we got inside. "Geez, you took long enough."

Aunt Verdella and Freeda peered over Evalee, who was still naked and grinning on the table. Aunt Verdella was about to blurt something out, then she folded her hands across her tummy and backed up, waiting for Freeda to speak.

"Winnalee, that's just heat rash," Freeda said.

Winnalee blinked up at her. "Is that bad?"

"It's nothin'," Freeda said. "Just bathe her and dry her off good and powder her. Leave her naked, but for her diaper. It's not supposed to drop below seventy-nine tonight. It'll be gone by morning."

"You sure? Because it might be measles. Did she have a shot for measles?"

"It's not goddamn measles, Winnalee. For crissakes, it's heat rash."

"It's heat rash, honey," Aunt Verdella confirmed. She tugged her neckline out from her chest. "Look, I even got a bit of it today."

Freeda laughed. "Then maybe we'd best strip you down to your undies and powder you up, too."

I would have thought Winnalee would have relaxed after Aunt Verdella confirmed Freeda's diagnosis, but instead she burst into tears.

"Winnalee, what's the matter?" Freeda asked.

Winnalee shrugged. "I just got scared, that's all."

"Yep, that's what we mothers do. Get used to it." She caressed Winnalee's back.

While Winnalee bathed Evalee, Freeda and Aunt Verdella and I meandered out to the porch, where it was a bit cooler. I thought they'd head home, but Freeda flopped into a chair and told Aunt Verdella to "take a load off."

"But Boohoo . . ."

"Rudy's there. Sit."

"But Freeda . . . ," Aunt Verdella said between her teeth, like Freeda wasn't getting something.

"Relax."

We left the yard light off because the moon was bright, and to have it on would only draw more mosquitoes. After Winnalee fed Evalee and got her down, Winnalee came out carrying a filled pitcher clinking with ice on the silver platter she'd found in the back of the cupboard and liked, even though it was tarnished. She had a small plate stacked with cookies, too.

Freeda reached for a glass and took a long gulp, smacking her lips as if it was hand-squeezed lemonade, rather than lime Kool-Aid. "Now don't I feel just like frikken Scarlett O'Hara, sitting on her veranda, getting waited on hand and foot. Thanks, honey," Freeda said.

"Oh, I loved that movie!" Aunt Verdella said as she took her glass and reached for a store-bought gingersnap. Freeda went to bat her hand, then stopped. "Oh hell, go at it," she said. "Gotta treat yourself now and then."

I scootched over so Winnalee could sit with me since there were only three chairs.

"My girlfriends and I went to see *Gone with the Wind* at least six times when it came out—and we cried at the end every time."

"You saw it when it was released?" I asked.

"Wasn't that about a hundred years ago?" Winnalee said, then sheepishly added, "Sorry."

Aunt Verdella laughed. "It was 1939. I was thirty . . . uh . . . thirty-six."

"Wow," Winnalee said and I nudged her with my elbow. "I know," she whispered in my hair, "but '39? Man."

"We were all madly in love with Rhett Butler," Aunt Verdella said. "But who wasn't? To this day, I think of him leaning on the banister, and well, put it this way, he could have parked his slippers under my bed any day."

I sputtered Kool-Aid onto my shirt.

"He had the breath of a dead fish, you know," Freeda said, and it was Winnalee's turn to spit her drink.

"Who? Rhett Butler?" Aunt Verdella asked.

"Well, Clark Gable," Freeda said, which kept Winnalee and me laughing. "Vivien Leigh said so. Anyway, that's what the women at the salon told me. One of them read it in a movie magazine. I guess it was from his dentures—doesn't make sense, though." She shrugged.

"You're kidding!" Aunt Verdella said this as though suddenly her chances for a juicy, sweet kiss from him were dashed.

Headlights glowed in the edges of the trees close to the road and Aunt Verdella got up and went to the screen. She turned to Freeda. "He's coming!"

"Who?" Winnalee and I asked in unison.

"Rhett Butler and Ashley Wilkes, by the looks of it," Freeda said when Tommy's truck pulled into the drive and Tommy and Craig stepped out.

"Oh my God," Winnalee said. "Do I have spit-up on my shirt?" I couldn't see in the dim light, so I pulled her hair over her shoulder.

Freeda stood up. "Tommy Smithy? Is that you? Get over here you little shit!"

Tommy looked shy when he stepped onto the porch and Freeda reached for him—either because he still had a crush on her, or because he was remembering when he did.

"My God," Freeda said when she let go of him. "Just look at you. All filled out, shoulders like a football player. I'll be damned."

Tommy hurried to introduce Craig, who was acting even

shyer than usual. I was waiting for Freeda to say something obnoxious to him, too, but she didn't.

"I left a message with Ada, asking Tommy to do a little favor for me," Aunt Verdella explained to Winnalee and me, her chest puffed with pride.

"Sorry I'm so late, Mrs. Peters," Tommy said. "Craig and I went fishing after we got done with the baler. Ma told me you called when I got back, and we headed right over to Hank's."

"Well I'm just glad you came. And, that you brought help. I was thinking you and Rudy could carry it in, but I worry about his back."

"Bring what in?" Winnalee asked.

"You'll see."

Winnalee and I waited on the porch with Freeda, while Tommy and Craig went to the back of Tommy's truck. "Jesus, I can't believe that Tommy Smithy. Wasn't he scrawny, and goofy lookin' as a squirrel when he was a kid?"

"Enough about Tommy," Winnalee whispered. "What about Craig? Isn't he a hunk? Did you see him looking at me?"

"Yeah, he's a cute one," Freeda said. "But sorry if I didn't notice him looking at you. I guess I was too busy watching Tommy with this one."

"Oh, don't expect Button to have noticed. Her radar is broken."

"Well, then I'll spell it out for you, Button," Freeda said. "Looks like that soldier boy of yours has some competition." I wished Jesse had heard her comment. He still hadn't written, even though he *had* to have gotten my picture by now.

Tommy backed his truck up to the porch door, and there was a big square box covered in tarp. "Be careful boys . . . don't drop it."

"Holy crap, Button. You see that? It's a TV set!" Winnalee shouted. "Wow, we can watch *Dark Shadows* and *American Bandstand* and everything, right here at home!"

"I paid Hank for it and told him I'd pick it up one way or another."

Winnalee and I wrapped Aunt Verdella with hugs as she followed the boys up the steps, telling them to be careful not to nick the cabinet because it was in good shape. "It's an older set, so the color might not be as good as it should be, but Hank said it works real good."

Tommy and Craig stood holding the giant console. "Where do you want it?" Tommy asked.

Winnalee and I looked around the living room and the guys waited as we women dickered over which corner it would look best in, then we stopped them before the legs touched the floor, because we changed our minds. Winnalee's the one who started saying, "Oh, fiddle-dee-dee," each time we changed our mind, and sent them to a different spot.

"There," we finally agreed. "We can see it good from the couch and the chair," Winnalee said. "And from the kitchen," I added.

Only the reception wasn't great in that corner, so they had to move it back to the first place we'd tried.

I couldn't resist teasing Tommy by saying, "Wait, on second thought . . ."

Tommy cut me off. "Frankly, Scarlett, I don't give a damn. It's stayin' right where it is."

Aunt Verdella waited until Tommy had the TV plugged in and the rabbit ears adjusted, then she thanked the guys for helping. "I'd better get back home. Rudy probably fell asleep in the lawn chair, and who knows what Boohoo's doing."

"I'll head back with you," Freeda said. "You'll likely need my help freeing Rudy from the web of twine Boohoo has him tangled in by now."

"Oh," Tommy said before they could get out the door. "Mom told me to tell you guys that she's having a big cookout next weekend to celebrate the end of haying season—if we get done. Probably on Sunday. She'll be calling you."

After they all left, Winnalee and I sat on the couch side by side and watched a stupid Western because that's all that was on, and we laughed as we remembered when we used to play that we were saloon girls. Then Winnalee got serious and said, "Craig looked right in my face when I showed him how cute Evalee was, and I don't think he checked out my ass once, did he?" I told her I didn't think so, either, and she smiled first, then frowned. "Wait a minute . . . is that a good thing, or a bad thing?"

CHAPTER 37

BRIGHT IDEA #87: On days when your head hurts on the outside because you didn't know when to get out of the sun, or on days when your head hurts so bad on the inside that you don't want to make pot holders because your ma got spilled, it can still turn out to be a good day if even one good person does one nice thing for you.

The morning after the Community Sale, Winnalee hung the old dresses in a line along the upstairs banister, and Boohoo helped spread the buttons and jewelry over the coffee table so she could see them as she sketched, until he lost interest in the buttons because *Captain Kangaroo* came on. He turned to Evalee, who was sitting beside him in her infant seat. "Watch this, Cupcake." He swerved her chair to face the TV. "I think Bun is gonna get clobbered this morning."

Boohoo turned to the couch, where we sat contemplating a neckline alteration. He was giggling. "Look at her legs," he said, pointing at Evalee, whose fists were punching and roly-poly legs were kicking. "She likes Cap'n, too."

I was just opening the waxy milk carton to fix Boohoo some cereal when Winnalee screamed out, "Boohoo!"

I poked my head out of the kitchen, just as Winnalee was snatching Evalee out of Boohoo's arms. "What are you doing? You know you're not supposed to pick her up!"

Boohoo looked indignant. "Her legs were going because she wanted to hop. Like Hoppy. So I was helping her get up."

Winnalee was patting Evalee's back as though she *had* been dropped, when I got in the room with the bowl of Quisp. I told Boohoo, "Toads hop, people don't."

He looked up at me with quiet defiance. "Uh-uh," he said. "Aunt Verdella hops."

Over the next few days, Winnalee sketched her alteration idea for each dress while I sewed. "Geesh, Winnalee, these are taking lots more time than I thought they would. I could have sewn this dress from scratch in the time it's taken me to do the alterations. And hand-sewing all that hardware on them? Geez."

"Then we'll charge an arm and a leg," she said. I wasn't sure anyone would buy them, but Winnalee was convinced that Cindy and her bridesmaids and the girls whose jeans I dressed up, would scarf up every one of them. Then their friends would see them and want some, and well, we'd have ourselves a little business going in no time.

"Was that the door?" Winnalee asked. Freeda's voice rang out, so we scooped up Evalee and hurried downstairs.

Freeda took the baby and smooched her cheeks with kisses, then asked if I'd found the canning jars that Aunt Verdella asked me to search for in the basement. I told her they were in the kitchen, washed, then, while Winnalee led Freeda there, I headed outside because I'd heard the mailman's car pull up.

"Here you go," he called as he leaned out the passenger window with my mail.

A letter from Jesse! I snatched it out of the mailman's hands, and it was thick between my thumb and fingers. Jesse *never* wrote more than a couple of paragraphs! I stood holding it, my quickened heart chasing away every thought but opening it and savoring every word.

I didn't want to go back into the house, because I knew Winnalee and Freeda would stand over my shoulder, eager to see what impression my photograph made. I only wanted to be alone with Jesse's letter, so I jumped in the Rambler and headed down the road.

I shocked myself when I turned down Fossard's drive, as if I'd forgotten I was ever terrified of the place. I didn't look to either side, but kept my eyes straight ahead, thinking of nothing but how I wanted to read my letter down where the fairies played. Where magical, good things could happen.

I drove as far as the ruts allowed, then left the Rambler sitting in the open. I tugged the bulky letter out of my pocket and held it tight to my middle as I half ran, half skidded down the bank. I didn't stop until I was safely on the rock where I'd found Winnalee the last time I was here. The sun was sparking off the water, and up above the falls, insects made miniature ripples as they skipped across the surface.

I drew my knees up and carefully tore Jesse's letter open at one end like I always did, so I wouldn't tear my name, written in his hand. I unfolded the letter—four pages long!—and smoothed it over my naked knees.

Dear Evy,

Sorry I haven't written in awhile, but things got a little crazy here, plus my buddy Bill got a "Dear John" letter from his girlfriend and was pretty messed up for awhile. They were supposed to marry on his leave. Poor bastard. But that's not the only reason you haven't heard from me.

Christ, Evy. I've been sitting here for twenty minutes now, chain-smoking while I try to get up enough courage to tell you something. Isn't that stupid? We've been close for years, and you've been writing me long letters—which I LOVE—spilling your guts to me about what's happening in your life, and your feelings. Why I should be nervous about THIS then, is beyond me. You've always been the one I could talk to about love. Yet I'm nervous as hell right now.

Jesse was going to talk to me about love? I knew it! *I just knew it!* A wave of joy whooshed over me like water over rocks, washing clean every doubt I ever had about Jesse being a snowflake and therefore, not for me. I flipped the filled page over, and the hem of my hair brushed over the paper like a painter's brush dipped in gold.

Remember awhile back, when I said I'd been granted a three-day pass and was going to Ulm? Bill and Deek and I went (this was before Bill's woman wrote that for-shit letter). Deek's married, Bill was engaged, so it wasn't like we were heading to Ulm to get some action. We were going to kick back, and have ourselves some good German brew. We went to this bar where a lot of the GIs go, a lot of whores, too. But it was too crowded, too damn hot, too tempting for my buddies maybe, so we found this bar off the beaten path. And well. Shit. I met somebody there, Evy. Yeah, yeah, I know. I've been spouting off about girls to you for the past four years, but wait. Wait until I'm finished because this has an unexpected ending.

My breath snagged on my ribs. Jesse had met someone? I pressed my hand over my mouth and my eyes darted side to side, as if desperate to find some better truth to look at, than the one I was seeing on paper.

My hands shook the paper, and the wind ruffled its corners. *Wait until I'm finished because this has an unexpected ending.* I read that line again. And again. Telling myself to swallow my fear and keep reading, because maybe, just maybe, what he was going to tell me was that he couldn't act on that attraction because when he tried to, all he could see was my picture hanging above his cot, and something kept tugging his heart back to me.

I don't know why I was drawn to her. She wasn't beautiful, maybe not even pretty. Yet there was just something about her that kept me glancing over at the table where she sat all alone.

Evy, you know me. I've probably had a girl for every foil wrapper in that crazy chain you made, but this is different. We spent that night together—the next night too. On the third day, she painted me—she watercolors and sells her paintings for big money. So okay, here's the kicker—SHE'S FORTY YEARS OLD! Almost as old as my mother! A widow, and she's got a grown kid a year younger than me. There's a sadness about her that just makes me want to . . .

The moan I made sounded muffled, like it was underwater. I couldn't read any more. I couldn't.

I tossed the letter to the side, and the wind pushed it against the boulder I sat on. I rocked myself as I cried for how stupid I'd been to think that any man but Uncle Rudy could love me, and how dumb I was to believe that anyone would really stay in my life forever.

I rocked myself until the sun disappeared behind rain clouds, and thunder rumbled in the distance. Then I stood up, wanting only to run. But I couldn't leave that letter at the falls and risk someone reading it and witnessing my humiliation. And I couldn't bring it home for the same reason.

The letter was too thick to rip in a stack, so I took the first page and pinned the others against me with my arm, then tore the sheet into tiny pieces, tossing them into the swirling water, where they fell like confetti that had lost its way to a party. One by one, I ripped the pages, the shame and anger I felt at myself and my broken radar making my hands strong.

I had the last page torn in half when I saw the P.S. at the bottom: *Hey, great picture! Deek said you were a babe and Bill asked if you were taken. I told him hands off, because you are far too sweet for him.* I ripped that page in even finer pieces, and choked on my sobs as the raging dark water swallowed the last bit of my hope.

The sky rumbled as I headed back to my car. But I couldn't go home. Not just yet. Winnalee would know something was wrong and drill me until she guessed the rest. Then she'd call Jesse a prick and tell me I was too good for him. And Freeda'd say the same, and tell me not to let any guy tear me down. Aunt Verdella would cry, of course, her expression the same one Ma wore when the only boy I had the guts to ask to the Sadie Hawkins dance when I was a freshman—Robert, a raindrop like me, with so many zits his chin looked like mincemeat—turned me down. If that's how they reacted, I knew I'd split open like a filleted fish. And with no backbone left and my panic and angst lying bare, I knew I'd pathetically plead with each of them to never, ever leave me.

I drove toward town in a blazing storm that both darkened and lit the sky at the same time. I didn't care if it blew me to bits, and I would have driven right through it, but the same wind that swirled the treetops was whipping sheets of rain at the windshield. Between the rain and my tears—and on a road I wasn't familiar with because of the detour—I could no longer see where I was going. I pulled over, leaned my head against the window, and cried with noise—something I hadn't done since Ma died. I'd cry as long and hard as I needed to in a desperate attempt to dump out every bit of disappointment I felt, so I wouldn't risk taking it home with me.

It wasn't the sound of knuckles whacking against my window that alerted me to the fact that I was no longer alone, but the glass shaking against my head. I startled and turned, and tried to make out the face obscured by rain, and the fog over the glass that my heavy sobs had made. "Evy?"

I swabbed my face with one hand, and rubbed a circle on the glass with the other. It took me a moment to recognize Craig, because his blond hair was darkened and flattened from the rain.

I wiped my face some more as Craig sprinted around the car and slipped in the passenger seat. His shirt was soaked and clinging to his shoulders. "You break down, or are you just waiting out the storm?"

"Waiting out the storm," I said, my voice hoarse. I looked straight ahead to hide my bloodshot eyes, and hoped he'd think the dampness on my cheeks was from the rain.

"Yeah, it's coming down pretty hard. I was heading home and saw your car. I just wanted to make sure you weren't having trouble." He rubbed the knuckles on his right hand as if they were sore, but he didn't say anything. I didn't know what to say, either.

"It looks like the rain's easing up a bit, so I guess I can get moving again," I said, though it didn't look like it was letting up at all. But storms never last forever.

"Yeah . . . Evy? Are you sure you're okay?" he asked.

I nodded and he stared at my profile for a second longer, then he nodded, too.

I watched the rain over the back window ripple his form as he trotted back to his car.

. . .

Before I reached Dauber, I had my plan. I'd open the shop with my key and pick through spools of lavender thread that I'd claim I needed for a new sewing project—which was true, even if I didn't need it immediately. I'd claim that I called inside that I was going, but they must not have heard me. Then I'd tell them that I'd gotten confused along the detour and drove almost to Porter before I realized how far out of the way I'd gone. I'd hint that it was my fear over the approaching storm that had me muddled, and that I hadn't wanted to leave town until the sky stopped sparking and the narrow streams running alongside the curbs had drained. And I'd never tell any of them about Jesse's letter. I'd only pretend to lose interest, so that hopefully, by the time Jesse got up the guts to tell his mom about this woman, enough time would have passed that they'd not expect it to sting me.

When I got home, Winnalee was on the couch, the TV blaring. A laundry basket stuffed with clothes was in the doorway.

I wasn't standing there more than fifteen seconds when Winnalee looked up. "Oh, you're back. Where'd you go?" she asked as she untangled her hair with her fingers.

I recited my fib, and she didn't question it. She only asked if I'd keep an ear out for Evalee so she could get the clothes washed.

Two people were kissing on TV, and I got up to shut it off. Out the window, I saw Winnalee, climbing up Aunt Verdella's front steps, the basket on her hip. She stopped and looked toward the driveway. I moved to another window and saw Tommy getting out of his truck. Winnalee looked over to our place as Tommy talked, his hands working like puppets. No doubt he'd spotted her and thought I was there, too. I knew why he'd come. Craig had told him how he'd found me earlier in the day, and now he was telling Winnalee.

I went into the kitchen and poured myself some water. On TV that's what they always gave people when they were upset. I didn't expect Tommy to walk in when I ignored his knocking, but he did.

"I just wanted to make sure you were okay," he said. I didn't say anything, so he followed it up with "I know, Evy."

"Of course you do. I knew Craig would blab."

"I don't just mean I knew you were crying. I mean, I know *why* you were crying."

I shut the faucet off. "What, are you psychic?"

I heard a noise, and strained to hear in case it was Evalee fussing. But I didn't hear anything but the thumping of my own pulse in my ears.

"No," Tommy said. "Craig and I stopped for a beer last night, and Amy was there. She was flappin' her gums to her friends about Jesse Dayne, and the letter she got from him. I guess she'd written to tell him she wanted to get back with him, and he told her he was seeing someone in Germany. He must have told you the same thing."

I turned away. "So? Why would that upset me? Jesse and I are friends. That's it. Just friends."

"He told you, didn't he? That's why you were so upset."

I turned away and grabbed the dishcloth—grateful that Winnalee always left droplets of milk, or crumbs of some kind or other on the counter. I kept my head down as I swirled the dishrag. "I wasn't crying. My face was wet from the rain."

Tommy sighed. "Why are you lying?"

I spun and faced him. "Well maybe I'm just trying to keep a little shred of dignity, okay?"

I don't know what I expected Tommy to do with that, but certainly not what he did. He came forward and before I could raise my arms to block him, he put his arms around me.

Tommy's skin had the faint smell of fresh hay clinging to

the scent of soap. I wanted to shove him away, but instead I fell against him. "I feel so dumb," I sobbed.

"We've all been that kind of dumb before," he said.

"Button?" Winnalee's voice rang from the other side of the house. Tommy backed away and I scraped the tears from my face.

"Honey?" Aunt Verdella and Freeda echoed, as if I was lost and they were my search party.

They came barreling into the kitchen, all three of them, their arms reaching.

"Jesse—that stupid asshole! Why didn't you tell me, Button?"

Aunt Verdella squeezed me to her. "Oh, honey, I'm so sorry! That boy's gotta be blind, if he can't see that the best girl he could ever find is right here in Dauber."

"I hope that old broad gives him crabs," Winnalee said.

"Don't you feel bad about yourself for this, Button," Freeda said.

Aunt Verdella and Freeda led me to the couch and sat down beside me. They wrapped their arms around me tighter than a turtleneck, and Winnalee crouched before me, her hands cupping my knees as though they were beautiful. Tommy slipped out the door, and Winnalee and Freeda and Aunt Verdella continued, saying all the things I knew they'd say. But while I expected to feel humiliated, I didn't. I only felt loved.

CHAPTER 38

BRIGHT IDEA #39: Don't start a greace fire if you don't know how to put one out.

You never really know how life is going to go. You make your plans, you have your hopes, you try to guess, but you never really know.

On the day of Ada's cookout, I took my bath at dawn so I wouldn't have to wait for Winnalee, who stayed in the tub forever once she finally got in. Then I rolled my damp hair in the big, plastic curlers I picked up last time I went to town, and hurried across the road to grab an oblong cake pan from Aunt Verdella. It wasn't seven o'clock yet, but Aunt Verdella always woke early on big days.

Aunt Verdella and Uncle Rudy were in the kitchen—

Freeda and Boohoo were still asleep. "Just look at what me and Freeda did yesterday," Aunt Verdella said, pointing to the rows of canned food lined on the counter and covering half of the table. "We put up eight quarts of tomatoes, ten quarts of beans, and we made six more jars of pickles last night."

Uncle Rudy looked up from his coffee. "I'm gonna have pickles comin' out of my ears," he said.

Aunt Verdella laughed. "Freeda did such a good job takin' care of that garden while Rudy was haying, that we'd probably have enough food canned for a lifetime, if they'd keep that long. And string beans—we can't keep up!"

I was crouched down digging in the cupboard for a cake pan when Uncle Rudy said he'd better go outside to see if his lawn chair needed any company. "We're gonna have a fun day," Aunt Verdella said. "One to remember."

"I'll dress Evalee," I told Winnalee, eager to share the surprise I'd been working on in snatches when I could sneak some sewing in.

It was impossible not to smooch Evalee's soft cheeks at least a hundred times every time you picked her up. I kissed her until her cheeks got red, then held her to me and peppered her head with soft kisses as I told her that she would always be special, no matter what boy failed to realize it.

Evalee looked like a little princess in the lavender dress I'd made her, with matching bloomers and enough ruffles to make Cindy Jamison faint. I tied the little eyelet bonnet under her chin. "There. This one won't bobble on you. See? Remember when Auntie Button measured your head?"

When we got downstairs, Winnalee was still in the bathroom, bent over so she could wrap a towel around her dripping hair. "I have a surprise to show you," I called.

"Fun!" she said.

I was holding Evalee out when she came out of the bathroom stark naked, and she squealed when she took her, "Oh, Button, she looks adorable!" And then she noticed the best part. The print on the fabric.

"*Fairies?* You found material with little *fairies* on it?" Her laughter rang through the house. She held Evalee high and twirled her in circles. "Look what I found in Dauber after all! My very own little fairy!"

"I made her this, too," I said. I slipped the strap for the quilted diaper bag in the same fabric down my arm. "So you don't have to carry her things in that ratty army bag."

"Aw, Button. That was *so* dang nice of you!"

I laughed. "'Dang'? I don't think I've ever heard you say 'dang' before. Not once. Not ever."

"Me and Freeda are turning over a new leaf," she explained. "We're not gonna swear around her—or any kids for that matter—anymore. We decided that if we can give up sex until we find somebody worth having it with, then we can probably give up cussing until these kids grow, too."

"Oh, lands sake, look at our Cupcake!" Aunt Verdella cried out when she spotted us crossing the road. Freeda scooted her purse up her arm and reached for Evalee, then the two of them fussed over her like it was the first time they'd laid eyes on her. Winnalee insisted we wear two of our "designs" because it would be good advertisement, so I wore bell-bottoms tacked with crocheted lace down one leg, and the lacy dress we converted into a long, empire-style shirt. We'd added new sleeves and random patches, made from scraps of other fabrics. I wasn't sure about the color and print combinations—akin to the pot holders Winnalee used to make—but the style was really cool. Winnalee was wearing one of our recycled dresses, I think from the forties, the waist and hem lifted to make it an empire-style minidress, but keeping the same princess neckline and capped sleeves. "And oh, look at the girls!" Aunt Verdella said to Freeda, and they fussed over our outfits as if we were every bit as lovely in them as Evalee was in hers.

"Wait until you see the rest," Winnalee told them. "We have four left to alter. When they're all finished, me and Button will put on a fashion show for you."

When we got to the Smithys', cars were crammed in the driveway and lined along the dirt road. Boohoo was in the backseat beside Evalee. "Hey, look!" he shouted. "Tommy's got his Piper out!" And there it was, sitting in the field, at the mouth of a makeshift runway mowed into the field.

"Far out!" Winnalee said. "I'm gonna make him take me up in it, too. He promised."

"He's gonna take me, too," Boohoo said, as he bounced on the seat. Even the thought of Boohoo up in the air in that old contraption was enough to make me sweat—not that I needed to figure out how to keep that from happening today. There was a thick haze hanging in the air (which hopefully wouldn't lift anytime soon), and Tommy wouldn't fly when visibility was poor.

We pulled over on the side of the road and parked. Aunt Verdella hopped ahead of us, staying close to the line of parked cars. "Oh my gosh, look at all these cars. Ada said her invite list had grown, but I had no idea. Everybody in Dauber must be here. Good thing she made it pot luck.

"Rudy, Rudy, is that Reece's car?" Aunt Verdella hurried to get a closer look before he could answer. "It is," she called back. Freeda, pretty in the same yellow shift she'd made spaghetti in, her hair glossy and ratted high at the crown, pretended not to hear.

Long tables made from boards propped on sawhorses and

adorned with a variety of tablecloths sat in the center of the yard, and clusters of metal lawn chairs borrowed from Ada's church were scattered here and there. Tommy and a couple of older men were manning two grills that filled the air with beef-scented smoky plumes. All around us people were chattering—about the length of time it took them to get there because of the road construction, about the haying season, their aches and pains, and just about anything else.

As we carried the food we'd brought to the table, Boohoo pointed across the yard at a boy about his size, who was running with a pack of little kids. "That's Rupert! He's from my school." Boohoo ran off to catch up with him, and Aunt Verdella and I sent trailing after him our warnings to stay in the yard and be good.

"Look who's here," Winnalee said. I turned, expecting to see Fanny Tilman, based on Winnalee's tone alone—and she *was* there—but she was pointing at Brody Bishop. He was standing in a group of young guys, his legs spread, his hands on his hips. Cigars with blue bands puffed his shirt pocket.

Winnalee lost interest in Brody when she spotted Tommy at the grill. She dragged me over to him. "Hey, you're taking me up in the Piper today, right?"

Tommy searched my face for some sign I was feeling better, as he answered, "If the haze lifts, I will."

"What difference does that make?" Winnalee asked.

Tommy blinked at her. "Well, I've kind of got to be able to see where I'm goin', don't I?"

Winnalee frowned at the sky.

Tommy flipped hamburgers as the two men helping him brought platters of steaks to the table. "Bishop's kid was born last night," he told me after Winnalee got swallowed up by a brood of older ladies who wanted to cluck over Evalee.

"Was he there when the baby was born?" I asked hopefully.

"Course not. He said he's going, but who knows."

Tommy got called away by Ada, and I watched Boohoo race ahead of Rupert and two smaller boys, trying to catch the tail of twine dangling behind him. Dad was standing over by the beer tub with Elroy Tilman, not more than twelve feet away, but I doubted he'd even said hello to Boohoo. Brody's little boy would suffer the same fate, and that made me hurt inside for him. And for Marls.

I've never liked those first awkward minutes after you get to a gathering, when everyone's broken off in groups and you don't quite know which one to join. So I was glad when Winnalee broke away from the older ladies and called me over to a cluster of girls about our age, one wearing a pair of bell-bottoms we'd tacked with crocheted lace. "They wanna see your shirt, Button." Winnalee spun me around so they could admire my shirt—dress, whatever it was supposed to be—and the girls fingered the ribbons dangling loose from the seams at the shoulders. "See? The same ribbons are gathering the long, puffy sleeves at her wrists. Cool, huh?" The girls wanted a shirt just like it, but Winnalee told them that we only make one-of-a-kind garments.

"We're gonna make a fortune," Winnalee told me as we left the girls, me pushing Evalee in her stroller. I grinned. Not because of her promise, but at the way she was moving, strolling like she was on a fashion runway, and stopping now and then to pause and strike poses that looked straight out of the Montgomery Ward catalog. And yeah, lots of people looked, but I don't think it dawned on Winnalee that at least some of those looks came from guys who remembered her from the cage at the Purple Haze (or, worse yet, from the back of her van), judging by the amount of them who gawked and grinned, while their girlfriends or wives crossed their arms, or swatted them on the cuff.

Tommy rang the bell near the house to let everyone know

it was time to dish up, and as I was filling plates for me and Winnalee, Rita Dayne and Jesse's dad came to the table. "Hi, Evy, don't you look pretty today. Did you change your hair?" Just seeing the shape of Rita's smile—so like Jesse's—made me get that carved-like-a-pumpkin feeling inside. She pumped me for any news I might have about Jesse, because she hadn't heard from him in at least three weeks. "Oh, he's been busy," Winnalee said, her tone sarcastic. "Taking care of some *old* business. Isn't that right, Button?"

I assured Rita that Jesse was fine, then quickly pointed to a casserole. "You want some of this, Winnalee?"

"Ew," she said. "There's celery in there."

"I'm sure Jesse told you that he's coming home on leave soon?" Rita said.

I wanted to pretend he did—and maybe he *had* in the letter I'd torn—but instead, I asked when.

"Soon," Rita said. "I'm not sure of the date, though. That's why I'm so eager to hear from him. So I can put together a little party. But you know men. Maybe he'll just pop in."

The Daynes moved down the table, and I worked hard to steady my hands and control the dread I felt at the thought of running into Jesse while he was on leave. Or worse yet, being at a party like this one, and him singling me out so he could get advice on how to tell his parents about his older woman.

"Reece, Reece, come eat," Aunt Verdella called over to where Dad sat, holding only a beer while the men around him ate from overflowing plates.

Freeda set her half-finished plate down. "Why don't you give me the baby so you can eat," she said to Winnalee. Freeda drifted off to the shade where we'd left Evalee's stroller near two lawn chairs, and only then did Dad start heading toward the table. "Oh dear," Aunt Verdella said, her eyes darting from Freeda to Dad. "There's something up with those two," she whispered to me. "Freeda was quiet while we canned yesterday, then she headed over there, late. She went straight upstairs when she got back, and she's not been herself all day."

"Hi, Uncle Reece," Winnalee called. "Have some of this Jell-O stuff. It's really good."

While Aunt Verdella was tapping spoonfuls of food over Dad's plate, Linda and Al came up to the table with empty paper plates, their napkins flapping. "I found work," Al told Dad. "A plumbing outfit down in Green Bay. I start next week. Crissakes, will be nice to bring in a check again."

Dad asked Al about his new job, and Aunt Verdella turned to Linda to ask the question screaming in my head. "What about the shop?"

Linda glanced at me under hooded eyes, then turned her attention to the potato salad. "Well, I don't want to say too much. I want to talk to Hazel and Marge first. And of course, Evy."

Linda scooted around Al, pretending a dish farther down the table had caught her eye. I looked up and grabbed a flap of skin in my mouth. Not biting, just holding on to it like a security blanket. I'd been at the party less than an hour, and already I'd gotten two bits of news that made me want to run off by myself.

Al followed Linda, and Dad stopped Aunt Verdella when the plate he was holding threatened to collapse from the weight. "Why don't you eat over by Freeda, Reece? She looks like she could use a little company." Dad looked over to Freeda, who bounced Evalee on her bare knee.

"Reece," Melvin Thompson called. He hurried to the table to ask Dad about some racket he'd heard under his hood on the way over. "We'll look at it after we eat," Dad told him, and Aunt Verdella sighed.

"Are you worried about the shop, honey?" Aunt Verdella asked me after the guys wandered off. I shook my head—

another lie. "Linda must have something planned. Maybe Hazel's taking it over. You just put it out of your head for now and have a good time." I nodded.

I didn't expect Tommy and Craig to join us as we carried our plates toward Freeda, but they did. Freeda put Evalee in her stroller, plugged her mouth with her pacifier, and excused herself to go talk with June.

Winnalee was cute, the way she tried to act all proper and shy around Craig. Dabbing at her mouth with her paper napkin, and talking a lot softer than she normally did. I could feel her glancing at me often, and when I sipped my lemonade instead of chugging it, she did the same. "What's up with you, Winnalee?" Tommy asked.

"What?" she asked. There was an edge to that *what,* and I could tell Winnalee was struggling to file her voice soft again.

Tommy grinned. "The girlie act," he said. He gave a slight nod toward Craig, who was watching Brody flirt with some blonde who looked like Amy, but wasn't. Winnalee reached out and jabbed Tommy in the thigh, then smiled sweetly at Craig when he turned.

Across the yard, Boohoo wrestled with Rupert, then the two of them took off around the back of the house. Dad dropped his plate in the trash barrel and followed Melvin out of the yard.

"I'm gonna bring Craig to fly over your house while he's still steering like a five-year-old on a two-wheeler," Tommy teased. I turned to see who he was talking to, me or Winnalee.

"Well, you'd better warn Button first," Winnalee said, "so she knows when to duck . . . or hightail it to Fossard's bomb shelter."

Tommy laughed, like it was absurd that I'd duck or run.

"She did, you know. She ducked! It was so funny . . ."

Tommy looked at me, his face reddening from a hearty laugh. "You really ducked?"

"She did. Just like this . . ." Winnalee set her plate on the grass and got up to reenact the scene.

"Okay, okay . . . so we were in the house and Boohoo shouted at us to come see—right after he beat me up with a broom, but wrong story. Anyway, Boohoo heard your plane. So I looked up . . ." Winnalee looked up, capping her hands above her eyes, even though the sun was so muted by fog that she didn't need to. "So me and Boohoo started going crazy, jumping up and down and shouting . . ." Winnalee reenacted that, too, being every bit as loud and boisterous as she was then.

Brody and two other guys I remembered from someplace—probably the Purple Haze—were drinking beer a few yards away, and looked over.

"So Tommy tipped the nose of the plane down"—she used her hand to demonstrate—"and it was coming right at us. Boohoo and me were all excited, and Button . . . oh my God. I turned and there she was . . ."

Winnalee squatted, oblivious to the fact that her dress had crawled up her legs, and that her knees were spread to keep her balance.

Brody and the other guys were standing right in eye-shot, and *they* noticed her creeping dress.

"Winnalee . . . ," I hissed, to alert her.

"I'm not making fun of you, Button," she said in a rush. "It was sweet." Then without missing a beat, she resumed her story.

"And *zoommmmm*, over the house the Piper went, and . . . and . . ."

"Winnalee," I hissed again, louder this time, because I could hear Brody and the other guys snickering. I knew Craig could, too, because he was watching them.

"I looked, and there was Button, crouched down, and she's got her arms wrapped around her head like this . . ." Winnalee was laughing so hard now that she was weak. She covered her head as I had, then put her hand on the grass to steady herself. "Like what?" she chortled. "If the Piper crashed on her, her head would be the only thing that was gonna get donked? And her arms could save her if that was the case, anyway?"

Winnalee was laughing so hard that she toppled over onto the grass, holding her stomach and rolling side to side as she laughed. Tommy gave me a gentle shove with his shoulder, as he laughed every bit as hard as Winnalee.

I saw the three shadows stretch over the grass. "Look at that, Pete. Winnalee felt so sorry for us, missing out on the cage show at the Purple Haze, that she decided to give us our thrills with a little picnic peep show." The three of them chuckled, Brody, the loudest, of course.

Winnalee sat up, only now realizing that her legs were spread, her dress hiked to her underpants (thank God she was wearing them!). She sprung to her feet.

"Hey," Brody said, looking at Tommy now. "We're talking about going up to the Willow Flowage tomorrow. Now that your haying's done, you guys wanna come?"

Winnalee's nostrils were huffing. "Just ignore him," I muttered, even though I knew she wouldn't. Evalee started to fuss and I stood up to lift her from her stroller. Winnalee shoved aside the guy to Brody's left, and butted her face up to his.

"What did you say about me?" Winnalee asked, her jaw so tight that her lips hardly moved.

"What?" Brody asked innocently, even though he was smirking.

Winnalee forgot all about being a lady then. She jutted her chin out like Boohoo did when he was mad. "Listen, you schmuck. I was telling a story. And not to you, so you can just keep your beer-buggy, bastard eyes to yourself. And that goes for your two slimy friends, too."

He turned to the guys and grinned. "Must have been a story about the big boy here," Brody said, jabbing his chest with his thumb. "She did look like she was enjoying herself, didn't she?"

"Come on, Bishop," Tommy said. "Knock it off."

"Listen, asshole," Winnalee spat. She paused, glanced over at Evalee, whom I was nervously bouncing on my hip, and hurried to clamp her hands over the sides of Evalee's bonnet. She held her hands there as she snipped, "I'm turning over a new leaf because I've got a kid to raise—you should try it—and I'd appreciate it if you'd stay out of my goddamn face with your smutty talk! You're nothing but a useless asshole, Bishop, and I don't want you talking *to* me, or *about* me ever again. Got it?"

"She was just as sassy in the sack," he said, nudging the guy to his right, who was gawking around, flushed-faced.

Winnalee let go of Evalee's head. "Cover her ears," she ordered me, then she charged forward. "You son of a bitch!" she shouted. Tommy got to his feet. But before either of the guys could say or do a thing, Winnalee hauled off and slapped Brody across the face. So hard that his head jerked. A raspberry-colored handprint instantly stained his cheek.

Brody's other cheek reddened to match it, and his lips pulled tight. He didn't have a chance to say or do a thing, though, because Tommy took his arm and backed him up. "Let it go, Bishop. You had that one coming."

Winnalee was so mad she was panting. She glared at the few who were gawking, and they quickly turned away. Then she looked at Evalee and brushed her hands together. "That, little girl," she said, "is how you treat disrespectful men."

Her pride drooped some, though, when she realized that

Craig was staring at her like she'd suddenly grown seven heads, and all of them pea-sized and sporting cocked eyes. Winnalee's shoulders dropped. "Oh, who am I trying to kid," she muttered to herself.

She looked back at Craig. "All that proper stuff you saw me doin' a bit ago? Wiping my mug, and talking all soft and sweet—that isn't me. That's Button. I'm loud lots of times, and scrappy when I need to be. And yeah, I was into free love and all that shit, and I danced at the Haze to make a dime . . ." She glanced over and I moved my hand up to Evalee's ears again, "and I'm still all for love, but it's not gonna be so free anymore. That's who I am, and if you don't like girls like that, that's okay by me, but it's who I am."

Craig stared at her a minute, then he smiled. He picked her plate up and held it out. "Your Jell-O's getting runny."

Winnalee smoothed the back of her dress and sat down like nothing had happened.

I once heard Fanny Tilman tell Aunt Verdella, "A person would be wise to watch how long and hard they laugh. Because you can bet that while you're carrying on, something bad is sneaking up to bite you from behind."

The four of us were joking around when Ada asked Tommy to bring out more beer and pop. Craig offered to give him a hand, but Tommy decided I should. We were almost to the shed—still laughing—when something above my head caught his attention. His eyes squinted. I turned to look, and saw Boohoo on his knees at the edge of the yard, next to the liquid propane tank. His ball of twine was on the ground, and he was wrapping the string around something. Rupert was standing a ways off, backing up, his fists clenched at his sides as he watched Boohoo. "Boohoo, don't!" Tommy shouted. Rupert took off running.

"Run, Boohoo, run!" Tommy shouted as he zipped past me, and sprinted toward him.

It all happened so fast I hardly knew what was happening: Boohoo jumping to his feet and batting the air, screaming like he was on fire.

When I got close enough, I saw the hornets' nest knocked to the grass, twine half draped around it, and hornets swirling Boohoo.

Tommy snatched Boohoo on the run and dropped him at the corner of the house. He started tearing at his clothes, while Boohoo flailed his arms and danced in place, screaming. Tears were streaming down Boohoo's cheeks, and his eyes were stretched wide with pain and terror.

Maybe Rupert told the others, or maybe they just heard the commotion. Either way, they came swarming into the backyard, Aunt Verdella out front, shouting, "Oh my Lord, what happened? What happened?"

Tommy picked Boohoo up, naked but for his underwear and socks. He moved him farther from the few stray hornets that still spun above us. I saw two stings on Tommy's hand, and somewhere on my arm, I felt one, too.

Boohoo was too heavy for Aunt Verdella to hold, so she slid him down her belly to stand, her arms hugging him close. "Oh, honey, my poor baby!" she cried as Boohoo bounced and bawled. She looked horrified when she turned to June. "Oh Lord, look how many times he was stung!"

Uncle Rudy reached us and knelt down on one knee. "You okay, little buddy?"

Everyone was talking at once then, loudly, because Boohoo would not be consoled. His reddened face swished across Aunt Verdella's belly and he looked up at Uncle Rudy, then at me, his eyes pleading for us to make the pain go away. "It's okay. It's okay. They're gone now, honey," Aunt Verdella kept repeating. My hand, shaky with fear, fluttered at my mouth.

I didn't know who was saying what, but I heard each comment:

"I told him to leave the nest alone, Mom."

"You've got to scrape out the stingers."

"Raw onions on the sting helps."

"You kids get in the front of the yard. No one in the back."

"He's teetering. That's not a good sign. Son, are you dizzy?"

"My brother almost died from *one* bee sting."

Seconds later, Uncle Rudy had to catch Boohoo's shoulder because he was staggering. Tears were streaming down Boohoo's face as Rudy wrapped his hand around his skinny neck. "A bee's in my throat," he told Uncle Rudy. His voice sounded thick.

"It feels like something's in your throat, honey?" I think it was Sally Thompson asking.

Aunt Verdella was gently patting Boohoo, and she leaned over to examine the big patches of plumping skin outlined in red that were starting to form on his back.

"Hives. He's getting hives, and his throat's closing," Sally Thompson said. "Get him to the hospital. He's having a reaction."

Uncle Rudy scooped Boohoo up. "Rudy, with that detour," some guy behind him said, "it's gonna take a good twenty, twenty-five minutes to get him there. Maybe thirty."

"You aren't going to have that long," Sally said, and someone else agreed. I covered my ears, as if their words were curse words *I* was too innocent to hear.

I looked up and saw Winnalee shoving her way between shoulders. "Fly him there, Tommy! You can get him there faster in the Piper, right?" The crowd stilled. Waited.

Freeda was behind Winnalee, Evalee in her arms. "Do it, Tommy. Do it!"

Suddenly, it was like my panic was gripping the limbs of time, slowing it down so it could hardly budge. Tommy's head moved in slow motion, and his Adam's apple rose with the pace of a rising sun. Boohoo said something, and I didn't know if *he* was speaking gibberish, or if my ears were only hearing it that way.

And then, just like that, things sped up. Raced at breakneck speed even.

"Craig, start the Piper!" Tommy shouted.

Craig took off, and Tommy snatched Boohoo from Uncle Rudy and followed him, Boohoo's limbs and head bouncing with every stride.

"This haze . . . ," someone said, and then Ada's voice: "My God. Be careful, Tommy!"

"I gassed it this morning," Tommy shouted up ahead, apparently because Craig had yelled back to ask. "Thirty gallons."

We moved like a swarm, Winnalee and I holding hands, Freeda running alongside us, Aunt Verdella moving faster than I ever thought she could, our neighbors close at our backs. "I'm going with Tommy!" Aunt Verdella shouted.

We gathered around the plane, the propellers a humming blur, the engine trembling the wings. *My God! My God!* I screamed inside as Tommy passed Boohoo to Uncle Rudy, then hurried to the pilot's side. Craig and Melvin Thompson helped Aunt Verdella into the plane.

"Hurry! Come on, hurry!" Tommy shouted as he slammed his door. I'd never touched an airplane before, and I cringed to feel the sides so flimsy that it seemed that if I leaned into it a bit harder, I'd dent it.

"That plane's never going to get off the ground with her in

it," a woman's voice behind me said, and Winnalee turned around and screamed, "Shut the fuck up, Fanny!"

Aunt Verdella drew her arms in tightly. "Oh dear, am I too heavy? I'm a hundred and seventy-six pounds. Is that too much?"

"You're fine," Tommy told her as Craig took Boohoo from Uncle Rudy and placed him on Aunt Verdella's lap. Boohoo was limp and confused, blotched with hives, his lips so swollen they didn't even look like lips anymore. The stings—so many of them—pocked his skin like miniature sinkholes.

"You're going for a ride in the Piper, Boohoo," I called. "Just like you wanted to." I meant for my voice to sound excited in a good way, but it sounded more like a siren. I glanced at Tommy, hoping to see confidence and calm on his face, like the heroes in TV shows always wore, but he didn't look like that at all. There were beads of sweat on his upper lip and dappling his temple. He seemed almost confused about what controls he needed to mess with. He gulped a deep breath, held it for a moment, then blew it out with force.

Uncle Rudy said something to Aunt Verdella, I couldn't make out what, then Craig shut the door and gave the plane one quick pat.

"Back up, everybody. Back up!" Craig shouted. Craig and Melvin—even Brody helped—spread their arms and herded the stunned spectators away from the plane.

"What's going on?" I turned when I heard Dad's voice. He was standing with Mr. Bishop, who looked every bit as confused as he.

We moved like one body, walking backward, and I could hear someone telling Dad what had happened. "Jesus Christ," Dad spat.

The Piper started moving, crawling at first, and the crowd hushed, their fingers near their lips.

"He's got to get it up to sixty miles an hour before it can lift," someone said as the plane grazed the field. People rocked to their toes, as if doing so would somehow help the plane lift all the faster. Together we sighed, when the Piper's wheels finally left the grass.

Someone was shouting orders to call the airport and the hospital, and a couple of women were flurrying toward the house. But most stood in huddles, talking among themselves, shaking their heads and rubbing their arms as if they were cold.

Craig came over to where Winnalee and Freeda and I were standing with Uncle Rudy. Dad made his way over to hear what he had to say. "Tommy will get him there in fifteen, sixteen minutes tops, and an ambulance will be waiting," he told us. "Tommy's an excellent pilot. He'll get the job done."

"But it's so foggy. He won't be able to see," I said. Ada appeared at my side, to ask Craig if it was too hazy for Tommy to fly—as if Craig was an experienced flyer who'd logged a million miles in the air, when in fact, he'd only had a couple of lessons so far, and not many more passenger trips.

"He'll ride right above the road and keep it low. Tommy knows every high spot around here, so don't you worry."

"Let's get to the hospital," Uncle Rudy said. His voice was gentle, as always, but there was an intensity in him that stretched his strides as he led us to the road.

"Evalee? Where's Evalee?" Winnalee asked as we hurried, her head cranking.

"Sally Thompson has her. She's gonna keep her until we get back." Winnalee's steps slowed, and Freeda pushed her to go faster. "It's okay. She's got formula and diapers. She'll be fine."

"Call me, call me!" Ada shouted after us.

Dad paused when we reached his truck, like maybe he was considering driving himself to town, but Winnalee tugged his arm as if it was a branch from our magic tree, that could keep her from falling into a scary world where little boys die of bee stings.

Dad lit a cigarette the second he got in Aunt Verdella's car, and Winnalee, who sat in the back with him—I was tucked in the front between Uncle Rudy and Freeda—reached over and opened his window so the wind would suck the smoke out.

"I can't believe this. I just can't believe it," Freeda kept saying, as she pressed her head to the window to watch the Piper moving above the road out ahead of us. I was too scared to look. "One minute everything was fine, and now this. For crissakes, if that ain't life."

"Why was he trying to tie up a hornets' nest anyway? He had to know it was a hive, didn't he?" Winnalee asked.

I felt sick to my stomach. Freeda squeezed my hand and told us everything would be okay. Then she spotted the road sign, and muttered a tense, "Goddamn detour. Goddamn it."

The tension in the car hung just as heavy and low as the haze above us, as Uncle Rudy turned on Pike's Peak Road and was forced to slow down to account for the thick spread of new gravel. I cranked my head, trying to spot the Piper, but distance and fog had swallowed it.

"Shouldn't we be praying or something?" Winnalee asked. "Isn't that what people do at times like this?"

"Our Boohoo's gonna be fine. Just fine," Uncle Rudy said. Freeda turned to look into the backseat, and mimicked his words.

And then Dad spoke, his words punching me in the back so hard they knocked the wind out of me. "Why in the hell weren't you watching him, Evy?"

Silence, the kind born out of shock, fell over the car for a second or two.

Uncle Rudy growled Dad's name, then squinted a warning glare in the rearview mirror.

Winnalee snapped, "Uncle Reece! I don't believe you just said that!"

Freeda cranked sideways so hard, her right boob butted up against my shoulder. "You miserable son of a bitch, you!" she screamed. "If I could reach back there, I'd pound the living shit right out of you for saying that! How dare you, after all this kid's been through . . . after how hard she works to pick up the fucking slack you leave. For crissakes, what's the matter with you, Reece Peters?"

"Okay, let's calm down now," Uncle Rudy said, his voice scraping like a razor over Freeda and Dad's rough-edged rage. "This won't help anybody right now."

Freeda turned back around, and drew me into her. I propped my hand between my face and her shoulder so I wouldn't soak her shirt. Her heart and breath were working hard, and her heel was tapping the floorboards, jiggling her leg and me.

Winnalee started praying awkwardly under her breath. "God is good, God is great. Let us thank Him if He gets Boohoo to the hospital in time. Amen."

I prayed after Winnalee did, but silently. And not to God, but to Ma. Asking her to please, please, if Boohoo came to her, selflessly send him back to us.

I was grateful when we finally reached the end of Circle Avenue and got back on the highway. I was holding Boohoo, Aunt Verdella, and Tommy so close in my mind and heart since we'd lost sight of them, that it was easy to believe that once we left the rocky terrain, they, too, were now sailing along more smoothly and swiftly.

When we reached town, Uncle Rudy put his emergency flashers on and honked at every car in front of us until they pulled aside and let us pass. Winnalee scooted forward until I could feel her arm crossways on my back, and her breath on my hair. "Go, Uncle Rudy! Go!"

We had to park in the visitors' lot and use the main doors that opened onto the second floor, even though two ambulances sitting alongside the hospital confirmed what Uncle Rudy remembered—that the emergency room was on the first level.

"Do you think Boohoo is here yet?" Winnalee asked, and Uncle Rudy told her he was sure he was.

Polished floors that echoed our hurried steps greeted us inside the hospital, as well as an elevator that moved so slowly that Freeda had time to fill it to the ceiling with cusswords before it let us out.

Maybe it was the whooshing of the elevator. Or maybe it was my rising panic, mixed with the hospital smells. Whatever it was, I suddenly felt like I was going to vomit. There was a short little couch with powder blue cushions and wooden arms tucked in an alcove near the elevator, and Freeda led me to it and told me to breathe through my nose. Dad and Uncle Rudy hurried down the hall, their work boots thumping.

"You okay?" Winnalee asked. But I couldn't answer her. I couldn't do anything but shake.

"Breathe," Freeda said, as she bent over me. She stood with us for a moment longer, then told Winnalee to stay with me, and hurried to follow the men.

"I'm sorry. I'm sorry," I said, as I struggled to find a shred of bravery.

"Don't be," Winnalee said. "Boohoo means everything to you. Of course you're scared. I'm scared, too." She sat down beside me, our sides touching, and we held hands.

I don't know how long we sat there. Minutes? Forever?

At one point, Freeda appeared at the end of the hall to say the doctor was with him and they were waiting. Winnalee shouted to her like we weren't in a hospital, telling her to let us know when the doctor came out.

"I'm so scared," I told Winnalee, and she squeezed my

hand harder. "I know. Boohoo means the world to you. To all of us."

We heard footsteps and I was almost afraid to look up, for fear I'd see a man dressed in green, a stethoscope dangling from his neck, coming to tell me that Boohoo was dead. I clamped my eyes shut and braced myself for the tragic, emotional storm I was sure was coming.

"Evy?"

It was Tommy. He squatted down next to the couch and I flinched. "Please . . . no," I said.

Tommy took my hands, prying them apart so he could hold one. "He's okay," he said gently.

I looked up, my throat so tight it hurt to swallow. "He's okay? You sure? You sure, Tommy?"

Tommy nodded, his closed lips curving into a reassuring smile.

"Even the doctors aren't sure how, because I guess with a reaction that severe, you usually only get ten, fifteen minutes tops, and it took us exactly fifteen-point-five minutes to get here, then maybe another minute before the paramedics shot him up with something to counter the allergic reaction."

"Oh my God," I said. My whole body sunk into relief and I started crying all the harder.

Winnalee was crying, too, and she wrapped her arms around me and Tommy, drawing us into a circle of relief.

"I couldn't tell if he was breathing when they gave him that shot," Tommy said when Winnalee let go. "It didn't look like it, but shit, *I* was hardly breathing by that point. Anyway, those paramedics were on the ball, waiting right near the runway. Boohoo was better before they even got him here."

Tommy put his hand on my arm, and the relief that radiated from his hand filled me. I exhaled a jagged breath and my tears kept spilling. "It's all okay now, Evy," he said, and I nodded, because my mind was powerless to find any words more momentous than "thank you."

The rule, I guess, was that only immediate family could go into the emergency room. When the nurse asked if we were *all* family, we said we were.

Boohoo was sitting up in bed when we got in his room, a purple Popsicle tucked between his swollen lips. "I gotta hold this here because my lips are fat," he mumbled around the icy, purple sphere. He had medicine pasted over the sting marks peppering his face, his arms, and his scrawny neck. Winnalee and I hurried to him, one on each side of the examining room table, and Boohoo tucked his head, the tip of his Popsicle tapping cold against my cheek as he giggled, "Oh no, here comes a love sandwich!

"Feel me," he said, touching his chest over his heart. "I'm still pounding kinda hard, right, nurse? Not like before, but still kinda hard."

"It's the epinephrine," she said. "It races the heart."

I think all of our hearts were pounding equally as hard.

"I flied the Piper, Evy. That's what Tommy said. Did you see me fly in the Piper?"

"Yes," I told him, looking up to laugh with relief along with the others.

"I flied the Piper, too," Aunt Verdella said. She was sitting in a chair designed like the couch I'd just left. Her eyes were almost as swollen as Boohoo's from all the crying she'd done, but she had a smile slow-dancing in them now. "The doctor had to give me something to calm me down," she said. She reached for Uncle Rudy and tugged on him to brace herself to rise, but a nurse stopped her. "Why don't you just sit for a bit, Mrs. Peters. You've had quite an ordeal."

"I sure did." She looked up at Uncle Rudy, and her eyes said all the things she couldn't say in front of Boohoo. "Course,

I hardly realized I was in the plane, as worried as I was. But boy, when that plane landed and the paramedics took over, I just went down. Plop! Look at this," she said, pointing to her bandaged knees. "That poor skinny guy—I don't know his name—tried to catch me, but . . . well, Freeda, let's just say that you'd better be slapping my hands a little more often than you already do, because I almost flattened the poor fellow."

We laughed, maybe louder than we would have otherwise, but relief does that to a person. Aunt Verdella laughed, too, then said, "Oooo, I feel fuzzy. I don't know what that doctor gave me, but whatever it was, I kinda like it."

I stepped back when Dad approached Boohoo's bed, though I wouldn't have needed to, because he didn't get that close. He just reached over and patted Boohoo's foot under the sheet. "You okay there, little buddy?" Boohoo told him he was, and Freeda watched to see if Dad would back away. He did, but—hopefully—only because the woman from the front desk asked him to come to the desk to fill out some forms.

"You're not going to go try lassoing any more hornets' nests, now are you, cowboy?" Tommy asked.

"I wasn't trying to lasso it, Tommy. Rupert is scared of 'em, so I was gonna put my web around it so the bees couldn't get out. It didn't work, though."

We had to hang around for a while so they could monitor Boohoo, and we stepped into the hall when a nurse came in to check "her patients."

Uncle Rudy clamped his hand on Tommy's shoulder and gave it a squeeze. He didn't say anything, but then I guess he didn't need to.

"You call your ma, Tommy?" Freeda asked.

"No, I suppose I should, though."

"Yes, you should," Freeda said. "You're her little boy, grown or not, and she needs to know you're safe, too."

Uncle Rudy was digging in his pocket to find change for

Tommy to use the pay phone when Dad walked past us and out the door. Freeda pursed her lips, then followed Dad out.

I could see them from the hallway window. Dad was smoking, his head down, one hand in his pants pocket, and Freeda was bent forward, her face enflamed with rage. A couple of nurses were soft-stepping around them to get to their cars.

There was a door up ahead, another outlet to the parking lot, and I knew if I slipped through it I could hear what Freeda was saying, without being noticed. But I didn't need to. I already knew. So I hurried along toward the restroom, recounting the whole awful event in my mind, exactly as I would have written it to Jesse.

CHAPTER 39

BRIGHT IDEA #29: Not all surprises make you happy like a new set of jacks, or a baton with pink rubber tips. Some surprises make you sad, and some surprises scare the crap out of you.

Boohoo was in the front yard, making little hay bales out of fresh grass clippings from the narrow trails Uncle Rudy's lawn mower was leaving, and tying them with gold yarn. He had them stacked on the front steps, his toy baler nearby. "They look like real ones, don't they, Evy?" I told him they did, and he added, "'Cept mine are green." I put my hand on the top of his sun-warmed head, just to feel him here.

Boohoo paused to scratch his stings, itchy in spite of the calamine lotion. His fingers still had a yellow tinge to them and were a bit puffy, but the doctor said that would go away in another day or two. "Is Cupcake awake?" He shouted to be heard over the mower, since Uncle Rudy's pattern had led him up close to the house again.

"Yep. Winnalee's giving her her bath."

"Okay. When I'm done haying, I'm gonna go see her. She's happy in the morning. Not like Freeda."

I waved to Uncle Rudy, and Boohoo got still. "That a bee, Evy?" he asked, his index finger all that moved as he pointed toward his hay bales.

"No, just a horsefly," I told him.

"Good. Because I don't like bees no more. If I get stung again, then Aunt Verdella has to give me a shot. She practiced a needle on an orange at the hospital, and she wasn't very good at it, either."

I wanted to smile, but couldn't. Boohoo would carry his fear of bees now, the same way I carried my fear of storms. "Bees won't sting unless you're by their hive," I told him, hoping Uncle Rudy was right about that.

It was Winnalee's idea to put on our fashion show for Freeda and Aunt Verdella that night, since I'd just finished altering the last dress. "It'll be fun. Like playing dress-up again." Not all the dresses fit us right, but most of them fit one of us well enough. So while Winnalee gave Evalee her bath, I was to hike over and ask Aunt Verdella and Freeda what time they could come over.

I could hear them shuffling in the kitchen as I neared the porch, and the sound of a spoon clinking against the rim of a coffee cup. The smell of dill and garlic wafted through the porch screens. I paused to give Knucklehead a pat. Even Uncle Rudy couldn't believe that he was still with us, and although I knew it wouldn't be long now, for today anyway, I was just grateful that he was.

"Oh, Freeda. I can hardly stand the thought of you leaving," Aunt Verdella was saying, as my foot reached for the step. I brought it back down.

"I know, but let's face it, I can't impose on you guys forever."

"'Impose'? Freeda, how can you even say that? You've been nothing but a blessing since you've been here. Taking over the garden so Rudy could hay, helping me with the house and Boohoo . . . helping me with my diet . . . giving me a friend to talk to. Helping Button . . ."

I stepped to the side so they wouldn't see me through the screen if either of them happened to look over from the table.

"But I've got a salon to run, Verdella. Terri's been great about holding down the fort since Winnalee took off—she needed the extra money—but she's got three little ones at home. I've got to get back, Verdella."

"I know, but I wish you didn't. When are you leaving?"

"I told Terri I'd be back to work next Monday. I think we'll pull out on Thursday. Evalee's got a doctor's appointment next week. We should get her back in time for that. And—"

I cupped my hand over my mouth.

"Winnalee's going, too?" Aunt Verdella asked, her voice soaked in dread. I snapped my eyes shut, and wished I could close my ears just as easily.

"Verdella, Winnalee's doing her best, but she needs my support right now. She'd have to take a night job if she stayed, and you know as well as I do that night jobs are scarce in Dauber. It would have been hard for the girls as it was—Button watching Cupcake during the day while Winnalee worked, Button sewing in snatches and doing the brunt of her work at night—but now that Linda's selling the shop, the girls will both be needing to look for jobs."

"Marge or Hazel aren't taking over Jewel's store? Button didn't tell me."

"Marge told Ada she doesn't want it, and neither does Hazel. It would be just too much for them at their age."

"Oh my," Aunt Verdella said.

"But it isn't just about the money, Verdella. Even though Winnalee pretends it is. Since Boohoo's run-in with the hornets, she's been fretting over every possible awful thing that could happen to that baby. She needs her mom right now. I wasn't there when she was little; I want to be here for her now. I guess you could say it will be my redemption. And I don't want to miss out on Evalee's first years."

"Oh my. Button will be devastated. Boohoo, too. And Reece . . ."

"Reece," Freeda said, as though she only meant to think his name.

"Verdella," Freeda said after a pause. "I know he's like a son to you. And I know you loved Jewel. But for a moment, could you please forget those things and listen only as my friend?"

"Of course," Aunt Verdella said, in a voice as soothing and gentle as hair brushing against your bare back.

"I'm in love with him, Verdella."

"I know, honey. I ain't blind."

"There've been times when I've wanted to use the oldest trick in the book to win that guy over—you know, like I never learned that that doesn't work in the end, anyway. I felt so desperate to try and force *something* to crack that hard shell of his. But he's not ready to love anybody yet. Not even himself."

"Oh, Freeda." There were tears in Aunt Verdella's voice.

"One night last week, we had a few beers at his place, and we kissed. He'd have gone to bed with me in five seconds if I hadn't pushed him away. But I had to. Because it would have only been sex to him, and it would have been making love to me. It's one thing to have a stranger turn away after sex, but the man you love?"

"He cares about you, Freeda. I know he does. Thursday, when I ran some of those creamed peas and that ham over to him, he grinned when I came in the door, and I could see he had to work hard to keep that smile on his face when he realized that you weren't coming in behind me."

"Sure. Because I can make him smile—outright laugh now and then. Well, I *could* anyway. Before I chewed his ass about what he said to Button after Boohoo got stung."

"What'd he say?"

Freeda ignored her question. "You know Reece. His heart is closed as tight as Fanny Tilman's asshole. The night before Ada's picnic, around dusk, I talked him into going for a walk . . ." *My dad went for a walk?* "We'd been working on his kitchen for weeks and he'd never even come close to opening up. But that night, he almost did. *Almost.* I stopped, and I had my hand on his arm, and I looked him straight in the eye and I said, 'What is it, Reece? What are you holding in there that keeps you locked away from me? From your kids?' He shook my hand off and told me to mind my own business."

"Oh, I knew something had happened between the two of you, Freeda. You looked so sad when you got back, and you haven't gone over there since, have you?"

Freeda's sigh sounded painful. "He'd have gotten past my prying if I'd backed off, but after the things I said to him the day Boohoo got stung, I'm afraid he's cemented shut any hairline cracks he might have had on his heart by now."

"Oh, Freeda," Aunt Verdella said. I waited, my hand resting on the scratchy gray siding to steady myself. The Malones had plans to leave, and Winnalee hadn't thought to tell me? And Freeda *was* in love with my dad? Everything felt surreal, but for the skin between my teeth, the itching on my arms, and the ache I felt for Freeda's anguish.

"Verdella," Freeda finally said, "Rudy was a widower when you met him. Was it hard for him to let you in?"

"Well, honey, I met Rudy long after Betty passed, so I guess it was different. He was ready for someone in his life by then. I wish Rudy would talk to him, but you know Rudy. He doesn't like to interfere. After Jewel died, he told Reece that he would always be here if he needed him, and he won't say it again because he thinks that's pryin'. I've tried talking to him about Reece, but all he says is 'Verdie, some winters just hang on longer than others.' "

They were quiet for a minute, and I heard a chair scrape the floor. Then Freeda spoke. "I don't know, sad of a thought as it is, I'm afraid Reece is going to live out the rest of his life cut off from everybody and everything, including himself. I have to accept that I can't change that."

"Oh, honey, I can see how this is breaking your heart."

Freeda cleared her throat. "Well, forget me for a second. Think about what he's doing to his kids." Freeda must have gone to refill her coffee cup, because there was a clink and the chair scraped the floor again. "Verdella, I hope you don't take this the wrong way, but it can't be a coincidence that Button's been pining away—for what, four years?—for some guy who only saw her as a friend. Using any scrap of attention from him that she got, to convince herself—even us—that he loved her in a romantic way. I'll bet you any money, that through the years you told Button often how much her dad loved her, and that he just wasn't good at showing it. I'd have said the same thing. But do you see a connection here?"

"Not really," Aunt Verdella said in a voice too small to be hers.

"Well, Verdella, if I learned anything from my past, I've learned that it's our fathers who teach us what to expect from men. When I was little I used to tell myself that if my dad knew what Dewey was doing to me, he'd protect me. Comfort me, even."

"Your dad was alive then?" Aunt Verdella asked.

"Yeah. He died when I was fifteen. It took me until therapy to admit that if I had truly believed he would've rescued me, I'd have told him instead. He was sitting in the living room, not even six feet away, when I told Hannah. He had to have heard her scream at me, and no doubt heard the slap. He waited until I was done cleaning up my vomit, then came into the kitchen. He stepped over me like I was a barn cat, and went to the stove for coffee. He never did buck Hannah."

"Oh, honey . . ."

"It's all right. I've dealt with it. But my point is this: Dewey may have taught me that the only value I had to any guy was for sex, but my dad taught me that no guy will ever love me enough to protect me or be there for me. And I've taken that attitude, that lack of trust, into every relationship I've ever had that could have been good."

"I'm so sorry . . . ," Aunt Verdella said.

"It doesn't matter anymore, Verdella. What does matter, though, is what's in *Evy's* present and in her future. What *she's* learned from *her* father. Reece ignored her when she was little, and although he may have given her some attention between the time we left and Jewel's death, he's been ignoring her ever since. What has she learned from him, but how to quietly hope for a man's attention, and make a meal out of any crumb she gets? How to love a man from afar? I'll bet any money, if Jesse came home tomorrow and professed his love for her, she'd not know how to deal with it. She'd only feel awkward, and almost wish he'd leave again so she could love him openly from a more familiar distance. Look at her with Tommy. She doesn't know what in the hell to make of him."

I swallowed hard in an attempt to dislodge the lump in my throat.

I could hear Aunt Verdella crying. "Rudy tries to give her what she needs."

"I know. And what he gives her is priceless. But she needs the same from her father. Verdella, think back. Wasn't your dad the very first man you fell in love with?"

"Well, I guess so. Ma said when I was three, I told her I was gonna marry him when I got big."

"And I guess you could say that's exactly what you did. I'll bet your dad was every bit as loving to you as Rudy. And that's my point."

I assumed Aunt Verdella nodded.

"Just listen to me," Freeda said with a humorless laugh, "sounding like a know-it-all. No wonder Reece won't hear me out. My kid doesn't even have a father. Neither does my grandkid. And I cut out on Winnalee, and she tried doing the same. Who in the hell am I to talk about the damage we do to our kids when it's taken me this long to deal with my own shit?"

"You're a kind heart, and a wise soul. That's who you are, Freeda Malone," Aunt Verdella said. "You're somebody who suffered over her mistakes and the mistakes of others, and you don't want to see anyone else suffer."

I heard the soft murmur of sniffles, and I turned and headed for home before they heard mine.

"What's the matter, Button?" Winnalee asked when I got in the door.

I turned to her, my voice hoarse from the words that were still stinging me. "When were you planning on telling me you're leaving, Winnalee? Or were you just going to slip out in the night without saying goodbye, like you did last time?"

Winnalee sighed herself to the couch, a spit-up baby T-shirt bunched in her hand. "I was holding out hope that I wouldn't have to tell you, period. That we'd make a mint off our dresses and I wouldn't have to go—I didn't know they'd take so long. But Freeda's right. Finding old clothes and making them over might bring in a few bucks, but not enough for me to raise a kid on."

"Well, what will be different in Michigan?"

"Freeda will work days, and I'll clean the salon after hours."

"I could have done the same for you if you found a night job here. And there *are* night jobs."

"But you'll need a job now, too, Button. Who's to say we'd find jobs fast, much less in opposite shifts like we'd need to?"

"Did everybody but me know Linda is closing Ma's shop and that you guys are leaving?"

"Button, I don't even have money for Cupcake's next case of formula. That shit's expensive, and I've got five dollars and fifty-three cents left to my name. That's it. Going with Freeda is the only option I can think of." Winnalee tossed the dirty T-shirt into the laundry basket waiting by the door. "But I'm coming back. I promise you I am. This is the only place left that really feels like home. You guys are my family, and I want my daughter to grow up here. Where she can play in the magic tree, and have people make her bunny pancakes, and look out for her and love her just like I do."

"Then stay," I begged. "I told you I'd help. So will Aunt Verdella. I don't pay rent here, so all I've got are my utility bills and what little food I buy. I've got enough to buy her formula. Diapers, too. We could figure it out."

Even as I spoke, I knew I was wasting my breath, because money and a job *wasn't* the sole reason she was leaving. "You just don't want to be apart from Freeda right now," I said. I sounded accusatory, even though I didn't mean to. "No, don't deny it, Winnalee. I don't blame you. I'd be with my mother, too, if that was possible."

"But still, it will only be for a while," she said. "You know, until I get the hang of being a mom. I'm coming back, though. I promise you, I am. I came back once, didn't I?"

"Yeah, nine years later."

"Well what was I supposed to do? Use my step stool to get in Freeda's truck and drive myself back here?"

"You could have at least written, after you got older."

"Yeah . . . but it's weird. You don't really know if someone you knew when you were nine would even remember you."

She sighed, then gave me a smile I knew she hoped would be contagious. "Hey, I *have* to come back. We haven't written our one hundredth idea yet."

I bit at my cheek and flinched at the pain. Her smile faded. "Don't you believe me?" she asked.

I got up and removed my box of stationery from the end table, closing the lid and slipping it into the drawer underneath. "Right now," I said, "I'm having a hard time believing in anything. Except that people you love leave."

CHAPTER
40

BRIGHT IDEA #97: A person doesn't need to be ugly and mean to tell a big lie. They don't have to be a stranger, either. Sometimes the biggest lies come from pretty people who are in your own family.

It was easier if you stayed busy. I suggested we sort through Winnalee's things. Pack what she wouldn't need before Thursday, and get the dirty laundry gathered to wash in the morning.

"No, leave those," Winnalee said, when I grabbed her buckskin dress with fringes and a couple of her granny dresses from the closet. "If I take everything, then that's just all the more I'll have to lug back here." I rehung the dresses, knowing full well that Winnalee believed with all her heart that she'd be back, whether it was true or not.

Evalee reached out to grab a fistful of my hair, but I tugged it gently out of her grasp before she could get it to her mouth. I lifted her up to my shoulder and pressed my cheek to her downy head.

"Oh, I forgot to tell you, Button. Yesterday Freeda took a phone call from one of those girls I pitched our dresses to at the picnic. She wants to know if she can come over with some of her friends and look at them on Sunday. I'll be gone by then, but I'm gonna price them today. Don't you cave when they try to talk you into taking less, either. Those dresses are one of a kind and supercool. They want them, they can pay for them."

I nodded, not caring.

The flies were particularly heavy, as they always were in late summer, so we were keeping the front door closed most of the day now so they couldn't shimmy in through the gap between the screen door and the door frame.

I didn't hear anybody knock. I was upstairs in the sewing room, pairing Winnalee's albums with their covers, and Winnalee was downstairs washing bottles. "Coming!" she shouted from the kitchen, then: "Uncle Reece!"

I slipped into the upstairs hallway to listen, trying to figure out why Dad was downstairs.

"Hi, kiddo," he said.

"Did you come to say goodbye to me and Cupcake?"

"Goodbye?"

"Yeah. We're pulling out on Thursday. We're heading back to Northville. But I'm coming back. By Christmas, I decided. Man, and we didn't have you over for supper. Not even once."

I heard Winnalee close the entrance door, and some quieter talk, then I thought I heard Dad say, "I came to talk to Evy, actually."

But that couldn't be right.

I waited, wondering if I'd heard wrong.

"Button!" Winnalee bellowed.

"Coming," I called back, hoping the weakness of my voice

would be interpreted as not wanting to wake Evalee. I smoothed my hair, then went down the stairs, trying my best to act like it was natural for Dad to be here, asking to see me.

He was standing by the door. "Hi, Dad," I said awkwardly. I was ashamed that the house was such a mess, the couch scattered with stiff, line-dried clothes, and folded jeans and shirts heaped in lopsided stacks on the back and arms of the chair. Paper plates with bread and potato chip crumbs were still on the coffee table, along with empty glasses and a baby bottle. I couldn't help but wonder if he was seeing *his* mother's judgmental face looking down at the mess.

Winnalee looked at me, then at Dad. And when nobody said anything, she asked me to keep an ear out for Evalee so she could run the last batch of dirty laundry to Aunt Verdella's. I nodded.

I didn't want Winnalee to go, but I couldn't say so with Dad standing right there.

I went to move Winnalee's clothes from the chair, but I didn't know where to set them, so I just put them back down. "You want some Kool-Aid or something? Well, I guess not 'or something,' because that's all we have, besides water. Oh, and coffee. I could make some of that."

"Sure," Dad said, though I didn't know which he was saying sure to, the Kool-Aid, the water, or the coffee.

Dad followed me into the kitchen—I was glad that I'd at least put away the bologna, stuffed the chip bag back in the box, and that Evalee's bottles were tipped upside down in the dish drainer. Dad sat down and lit a cigarette. I didn't have an ashtray, so I brought him a glass candy dish.

I had one hand on the handle of the cupboard, and one hand on the fridge. I turned. "Which drink do you want?" I asked nervously.

"Anything's fine," he said. I never saw Dad drink water unless he was overheated, and coffee would take awkward minutes to brew, so I pulled out the Kool-Aid and filled two glasses with ice. "It's grape," I said as I poured. "Boohoo's favorite." I scratched my hairline at the top of my neck, though I wasn't sure I'd felt an itch.

"I guess I should know that, shouldn't I?"

Dad asked me to sit. I took a sip from my glass; it tasted too sweet. But that's how Winnalee and Boohoo liked it. I hoped Dad did, too.

"Evy, I want to apologize for snapping at you like I did on the way to the hospital. I guess I'm so used to you looking out for your brother, that you were the first one I thought to blame."

"That's okay," I said, because that's what you say when somebody apologizes, whether it's okay or not.

"Pretty goddamn pathetic, isn't it? I mean, I'm his old man, and I haven't looked out for him once in the last four years. Probably longer. Yet I was blaming you."

I glanced up. Dad's face had stubble on it, and he was wearing those familiar smudges under his eyes that made it look like he hadn't slept in days. I looked down at his glass and watched the gray smoke from his cigarette circle it.

"Well, I *should* have been watching him, instead of horsing around," I told him. "Boohoo's into mischief all the time, and I knew Aunt Verdella was busy."

Dad shook his head. "No, you should have been horsing around. *I* should have been looking out for him."

Dad hadn't touched his Kool-Aid, and I decided I should have made coffee instead.

"Evy," he said as he crushed his cigarette out. He got up and paced a little, then turned away and leaned on one leg, his fingertips tucking into the back pockets of his jeans. "I know I've been a shitty father. The last four years especially. But every single time I look at you kids . . ." He suddenly sounded like he was being strangled. He took a deep breath, looked up at the ceiling, and started again. "Every time I look at you and your brother, I'm reminded of how it's my fault you don't have a mother anymore."

For four years, I'd waited for Dad to take responsibility for Ma's death. To blame himself, hate himself even. But now that he was, I felt no glory. Only a rising desperation to take his remorse away.

"It's not your fault," I said.

He turned and his dark brows, made heavy with guilt, sagged above his strained eyes. "But it is. I know it, and you know it. How many times did your ma ask me to level that washer and secure that goddamn sump pump anyway? The basement had flooded just two weeks before that."

"Guys are always letting things go," I said. "Every time I'm around more than one or two married women, they're always complaining or joking about their men doing everything for everybody else, but letting jobs at home go."

Dad ignored my attempt to pardon him. "Every day I live with knowing I robbed you kids of a mother, and your ma of what should have been a long life. All because I was too damn lazy to go downstairs and do what needed being done."

Dad came back to the table and braced himself on bent knuckles, his head down. "You think I don't know that that's why you can't even look at me anymore, Evy? Why you turn away every time you come in the house? But who can blame you? I can't even look at myself in the mirror to shave my goddamn face half the time."

"That's not why I turn away," I protested, my words coming out thick with anguish. I opened my mouth to remind him that for most of my life he looked through me as if I was made of fog, that for most of my life we'd been uncomfortable with each other. But I couldn't say that. It would have only made him feel worse.

I put my head down and wished for the awkward silence

and his anguish to go away. When it didn't, I blurted out, "It wasn't your fault, Dad. It was mine."

Dad peeked at me. "Yours? Come on, Evy, what—"

"It's true! Ma asked me to go down there and redistribute the clothes because she was busy washing Boohoo's hands. But I was stitching something I was making, and almost had the hem done, so I ignored her. She told me again to go, and I got huffy with her and said I was just as busy as she was."

"You always listened to your mother."

"But not that time. If I'd listened to her, she'd still be here."

Dad leaned across the table. "You really think your ma would have rather it had been you instead? God, Evy. She wouldn't have been able to live with herself if she'd sent you down there."

"But it wouldn't have been either of us," I insisted. "Uncle Rudy had taught me how lightning works with metal and around water. I would have been too scared to step on that soppy floor. And by the time she went down there in my place, that strike would have come and gone." I squinted my wet eyes shut, hiding them from Dad like a little kid who thinks she can't be seen because her head alone is hidden.

Dad hurried around the table, and put his arms around my shoulders. "Crissakes, Evy. You've been blaming *yourself* this whole time?" he asked. "Is this why you can't look me in the eye anymore?"

I sobbed as I nodded.

Dad's arm was around my neck, his head touching mine. And I swear, he even smelled like guilt. I nodded as hard as I could with my head held so tightly.

"Oh, Evy. Don't blame yourself. Blame me. Blame God. But don't blame *yourself*. Please. Guilt is such a heavy burden to carry."

Dad hadn't made a sound when his eyes filled at Ma's funeral. But he cried with sobs that convulsed his stomach and sounded agonizingly painful now.

He let go of me and stood back, as if suddenly embarrassed over his outburst—or maybe ashamed over the relief he felt when he learned that I avoided him out of guilt, not blame.

I got up and grabbed a dish towel and wiped my face, while Dad swabbed his eyes with calloused fingers. "Let's make a deal. *I'll* stop blaming myself, if *you'll* stop blaming yourself. I mean it, Dad. I'll never be able to feel it's okay to let go of my guilt, if you don't think it's okay to let go of yours."

"I'll do it," Dad said, nodding his head in determination. "I'll find a way to let it go."

He cleared his throat and sat down. He lit another cigarette, and after a few moments of silence, he drank his Kool-Aid like it wasn't too sweet, and asked me if I'd been checking my oil. I nodded.

When Dad said he had to go, I walked him to the door. "Thanks for coming," I said.

He opened the door and it squealed. He swung it back and forth a couple of times. "I'll stop by and bring some WD-40 for these hinges," he said.

"That would be nice," I told him.

He went outside and I stood on the front steps. He turned. "I'm gonna do better by Boohoo, too," he said. He looked up at the fat-bodied moths swarming the yard light above me, like he was thinking of something else to say. Across the road, I could see two heads in the window, and I knew that Aunt Verdella and Winnalee were watching. Watching and hoping, while Freeda kept herself busy in another room, the same way I did now when the mailman came. "Dad?" I asked. "Can you not tell Aunt Verdella that I refused to go downstairs when Ma asked?"

Dad's face was lost in the shadows under the brim of his

cap, but his gratitude for having some way to help me wasn't. "You don't even need to ask."

As soon as he pulled out of the drive, the front door opened and Winnalee and Aunt Verdella came hurrying out, both calling my name. Above them, the wispy clouds had passed across the sliver moon, and I felt as though Ma was calling to me, too. Assuring me that she knew there *was* a difference between a lie that hurts and a lie that heals.

I was lying on the bed, holding the picture Uncle Rudy gave me of the tree growing on the top of a big rock jutting out of the water, no soil beneath it, when Winnalee crawled into bed. She scooted over and laid her head on my shoulder to stare up at the picture.

"Uncle Rudy gave me this the morning after Ma died. When he found me sleeping in the magic tree."

"You fell asleep in our magic tree that night?" she asked quietly.

"Yeah."

"Aw," she said.

"I think he wanted me to see myself as this tree, and my love for Ma the roots, stretching across space and sky, so that I'd never forget that Ma and me will always be connected."

"That's beautiful, Button."

I stared at the roots. "It's weird, though, how I never noticed until a few minutes ago, that this isn't one thick root, like I thought it was. Look. It's made up of many roots entwined together."

Winnalee lifted her head and peered more closely. "Oh yeah," she said, like she found my discovery every bit as astonishing as I did. She swiped her finger along the root, saying what I was thinking. "Like there's one root to keep you connected to your mom, and one to Aunt Verdella. One for Uncle Rudy, and for Boohoo, and for your dad. And one for me, too, and Freeda, and Evalee. One for everybody you love. To remind you that you're connected to all of us, no matter where we are."

"But I wish I could wrap all of you around me, and keep you right next to me forever."

"Maybe Boohoo could help you out with that," Winnalee said, and we both chuckled softly.

"Button? If Freeda could have made your dad happy, would you have been okay with them being together?"

"Yes."

"What about your ma? If people do look down on us from Heaven, do you think she would have been okay with it, too?"

"Yes," I told her. "In the same way that I think, that while she once resented my attachment to Aunt Verdella, she was happy for it after she had to leave me."

"I think so, too." She sucked her tongue against her teeth, then said, "I was waiting, hoping that after your dad talked to you, he'd come over and ask to talk to Freeda alone, too. And tell her he loved her, and that he wanted her to stay."

I didn't need to tell her that I had hoped for the same thing. She knew it. And our sighs rose and fell together.

CHAPTER

41

BRIGHT IDEA #81: If someone asks you why you carry your ma in a jar, just tell them that sometimes it takes a long, long time to find a final resting place.

For the next couple of days, I pretended that the Malones weren't leaving. I went blind when I stepped around the bags and boxes lined near my front door, and when I was at Aunt Verdella's, I pretended the box stuffed with filled bell jars on the counter were waiting to go into the basement for winter and not in Freeda's car.

On Tuesday, Freeda made us heaping bowls of garden salad for lunch, with homemade dressing, and we ate out on the picnic table. We laughed ourselves silly as we recounted every detail of Fanny Tilman catching us doing the "naked lady dance," then laughed even harder during the retelling, when Aunt Verdella bunny-hopped to the house, her legs pressed together to the knees, ha-ha'ing as she pleaded with us to stop making her laugh. And the whole time while we laughed, I pretended that our recounting the funniest event of our two months together wasn't an attempt to sear that memory in our minds forever, so we'd have something to smile over when we missed one another.

But by Thursday morning, there could be no more pretending. Dad hadn't come to profess his love to Freeda and beg her to stay, and the girls who wanted our dresses hadn't come early and paid us an outrageous sum so that at least Winnalee and the baby could stay. And because those things hadn't happened, the Malones were leaving at noon, and that heavy feeling you get in your stomach when you're full of loss woke me before dawn.

I picked Evalee up when she stirred, and took her downstairs to change and bathe her, because I knew that Winnalee could use the extra sleep. She had a long drive ahead of her.

I talked to Evalee as I tended her, telling her everything I wished her to know, in case I'd never get the chance to say them. Mostly how much I loved her, and wanted her to always love herself. Sure, Winnalee would tell her the same things. So would Freeda. But I wanted her to have many roots to cling to in the event she ever found herself standing alone, feeling disconnected from life and love.

Winnalee woke early and took her bath, and we hiked over to Aunt Verdella's by seven-thirty. The morning was cool, and the sky so clear that it was easy to believe that all of summer's storms were behind us.

Freeda's car wasn't in the drive, nor was Uncle Rudy's truck. Aunt Verdella was in the kitchen, though, and Boohoo was in the tub. "He wouldn't take his bath last night. He was upset," she said, her gaze swooping over Winnalee and Evalee to tip me off as to why, as if I didn't know.

Aunt Verdella's morning hugs were a little longer, a little

tighter than usual. She forced a smile when she let go of Winnalee, but her eyes didn't crinkle. She reached for Evalee. "Awwww, come to Auntie Verdella," she said, and she cuddled her close before passing her to me so she could turn the eggs.

Boohoo didn't take more than a quick splash, and when he came out, he tried giving me a comb. "I can't make that part thing," he said, as if he had to, when his hair never saw a part unless we were going somewhere.

I was holding Evalee, so Winnalee grabbed the comb. Boohoo jumped and snatched it back, saying to me, "Give Winnalee her creepy baby back, so you can do it."

I expected Winnalee to get upset, but she didn't. I guess she knew, as I did, that Boohoo was only trying to protect his heart from hurting after they left.

Boohoo's hair was only half wet, and there was a wad of fuzzy soap on the dry half, but still, I made a neat part, and tucked his striped shirt into his pants as Aunt Verdella instructed me to.

"Where's Uncle Rudy?" Boohoo asked, when he noticed his truck was gone.

"He went over to your dad's to grab some quarts of oil, so he can have the girls' vehicles in tip-top shape for . . ." She stopped talking and got busy instead.

I turned Evalee outward over my arm because she was squirming, and her legs started kicking when she saw Boohoo. "Awwwww, look how Cupcake loves you, Boohoo. She's waiting for you to smile at her."

Aunt Verdella grimaced when Boohoo turned his back to the baby. "Honey, I know you're upset, but Evalee doesn't understand why you're not being her fun and sweet Uncle Boohoo right now."

"I am not upset. I just don't want to see that creepy, poopy little baby today, that's all. I don't even like her. And I don't care if she's moving away, either. I'm gonna look for Hoppy, 'cause I'd rather have a toad for a friend anyway."

Winnalee asked where Freeda was.

Aunt Verdella gave her a just-a-minute glance, then told Boohoo to go upstairs and get a clean pair of socks, because she'd forgotten to bring some down. He went quickly—maybe to avoid Evalee.

"She was running to The Corner Store first, then she was going to Jewel's grave. She just left a few minutes ago." Her face bunched first with sadness, then with worry. "Button, she wanted me—and Boohoo—to go with her. But I wanted to talk it over with you, first. Honey, I think we should go. All of us. Even Boohoo."

"I want to go," Winnalee said quietly, watching for my reaction from the corner of her eye.

I sighed and looked down at my hands. With Knucklehead doing so poorly, I knew we couldn't avoid the topic of death forever. As Freeda pointed out, we shouldn't be avoiding the topic at all. So I nodded. It was a day of dread, anyway.

As Boohoo thumped down the stairs, Aunt Verdella looked at me. "I'm glad we're doing this while the Malones are here. We could use the extra support today."

I nodded, then put my head down. *We could use the Malones' support every day, just as they could use ours.*

Boohoo seemed to forget his cranky mood once Aunt Verdella told him we—all of us—were going on "an outing." He ran to find his shoes, and came back wearing them, and his towel cape. Aunt Verdella fidgeted, and I knew she was thinking it would be disrespectful to go to the cemetery in a makeshift costume. But I guess she decided it wasn't worth the tug-of-war to get the towel off of him. Either that, or she forgot about it mid-thought, because she just remembered that she needed to slip Boohoo's bee kit into her purse.

"Where we going, Evy?" Boohoo asked as Aunt Verdella turned the car down Shady Road.

"You'll see," I said.

"Do they sell root beer where we're going? Because I could use a root beer."

"No," I told him, quickly, and quietly. I looked over at Winnalee, who was jiggling a bouquet of lilac-colored asters, fireweed, and goldenrod that she'd picked for Ma from the edge of the yard, to get Evalee's attention.

Aunt Verdella slowed down as the first rows of gravestones came into view, and Boohoo's bony elbow cut into my thigh as he leaned over me to get a better look. "What's this place?" he asked.

"A cemetery," Aunt Verdella told him.

"What's a cemetery?"

"Auntie will explain in a minute, honey."

We pulled under a cast-iron archway with Shady Lawn Cemetery formed in sympathy-card-shaped letters at the top. Just inside the entrance, the smooth pavement circled a six-foot granite angel. When I was a kid, I didn't believe the statue was an angel, like Aunt Verdella said. It wasn't pretty like the baby angels on Valentine cards, or the beautiful, sweet-faced lady angels that we topped our Christmas trees with. It was a male angel who looked serious as a soldier. And he didn't have delicate-looking wings like a dragonfly, or those butterfly-shaped ones made of duck feathers. Instead he had spiny wings that pointed straight up from behind his head, the tips sharp as arrows. His head was bowed, and one hand curled into a fist lifted high. The other hand was resting over his heart. With his stoic face and sharp, angular lines, he looked more like a sleepy superhero villain tangled in a bedsheet than a vision of comfort for grieving hearts. I guess Boohoo thought the same, because after climbing onto my lap to peep through the opened window, he said, "Cool. Do they have Spider-Man here, too?"

Winnalee giggled, then gave me an apologetic look.

Aunt Verdella veered to the right when she reached the fork in the road, and pulled the car over as far as she could without making tire tracks in the grass.

She turned sideways on the seat, and blew out a deep breath before she began. I bit my cheek.

"Boohoo, when people get old, or get hurt and their body breaks so bad that they can't be fixed with a shot or an operation, they leave them. Kind of like they're taking off a pair of pants or a shirt or something, and they go off to Heaven to live with God."

"You mean they go there naked? Like how I went to the hospital?" Boohoo asked.

Winnalee lifted the flower blooms up to cover her face.

"Well, no. They go like, well, spirits. Their spirit goes there."

Boohoo nodded. "Like a ghost then." He cocked his head in thought, then nodded slowly. "Yeah, I guess that's right, because Casper the Ghost doesn't wear clothes."

"She doesn't mean like a Halloween or a cartoon ghost," I said, and Boohoo looked more confused than ever.

"Anyway, after they go off to Heaven, we have to do something with their bodies after they leave them. So we bring them here to the cemetery and we bury them under the ground in a box. Then we put one of those pretty gravestones on top so we can find where we buried them when we come to pay our respects."

Boohoo looked at Aunt Verdella, his eyes squinted in thought. Then they shot open. "Wait . . . are you talking about people being *dead*?"

You can't grow up in the country, much less on a farm, without seeing dead things—birds, deer, raccoons, rabbits, fish. I never gave this much thought until one of Uncle Rudy's cows gave birth and the calf died two days later. I'd taken a liking to the calf, a girl like me, with huge eyes and lashes long as my fingers. When Uncle Rudy and I found her dead on the third morning, it wasn't just an unfortunate accident that happened to some wild animal with fur or feathers: It was something that happened to my friend. I remembered looking up at Uncle Rudy as we were leaving the barn, and asking him if people die like that, too. He told me they did, and reminded me of Grandma Mae. That night I had nightmares, and between then and when Ma died—and even a couple times since when I thought of *me* dying, I got so scared I could hardly breathe. I looked at Boohoo, my whole insides tense, as I waited to see if he was having the same reaction.

Boohoo scratched his head. "You mean, this is where they put *people* when they die?"

"Oh dear. He's itching," Aunt Verdella said.

I quickly looked at Boohoo's tanned arms for signs of a peppery rash.

"We should have made him rinse his head better," Aunt Verdella said.

Boohoo tapped her arm. "Is it, Aunt Verdella? Is this where they put dead people?"

"Well, yes, Boohoo."

Confusion twisted his mouth. He looked up at me. "Evy, why do they go through all that bother with dead people? Why don't they just throw them on the road, like they do the dead animals?"

Maybe it was the stress of the day, the moment, and the relief that came when we realized Boohoo wasn't going to be traumatized for life. Whatever the reason, we busted out laughing. Well, at least Winnalee and I did. Aunt Verdella only pressed her hand to the side of her face and said, "Oh dear."

Aunt Verdella put the car in gear, and we crawled reverently down the road toward the center plots.

"Hey, that's Freeda's car," Boohoo said, pointing up ahead.

Freeda was standing before Ma's grave when we pulled up behind her Ford. There was a softness in her stance. Our moods grew solemn as we got out of the car. Winnalee walked so close to me that our shoulders bumped, and I put my hand on Boohoo's head when he asked why we had to come here.

With a breeze rustling the leaves in the scattering of trees, I think Freeda sensed us more than heard us. She had a sad smile on her face when she turned. She pulled Aunt Verdella and me to stand on each side of her, then tilted her head to rest against Aunt Verdella's.

"Hey, that rock there says Peters. Ma Peters."

"It's Mae, honey," Aunt Verdella said. "That's where your grandma—your dad and Uncle Rudy's ma—is buried."

Aunt Verdella led Boohoo by the shoulders, and leaned over him to point. "Honey," she said, in a church-quiet voice. "You see this pretty white stone here? It says Jewel Peters. And this is the year she was born, and this, the year that she passed away."

Aunt Verdella fumbled in her purse and took out a black-and-white photograph. She handed it to Boohoo. "This is a picture of her," she said. "That's her, standing right there next to your daddy."

I filled my lungs and squeezed the breath to me. Winnalee reached out and took my hand, and Freeda's hand came to rest on my back.

"She died when you were just two years old," Aunt Verdella said. She glanced up at me, anguish tugging the outer corners of her eyes, then looked back down at Boohoo. "She was your mama, Boohoo. The one who brought you into this world."

Boohoo stared at the stone, and I swallowed hard in an effort to force the lump in my throat to go down.

"We're real sorry that we never told you about her until now. We should have. We just didn't want—"

Boohoo looked up. "That's okay. 'Cause I already know about her. Uncle Rudy told me."

We all looked at Boohoo. "What?" Aunt Verdella asked. She bent farther over, as if she hadn't heard right.

"I said, Uncle Rudy already told me about her. Jewel. My mom. He told me a long time ago. Maybe when I was in kindergarten."

"He told you about your ma?" Aunt Verdella looked up, her mouth hanging open, like it was the most implausible thing in the world. "Rudy never told me he'd told him," she said. "Why wouldn't he tell me?"

"Because it was boy talk, probably," Boohoo said.

"Boy talk?" I asked.

"Yeah. The stuff you don't say around ladies or girls, because they're gonna get crabby or they're gonna start bawling."

"He asked you not to say anything to us?"

"No. I just didn't. Because Uncle Rudy said she was *dead*. And you guys get all weird when something's dead. Even almost dead, like Knucklehead. You make me not look, then you start lookin' at me all funny, trying not to cry. Evy chews on her mouth, and you start hugging me to your belly until I can't hardly breathe."

Aunt Verdella straightened up and put her hands on the slight indent of her waist. She shook her head. "I can't believe this. I just can't believe it."

"What did Uncle Rudy tell you?" I asked.

"He told me what I already knowed. That everything that is born, dies in time. Like the flowers. And cows. And dogs. *And* people. Well, I didn't know that part about people until he told me, but I woulda figured it out."

Aunt Verdella still had her hands propped on her hips, and

she was stepping slowly in place. “I can’t believe he already knows,” she said.

“But he didn’t tell me about cemeteries,” Boohoo said, like he was trying to make up for ruining a surprise. “I didn’t know that part. I just thought *all* of my ma went to Heaven.”

“What did he tell you about your ma?” Freeda asked softly.

“He told me that she died even when she didn’t want to, because she had an accident, and that now she lives in Heaven. And he said she was a very nice ma and a good person. And that she kinda looked like Evy, and she liked to clean things and sew. Oh, and that she loved me very much.”

Aunt Verdella felt shaky, so Freeda helped her lower herself to the ground. My legs weren’t feeling so peppy, either, so I sat down beside her. “Lands sake,” she said. “I can’t believe he knew about Jewel this whole time. Can you believe it, Button? And there we were, keeping and fretting over this secret for years.”

Freeda and Winnalee sat down, too, Evalee straddling Winnalee’s leg.

“Do you remember anything about her?” Winnalee asked.

“No,” Boohoo said, as he nestled down between Winnalee and Aunt Verdella. “I don’t remember her. Just Evy and Aunt Verdella ’cause they got to be my mas when my other ma got dead.” He leaned over and pressed his cheek to Aunt Verdella’s bare arm. “We should have brought a picnic lunch,” he said. “And root beer.”

And with that, Boohoo ran off, circling the gravestones with arms spread airplane-style, his towel cape flapping, the forgetfulness of babyhood holding him high above the grief of mother-loss.

CHAPTER 42

BRIGHT IDEA #45: Sometimes when there's nothing left to say, people just say Don't take any wooden knickles.

An hour later, Winnalee's van was backed up into the yard, just feet from the porch. The screen door was propped open with the broom, the inside door left open. Winnalee was changing Evalee's diaper on the couch when I got inside after carrying a box to her van, and Aunt Verdella was standing nearby.

"Did you see Boohoo in his sandbox?" Aunt Verdella asked me. "He's been there since we got back, and he's refusing to come over. I told Rudy to stay with him. Is Rudy out there?"

"Yes, they're both out there," I told her.

"Poor kid," Freeda said. She went to the couch and smiled at Evalee, who was making bubbles as she cooed. "You have everything from upstairs now, Winnalee?"

"I think so."

"I'll check," I said, eager to get out of that living room where everyone was trying hard to pretend that their hearts weren't breaking.

Tommy was coming down the stairs with Evalee's folded playpen, and we did that side-to-side dance that people do when they come face-to-face and are heading in opposite directions. I moved aside to let him pass, then hurried upstairs.

Winnalee had insisted on cleaning the bedroom before we turned in the previous night, "so it can look just like it did before I came," she'd said. I stood in the doorway and looked at the dresser top, bare for the first time in almost three months, and the floor that she'd swept. There were streaks over the furniture and on the vanity mirror, and dust bunnies were crowded around the legs of the bed, as if she didn't have the heart to sweep them away. Not that it mattered. Even if she'd gotten the room hospital-clean, it—as well as our lives—would not go back to what it was before she came back.

I peeked in each dresser drawer to make sure none of Winnalee's things were there, and looked under the bed. I spotted one of Evalee's pacifiers, and grabbed it. And as I was getting up, I braced my hand on the nightstand and felt our Book of Bright Ideas under my fingers. My stomach did one of those flutter-flips, and I picked it up. I ran my hand over the embossed words, *Great Expectations,* then rummaged for a pen. I flipped to the remaining page, and under Winnalee's last entry nine years ago, I wrote: *Winnalee, it can be your turn to keep our book. Bring it when we meet again so we can write our 100th idea. Then we'll know everything there is about how to live good and not make the same mistakes we, or our parents, already made. Okay? Your best friend, Button.*

They were all outside when I got downstairs. Tommy had Evalee's playpen propped against the van, trying to redistribute the heap of bags and boxes before he slipped it in, so that everything wouldn't come crashing down on the first curve she took. After he closed the door, we stood like statues wearing granite smiles. "Here comes Uncle Rudy to say goodbye," Aunt Verdella said. Boohoo was still in the sandbox, his head bent over the towers of sand he was making with his plastic pail.

I handed Winnalee our book, opened to what I'd written, and as she read my words the wind at her back blew her hair around to hug me.

Aunt Verdella grabbed Uncle Rudy when he reached us, and she hugged him as though he was leaving. She muttered something against his shirt, and he patted her back.

We all stood there, then, as if in silent agreement that we wouldn't cry. But when Aunt Verdella touched my arm, that soft rub over my skin was enough to wipe any sort of agreement away. I started crying, which made her cry, too, and the tears spread like a wildfire. We passed out hugs, and Winnalee made promises I hoped she'd keep. And then the inevitable moment came. "Everything in?" Tommy asked. The Malones nodded, so he slammed the van door shut.

Boohoo's head lifted with the bang, and he sprang to his feet. With his ball of twine cradled in his arm, he came running, his skinny legs pumping. "Aunt Verdella! Aunt Verdella!" he cried. "Don't let them go! Sit on them, Aunt Verdella! Sit on them!"

"Oh, honey," she moaned.

A strand of hair was glued to Winnalee's cheek with tears, and she pulled it loose. "I'm bringing your Cupcake back in a couple of months, Boohoo," she told him. "Probably before Christmas."

"But I don't want you to go *now*!"

Boohoo's fingers fumbled to find the loose strand of twine,

and he let the sphere thud to the ground when he got ahold of it. He wrapped it around Evalee's ankles, twirling it frantically up her leg as he sobbed, as if he could tie her to him forever.

Winnalee grabbed at the web he was making. "Boohoo . . . ," she said softly. He ran the twine behind Winnalee, then raced the string around the back of me. Freeda turned and stopped him when the twine reached her. She didn't say anything. She just grabbed him and tried holding him. He jerked away and sobbed through gritted teeth.

"Hey, Boohoo," Uncle Rudy said calmly. "I was thinking about going down to the crick to see if there's any trout who wanna be our supper. Why don't you go get our poles out of the shed?"

Boohoo handed out one last scowl to the Malones, to all of us, then stomped away, his arm crooked as he rubbed his sleeve across his eyes.

We just stood there, silent, but for Aunt Verdella, who was watching Boohoo go and sniffling hard. Uncle Rudy jiggled the brim of his cap, staring off, seemingly at nothing. Then he pointed to the red maple sitting on the edge of the front lawn. He put his arm across Aunt Verdella's shoulder, his hand reaching to mine. "Verdie," he said, "you remember that ice storm we had a good twenty-four, twenty-five years ago? That maple wasn't much taller than me when that storm happened. Remember? Left the trees with a good inch-thick coating of ice, and that one bent till it was almost touching the ground. Remember how worried you were when a couple of its branches snapped off under the weight of the ice? But then the sun came out again, the ice melted, and that tree straightened itself right back up. And missing a couple branches or not, it grew. Just look at it now, nearly twenty-five feet tall." Uncle Rudy dropped his arm and looked across the road, where Boohoo was shoving the shed door open. "Don't you girls worry about that boy. He's a strong sapling, that one."

Uncle Rudy gave Freeda and Winnalee a hug, and jostled Evalee's foot. "You girls drive safely now, and remember that you're always welcome here." Then he headed for home.

And that was it.

Freeda climbed into her car.

Winnalee tucked Evalee and her diaper bag into the van, then scooted behind the wheel.

We waved, and called *I love you* and *I'll miss you* through their opened windows.

Throughout the day, my insides had felt like a rain barrel under a monsoon, and the second the dust settled behind them, and Aunt Verdella headed home to check on Boohoo before they left to fish, I hurried into the house and fell facedown on the couch that smelled like baby powder. That rain barrel I was holding inside tipped over as I did, and my grief over the Malones, Ma, Jesse, the dress shop, everything came spilling out. And while I cried, Tommy came inside and sat down and began unwrapping a stick of gum.

CHAPTER 43

BRIGHT IDEA #89: If you ever don't know which direction to go in, or you start moving in the right direction but then get lost along the way, don't get rattled and start moving fast, this way and that. Instead, stand still and be quiet. Then you'll be showed which way to go.

Winnalee always said that you've gotta believe in something, or what's the point. I cried for a good hour, then decided I had no choice but to believe that Winnalee was coming back, and that the winds of change would carry us all into a future where we'd find some happiness.

And it did.

The Malones only got as far as Milwaukee before they decided they were done running and that they would be coming back. Winnalee, right then, and Freeda after she sold her salon in Michigan.

A week after Winnalee returned, Linda announced that she would stay in Dauber until we finished the fall orders, then she was putting the store up for sale and joining Al in Green

Bay. Before that could happen, though, Dad showed up with a check for five thousand dollars—my share of the life insurance money he'd been keeping for Boohoo and me since Ma's death. "It's enough for a down payment on Ma's shop, if you want it. I'll cosign the loan for you."

But Dad didn't need to cosign the loan, because by the time Freeda returned two months later, profit in hand, I had already talked to Ma and felt I had her blessing to pitch the Malones my brightest idea to date: turning Jewel's Bridal Boutique into the Magic Tree. A place for women—sixteen to ninety-six, darning-needle-skinny to fatter than Fred—to get a makeover for their hair, their clothes, and their attitudes about themselves.

Dad helped us remodel the shop, and Winnalee painted a bright, playful mural of ladies of every shape and size dancing naked around a tree. We took out the tables and some of the fabric cubbyholes, and put in a workstation for each of us: a sink and vanity where Freeda now gives the women the best hairdo for the shape of their face and personality, a desk and easel where Winnalee sketches out their body type and shows them how the art of distraction works. And a sewing corner for me, where I sew the outfits Winnalee designs on Ma's Singer, in fabrics and colors and patterns that will look best with their coloring and size and shape.

We took out the file cabinet where the patterns were kept in the front room, and added the clothing racks where our newest designs and the reworked clothes Aunt Verdella picks up for us at the Community Sale hang. We also sell makeup, hair products, homemade jewelry, cloth purses, candles, wind chimes, and whatever other gift items we decide to make at the time.

I thought Winnalee was going to croak when I stopped her from tossing out the bridal gown from the old window display while we were remodeling, and told her I was planning on wearing it at my wedding. "I knew it!" she shouted. "I just knew you'd do this, the minute I came downstairs and saw him going at your neck like a . . . a vacuum cleaner. Just friends . . . just friends my ass! But man, Button. Marriage? Are you nuts? Cripes, just get on the Pill and have at it."

Winnalee reacted just as I knew she would. And so did the rest of them. Freeda fretted about me making such a big decision at my age, and so fast. Uncle Rudy and Dad smiled and gave me quick pats to my back, and Aunt Verdella busted into happy tears and hugged me so hard I nearly lost my breath.

But Winnalee came around, and when we took the gown to the cleaners in Porter, she looked peacock proud when she plunked the dress box on the counter and said, "This is my best friend here, and she's a virgin, so you'd better get this dress white as snow. And hurry about it, too, because I've gotta update this butt-ass-ugly thing, and that's gonna take some time."

Needless to say, Winnalee didn't make the same comment about the need for a snow-white gown for Freeda, when she and Dad announced that they were getting married a year and a half later. In fact, she suggested a dress in the color of my cheeks when she made her comment to the dry cleaner. If I remember correctly, Freeda called her a "little shit," and tossed a hair comb at her.

Epilogue—1978

Winnalee and I are going to meet at Aunt Verdella's a half an hour earlier than usual. I pull into Dad's yard on my way and honk to let Freeda know I'm here. I often pick her up on the way, because she says it does her good to start her day with Aunt Verdella's ha-has.

Wood smoke is curling from the chimney in Dad's garage, telling me that he and Boohoo are inside, working on the 1934 Ford that Dad started restoring years ago, but never finished. I zip up my jacket and Boohoo's dog, Knucklehop, tags me to the garage.

Dad turns down the radio when I come in. He makes a bit of small talk, and I smile. Not over anything he says, but because when I look in his eyes, I see happiness there. And because he doesn't turn away.

Freeda barges into the garage. She's in her forties now, and her hair sits just below her shoulders. Because, like she says, if she's going to have hair down to her ass when she's old, she's got to get a good start now. She kisses on Dad like he's Uncle Rudy and she's Aunt Verdella, and reminds Boohoo to make his bed or there will be hell to pay. "Okay, gotta go," she says.

Freeda and I surround Boohoo. "Love sandwich!" I shout. Boohoo winces and says, "Come on, are you guys gonna still be doing that when I'm thirty?"

Aunt Verdella is at the stove dropping bunny pancakes on the griddle when we get there, and the kitchen is toasty warm and swaddled in breakfast smells. Winnalee is lifting browned sausage links from the fry pan onto a paper-towel-lined plate.

"I wonder how many of those things you've made over the years?" I say, as I prop my chin on Aunt Verdella's shoulder and watch her drop in the raisin eyes. Her hair—a light reddish brown, because that's what Freeda gave her—tickles my cheek. She laughs. "Oh Lord, I don't know. Lots of them!

"You two have time for coffee?" she asks, as she gives Freeda her morning hug. I glance up at the clock, decide we have time for a half a cup, and tell her I'll get it.

"Oh, you'll never guess who Rudy and I ran into in Eagle River over the weekend," she tells us. "Marls Bishop. Well, she's not Marls Bishop anymore. She married a nice guy named Allen, and they've got three more little ones. She said her boy's doing real good. Brody gave up custody so Allen could adopt him. Did you know that?"

Aunt Verdella takes the platter of pancakes to the table and reaches for a sausage link. Before she gets it to her mouth, Freeda taps her hand. Aunt Verdella groans. "Look at that. I was gonna stuff that thing in my mouth without giving it an ounce of thought. I'm never gonna get below a hundred and eighty again if I keep pickin' like this. I didn't even know I was doin' it." Her eyes get huge then and she turns to me. "Speakin' of not knowing what you're doing, did Ada tell you what happened with Fanny on Monday?"

"I haven't seen Ada in a couple of days," I tell her.

"Well," she says. "Ada had to call Fanny's son in Indiana and tell him something has to be done with her, because she ain't in her right mind."

"Was she ever?" Winnalee asks, and I stifle a giggle.

Aunt Verdella continues, like she didn't hear the comment. "Ada said Fanny came into The Corner Store, and she was shuffling in these tiny baby steps, like her feet were having trouble moving. Ada was afraid she'd go crashing into the bread rack, so she hurried around the counter to help steady her. And then she saw the problem. Fanny's bloomers had slipped right down from under her dress, and were all tangled around her ankles!"

"Maybe she finally got too warm," I say. And Winnalee adds, "And decided to do the naked lady dance to cool off." Freeda laughs. But then, because Aunt Verdella looks serious, I say, "She didn't even notice?"

"No. Not even when Ada told her. Ada didn't have any choice then but to coax her to step out of them before she fell."

"I bet she was wearing long, wool underwear," Winnalee says.

Aunt Verdella's eyes are round. "Well, that's the strange part. I came in right after it happened, and there was Ada, holding this pair of these red, silky underpanties! I thought she was pulling my leg when she said they'd just dropped off of Fanny."

As Winnalee and I roar, Freeda shouts, "Fanny Tilman. Wool on the outside, silk underneath! Who would have guessed?"

"Her son is coming up today and putting her in the nursing home. I'll have to go see her tomorrow."

I smile, because that's Aunt Verdella for you.

Upstairs, there is a scurry of footsteps, followed by an "Ouch!"

"Oh lordy, what are those kids up to now. Rudy?" Aunt Verdella calls. She turns to us. "You wouldn't think he could still be sleeping with all that racket," she says. Then she belts out, "Breakfast!"

The same fluttery footsteps join the heavy, slow ones descending the stairs.

"Lookie what came jumping on my bed to wake me up this morning," Uncle Rudy says as he comes into the kitchen. "Two pretty little dancing fairies."

Winnalee and I squeal with delight. "Our old tu-tus!" we yell in unison, and we barrage Aunt Verdella with questions.

"Well, I don't really know how they ended up here. But you know me, I'm a pack rat. I found them last night and laid them out for the girls to find this morning. Oh, don't those two look darling!"

The girls giggle as Uncle Rudy lifts their hands and twirls them in circles, one at each side. Eight-year-old Evalee, pudgy-bellied and beautiful with her sugar-cookie skin, silky straight blond hair, and angelic face, holds out the pink mesh skirt delicately as she slowly spins, while Jewelee—a year and a half younger, but already nearly as tall—dances, her skinny free arm whipping in circles like she's winding up to throw a lasso. She's wearing an impish grin, and her long hair—lighter than mine, but every bit as curly as Tommy's—bounces.

Uncle Rudy lets go of their hands, and while Freeda asks them if they had fun at their pajama party with Aunt Verdella, Jewelee twirls in high-speed spins around the table, her arms above her head, her hands clasped. She bumps into Aunt

Verdella's belly and Aunt Verdella ha-has as she catches her with a hug, then warns her to be careful because Uncle Rudy's got hot coffee.

Evalee comes to me, her head half bowed, her mouth pouty. I grab her and she melts against me. "Auntie Button," she says. "Jewelee pulled my hair when we were putting on our dancing dresses. All because she wanted to wear this one. But that one was littler, like her."

I can feel my lips pull tight like Ma's used to, even if I don't want them to, and I call Jewelee to me. "What did we tell you about being naughty?"

Jewelee juts out her chin. Her neck is every bit as wrist-skinny as Boohoo's used to be. "That if I don't stop it, Aunt Freeda is gonna sit on me."

"Don't think I won't, either," Freeda says, and Winnalee adds, "Ask your uncle Boohoo."

"I swear," Aunt Verdella says, looking first at me, then at Winnalee. "If I didn't know it was impossible, I'd say your daughters were switched at birth." We've all said this a thousand times already.

I pull a ponytail holder out of my purse and pat my lap. Jewelee hops up and caps her knobby knees with her hands. "Speaking of your uncle Boohoo," I say, as I gather handfuls of her wild curls, "he's stopping over here with Grandpa today." The girls cheer, and Aunt Verdella smiles.

"Soon?" Evalee asks, and I tell her no. "He and Grandpa are going to help Uncle Tommy put up snow fence as soon as he gets back from the hardware store."

"Andy's gonna help do snow fence, too," Jewelee says, and Aunt Verdella marvels out loud over how attached my five-year-old son is to his daddy. I tell her how Andy had his little tool set strapped around him when I left home, even though I told him that the hardware store wouldn't be opening for another two hours.

"Hey," Evalee says, her voice soft with thoughtfulness. "Where is Uncle Boohoo's home, anyway?"

"At Grandpa and Freeda's," Jewelee pipes up. "'Cause that's where his toys are." She's talking about the model airplanes that hang from the ceiling with twine in my old room.

"But he's got a room at my house. And your house, too," Evalee reminds her. "Even one upstairs here. And there's old toys up there, too."

Aunt Verdella and I exchange smiles because even at fourteen, Boohoo remains tied to us all.

The straps of Jewelee's costume slip down her shoulders and while Aunt Verdella comments that she'll have to take them both in, I lift the straps above Jewelee's head and crisscross them. A strap catches on her perfect little ear, and she yelps. I give her a kiss, ask her if she apologized to Evalee, and she hops down and scoots onto the same chair as Evalee. Jewelee puts her arm around her and kisses her cheek. She says she's sorry, and just like that, they're best friends again.

"I'm glad you don't have to go to school today, Cupcake," Jewelee says. "We can play in our house now." Their "house" is Winnalee's old, broken-down hippie van that's parked alongside Grandma Mae's house, where Winnalee and Bradley, her fiancé, live. Bradley—the guy she loves to kiss, who came after her five-year live-in relationship with Craig, a miscarriage, then a quick romance with a guy named Darrin, followed by one with a guy named Kevin—installed a little heater in the van for the girls, and now it's filled with dress-up clothes, a pink plastic kitchen, Community Sale toys, and memories to last them a lifetime.

Jewelee's left arm still looks bleached where her cast was until last week, and I remind her to keep her feet on the ground today.

"I didn't climb on anything high the last day we played," she said. "Did I, Cupcake?"

Evalee shakes her head, her blue eyes bright with innocence. "She didn't, Aunt Button. I saw her not do it."

I glance at the clock and tell Winnalee that we'd better get moving. Winnalee digs in her tote bag and pulls out our Book of Bright Ideas. I grab a pen, and we start for the door.

"Sit. We'll be right back," Winnalee tells Freeda, who is trying to down her coffee quickly.

It's late fall, and leaves crackle under our shoes as we step off the back porch. Above us, the clouds are dropping a soft, cold rain.

We are twenty-six years old, but we giggle like little girls as we unlatch the fence that encloses the side yard. Winnalee kicks a lopsided beach ball out of the way, and we sidestep a doll stroller. We slip off our shoes and put them in Boohoo's old wagon. We leave our socks on, though, because it's chilly. Winnalee climbs up first. The pen jabs my hip as I swing myself up.

We shuffle our feet to wedge them in the platform between the three sturdy trunks, and the bare wood is cool and slippery against our socks. I look up once we're situated. The leaves are mostly gone now, sitting in a scattered heap across the yard, but for a few that still cling, their color a blaze of orange.

Winnalee strokes the leather-bound cover of our book with fingers that are already pinkening at the tips. I reach over and pull her hood up over her head, and her long loops waver in the breeze. "I can't believe it's been seventeen years since I started this book," she says. I tell her that I can't believe we're just now going to write our one hundredth idea, and she reminds me that we needed that long to find it.

Winnalee looks off in the distance, and I know she's thinking of all the things that happened in those years, just as I am: the urn, the book, the lies, the love, the losses, and suddenly we're not in our special tree anymore. We're in that place called "bittersweet." That place, I reasoned when I was a girl, that if you could find it on a map, would be the mountain that sits between happy and sad. The place where you can almost feel God's hand on your head and just know, deep down inside, that there was a good reason for every single thing that happened.

We're quiet for a time, then Winnalee's mouth slowly drops open. "Oh my God, Button. You and me are older than Mom was when we pulled into town the first time. Unreal."

I smile, not at the revelation, but because I never tire of hearing Winnalee call Freeda *Mom* (which she switched to after Evalee said *Mama* for the first time). I don't think Freeda ever tires of it, either.

We become thoughtful and silent again. Winnalee gently pats the cover of our book, and the diamond in her engagement ring glitters like fairy wings. We look at each other with smiles made soft from our thoughts, then Winnalee holds out the book.

"You go first," she says.

As I write, a raindrop lands on the page to dot an *i*, and Winnalee puffs warm breath into her cupped hands. She reads my entry when I'm finished, and tilts her head and smiles.

I hand her the pen, and slip my stiff hands into my pocket while I wait.

Winnalee finishes, and hands me the book so I can read it. I laugh. We share a hug made awkward by our fear of falling, then Winnalee asks, "Where to?"

I grin. "The Magic Tree!"

Winnalee makes the same engine noises she used to make, and we jump down. We slip our shoes back on and race back to the house, as the rain changes to snow.

Bright Idea #100:

If you don't want to keep making the same mistakes that you, or your parents already made, find a book with nothing inside it and write down the things you think might be clues to the secrets of life. It won't keep you from making every mistake, and you won't have all the answers by the time you reach 100, but it will keep you mindful and help you not make as many. And when you read it years later, you'll see just how much you've grown. Past that, just love yourself, and others. And on bad days, when you feel like you're stuck on a rock in the middle of nowhere, with no earth beneath you to sink your roots in, and no breeze to push your life forward, reach out to all those who ever gave you love, and believe with the faith of a child.

And revisit your favorite childhood places (if only in your mind) and remember catching fireflies, and eating bunny pancakes, and playing dress-up. Then call your best friends together and have a pajama party, share stories, eat good food, paint your faces, and dance naked in the rain. And never, ever be afraid to believe in things that others say don't exist.

ACKNOWLEDGMENTS

My heartfelt gratitude to the following people, each of whom played a vital role in helping to bring the Peterses and Malones back to life:

To my new publisher, Jane von Mehren: Thank you for your enthusiasm. To my former editor, Kerri Buckley, who lovingly took this book near to its completion, then handed it with confidence into the apt hands of my current editor, Jennifer Smith, whose depth and skill nurtured it to fulfillment. To my agent, Catherine Fowler, who guides me with wisdom and love. My thanks to each of you for being champions of my work.

To pilots Joe Sanfilippo and Cade Lowell Woodward, whose knowledge of the Piper PA-12 Super Cruiser allowed Tommy to take to the skies, and to seamstress Sandy Swenson, whose skilled hands and love for what she does became Evy's. To Dr. Sytinderpal Judge, who patiently imparted his expertise on bee stings and allergic reactions, and who takes such good care of my allergy-prone daughter. To Patricia Martini, who gave me the inspiring photograph that ended up on Button's nightstand, and to Kerry Kring who answered my endless questions on the nature of trees. To Dan Jendrzejewski, who clued me in to the fact that Spider-Man does *not* wear a cape (Boohoo didn't listen, but I did). To my daughter Shannon Kring Buset, who offered valuable feedback on grown-up Button's voice, and to my daughter Natalie Kring who edits my punctuation when I need it (and I need it often!). To my son, Neil, who drags me away from the computer for an occasional movie or basketball game when I need a break but don't know it, and to my writing bud and friend, Christopher Pimental. Our endless conversations over the most minuscule aspects of writing provide an outlet for my love of the craft, and keep me—and those who come into contact with me—sane.

To the wonderful people at "my office," who not only hand-sell my books with zeal, but welcome my almost daily visits and my chatter, and who share their stories with me. I appreciate each one of you and am happy to call you my friends.

And last, but not least, to the many booksellers, librarians, book clubs, and individuals who read my books and recommend them to others. None of this is possible without you.

A LIFE OF BRIGHT IDEAS

A NOVEL

SANDRA KRING

A Reader's Guide

A Conversation with Sandra Kring

RANDOM HOUSE READER'S CIRCLE: What made you decide to write a follow-up to *The Book of Bright Ideas*?

SANDRA KRING: At least 98 percent of the readers who wrote to tell me how much they loved *The Book of Bright Ideas* pleaded with me to write a sequel. They wanted to know if Button and Winnalee were ever reunited, if the changes in the Peters family lasted, where the Malones went, and if Freeda and Winnalee made their peace. Each time I replied, I had to explain that I only knew the story to the point where the book ended. In time, though, I started asking myself these same questions, and realized that I could not turn my back on these characters, nor on the readers who came to love them like family.

RHRC: Do you think the unforgettable duo of Evy (Button) and Winnalee will ever appear in any of your future novels?

SK: Yes, I'd say it's very likely I'll revisit these characters again. Not in my next book, but perhaps the one after that.

RHRC: How long did it take you to write this book?

SK: Believe it or not, I have no clue! Time both stands still *and* whooshes along when I'm writing. Couple that with the fact that I have practically *no* sense of time to begin with, and I'm completely stumped. All I can say for certain is that I loved every moment I was writing it.

RHRC: What is your writing process like?

SK: I go straight to my computer first thing in the morning. When I'm at the awkward beginning stages of a novel, I'm not as quick to rise, and I have to push myself to stick with writing for even five or six hours. But in no time, the characters start breathing on their own, and the story begins sailing along. Once I've reached this point, I eagerly wake before sunrise, and I could easily write for ten to twelve hours a day, if I didn't discipline myself otherwise. While I love long writing days, my wrists and back do not.

RHRC: You tend to write about tightly-knit families in small towns. Did you grow up in a small town? How have your experiences shaped your writing?

SK: I spent the majority of my life living in a township of 399 people and often joke that I started writing fiction because I knew that if I didn't create people, I'd never meet another new person in my life! I was in my early forties before I even visited a large city, and the first few visits gave me sensory overload. Eventually, though, I came to love the energy of large cities, and I now visit them every chance I get. I'd live in one, but I fear that with my love of meeting new people and experiencing new places, I'd never get any writing done. I write what I know, so I write what I know best: about complex families living in simple places.

RHRC: How much interaction do you have with book clubs, and how have your experiences with them been? Are you part of one yourself?

SK: If there is one aspect of being a writer that I *don't* enjoy, it's spending vast amounts of time in isolation. I am a people person and lose energy if I don't have a certain amount of interaction with others. Visiting book clubs (in person, and via Skype) is a wonderful way for me to connect with the public, and to meet my readers. And, yes, I have been a member of a book club for years. You can read about our crazy crew on my website: http://www.sandrakring.com.

RHRC: What are some of your own favorite books?

SK: Unfortunately, I'm one of those writers who cannot read and write at the same time (it's like listening to two radios at once, each tuned to different stations) and I always seem to be writing. So while once I read four to six books a week, I'm now lucky if I get to read that many in a year. Some of my all-time favorites include *Of Mice and Men*, *A Tree Grows in Brooklyn*, *To Kill a Mockingbird*, and *The Education of Little Tree*. I did manage to sneak in *The Help* (and loved it!) in the week I took off after finishing *A Life of Bright Ideas*. The books on my ever-growing stack of to-be-read list are waiting patiently.

RHRC: We'd love to know what you're working on next. Can you share any details of your next book?

SK: I hesitate to say too much about a plot that's still unfolding, but I can tell you a little about the characters. There's Sada Flitchart, who, at ninety-four, wants only to let go of this life and join her beloved husband in the next—though she has unfinished business to tend to first. And there's Sada's wig-wearing friend, Loretta Brewster, who is hiding more than her balding head. The story is told through a series of flashbacks that spans their lifelong friendship, and is supported by the presence of Carly Butters, the fanciful seven-year-old girl who visits them at Peaceful Heart Rest Home. As their story unfolds, both women just may learn that there's truth to what their young friend says: that if you get to the end of the story and the ending is sad or scary, it only means that the story isn't over yet.

Questions for Discussion

1. This novel has many strong themes: family, friendship, love, loss, and healing, among others. Which one resonated with you the most?

2. Evy and Winnalee are best friends, but have such different personalities. What are the dynamics of their relationship, and how does their friendship work so well? In your own experience, are you more drawn to people who are similar to or different from you?

3. What has changed about the two girls' outlooks on life since they wrote their "book of bright ideas"? What has stayed the same?

4. How does the book deal with the theme of loss and how we can be healed? What roles do family and community play in healing?

5. How were both Evy and Winnalee affected during their adolescence and early adulthood by the heady times of the sixties? For you, what was most evocative of the sixties in the book, and how have things changed?

6. Winnalee tells Evy to "say it, don't scratch it." What facilitates Evy's journey from self-harm and bottling up her emotions to expressing herself with others?

7. Like her mother, Freeda, Winnalee struggles with adult responsibilities. How does she ultimately come to terms with them?

8. What does this novel have to say about passing down problems from generation to generation? Is it possible to break the cycle?

9. Evy cherishes a picture of a tree that perches improbably on a rock, far from the nurturing soil of the bluffs. She realizes that there are many small roots that reach back to the bluff, anchoring the tree to the soil. What is the significance of this?

10. What is it that makes Dauber, Wisconsin, so special? Would you like to live in a town like this? Why or why not?

Read on for an excerpt

from Sandra Kring's

The Book of Bright Ideas

CHAPTER 1

I should have known that summer of 1961 was gonna be the biggest summer of our lives. I should have known it the minute I saw Freeda Malone step out of that pickup, her hair lit up in the sun like hot flames. I should have known it, because Uncle Rudy told me what happens when a wildfire comes along.

We were standing in his yard, Uncle Rudy and I, at the foot of a red pine that seemed to stretch to heaven, when a squirrel began knocking pinecones to the ground with soft thuds. Uncle Rudy bent over with a grunt and picked one of the green cones up, rolling it a bit in his callused palm before handing it to me. It was cool in my hands. Sap dripped down the side like tears.

"Here's somethin' I bet you don't know, Button," he said, using the nickname he himself gave me. "That cone there, it ain't like the cones of most other trees. Most cones, all they need is time, or a squirrel to crack 'em open so they can drop their seeds and start a new tree. But that cone there, it ain't gonna open up and drop its seeds unless a wildfire comes through here."

"A wildfire?"

"That's right," Uncle Rudy said, scraping the scalp under his cap with his dirty fingernail. "See them little scales there, how they're closed up tight like window shutters? Underneath 'em are the seeds—flat little things, flimsy as a baby's fingernails—with a point at one end. If a fire comes along, the heat is gonna cause those scales to peel back and drop their seeds, while the ground is still scorching hot. Then that tiny seed is gonna burrow in and take root."

I was nine years old the summer Freeda and Winnalee Malone rushed across our lives like red-hot flames, peeling back the shutters that sat over our hearts and our minds, setting free our sweetest dreams and our worst nightmares. Too young to know at the onset that anything out of the ordinary was about to happen.

I was sitting on my knees behind the counter at The Corner Store playing with my new Barbie doll, her tiny outfits lined up on the scuffed linoleum. It was the first day of summer vacation, and Aunt Verdella was watching me because my ma was working for Dr. Wagner, the dentist, taking appointments and sending out bills and stuff like that. Aunt Verdella didn't work, like my ma, but she'd been filling in at the store for Ada Smithy (who was having a recuperation from an operation, because she'd had some ladies' troubles). It was Aunt Verdella's last day, then Ada was coming back, and we could stay at Aunt Verdella's while she looked after me.

Aunt Verdella was standing next to me, the hem of her dress like a blue umbrella above me. She was talking to Fanny Tilman about Ada, and Aunt Verdella's voice sounded almost like it was crying when she said, "Such a pity, such a pity," and Fanny Tilman asked her what the pity was for, anyway. "Ada's well past her prime, so seems to me that not getting the curse from here on out should be more of a blessing than a pity," she said, and Aunt Verdella said, "But still . . ."

While they talked, I was trying to get Barbie's tweed

jacket on, which wasn't easy because her elbows didn't bend, and that tiny hand of hers kept snagging on the sleeve. While I was tugging, I was itching. I was looking at the little clothes spread out and trying hard to remember if she was supposed to wear the red jacket with the brown skirt or the green skirt. I cleared my throat a few times, like I always did when I didn't know what I was supposed to do next, and Aunt Verdella looked down at me. "Button, you're doin' that thing with your throat again. What's the matter, honey?" Aunt Verdella's voice was loud, so loud that sometimes it pained my ears when she wasn't even yelling, and her body always reminded me of a snowman made with two balls instead of three. The littlest ball was her head, sitting right on top of one big, fat ball.

I stood up. My knees felt gritty and I glanced down at them, hoping they weren't getting too dirty, because I knew Ma's lips were gonna pull so tight they'd turn white, like they always did when Aunt Verdella brought me home looking all grubby. "I can't get her jacket on," I said.

I handed Aunt Verdella my Barbie, the tweed jacket flapping at her back. Aunt Verdella laughed as she took it. Fanny Tilman peered at me, her puffy eyes puckering. "Is that Reece and Jewel's little one?" she said, like Aunt Verdella could hear her but I couldn't. I put my head down and stared at a gouge in the gray countertop.

"Yep, this is our Button," Aunt Verdella said. She wrapped her freckly arm—stick-skinny like her legs—around me and pulled me to her biggest ball. It was soft and warm, not snowman-cold at all.

"She looks like Jewel," Mrs. Tilman said, and she sounded a bit sorry about this. I saw her looking at my ears, which were too big for my head, and the face she made made me feel smaller than I already was. Aunt Verdella thought that long hair would hide my ears until I grew into them, but Ma said long hair was too much work to keep neat and she already had enough to do. Every couple of months, she'd snip it short, thin it with those scissors that have missing teeth, then curl it with a Tony perm. When she was done, my hair was bunched up in ten or eleven little pale brown knots. I wanted hair long enough to hang loose past my shoulders and cover my ears when I was around people, and to put up in a ponytail that swished my back when I wasn't. But shoot, I knew I'd never have anything but those stubby knots.

Aunt Verdella finished dressing Barbie, then handed her to me. I stood there a minute, wanting to ask her which skirt matched, but I didn't want to talk with Fanny Tilman still looking at me, so I sat back down on the linoleum and stared at the two skirts some more.

Aunt Verdella had the door propped open with a big rock, because it was nice outside and the store was too hot with the sun beating through the windows. I was staring at the doll clothes when the sound of metal scraping on pavement filled the store.

"Uh-oh, somebody's losing their muffler," Aunt Verdella said. The racket from the scraping muffler got louder and sharper before it came to a stop. Aunt Verdella got up on her tiptoes, the tops of her white shoes making folds like Uncle Rudy's forehead did when she brought home a whole trunkload of junk from the community sale.

"Good Lord, look what the cat's drug into town now," Fanny Tilman said. "Just what we need, a band of gypsies."

"Oh, Fanny!" Aunt Verdella said.

I heard a door creak open, then slam shut. A lady's voice started talking, but I couldn't make out what it was saying. I heard some banging and then, "Jesus H. Christ! Is anybody gonna come pump my gas or not?" Folks who got gas at The Corner Store pumped their own gas, except for a couple of old ladies and the outsiders. Aunt Verdella called out, "I'll be right there, dear!"

"Excuse me, Button," she said as she stepped over me and hurried around the counter. I put my fingertips on the counter and pulled myself up to take a peek. Mrs. Tilman was standing in the open doorway, her purse clutched in her arms like she thought the "gypsies" were going to try swiping it. She was busy gawking, so I stood all the way up and peeked out between the handmade signs Scotch-taped to the window.

The bed of the red pickup truck at the pumps, and the wagon towed behind it, were piled high with junky furniture I *knew* didn't match and boxes stuffed with bunched-up clothes and dishes that spilled out over the tops.

My eyes almost bugged out of my head when I saw the lady who was standing next to the truck while Aunt Verdella pumped her gas. She had the prettiest color hair I'd ever seen. Red, but like a red I'd never set eyes on before: shiny like a pot of melted copper pennies. Not dark, not light, but somewhere in between, and bright like fire. She stretched like a cat, the sleeveless blouse tied at her waist riding up a belly that was flat and the color of buttered toast. She was made like my Barbie doll, with two big bumps under her blouse, a skinny waist, and long legs under kelly-green pedal pushers. She was wearing a pair of sunglasses with a row of rhinestones at the corners that shot rays into my eyes when she turned toward the store. There was something about the lady too, that shined just as bright as her hair and those rhinestones. Not a warm kind of shining, but a sharp kind, like bright sun jabbing through the window and stinging your eyes.

Aunt Verdella cranked her head toward the store and yelled, "Button, bring Auntie the restroom key, will ya?"

I stepped up on the wooden stool and reached for the key, which was taped to a ruler so it couldn't get lost easy, and I hurried it outside. As much as I hated meeting new people, I wanted to see the pretty lady up close.

The Barbie lady took off her sunglasses and poked them

into her fiery hair, which was piled high on her head in a messy sort of way. She had green eyes like a cat's, and her eyelids were sparkly with the same color, clear up to her eyebrows. She had real nice ears too. Tiny, and laying flat to her head like ears are supposed to. I handed Aunt Verdella the key, and she gave it to the pretty lady, who was glaring at the truck, a crabby look on her face. "The ladies' restroom is right around the west side of the building, honey," Aunt Verdella told her.

The pretty lady tapped the ruler against her thigh. "Winnalee Malone, I'm gonna blister your ass if you don't get out of that truck this instant and go pee. You hear me?" I'd never heard a lady swear before, so I know my eyes must have stretched as big as my ears.

The windshield of the truck was blue-black in the sun, so I couldn't see who she was talking to. Aunt Verdella put the gas handle back onto the hook alongside the pump, then headed over to the driver's door where the Barbie lady was standing, still tapping the ruler on her leg. "Oh my," Aunt Verdella said. "Ain't you the prettiest little thing! You've got a face like a cherub." Aunt Verdella said "cherub" more like "cherry-up." "Why don't you come out here and say hello? I got Popsicles inside. A free one for the first pretty little customer who uses the restroom today." Aunt Verdella looked at the lady and winked, then turned back to the truck. "Come on, now, honey. We don't bite."

The Barbie lady lifted her arms and slapped them against the sides of her thighs. "Ah, to hell with you, Winnalee. If you're gonna be stubborn, then sit there till your bladder bursts, for all I care. I'm too tired to argue with you."

"Winnalee? Now, ain't that the prettiest name. Where'd you get a pretty name like that?" Aunt Verdella asked.

"From my ma," said a voice from inside the truck. "It's a homemade name."

The lady cussed again, like ladies aren't supposed to do,

then she said, "Winnalee, I'm not going to stand here and piss my pants waiting for you. You coming or not?"

Aunt Verdella cranked her head around. "You go on to the restroom, dear. I got a way with children," she said, then she winked again. The pretty lady made a growly sound in her throat, then she headed toward the building, her heels clacking against the pavement.

It took a while, but finally Aunt Verdella coaxed Winnalee out. When I saw her, I could hardly believe my eyes: She had long, loopy hair the color of that stringy part inside a cob of corn, but with some yellow mixed in too, and it hung clear down to her butt. It didn't have any rubber bands or barrettes in it, so it floated in the breeze like a mermaid's hair under water. Her face was round and pink, with little lips that looked like they had lipstick on them. She was wearing a lady's mesh slip, and it was rolled up at her round belly to keep it from falling down. She had on a white sleeveless blouse that belonged on a grown-up too. One side of it slipped down her arm and she crooked her elbow to keep it from falling all the way off. She didn't look at us but turned to reach for something on the seat. I scootched over by Aunt Verdella to see what the mermaid girl was getting.

"Well, my, what do you have there, Winnalee?" Aunt Verdella asked as the girl slid out of the truck holding a capped, shiny silver vase in her arms, cradling it like it was a baby doll.

"It's my ma," Winnalee said.

"Your ma?" Aunt Verdella asked, suddenly looking a bit shook up.

It was like Aunt Verdella didn't know what to say—which I was sure was because she was thinking the same thought as me. That there wasn't a lady anywhere small enough to fit into that vase. Either Winnalee was funning us, or else she was just plain nuts. Instead, Aunt Verdella asked her about the thick book she had tucked under her armpit. "Button likes to read big books too, don't you Button?" she said, putting an arm around me.

"It's her Book of Bright Ideas," said a voice behind us in the same tone that the snotty big kids who picked on us little kids at recess used. I turned and saw the pretty lady standing there, her hands on her hips, her legs parted. She was looking up and down the street.

It was like Aunt Verdella didn't know what to say again, so she said nothing except that if Winnalee was a good little girl and went potty, she'd give her a Popsicle or an ice cream bar.

The lady grabbed a big black purse off of the seat of the truck and we all headed toward the store, Winnalee's loopy hair dancing, her mesh slip flapping in the breeze like fins.

Fanny Tilman backed out of the doorway and slipped behind a grocery shelf, where I knew she was gonna stay hid, like a mouse waiting for somebody to drop some crumbs.

"Where you people from?" Aunt Verdella asked as she scooted behind the counter. The pretty lady took a bottle of RC Cola and one of root beer from the cooler, then set them down on the counter alongside her purse. Winnalee was behind her.

"Gary," she says. "Gary, Indiana. We drove straight through."

"Yeah," Winnalee said. "We had to leave in the middle of the night. All because Freeda went dancing with some guy from the meat factory, when she was supposed to be Harley Hoffesteader's girl. Harley got so pissed he was coming after her with a shotgun. Probably would have killed both of us dead if we hadn't gotten out of there fast. It don't matter, though. Freeda would've moved us anyways. She always does." The lady cuffed her on the top of her head and Winnalee cried out, "Ouch!" Aunt Verdella flinched and told Winnalee that maybe she should go potty now, and would she like me or her to go with her. Winnalee's nose crinkled. "I'm not a baby," she said, then she grabbed the key from the counter and marched out the door.

"Oh my. Gary. That's quite a drive. That must be, what, a good three fifty, four hundred miles from here?"

"I don't know." Freeda shook her head so that wispy strands wobbled against her long neck. "Hell, I don't even know where we are."

"You're in Dauber, Wisconsin, dear. Population 3,263," Aunt Verdella said proudly. "You thinking of settling here, or are you just passing through?"

Freeda shrugged. "I guess one place is as good as another. There any places to rent around here?"

I swear I heard Fanny Tilman (who was peeking up over the bread rack) gasp.

Aunt Verdella squeaked her tongue against her teeth as she thought. Then her puffy lips made a circle like a doughnut. "Ohhhh, well, actually, there just might be! Well, if you don't mind living in a place that's being fixed up, that is. You see, my husband, Rudy, and his brother, Reece, their ma passed away a couple a years ago, and we've been talking about renting her place out once Reece gets it fixed up. I keep saying that a house that sits empty falls to ruin fast, but you know how men are. Reece—that's Button here's daddy—he ain't gotten around to the repairs yet, but if you don't mind him coming and going, I don't see why we can't rent it to you now."

Winnalee came back in and held the key out to me, but looked at Freeda. "Hey, you said we were going to Detroit! She lies," she said to me, her thumb jabbing toward Freeda. Then she leaned over and peered at the mesh slip she was wearing. "Can you see my undies through this thing?" I looked, saw a bit of white, and told her I could. She rolled her big, lake-on-a-sunny-day-colored eyes and sighed. "I tried to tell Freeda that I was in my underwear, but she went and packed up my clothes anyway."

Freeda grunted. "Like it matters. You're in dress-up clothes half the time, anyway, Winnalee."

Aunt Verdella talked about Grandma Mae's place, bragging about the nice closed-in porch with good screens (all but for the one a barn cat shredded) and about the flower garden that was already shooting up daffodils and hyacinths, while she went to the freezer so Winnalee could pick out a treat. She called me over to have something too.

"Oh dear, where *are* my manners," she said all of a sudden. "I didn't even introduce myself yet. I'm Verdella Peters, and this here is my niece, Evelyn Mae, but we all call her Button. She's nine years old. How old are you, Winnalee?"

"I'm gonna be ten on September first," she said.

Freeda smiled for the first time, and her smile was as pretty as her hair. "I'm Freeda Malone, and you already know the sassy one. She's my kid sister."

Things happened fast then. While Freeda Malone was paying for her gas and the pop, Aunt Verdella told her they could get something to eat at the Spot Café. "You girls come back after you're done eating," Aunt Verdella said. "I'm closin' up in an hour, and you can follow me then." While Aunt Verdella chattered, I watched Winnalee eat her grape Popsicle. She didn't seem to have one bit of worry about the purple dripping down her hand and streaking her arm. I had my wrapper cupped around my stick, like you're supposed to, so I didn't have to worry about getting all sticky and stained.

The minute the Malones left, Aunt Verdella got as light and floaty as bubbles. Fanny Tilman came out of her hiding place then, looking like a gray mouse in her wool coat, even though it was too warm for even a little jacket.

"Verdella! Jewel is gonna be fit to be tied, you offering Mae's house like that! And to some gypsy drifters, to boot!"

Aunt Verdella waved Fanny Tilman's comment away. "It's gonna be real nice having people in that house, Fanny. I get so lonely when I look across the road and see that big, empty place. Mae didn't take to me much, but still, it was just nice knowing someone was there." She looked down at me and grinned. "And Button here sure could use a little friend, couldn't you, Button?"

Mrs. Tilman's mouth pinched. "Good heavens, Verdella. It's not like bringing home a litter of abandoned kittens, you know. These are strangers, and most likely trouble, by the looks of them."

When the Malones came back, Winnalee had ketchup splotched on her blouse, right over one of those points sticking out front like two witch's hats. Her eyes were a little red, and her cheeks had white streaks on them where a few tears had washed them. She didn't look unhappy at the moment, though, as she squatted to examine the tops of some canned goods where rainbowy shadows made by something shiny hanging in the window were flickering.

Aunt Verdella took her pay out of the till like she was told to—one dollar for every hour she worked this week—while I packed up my doll. She folded the envelope in threes and tucked it into her bra to take home and put in her jewelry box, where she kept all the money that was going toward the RCA color television set she wanted. A magazine ad of it was tacked to her fridge door, where it had hung since I was in the first grade. When she first came over with that ad, saying she was gonna save up and buy it even if it took her a lifetime, Ma had taken the *TV Guide* and showed Aunt Verdella how, at best, she'd only get three hours of color TV time a day. Mom repeated this story whenever she wanted to make Aunt Verdella look foolish. "I told her, look here, on Mondays, you'll only get forty-five minutes! But Verdella just laughed and said, 'Long as two of those hours are used up by *As the World Turns* and Arthur Godfrey, I'll be happy. Besides, by the time I save up $495, who knows, they might *all* be in living color!'" Aunt

Verdella had no idea how much that TV set was gonna cost her once she finally saved up enough, but she still faithfully put away every spare dime she had to buy it.

Aunt Verdella locked up The Corner Store and we climbed into her turquoise and white Bel Air, which was cluttered with junk. A Raggedy Ann and Andy—bought from the community sale last summer, just because they were cute—were propped on the bag of romance magazines that somebody gave her weeks ago, and wadded-up candy and chip wrappers littered the floor. Aunt Verdella checked my door three times to make sure it was locked, so I wouldn't lean on it and fall out, then made me set down my Barbie case and climb over the seat to watch out the back window as she backed out, so she didn't run anybody over.

"It's okay," I said.

Once we got going, I climbed back into the front seat. I sat close to Aunt Verdella, her arm warm against my cheek. Aunt Verdella kept looking in the rearview mirror, making sure that the Malones were still following us.

The shortest way home was down Highway 8, but Aunt Verdella wouldn't drive on the highway, so we kicked up dust down one town road after another, driving for what seemed forever. By the time we got out of the city limits the insides of my arms were splotched with the red, pimply rash that sprouted up on them whenever I got rattled. I knew Ma wasn't gonna be happy. Not about my dirty knees, and not about the Malones. I slid my jaw over a bit so my teeth could grab at the bumpy clump of skin inside my cheek, even though Dr. Wagner told me that if I kept up the nasty habit, I was gonna bite a hole clear through my face. Aunt Verdella wasn't worried like me though. She sang lines from one of those country songs she always played on her record player and grinned like she was bringing home Christmas. The rash itchin' my arms, though, told me that maybe this was a package we weren't supposed to open.

ABOUT THE AUTHOR

SANDRA KRING lives in Wisconsin. Her debut novel, *Carry Me Home*, was a Book Sense Notable Pick and a 2005 Midwest Booksellers' Choice Award Nominee. *The Book of Bright Ideas* was named to the New York Public Library's Books for the Teen Age list in 2007. Visit her on the Web at www.sandrakring.com.